NEWPOINTE
9 1 1

WORD OF HONOR

TERRI BLACKSTOCK

ZONDERVAN™

GRAND RAPIDS, MICHIGAN 49530

This book is lovingly dedicated to the Nazarene

ZONDERVAN™

Word of Honor
Copyright © 1999 by Terri Blackstock

Requests for information should be addressed to:

Zondervan, *Grand Rapids, Michigan 49530*

Library of Congress Cataloging-in-Publication Data

Blackstock, Terri, 1957-
   Word of honor.
      p. cm.--(Newpointe 911)
   ISBN: 0-310-21759-8 (pbk.)
   I. Series: Blackstock, Terri, 1957- Newpointe 911.
PS3552.L34285W67 1999
813'.54--dc 21   99-30016

Published in association with the literary agency of Alive Communications, Inc., 7680 Goddard Street, Suite 200, Colorado Springs, CO 80920.

Interior design by Jody DeNeef

Printed in the United States of America

04 05 06 07 08 09 /❖ DC/ 23 22 21 20

WORD OF HONOR

Books by Terri Blackstock

Cape Refuge (Book 1 in series)
Emerald Windows

Newpointe 911
Private Justice
Shadow of Doubt
Trial by Fire
Word of Honor

Sun Coast Chronicles
Evidence of Mercy
Justifiable Means
Ulterior Motives
Presumption of Guilt

Second Chances
Never Again Good-bye
When Dreams Cross
Blind Trust
Broken Wings

With Beverly LaHaye
Seasons Under Heaven
Showers in Season
Times and Seasons

Novellas
Seaside

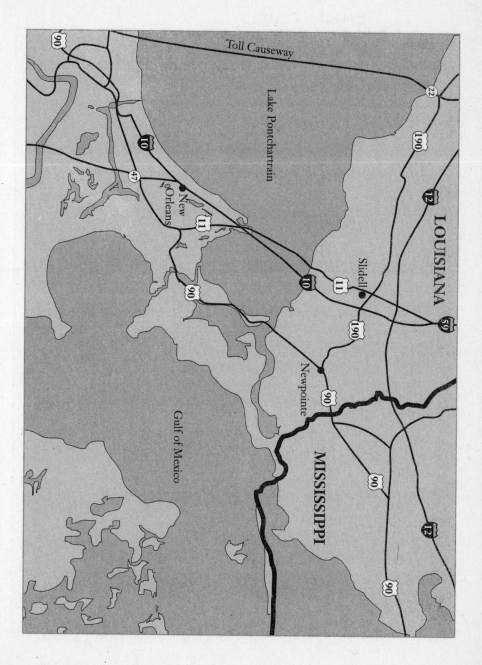

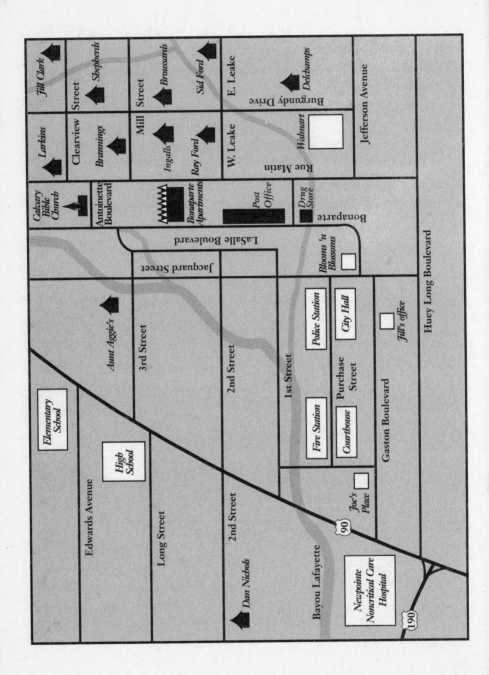

Chapter One

• • •

The small, hot post office smelled of mold and dust and hummed with the sound of several air conditioning units placed in windows around the building. Cliff Bertrand, the Newpointe postmaster, held his hand in front of one of the vents, and realized it was blowing hot air. No wonder the building was so warm. He gave the side of it a bang with the heel of his hand, as if that would shock it into spitting out cold air. But he knew it wouldn't work.

Sue Ellen will be whining all day, he thought. He looked over his shoulder at Sue Ellen Hanover, his postal clerk, who stood at the counter fanning herself as she waited on a customer. With a fake fingernail, she punched out the amount of postage that Mary Hampton's packages would need.

"You wouldn't know it was July," she commented as she applied the sticky metered strips to the boxes. "You'd think it was Christmas, what with all these packages."

"Just some of Mama's stuff," Mary said. "She went to live with my brother over in Waco, so I'm shippin' her some of her things."

"You two couldn't get along?" Sue Ellen asked sweetly.

Mary looked offended.

Cliff knew it did little good to scold her, but he gave it a shot, anyway. "Sue Ellen, that was rude. Everybody knows her mama just went to help with her new grandbaby."

Sue Ellen shot him a look that said his intrusion wasn't appreciated. "Cliff, you really need to fix that air conditioner. It's hot as blazes in here." She fanned herself with a manila envelope and turned back to Mary. "Yep, them babies always do outshine the older grandkids. Where's your youngun, anyways?"

"Out there." Mary nodded through the glass doors at the child playing on the floor with a toy fire truck.

"Scrawny little thing," Sue Ellen said, taking Mary's check. "Can I see some ID, please?"

Cliff shook his head at the absurdity of the request, since Sue Ellen knew Mary well enough to wag her tongue all over town every time the single mother stepped outside her house. He heard Sue Ellen tapping her fake fingernails on the counter, as if she had a million better things to do than wait for Mary to dig her driver's license out of her purse.

Disgusted, he grabbed his keys and the refills for the stamp machine, and headed out to reload it. As he pushed through the door into the outer room, he saw Mary's sandy-haired five-year-old crawling along the wall, running his fire truck as fast as he could. He smiled, but the boy hardly noticed him.

Cliff jangled his keys and opened the machine.

Instantly, the boy was on his feet, peering into the machine as if glimpsing something sacred. "Hey, there," Cliff said.

"Hey." The boy watched, fascinated, as he stacked the packages of stamps in the appropriate places. "Can I do one?"

Cliff grinned and handed him a stack. "Put those right here."

The boy's eyes rounded, and he slid them carefully into their slot.

"Good job. What's your name, son?"

The child looked up at him. "Peter Jacob Hampton."

Cliff held out his hand. "Nice to meet you, Peter Jacob Hampton. I'm Clifford Wayne Bertrand. How do you do?"

The little boy shook. "D'you do this everyday?"

"Every single one, except weekends," he said, closing the machine back. He looked down at the truck lying on the concrete floor. "Nice truck you got there."

"Thanks." Pete fell back to his knees and began making an engine noise as he ran along the wall.

Cliff chuckled and picked up his box. "See you later, Pete."

"Bye."

As Cliff pushed through the door in the back room, he glanced back and saw the child watching him with awe, as if wondering what treasures lay behind the mailboxes.

• • •

Pete watched the door close behind the man, and decided on the spot that he was going to be a mailman when he grew up. That, and a fireman. He went back to pushing his truck.

The door at the far end of the building opened, and Pete's attention shifted to the man coming in from outside. He was sweating hard and breathing fast, and carrying a box that looked like it held a big present. Pete stopped pushing the truck and sat up, trying to imagine what could be inside. The man stepped past him and set the box down against the wall, then started back to the door.

"That ain't where you put that, Mister," Pete said. "It goes over there." He pointed to the slots in the wall.

"That's right where I want it, kid." The man hesitated as he looked down at him. Pete noticed that the man was missing some fingers, and he bent some of his own to see how it felt. He started to ask him what had happened to them, but the man spoke first. "Hey, you know, that truck sure would fly on that half wall outside. Why don't you go out there and try it?" Not waiting for an answer, the man pushed back through the door he'd come in. Pete watched through the glass doors as the man climbed into the passenger seat of the blue pickup. The driver pulled away.

Quickly, Pete's attention moved from the blue pickup to the half wall he'd suggested outside the building. He glanced through the glass doors and saw his mother paying for their package. If he went outside, just this once, would he get in trouble?

Deciding that the wall's incline was worth the trouble it would cost him, he pushed through the door and hurried to the wall. His throat made a rumbling sound as he set his truck on the wall and gave it a shove.

He would never see it hit the bottom of the incline.

• • •

The explosion was so loud Jerry Ingalls heard it from half a mile away. "What in the—?" He slammed on his brakes. The blue pickup skidded across the street.

"What are you doing?" Frank shouted. "Drive, man! Drive!"

As Jerry tried to right his pickup, he looked back through the rear window. He could see the black smoke rising from where they'd been, filling the sky. "That's the post office!" he said.

"Up here," Frank said. "Take a right up here."

Sirens began to blare a few blocks away. Jerry turned in the direction he'd been told, his heart racing. "Do you know anything about what happened back there?"

"Yes," Frank said. He was dripping with sweat now, and the humid Louisiana air crept through the pickup in spite of the air conditioning. "But I can't tell you about it now. Just drive."

"Drive where?" Jerry demanded. "If you're involved in something, man—"

"I need your help!" Frank's bellowed statement left no room for argument. "Drive to the Delchamps parking lot. I have a car. Drop me off, then you head for Chalmette. There's a motel right on the outskirts of Chalmette. The only one in town. The Flagstaff, I think it is. Go there and rent me a room. Don't use my name or yours. Tie a hand towel over the knob so I can find you. I'll meet you there tonight and tell you everything."

Jerry's head was reeling from the orders. "Frank, if you had a car, why did you just have me drive you to the post office? What have you gotten me into?"

"A fight for your country!" Frank yelled back. "You're in, now. There's no turning back. You owe me, Jerry! And you owe your country."

"My country?" Jerry asked. "What are you talking about, man? The war's been over for twenty-five years!"

"I've been a POW, Jerry. For twenty-five years, and there were others there with me. They told you the war was over, but it came home with us. Communism is infiltrating our government, Jerry. The captain was part of it."

"The captain? What captain?"

"Bertrand, man! He works for the feds, and he's part of the whole thing."

"*Cliff Bertrand?* Frank, he's retired from the army. He's just a postal clerk, not some kind of spy."

"He's helping them to take over, Jerry. I don't expect you to understand. You weren't held all those years, like I was. But we have to stop it."

Jerry gaped at him. "Frank, you weren't a POW. You were in a VA hospital."

"That's what they want you to think, but there were others held there," he said. "You don't know what's going on. It's worse than the Viet Cong. They're going to take away everything, Jerry. They're trying to lull us into a false sense of security, and then we'll let them do anything they want. They already have our government."

Jerry's heart was racing. He pulled into the Delchamps parking lot and turned his pickup so he could see the black smoke still hovering above the post office. "Man, you didn't blow up that post office, did you?"

"You just don't understand," Frank said. "But I'll explain everything. I'll tell you at the motel. Be there. You owe me, Jerry."

With that, he launched out of the pickup and took off between the cars.

Jerry didn't wait to see which car was his. The sirens were getting louder, and the smoke billowed with urgent fury as he pulled out of the parking lot. Something told him he had just become a wanted man.

He reached behind him, got his hunting rifle from its rack, and set it on the seat next to him. He hoped he wouldn't need it, but he had a real bad feeling.

Frank was right. He did owe him. He could at least meet him and find out what was going on. Maybe he could talk him out of pulling any more sick stunts, make him go back to the hospital that had been his home for so long.

As he headed out of town, he looked back toward the post office. The black smoke of Frank's iniquities rose like a tragic prayer into the sky.

Chapter Two

● ● ●

The ambulance at Midtown Fire Station pulled out of the driveway first, just moments after the explosion six blocks away. The firefighters, who had just settled down to a lunch of shrimp gumbo, headed for their turnout pants.

Dan Nichols stepped into his rubber boots and pulled the pants up. As he snapped them shut, he grabbed his turnout coat and helmet. "Where's the fire?" he yelled as George Broussard, already decked out, jumped onto the pumper truck.

"Post office," George answered. "Explosion of some sort."

"Felt like next door!" Dan got into the truck. As the siren came on and Mark Branning pulled the truck out of the bay, Dan peered up through the windshield. The black smoke from the explosion just six blocks away had already made its way down Purchase Street and was billowing up into the sky, visible to everyone.

"Mail bomb?" Dan asked.

"Probably," Mark said.

As they rounded the corner and reached the block where the post office was, all three of the firemen on the truck went silent.

Dan had never seen anything like it. The roof and two of the walls were gone, and the walls left standing were consumed in flames at least twenty feet high. Fallen electrical wires sizzled and sparked. Dan dreaded the idea of digging through live wires and burning rubble to get to any bodies that might be under it all.

The ambulance was already there. Issie Mattreaux, the paramedic, climbed from the truck, joined by Bob Sigrest, an EMT.

Dan jumped out and waved to them. "Stay back!" he commanded. "Stay with the ambulance!"

They nodded, understanding. Since the ambulance squads weren't equipped to head into heavy smoke, it was up to him and the other firefighters, also trained as EMTs, to find any survivors.

Dan snapped down his face shield and pulled on his air pack. He pulled the gauntlets of his sleeves over his gloves to protect his skin, but he could already feel the skin-melting heat of the explosion, heavy on the July air. He wondered how any of them would make it through this. The breathing tank weighed thirty to forty pounds, a lot to carry when they were digging through bricks, steel, and glass. It had only about twenty minutes of air, not nearly enough for a job like this. They'd be swapping tanks left and right for the next few hours. He hoped the 911 dispatcher had radioed Slidell to send backup crews.

"Here! Help, here!"

Through the haze Dan spotted Penelope Houston, the owner of the drugstore across the street. Her face was smoke-stained, and she was coughing. Wildly, her arms gestured toward a body on the ground. *A child*, Dan realized, his heart jolting. He ran to the ambulance. "There's a child! Give me the megaduffel! He'll need oxygen."

Issie thrust the equipment at him, then handed Mark the spineboard and pediatric collar. Grabbing the gear, they took off into the smoke.

The child looked tiny on the scorched pavement, and he didn't seem to be breathing. He had been thrown in the explosion. Blood pooled on the ground from a wound on the back of his head, and his body was covered with glass and soot.

Wasting no time, they got the neck splint on him, slapped the oxygen mask on his face, and carefully moved him onto the board. Then they ran him back to the ambulance. "He's not breathing!" Dan yelled. "And he's got a bad head wound."

Even as he spoke, Issie began running a tube down the child's trachea to clear his airway. Dan fought the urge to watch to see if the soot-covered boy would live. Already, Mark was going back into the smoke to look for more survivors. Dan grabbed Penelope Houston. "Penelope, do you know of any other survivors?"

Penelope's face was streaked with smoke and tears as she babbled hysterically. "I heard the explosion, Dan." She coughed. Her voice was cracked and broken. "It shook the building and knocked my windows out. I . . . I come out and seen . . . all the smoke and flames . . . and this little boy was layin' here like he'd been throwed. I didn't see nobody else."

The town's other ambulance unit was just arriving, along with a convoy of other fire trucks and rescue units from neighboring towns. Dan waved for Steve Winder as he got out of the rig. "Steve, get her on some oxygen and out of this smoke!"

Steve tried to usher her back to his unit as Ray Ford, the fire chief, pulled to the curb between two of the trucks. He was dressed in full gear, face shield down, as he approached Dan. "Anybody inside?"

"Of course there was somebody inside!" Penelope shouted, turning back from Steve's ambulance. "Sue Ellen Hanover was there. And Cliff Bertrand. They're always there. They never leave, not even for lunch!" Again, she surrendered to a series of coughs.

"So we need to look for Sue Ellen and Cliff," Ray shouted. "How many cars in the parking lot?"

"Looks like a couple," Dan said.

Stan Shepherd, the town's only detective, came running up to the ambulances. "What in the sam hill—"

"Those cars could be Sue Ellen's and Cliff's," Ray cut in. "Who's the kid?"

Still coughing, Penelope turned around and shouted back, "That's Mary Hampton's boy. They were in the drugstore before they went to the post office."

Stan swung around. "Are you sure? Mary and Pete?"

"You know them?" Dan asked.

"Yeah," Stan said. "She goes to our church. Divorced. Some of the guys put a new roof on her house last year." He went to the ambulance and looked down at the boy as Issie struggled to stabilize him. "Pete's five years old. I've taken him to a couple of Saints games. Where's his mother?"

"He's all I've found so far," Dan said. He closed the doors of the ambulance to keep the smoke out, and ignored the stunned look on Stan's face. "Get out of the smoke, Stan. Keep everybody back."

As Stan ran to where they were setting up a barricade at the end of the street, Dan headed back into the heat to look for any survivors. But even as he did, he knew that there wouldn't be any. No one would have survived this blast. It was a miracle that the boy was still alive.

Chapter Three

● ● ●

Celia Shepherd had been shedding a lot of hormonal tears lately, and she suspected it would get worse as these last three weeks of her pregnancy passed. But the news of Mary Hampton's death, and the deaths of Sue Ellen Hanover and Cliff Bertrand, had sent her over the edge of her emotional precipice. She hadn't been able to stop the tears for Pete, the funny little boy in her Sunday school class. The thought that he had been orphaned in the space of a moment was too much to bear.

So she had gotten into her car and headed to Slidell, where he'd been transported. Pete's father had run off with his secretary two years earlier, and the boy had undergone quite a bit of emotional upheaval since then. No one knew where the father was, or how to reach him. And his grandmother, who had been living with them, had recently gone to live with her son.

The child was incredibly alone.

Celia's tears streamed down her face and she wiped them away as she drove. She set her hand gently on her pregnant belly and felt her own child kick within her. What a terrible thing it would be to leave your child behind. What a horrible nightmare for a little boy, to wake up from an accident and learn that the person he loved and needed most in the world was gone.

Trying to see through her tears to drive, she picked up her cell phone and dialed out her husband's number at the police department. "Stan Shepherd, please."

"Celia, Stan ain't in." She recognized the voice of LaTonya Mason, the rookie cop who did desk duty. "He's still at the post office. I'll leave him a note that you called."

"Just tell him I'm going to the Slidell Hospital."

LaTonya gasped. "The baby?"

"No, no. I want to go see about Pete Hampton—the little guy who was in the explosion. Just tell him he can get me on my cell phone."

She clicked the phone off, then dialed her Aunt Aggie and waited for the old Cajun woman to get to the phone. "*Hola?*"

"Aunt Aggie, it's me," she said. "Did you hear about the post office?"

"Hear 'bout it?" Aunt Aggie asked. "Near wet my pants when I heard that bang. And the smoke . . . it's still arrywhere."

"Aunt Aggie, Mary Hampton was killed, and her little boy was injured . . ."

"The little blonde, T-Celia?" The Cajun prefix was a shortened version of *petite*, her version of "little Celia." Aunt Aggie had called her that since she'd been a child.

Celia sniffed and wiped her tears. She could hardly see through them to drive. "Yes. The one in my Sunday school class. The one you said would be a heartbreaker someday."

"Celia, don't tell me—"

"It was him," she cut in. "His mother's dead, Aunt Aggie. And he's pretty badly injured. I just wanted to let you know I'm heading for Slidell to be with him."

"You okay, *sha?*" Aunt Aggie asked, using her drawled form of *chere*.

"I'm fine," she choked out. "I just can't believe they're all dead. Mary and Sue Ellen and Cliff."

"They got the crazy yet?"

"I don't know. I haven't been able to talk to Stan. Oh, pray, Aunt Aggie. Pray that they catch the person who orphaned that little boy."

Aunt Aggie paused for a moment. "You sure you don't want me comin' with ya?"

"I'm halfway there already."

"You take care of your baby, you hear? That little boy's gon' be all right."

"I'm fine," Celia said. "He doesn't have anyone, Aunt Aggie. I have to go help. At least until his grandmother gets back to town."

"You could try findin' that no-count daddy of his."

"He hasn't been heard from since he left them. I doubt seriously he'll turn up now."

"You might be surprised," Aunt Aggie said. "If he knew his wife was dead."

"I wouldn't have a clue where to start. Anyway, I'm almost there, and I'm fine, so don't worry about me. I just wanted to let you know."

"Okay, *sha*. You be careful, hear?"

Celia hung up the phone as she reached the outskirts of Slidell and checked her watch. The boy would have been here about half an hour by now. She wondered if anyone had notified his next of kin. She wondered if they even knew how.

She began to weep again, and not knowing what else to do, she picked up the cell phone and dialed out Nick Foster's number. He was the preacher at her church—a bivocational pastor who worked part-time as a firefighter. She had no idea if he was on duty right now. Even the off-duty firefighters were, no doubt, still working on the fire at the post office.

His voice mail picked up. "Your call is very important to me," he said, and she knew he meant it. "Please leave your name and number and I promise I'll call you back as soon as I can." She waited through the series of beeps that testified to the number of messages he had waiting already, then after the long beep added her own. "Nick, it's Celia. I just wanted to let you know that I'm headed to Slidell Hospital to be with little Pete Hampton. If you get a chance to come over there, would you do it, please? I'm kind of at a loss as to how to deal with things. I know it would help the relatives if you were there when they get there, and Mary's mother really likes you. Not to mention Pete." Her voice trailed off, and she cut off the phone and wiped her eyes again. What in the world was she going to say to that little boy? What in the world could she do for him?

She reached the hospital parking lot and parked near the emergency room. She hurried in to the receptionist booth in the ER.

"Maternity?" the receptionist asked through the glass.

"No," she said. "I'm looking for Pete Hampton. The little boy who was brought in from the explosion in Newpointe."

"Are you his mother?"

"No." She swallowed, and her lips trembled as she said, "His mother was killed in the blast."

The receptionist, who probably saw all kinds of tragedies on a daily basis, looked stricken. "I didn't know. That poor little boy. Are you a relative?"

"No, but he doesn't have anyone here, and he needs somebody. I'm his Sunday school teacher, that's all, but I love him, and no one else here even knows him." She broke into tears again.

The nurse peered up at her as if trying to decide whether to let her go back. Celia hoped she didn't recognize her. She'd had a colored past, and people who remembered her not-so-distant history often looked at her as if they'd spotted Al Capone.

"Just a minute, let me ask someone." She got up and headed through the swinging doors, and Celia began to pace in front of the window, back and forth, back and forth. This place brought back so many memories. So many close calls with death, so many friends in the midst of refining fires. All of Newpointe's crises seemed to culminate here.

She caught her reflection in the mirror, her blonde hair and wet blue eyes, her huge belly just weeks away from delivery. Again, she looked down and patted her stomach. "It's gonna be okay," she whispered to her baby. "We've just gotta go be with Pete."

In a moment, the nurse came back out. "The doctor said you can go back. It's through those doors, the third door on the left."

Celia searched the woman's face. "How is he? Is he gonna make it?"

"He's still unconscious," she said.

Celia headed through the emergency room doors and down the hall until she came to the room where Pete lay on the bed, surrounded by a team of doctors and nurses. A tube ran down his throat, his face was bruised, and his eyes were swollen shut. She threw her hand over her mouth to muffle her horror. "Is he . . . is he okay?"

The doctor left the bedside and met her at the door. "He has a skull fracture and a concussion," he said. "Both lungs have collapsed, so we've put him on a ventilator. Looks like he was thrown a good distance in the explosion. Fortunately, he was far enough away that he didn't sustain any burns. He's got a broken arm and multiple lacerations. He's unconscious right now, but he did wake up on the way to the hospital and spoke. Then he slipped back into a coma. We're running some tests to determine if there's any swelling in his brain. We're probably going to have to transport him to New Orleans, since they have a better equipped head trauma unit there, and a pulmonary specialist who has more advanced equipment. You're not one of his relatives?"

"No . . . I'm his Sunday school teacher. His mother . . ." She lowered her voice to a whisper, in case Pete could hear. ". . . was killed."

His face slackened. "The paramedics weren't sure when they brought him in. Do you have any way of getting in touch with his relatives?"

"I can try," she said. "I should have done it before now, but I wasn't thinking clearly."

"He may not wake up for a while. Right now, it would be a huge help if you could find his relatives. Where is his father?"

"No one knows," she said as a wave of anger surged through her. "But his grandmother . . . she lived with them until a couple of weeks ago, and then she went to stay with her son because his wife had a baby. It's so sad . . . because . . . she didn't know when she left that she'd never see her daughter again." She covered her eyes and sucked in a deep sigh. "Oh, what if she hasn't been notified yet? Shouldn't I wait until the coroner or somebody gets in touch with her?"

He touched her shoulder gently. "It's very important that we reach her right away. We need consent forms signed, decisions need to be made . . ."

"Yes, of course," she said. "Okay, I'll do what I can. Can I . . . just see him first?"

"Of course." He escorted her to the side of the bed, and she looked down at the tiny, limp body. He was a rascal in Sunday school, always asking the hard questions, delighting in everything they did. He had an imagination that never quit, and he soaked up stories of Joseph and David and Daniel like they were local heroes. She didn't remember ever seeing him quite this still. With all the tubes and wires they had attached to him, she hardly recognized him at all.

The fact that his mother wouldn't be here to nurse him back to health overwhelmed her. She lifted his little hand. It was limp in hers, but she could feel a light pulse beneath his wrist. "Hang in there, Pete," she whispered. "Hang in there. Don't let go." But even as she said the words, she wondered if, maybe, he *should* let go. Maybe staying in this life was going to be too tough. Orphaned, possibly brain damaged, even crippled. She just didn't know. Was this more than a little child could bear?

She leaned over and pressed a kiss on his little forehead, then stroked his cheek gently. "You're gonna be all right, Pete," she said. "You're gonna be fine. Can you hear me?"

No answer.

"Pete, this is Miss Celia. You just keep fighting, okay? I'll be here fighting right beside you."

There was no indication that he heard a word she said. She let go of his hand and looked up at the doctor. "I'll go try to make some phone calls," she said. "I know his grandmother is with his uncle. I'm just not sure what his uncle's name is. Maybe their neighbors know."

The doctor nodded. "As soon as we can stabilize him, we're going to be transporting him to New Orleans where they have better head trauma facilities and a team of neurosurgeons. If they have to do surgery, they'll need consent right away."

"I understand. I just don't know if I can make it through that phone call."

"Somebody's got to do it," the doctor said firmly. "It's better coming from a friend of the family."

She took strength from the doctor's calm, insistent gaze. Turning, she left the room to find a phone.

• • •

Four phone calls later, Celia had the name and number of Zack Lewis, Mary Hampton's brother in Waco. She was about to dial when Allie Branning pushed through the doors to the emergency room.

"Celia, is Pete all right?"

"No," Celia said, as Allie pulled her into a hug. "He's not. I'm trying to reach his relatives." She released Allie and wiped her tears. "Where's Justin?"

Allie was rarely seen without her eight-month-old baby. "I left him with a sitter. Mark's still working the fire at the post office."

"Well, I'm glad you came." Celia turned back to the phone. "Right now, I've got to do one of the hardest things I've ever done."

"You've done a lot of hard things," Allie said. "What could be so bad?"

"I've got to track down Mary Hampton's mother," she said. "And when I get her on the phone I have to tell her that her daughter has died, and that her grandchild is lying here, unconscious, with a crack in his skull." She pulled her tissue from her pocket and blew her nose, then picked up the phone and began to dial. Her eyes locked with Allie's as the phone began to ring. She almost hoped no one was there.

A man answered the phone. "Hello?"

"Uh . . . yes." She swallowed hard and cleared her throat. "My name is Celia Shepherd. I live in Newpointe, Louisiana. I'm looking for Thelma Lewis . . . or Zack Lewis. I'm a friend of Mary's."

"Yes," he said. "This is Zack, her brother."

She pinched her tear ducts. She could tell from his tone that he didn't know of his sister's death. For a moment, she hesitated, wondering if she should ask to speak to his mother or give the news to him directly. She wasn't sure what was the right thing to do.

"Is there something wrong?" he asked.

"Yes, I'm afraid there is." Her voice trembled as she spoke. "There was an explosion at the post office here."

"An explosion?"

"Mary . . . uh . . . she was there . . . inside . . ."

Silence settled like dust between them.

"I'm so sorry, but your sister was killed in the blast."

She heard the phone drop, heard him talking to someone else, heard a woman's wail. She covered her face and pressed it against the phone. Allie touched her back. Suddenly, the man picked the phone back up. "What about Pete?" he asked breathlessly.

"He's in the hospital," she said. "That's where I'm calling from. He was injured badly, but he's still alive. He's in critical condition at Slidell Hospital, but they plan to transport him to New Orleans to a head trauma unit as soon as he's stabilized."

"Head trauma?"

"Yes. He's got a fracture in his skull, and they don't know if there's any swelling in his brain or not. He's got a broken arm, and some cuts and bruises, and two collapsed lungs. Fortunately, no burns. They need his next of kin to sign consent forms for treatment . . ."

Zack was having trouble speaking. "We're gonna call the airport right now," he said. "If we can't get a plane tonight, we'll just drive. We'll be there as soon as we can. Meanwhile, maybe we could fax our consent. If someone from the hospital could call us on my cell phone—"

"That would be good," she said. She took down his cell phone number. "Pete's gonna need someone here in his corner. I'll stay until you come. When he wakes up, he's going to need to be told . . ."

She heard the man comforting his mother, who was still wailing. Then in a broken voice he asked, "You'll stay with him?"

"Yes. And here's my cell phone number, in case you need to get in touch. I'll keep it with me." She called it out to him. "I'm so sorry to give you this news."

He couldn't answer.

"I understand the shock. I'm kind of in shock myself. Please hurry."

She hung up the phone and fell into Allie's arms. The two women wept together for several moments, before Celia could muster the strength to go back to Pete's room.

Chapter Four

● ● ●

The firefighters at the Midtown Station were exhausted and emotionally spent as they returned from fighting the blaze. It had taken hours to make sure the fire was out, and a pall of death hung over them like the smoke that still hadn't cleared entirely. They had found partial remains of three unidentifiable bodies, and could only conclude that they were Sue Ellen Hanover, Cliff Bertrand, and Mary Hampton. Five firefighters, two from Newpointe and three from other towns nearby, had been treated for heat exhaustion, and six utility workers who'd come to help with the electrical lines had been treated for smoke inhalation.

The firefighters peeled out of their heavy coats and stepped out of their pants. Drenched with sweat, they grabbed jugs of ice water and went into the TV room to soak up the air conditioning before they showered. None of them had eaten lunch, but few of them had appetites. Some of them coughed and gagged on the smoke caught in their lungs. Though they tried to remain protected at all times, there were times when they didn't have access to their tanks, and they inevitably breathed what they shouldn't.

Dan and Nick couldn't get cool, so they headed for the cold showers. "Man, I thought my bunkers were gonna shrivel right off of me," Dan said.

Nick, the bivocational preacher who also served as the protective services' chaplain, had mistakenly taken off his hood and face shield once to cool off, and as a result, had soot streaks and blisters on his face from the smoke. "I thought my *skin* was gonna shrivel right off of me. Man, I'll never cool off."

As they cut through the kitchen, Nick noticed Issie Mattreaux standing at the back door of the fire station, her face and arms stained black from the smoke. She had a vacant, dull look in her eyes as she stared out the door. Tentatively, Nick approached her. "You okay, Issie?"

His question seemed to startle her out of her reverie. "Yeah … uh, sure." A moment of contemplation followed, then, "No …"

"Need to talk?"

She looked up at him for a moment, as though that concept surprised her. Then without a word, she pushed out the screen door and stepped onto the back lawn. Issie wasn't as hot as he— she'd been in a cool ambulance for some of the afternoon as she'd transported Pete Hampton and treated the firemen and electrical workers. Despite how badly he wanted to step under that cold spray of water in the shower, Nick followed her, wondering if he was supposed to. It was a sweltering July day in south Louisiana, and the humidity hung in the air like a curtain blocking any breeze. The smell of smoke still hung in the air. He imagined there was no place in the small town where it could be escaped.

He felt drained and dizzy, but he'd been praying for Issie, and didn't want to lose a chance to talk to her about her spiritual condition. He figured that if he passed out, she'd understand.

Issie went quietly to a bench near the bayou running behind them. It was a beautiful bayou, well-maintained and part of the pride of Newpointe. Ski boats pulled skiers behind them further down, where it was wider, but here, only an occasional fishing boat drifted by without an engine. Patricia Castor, the mayor, had outlawed boat engines in this part of the bayou, mainly because her city hall office was across the street and she wasn't big on noise pollution. They had all half expected her to outlaw sirens, as well, but she hadn't found a way to do that yet.

Nick watched Issie sink down on a bench under a tree dripping with Spanish moss. She had her black hair pulled back in a ponytail, as she always did at work, but wisps of it hung around her face in thoughtless disarray. He wondered if she knew her face was stained with smoke, or if she cared. He knew his was, but it was the least of his worries. He sat down next to her, his elbows on his knees. "Talk to me," he said.

She looked out over the water. "It's just . . . the kid. I don't understand."

"Understand what?"

"What happened to him." Her voice was hoarse, raspy from the smoke, and she turned her big, dark eyes to Nick's and locked into them so tight that it felt like she was clinging to him. But Issie didn't cling, and they weren't even touching. "He came to for just a few minutes when we were en route."

"He did?" Nick asked. "Well, that's good news, isn't it?"

Her eyes ripped away and scanned the still water again. "He was crying for his mom."

"Did he know?"

"No, I couldn't tell him." She pulled her feet up onto the bench with her and set her chin on her knees. "That's the worst thing a child could ever hear."

Nick tried to put himself in the child's place. "I'm sure you're right." Again, silence ticked off the seconds. He saw tears well up in Issie's eyes, the first of her tears he'd ever seen. She wasn't the kind to cry at the slightest emotional tug, but they were each going to suffer the aftermath of this crisis in their own way. He saw how hard she tried to keep those tears from shattering and rolling down her face. Her throat moved as she swallowed hard.

"I don't get it," she whispered.

He wasn't sure he'd heard her right. "You don't get what?"

"I don't get why a good mother like Mary Hampton has to die, when there are so many crummy mothers who don't care a thing about their kids." Her voice trailed off as her own memories assaulted her, and he could see in her eyes that whatever those memories were, they were costing her.

"It didn't have anything to do with what kind of mother she was, Issie. It just happened, that's all."

She stared out at the bayou, as those memories warred in her mind. "I didn't grieve when my mother died last year. Neither did my brother."

He couldn't believe she was opening up to him. Most of the time, she went to great lengths to avoid any serious conversations with him. Something about his preacher status normally made her uncomfortable.

He didn't prod her on, didn't ask any questions that would make it easier for her to continue. Afraid of frightening her away, he simply waited, his eyes on those tears still balancing in the rims of her eyes.

"My brother and I practically raised ourselves. She worked nights in a bar, and when she was off she was out with some man. Men were a top priority for her. Way higher than me."

Nick's face changed, and he unfolded and sat up straight, gazing at her as the tear finally let go and made its slow path down her face. "Where was your father?" He asked.

She breathed a mirthless laugh. "Who knew? He took off shortly after I was born."

"I'm sorry, Issie," he said. "Is he still living?"

"Nope. Alcoholics don't live that long. He died two years ago."

"So you lost both parents within a year of each other? That must have been hard."

She wiped the tears from her face and stared down at her wet hands. "It wasn't. You can't grieve for something you never had."

But he could see that she was grieving now.

After a moment, she brought her eyes back to his. "So tell me, Nick. If there's a God, does he hate little children?"

"Of course he doesn't. Issie, he's going to see Pete through this. He has a plan for him, and he has one for you …"

"Don't do it," Issie warned. "Don't preach to me, Nick. It'll just make me mad, unless you can explain to me how somebody could walk into a post office and leave a bomb, hoping to blow a little kid's mom to smithereens."

"The same way your parents could fail you. We live in a sinful world, and so there's unspeakable evil in it. You can't put the blame on God. He's—"

She shot him a look, cutting off his words. "Don't do it, Nick. Don't you preach to me."

"I'm not preaching," he said. "I'm trying to answer your question."

"You can't, and you know it." Another tear ran down her face, making a trail through the smoke smudges.

"No, I can't. Not the way you want, anyway. Issie, you're not the only paramedic or EMT who's ever come to me with that question. As the chaplain of all of the protective services, I hear from firefighters and cops and you guys all the time. It's an occupational hazard, to hit that wall of despair." He rubbed his dirty face. "It's gonna hit each of us hard, this one. It's tough finding people you know blown to bits and burnt beyond recognition."

She breathed in a deep sigh and then blew it out. "I gotta get a better line of work."

"Like what?"

"I don't know. I could go to nursing school and treat appendectomies and viruses. Give flu shots."

"You wouldn't be happy doing that."

She shot him a look. "Why would you say that?"

"Because you like living on the edge. That emergency feeling that keeps that adrenaline pumping. That life or death scenario."

"How do you know that?"

"Because I like it, too," he said.

"In the pulpit, or in the fire truck?"

He chuckled. "Both, actually."

Aunt Aggie, the eighty-one-year-old dynamo who cooked all of the fire department's meals, opened the door and shouted for both of them. "Come eat, T-Nick! Issie, you hungry? I got cold fruit and watermelon."

"I'm already off duty, Aunt Aggie," Issie said. "If you don't have enough, I'll just—"

"Have enough? You insultin' me, *sha?* I always got enough."

"I'll be there in a minute, Aunt Aggie," Nick called.

The old woman, dressed in a gold-glittery blouse and black wind-suit pants, looked as if she'd taken special care with her looks today. Her white hair looked freshly done, and she sported a smile that Nick knew was for their benefit. Aunt Aggie always liked to cheer them up when they'd fought a battle like the one today. "y'all need to get outa that heat and get some liquids down, not to mention food. I'm gon' have folks droppin' like flies around here, me."

They watched her go back inside, fussing and mumbling. "I wish I had answers for you," Nick told Issie softly. "All I know is that God is still in control. He was when you were a kid, and he still is."

"Why do you religious people always say that? That God's in control? It's like the catch-all answer."

"It's *exactly* the catch-all answer. In a world that doesn't always make sense, we can only trust in him."

"Trust him for what?" Issie demanded, growing angry now. "What can that little boy trust in him for? His mother trusted. She was one of your church members, wasn't she?"

"Yep. Sure was."

"Then how could this happen?"

"We may never know," Nick said. "But God will be faithful. I know that. Regardless of what happened ... regardless of how tragic this was ... God has a plan, and he will be faithful to carry it out."

"Well, excuse me for saying so, but if that's his plan for Mary Hampton ... for Sue Ellen Hanover ... for Cliff ... for Pete ... If it was his plan for me when I was eight years old ... I don't know that I want God's plan in my life." She got up and headed back inside.

Nick sat motionless, realizing that he hadn't helped at all. Once again, he had failed. This woman for whom he had prayed so many times had finally come to him with a spiritual question. And he had not had answers that satisfied her.

The screen door opened and Aunt Aggie came out again. "You awright, Nick?" she asked him.

He looked up at her. "I guess. I just ... Issie was asking me some questions about God. I didn't help her much."

"You prob'ly helped more than you know, *enfant.*"

"No, Aunt Aggie." He got up, took off his glasses, and cleaned them on his shirt. "Everything I say just goes in one ear and out the other. She just thinks I'm a big joke with silly ideas."

"Ain't that what I use ta think?" Aunt Aggie asked. "Used to say so, right to your face. I thought you was no better than a con artist, peddlin' your bill o' goods to that church full of folks. But look at me."

Nick couldn't help smiling. Aunt Aggie had been as close to a lost cause as he'd ever seen in his life. But a few months ago, she had shocked the town by showing up in church, and had almost caused collective coronary arrest when she'd gone down the aisle to tell him that she'd met Christ. "Tell me something, Aunt Aggie. Back then ... when you equated me with a con artist ... did anything I said ever sink in?"

"Arrything you said sunk in," she said. "I just didn't know it. One day, it all came cavin' in on me, all at once. You keep workin' on that Issie, *sha.* She'll come around."

Wearily, Nick followed Aunt Aggie back inside. The table was filling up with tired, quiet firemen.

Dan was out of the shower and stood in front of the mirror combing his hair, as if the right style might hide his receding hairline. Mark Branning was on the telephone, and when he got off, he turned to the rest of the guys.

"Do y'all have any idea where Pete Hampton's father is?"

Ray Ford, the fire chief, was just coming in as Mark asked the question. Ray frowned and took his place at the head of the table. "I knew Pete's daddy, Larry, when he was still here. We went to school together. Even played ball on the same team. He worked as an insurance salesman over on Bonaparte Street. Up and disappeared one day with his secretary. Hasn't been heard from since."

"The kid needs somebody. Allie said his uncle and his grandmother are on their way, but if we could locate his father . . ."

"I'll make some phone calls," Ray said, "soon as I get back to the office. Maybe we can come up with some leads and find him. But if I remember his daddy, I think little Pete might be better off with his grammaw."

Nick met Issie's eyes across the table. Those tears had sprung back into her eyes.

Chapter Five

● ● ●

Jill Clark didn't think she had the energy left to make it back across Lake Pontchartrain from Chalmette, where she'd spent ten hours taking depositions today. She didn't know how the injured Cajun roughneck had found her, but he had begged her to represent him in his lawsuit against the oil company responsible for the loss of his leg. Since most of the work required being away from Newpointe, she had tried to get everything done in one day.

But she hadn't finished, so she would have to be there early tomorrow morning. It was hardly worth it to drive the hour back to Newpointe. As she drove the outskirts of Chalmette, she looked for a motel where she could crash.

The song on the radio was grating on her nerves. She was reaching over to turn it off when a news bulletin cut in.

"Newpointe police are investigating an explosion that took place at the post office on Bonaparte Boulevard at 4:00 this afternoon . . ."

She caught her breath and turned it up.

"The source of the explosion is under investigation. Three people are dead, and one survivor—a child—is in critical condition."

Jill raked a hand through her short brown hair and tried to think. Three people dead at the post office? Sue Ellen Hanover and Cliff Bertrand had to be two of them, she realized as her heart sank. An explosion? How could it have happened?

She was distracted as she pulled into the parking lot of the Flagstaff Motel, and sat there a moment, punching different stations on the radio, trying to get more news. But all she heard was crying-in-your-beer tunes, knee-slapping zydeco, heavy metal ...

Quickly, she got out and went to the office, checked in, then hurried to her room. She dropped her few things onto the bed and grabbed the telephone. By rote, she dialed the number of the fire department, tapping her foot as she waited for someone there to answer the phone.

"Midtown." It was Dan Nichols. She knew his voice immediately, and wondered if she had been wise to call. It had been eight months since their relationship had ended, yet every time they passed or saw each other, she still got that little pang in her heart.

"Dan?"

"Jill?" He recognized her voice, too, and she wondered why that warmed her.

"I'm sorry to bother you, Dan," she said. "It's just that I've been in Chalmette, and I just heard about the explosion."

"Yeah, it was bad. Sue Ellen Hanover is dead, and so is Cliff Bertrand. And Mary Hampton was killed."

"So the child ..."

"Mary's little boy. He's in a coma."

She sank onto the bed with her hand over her mouth. "Dan, what happened?"

"We're not sure yet. Looks like a bomb. A couple of witnesses saw a pickup truck there just before the blast. Apparently, they've identified a suspect."

"Any guess why he did it? Was it terrorism?"

"In Newpointe? Doubtful."

"Was he trying to get revenge for something? Has Cliff fired anybody lately?"

"I don't know, Jill. The cops are playing this one close to the vest. Looks like the FBI's getting involved, too, since it was a government building. We'll just have to see how it plays out."

That was it, she thought. That was as much as she was going to get. She took a deep breath as her head reeled with the information. She was about to thank him, when he spoke again, his baritone timber softening. "So how are you doing?"

She tried to line her thoughts back up. "Uh . . . fine. Just fine. And you?"

"I'm okay. It's been a long day. So you're in Chalmette, huh?"

"Yeah. I decided to stay in a motel since I have to be back at the courthouse at seven in the morning. I'm at the Flagstaff."

He was quiet for a moment. "Jill, it's good to talk to you. Real good."

She smiled and looked into the mirror above the bureau. Her brown hair was tousled from a long day of raking tense hands through it, and her blue eyes looked tired and red. As she stared at her reflection, she was painfully aware that Dan's tastes ran blonder and more petite. Pageant material, Jill was not. "It's good to talk to you, too, Dan. You sound a little raspy."

"Yeah, there was a lot of smoke at the post office. We fought the fire for hours. It was the worst I've ever seen."

She sat back on the bed. "Who found the bodies?"

Again, seconds of silence ticked by.

"Dan? Was it you?"

"I made a few discoveries," he said.

She sighed. People thought Dan was self-centered and egocentric. He was, in some cases, but he also had a gentle, sensitive side that she cherished. "What did that cost you, Dan?"

"A lot." The words seemed to take a lot out of him.

"I'll bet. Wanna talk about it?"

"Maybe when you get back."

She tried not to let that statement give her hope. He was just feeling lonely and vulnerable. Death did that to you. It didn't mean anything.

A rap on the door made her jump, and she dropped the telephone. It clanged and she picked it back up, put the phone back to her ear. "Dan ... hold on a second. Somebody's here."

She went to the door, looked out through the peephole, and saw blue lights flashing. Startled, she pulled back the curtain and peered out. The parking lot was full of police cars, with lights flashing in a broad array of blue and red. The knocking sounded again, and she realized they were not at her door, but at the room next to hers. When there was no answer, one of them shouted for the occupant to open it.

Shaken, she went back to the telephone. "Uh ... Dan, this is really weird. The parking lot's full of cops, and they're banging on the door next door—"

A gunshot ripped through her words as it tore through the adjoining door, and she screamed and hit the floor. The phone crashed to the ground. Another shot whizzed past her head, and she rolled out of the way. The door crashed open, and a man with a rifle burst in, his eyes panicked. He got one look at her and bolted toward her, knocking over a chair to get to her. He grabbed her up and thrust the nose of his rifle at her throat.

She heard the police breaking down the door to his room, yelling at fever pitch as they filled it. One mistake, and it would all be over, she thought. One overzealous police officer, one overactive twitch of this guy's finger on that trigger ...

Two cops came to the door, their guns aimed at the man. "Drop the rifle!" one of them shouted.

"I'll kill her!" the man holding her yelled. "One more step and I'll kill her!"

She screamed again as he jabbed the barrel of the gun harder into her throat. He twisted her arm behind her to hold her still. She felt him shaking as he held her.

"Back up!" he bellowed. "Back up and close the door. Now!"

Slowly, the police backed away. "Just drop the gun and nobody'll get hurt."

"Shut the door! Now!" the man shouted. "I'm telling you, I'm gonna pull this trigger."

Jill's muffled scream frightened the cops back, and the door closed between them. Dragging her with him, the man kicked the door on their side shut. Jill screamed again.

Chapter Six

● ● ●

The sound of the gunshot shattered through Dan's brain with as much impact as if the bullet had traveled the phone line. He clutched the phone and shouted, "Jill! Jill!" She was no longer holding the phone, and he could hear screaming in the background, things crashing, people yelling.

Then the phone went dead.

"You okay?" Mark Branning had just come in from the truck bay, and stood there staring at Dan.

"No!" Dan slammed the phone down.

"What is it?"

"Jill! I've gotta run next door." He dashed out of the station and crossed the yard to the police station adjacent to the fire department, bolted up the steps, and pushed through the glass doors. Stan was heading out, and Dan almost ran into him.

"Stan, I was just talking to Jill at a motel in Chalmette, and something happened. There were police cars there, and I heard a gunshot, then we got cut off."

"The Flagstaff?" Stan asked, shooting him a look. "That's where I'm going."

"What's going on there?"

"We've got the suspect for the post office bombing cornered there," Stan said, trotting down the steps. "We had an APB on the pickup someone identified at the post office just before the bombing, and they spotted it at the Flagstaff. Apparently they've got the right guy if he's shooting back."

"He's not *just* shooting back!" Dan shouted, as if Stan had orchestrated the whole thing. "Stan, he's got Jill!"

"What?" Stan had reached his car and was unlocking it. "What do you mean?"

"I was talking to her and I heard a gunshot and *he came into her room!*"

"No way." He got into the car.

"I heard her screaming, Stan!" Dan opened Stan's passenger door and slid in. "I'm coming with you."

"No, you're not!" Stan said.

"He's taken Jill hostage!" Dan cried. "Call them and ask. You'll see."

Stan picked up his radio mike to check out the claim. In moments, he had someone from the St. Bernard Parish Sheriff's Department confirming that a hostage had been taken. "Okay, Dan. You're right. He has a hostage. But are you *sure* it's Jill?"

"*Yes!* Now, drive! I'm coming with you."

"All right." Stan turned on the flashing grill lights of his unmarked car and pulled out into the street.

Chapter Seven

● ● ●

The tortured dreams of napalm and Molotov cocktails, machine gun fire and mines, haunted Frank Harper, and in his sleep, he tried to cry out. But his screams were smothered by the sound of war, muted by the terror of death, or worse. He dreamed of comrades falling around him, of his captain's orders being bellowed over the fray. He dreamed of the pain that rent through him as a mine exploded, and the fingers tearing from his hands. He told himself it was a dream and tried to wake up, but the darkness was so profound, so dense, that he began to scream again, loud, agonized screams that went unheard and unheeded.

He tried to breathe, tried to remember where he was, tried to grope around for some sign. He was flat on his back, and he reached up and touched a wall above him, on each side of him, below him. A coffin, he thought, gulping in the air. He had been buried for his country.

Something crept across his leg, and he yelled again, then rolled onto his stomach and began to crawl away. The coffin wasn't closed on the ends. It was too long, and the farther he crawled, the more fresh air he felt. He crawled faster, faster.

It wasn't until he reached the end that he realized he wasn't in a coffin, but a culvert. He had hidden here.

He reached the end and pulled out, stretching to his full height, and looked up at the star-sprinkled sky.

It all came back to him, and he remembered stealing the Civic from the Delchamps parking lot after Jerry let him out, hearing the sirens as he hid under the bridge, hiding in the culvert to escape . . .

He looked around him in the darkness and wondered what he'd done with the detonation devices, the explosives, the wires . . . He was standing on the edge of Lake Pontchartrain, he realized. Maybe he'd thrown the explosives in.

But no . . . he'd needed them. He would not have gotten rid of them . . . not yet.

Had he left them in the culvert? He realized that he had, but couldn't—wouldn't—go back in to get them. What was he going to do now?

Jerry, he thought. He was supposed to meet Jerry . . . at some motel on the way to Chalmette. Would Jerry still be waiting? Had he slept too long?

He looked around, trying to orient himself. The bridge was too long, too far, to cross on foot. By now, they'd be looking for the stolen car. He'd have to find another one somewhere. He hoped that Jerry would wait.

Chapter Eight

● ● ●

The man let Jill go, and she reeled back into the wall, putting as much distance between herself and him as possible. He was breathing hard and beginning to sweat. The hum of the air conditioner gave a surreal feeling to the room, as if there wasn't a team of cops outside waiting to gun him down.

He pulled the chest of drawers in front of the adjoining door to make sure no one could come through, then satisfied, turned back to her. For the first time, he met her eyes, and she told herself not to shrink away.

There were certain things she'd learned in her years of dealing with clients who were both victims and criminals. Talk to them, she'd heard victims say. It was harder for them to kill people who seemed human to them. She'd also learned in dealing with criminals who occasionally wanted her to defend them that it didn't pay to let them know you were afraid. She lifted her chin and desperately tried to appear calm as she watched him get the phone off the floor and hang it up. But she knew her shallow, rapid breathing belied that calm.

Talk to him, she told herself. *Remind him you're a person.* "Why are they after you?" she managed to ask.

He turned to look at her with a surprised look on his face. Had he expected her not to speak? Or was it the question itself that stumped him? "I don't know," he said finally.

"You don't know?" she repeated. "Your motel room is surrounded by police, you've taken a hostage, and you don't know why?"

The phone began to ring, and he stared down at it as if it were some kind of live thing that threatened him. He made no move to answer it, and it kept ringing. Jill wondered if it was Dan calling back. She must have frightened him to death—the screaming and crashing. "Do you … want me to answer it?" she asked.

He seemed to think it over for a minute, then shook his head. "No. Let it ring."

"But … maybe it's them. The police, I mean. You could … I don't know … talk to them and … straighten this out."

He rubbed his perspiring face with one hand as he clutched the rifle with the other. The expression on his face and his defensive body language gave Jill courage.

The phone kept ringing … ringing … ringing …

"You must have some idea why they're out there. I mean, you're armed and holed up in here with me."

He aimed the rifle at her. "Get on the bed."

She eyed the bed where she had dropped her things. Dread overwhelmed her, and she struggled to find a weapon. The lamp, a ballpoint pen …

He seemed to reconsider. "Wait."

The phone continued to ring … ring … ring …

He ignored it and, still holding the gun to her, grabbed her briefcase and opened it. He pulled out the files, the documents, the day planner, the computer organizer, the pens. Satisfied, he put it all back, closed it, and put it on top of the chest of drawers blocking the adjoining door.

Surprised that he hadn't carelessly dumped it, she met his eyes. They were intelligent, not crazed, and she wasn't sure whether that comforted or disturbed her. Intelligence could be more deadly … more calculated …

The phone kept ringing …

"Jerry!" The bullhorn voice buzzed over the hum of the air conditioner, startling them both. "Jerry, pick up the phone," the police voice said. "We need to talk to you, so we can bring a resolution to this. Just pick up the phone."

He walked closer to Jill, the barrel of the rifle against her temple, as if they could see him and infer that he was serious. She squeezed her eyes shut, bracing herself. "Go to the bed," he said again through his teeth. She moved toward the bed with the gun at her back. Why did he want her there? Was he going to hurt her? She got on the mattress and leaned back against the headboard, hugging her knees. As he got on the bed next to her, she squeezed her eyes shut. Her heart rampaged, making her dizzy. She had never been so afraid.

The phone kept ringing . . .

Suddenly, he snatched it up. *"What?"*

She opened her eyes and saw the gun still aimed at her temple, but he wasn't looking at her. "Jerry, this is Mills Bryan, FBI." She could hear the telephone voice from where she sat. "You should know that you're making the situation worse for yourself. Keeping a hostage is going to hurt you more than anyone else. There are already three people dead. You don't want to add one more to that list."

Three people, she thought. He had killed three people.

"I didn't do it," he said. "You've got the wrong guy. I didn't have anything to do with that post office bombing."

She caught her breath as she realized that the man holding a rifle aimed at her head might very well be the terrorist that had killed three friends today.

"We can talk about that when you come out," the caller said. "Just let your hostage go and come to the door. Jerry, it would be so much better for you if you stop this now."

"How?" he shouted. "So you can gun me down and go on TV telling everybody that you caught the guy? *I didn't do it!*" He slammed down the phone and turned his raging eyes to her.

She balled herself tighter, and realized she was trembling. "Look . . . you don't have to keep that gun on me," she said. "Just . . . just put it down. I won't try to get away. I'll just sit here . . ."

"Shut up!" he said. "I have to think." He kept the gun aimed at her, but thankfully got off the bed and began pacing back and forth, back and forth. She was able to breathe again. Occasionally, he looked at her, started to speak, then stopped. She didn't move.

Talk, she told herself. She had to keep talking. "I believe you didn't do it," she lied.

He stopped cold and turned around, that gun still aimed at her. He looked almost amused as he stared down at her. "You couldn't possibly."

"I do. I'm a good judge of character. You're not the kind of man who would kill anybody."

His scowl returned, and he shook his head hard. "You don't know what kind of man I am. You'll say anything to keep me from hurting you."

"No," she insisted. "I know because . . . the briefcase. You didn't throw it or dump it. You were almost . . . respectful. I believe you wouldn't hurt anyone. Even me." She prayed it would be a self-fulfilling prophecy.

He looked at her for a moment as if trying to decide whether to gun her down or befriend her. She had to keep talking. "Why do they think you did it, Jerry?"

He seemed to flinch at her use of his name, then tried to consider her question. His eyes went back and forth from the window to the bed as he turned that over in his mind. "My truck. It must be my truck. I was stupid. I should have known they'd be looking for it!"

Then he *did* do it, she told herself. They were looking for his truck, and they'd found it.

"There must have been witnesses," he went on as he paced. "I should have known. I should have said no."

"What do you mean?" she asked.

He seemed unable to go on as emotion overwhelmed him. He groped for the chair, pulled it out from the table, and sank down. "Debbie's gonna die."

She swallowed hard. "Who's Debbie?"

"My wife." He looked up at her, those probing eyes searching her face. "What's a matter? You don't think somebody like
me could have a wife? I have kids, too. All these years, I've tried
to protect them . . . and now this." His face twisted in pain, and
tears shone in his eyes. As if to compensate, he aimed the gun at
her again.

"Please . . ." she whispered. "Please put that away. If it went
off . . . that would be four dead . . ."

"I didn't kill the other three. I didn't leave that bomb!"

"I know . . . I know you didn't. I just meant . . . four deaths
that you'd be accused of."

"You don't know!" he flung back at her. "Don't pretend you
know. For all you know I'm some kind of raving maniac whose
elevator doesn't go all the way to the top. You don't know me."

"I know what you said."

"And why would you believe some guy who bursts into your
motel room and holds a gun to your head? Huh?" His question
was angry, insistent.

She knew he had her there. "I don't know. Instinct. I told
you. The briefcase."

"Give me a break!" he shouted. "It's called *survival* instinct.
Tell him what he wants to hear so he won't hurt you." He leaned
back hard in the chair and leaned his head against the wall.
"Look, I don't want to hurt you. I don't know who you are, don't
care to know. All I do know is that I'm in a mess and I need time
to think. You're buying me that time."

Somehow, she did believe him . . . but she didn't know if she
should. "My name is Jill. Jill Clark." She hoped knowing her
name would make it harder to pull that trigger.

He didn't answer for a long time, then leaned his elbows on
his knees and gave her a tentative look. "Who were you talking
to on the phone when I came in?"

She swallowed and tried to gauge whether his finger was
right over the trigger. "A friend at the Newpointe Fire

Department. I had heard about the bombing on the radio, and I called to ask him what he knew about it."

"Small world, huh?"

"Yeah. It is something of a coincidence."

"And so . . . what did he say?" His eyes didn't look like those of a criminal. They were clear and green, and she imagined that he wasn't a bad-looking man when he wasn't drenched with sweat and waving a rifle. "Who were the three people killed?" he asked.

"Sue Ellen Hanover, the postal clerk, and Cliff Bertrand, the postmaster. And a customer . . . Mary Hampton. Her little boy, Pete, is in the hospital in critical condition."

His eyes widened with what looked like despair, and he turned his face away. "What have you done?" he whispered. She wondered if he was talking to himself. He brought his gaze back to her. "This . . . little boy. How old is he?"

"Five, I think."

"And his mama's dead?"

She nodded.

He took in a deep breath and wilted as his elbows hit his knees again. Slowly, he reached into his back pocket and pulled out his wallet. He took out a sheaf of pictures, tossed it on the bed. "That's my five-year-old."

Reluctantly, Jill picked up the pictures and studied the shot of the precious little boy in a baseball cap that was bigger than his head.

"You think a man with a kid that age would deliberately take a boy's mama from him?"

"No," she said. "Not deliberately."

"Not even accidentally," he said. He got up and grabbed the pictures back, turned the page, and showed her a little girl of about three. "This is my daughter. And my wife. I have a family. And a job. I'm a human, with feelings and a conscience. I don't kill people."

He waved the gun wildly as he spoke, and she held her breath, praying it wouldn't go off. His tears wet his face, and his nose was running, and he wiped it with the hand that held the gun. "I'll probably never see them again. My kids'll grow up thinking I'm a terrorist. My wife will wish she'd never met me." He batted at the tears on his face and breathed in a sob. "And I didn't do it!"

"Then tell them," Jill said, trying to keep her voice calm. "Go out there and tell them exactly what happened. Explain. If you didn't do it, you can prove it."

"No, I can't," he said. "Don't you think I've thought of this? I don't have an alibi. My truck was at the scene of the crime. They're gonna nail me to the wall. Only rich people are found innocent in this country. The rest of us poor Joes are automatically guilty. We don't have dream teams of attorneys spinning and posing for us."

"If you're innocent," she said, "then why *don't* you have an alibi? Why was your truck there?"

He just shook his head, got up, and began to pace again. When he refused to answer, she took a risk. "Jerry, I'm a lawyer. Not the five-hundred-dollars-an-hour kind, but I have a good reputation in Newpointe. They'll listen to me. You can turn yourself in, and I'll tell them you didn't hurt me. I'll help you prove that you weren't involved in the bombing. You have to try for your kids and your wife, Jerry. If you're not a criminal, don't become one just to avoid the fight."

He stopped pacing in front of the air conditioner unit and let it cool his back. "I didn't say I wasn't a criminal," he told her. "When they look at my rap sheet, they'll think I am one. But my record doesn't account for anything that's happened to me in the last ten years. They won't care who I am now. They'll only care about who I was then."

Her heart sank. So he did have a criminal record. Her hope that he was just a nice guy in a bad situation fled.

Keeping the gun trained on her, he came to the bed. She watched him—her breath held—wondering what he would do next.

Chapter Nine

● ● ●

Back in Newpointe, Jim Shoemaker, the police chief, hung up the phone and looked at the two federal agents in his office. "It's confirmed. The owner of the truck at the Flagstaff is a resident of Newpointe. He moved here six months ago when his wife's aunt died and left them her house. I knew the aunt. Good woman. Hard to believe she'd have a terrorist for a relative."

"What's his name?"

"Jerry Ingalls. Designs websites for a living, so he hasn't had occasion to get to know many of the townspeople yet. Kids aren't old enough for school, either, so the family kind of keeps to themselves."

"Are you sure it was him? The truck wasn't stolen, was it?"

"Nope. The men I sent over interviewed his wife. She said she hasn't seen her husband all afternoon. Apparently, he's the one in the truck."

"He's probably not working alone."

"Maybe not. But I have people going through his history, looking for affiliations and associations, groups he might have been involved with."

The door flew open, and Jim leaped to his feet. The agents swung around.

Patricia Castor, the mayor, bolted in. "Jim, I want to know what you know about that bomber. I can't have any more buildings go up in flames around Newpointe. Is he just targeting federal buildings, or government buildings in general? Should we evacuate?"

Jim frowned and looked at the two agents. "Uh ... gentlemen ... this is our mayor, Patricia Castor. Pat, these are FBI agents here working on the case."

"Then you tell me," she demanded, turning to them. "It's gotten so I'm scared to go to work tomorrow. Should we evacuate, or not?"

"Evacuate what?" one of the agents asked.

"The local government buildings. The social security office. The courthouse. City hall. This building right here! The homes around the downtown area."

"Pat, we can't evacuate all of Newpointe without cause."

"We have no reason to believe that other buildings are targeted, ma'am," one of the agents said. "We don't recommend random evacuations, but the minute we have reason to think evacuation necessary, we would let you know right away."

Pat wasn't satisfied. "I'm not so sure. You people blew the Kennedy investigation. I still haven't gotten over that."

Jim came around the desk, took Pat's arm, and gently turned her back to the door. "Pat, I promise, I'll keep in close touch with you about this. But right now, we have an emergency on our hands. We think we have the bomber holed up in a motel in Chalmette. We really need to get back to work on this."

"In Chalmette? Well, why on earth are you flapping your jaws in here, when you oughta be there?"

"There are dozens of law enforcement people there, Pat. Some of our own men. I'm working things from this end."

"Well, all right," she said, looking skeptically from Jim to the two agents. "As long as you catch him. You tell me the minute you do, Jim. I want to come over here and question him myself. I can't have people blowing up buildings in my town. What are we gonna do without our post office? Do you have any idea the position this puts me in, as the mayor? People will be looking to me for answers."

"I know," Jim said sarcastically. "Creates a lot of paperwork, doesn't it?"

"Now, don't you get smart with me, Jim Shoemaker! You know I care about the dead. I'm at practically every funeral in this town, whether they can vote or not." She stormed out of the office. Before Jim could close the door, she yelled, "You let me know the minute you get him, you understand?"

Jim closed the door and turned back to the agents. They probably thought they'd stumbled into an episode of the *Twilight Zone* in Mayberry. He hoped they wouldn't decide to disregard his department's help altogether.

Chapter Ten

● ● ●

In Slidell, Celia stood helplessly on the sidewalk of the Slidell Memorial Hospital as they loaded Pete into the ambulance to transport him to New Orleans. He still wasn't conscious, and some dreadful voice in the weariest part of her brain told her that he wasn't going to wake up. They had taken so long to stabilize him that she had almost believed they'd changed their minds about transferring him. When the ambulance had finally come, she had considered riding with him, but since she had her car here, she decided to follow behind them. She had tried to reach his uncle and grandmother to tell them where he would be taken, but hadn't been able to connect with their cell phone. Maybe they had gotten a flight out, she thought, and they were on the way.

"Celia." Allie stood next to her, looking distraught too. "Are you sure you don't want me to go with you?"

"No, no," Celia said. "You need to get back for the baby."

"But he'll be all right for just a little longer. I could follow behind you . . ."

"Really, it's okay. I'm just going to stay with him until his grandmother gets there."

"I don't want you to wear yourself out now," Allie said, patting Celia's belly.

She fanned herself with her hand. "If it just wasn't so hot . . . and it looks like rain."

They got the child into the ambulance, and Celia wiped her eyes again. "I hope he doesn't wake up in there and ask for his mother."

54

When they closed the doors, Allie hugged her. Wrenching herself away, Celia got into her car and followed the ambulance.

The ambulance made no attempt to move Pete there quickly, as she had expected. The siren wasn't on, and neither were the flashing lights, and she began to get nervous. Why were they wasting so much time? What if the child needed immediate attention?

Then she told herself to calm down, that they knew what they were doing. Maybe a smooth ride was more important than a fast ride. If they'd needed to hurry, they would.

She turned on the radio to divert her attention from her worries and fears, and flipped around until she came to the news. It was an update on the explosion, and she turned the volume up.

"The suspect is apparently cornered at the Flagstaff Motel in Chalmette, Bob. We are standing a good distance from the motel, since the suspect is armed. A few moments ago we heard gunshots, and it has just been confirmed that the gunman shot through the adjoining door in his room and took a hostage."

Celia brought her hand to her face. "Oh, Lord," she whispered, "don't let him kill anybody else." Quickly, she picked up her cell phone and began to dial Stan's number with her thumb. LaTonya Mason answered at his desk again.

"LaTonya, is Stan there?"

"No, he gone to Chalmette. They got the post office bomber there."

"I heard," she said. "So Stan's at the Flagstaff . . . right in the middle of all that?"

"He's on his way."

"And the man is armed?"

"That's what I hear."

Celia swallowed back her protests. "All right. Just leave him a note that Pete Hampton's being transported to New Orleans. I'm going with him."

"All right."

She hung up the phone and realized that her heart was racing. Her husband was on his way to a motel where they had backed an armed, desperate man into a corner. There had already been gunfire. There was likely to be more.

Blinking back her tears, she stroked her swollen stomach as she drove and prayed silently that no one else would have to die.

Chapter Eleven

● ● ●

Outside, Stan Shepherd arrived on the scene with Dan Nichols. Dan leaped out before Stan could cut his engine off. Sid Ford—another Newpointe cop—was already there, and so were a dozen or so FBI and ATF agents, as well as the sheriff's department for St. Bernard's Parish.

"What are the feds doing in on this?" Dan asked Stan.

"Somebody blew up a federal post office. Everybody and his brother is going to be in on this."

Because of Stan's emergency lights, no one asked for either of their IDs. Dan pushed through the officers to Sid Ford, who had been the first Newpointe officer to arrive on the scene. "Sid, how's Jill?"

"We think she's okay," Sid said, distracted as he studied the blueprint someone had given him of the motel.

"Is that the blueprint of the motel? I can go in there," Dan said. "I could go through the attic . . ."

Sid looked up, disgusted. "Dan, whatchu even *doin'* here? You ain't a police officer. Since when have the Newpointe firefighters responded to calls in Chalmette?"

"I came with Stan," he said. "I was talking to Jill on the phone when he took her hostage. Sid, you gotta let me go in."

Sid shook his head as if his friend had lost his mind. "I ain't even in charge here," he said. "We got all kinds of jurisdiction problems. The FBI's headin' this thing up. Local sheriff's

57

department is already buttin' heads with 'em. Our best bet is to stay out of the way."

Dan wasn't satisfied. He scanned the federal agents until he saw one who seemed to be in charge. Dan pushed through the police and reached him. "Let me try to go in," he said, but as he did, Stan came up behind him, presumably to pull him away.

Preoccupied, the man gave him a sideways glance. "Who are you?"

"I'm Dan Nichols. I'm a firefighter from Newpointe, and if I just study the blueprint I can figure out—"

Stan stopped him with a firm grip on his arm. "I'm Detective Stan Shepherd from Newpointe," he cut in, reaching to shake the FBI agent's hand. "Excuse me a minute." He turned his back to the man and in a low voice said, "Dan, you need to get out of the way. You don't belong here, and you're just calling attention to yourself."

"But *somebody* needs to go in there."

"And what are you gonna do? Shoot him from one of the air conditioner vents? I'm telling you, get out of the way or I'll have to arrest you."

"You've got to be kidding," Dan said.

Stan's eyes pierced into him. "I'm not."

Dan stepped aside, and Stan engaged the FBI agent to see where they were on the case.

Sid was shaking his head as Dan came back to him. "Man, what is wrong with you?"

Dan's eyes flashed. "Jill is in there," he said through his teeth. "A homicidal maniac is holding her hostage! What's wrong with *you?*"

"Jill's tough," Sid said. "She can handle this." He touched Dan's arm, and Dan jerked away and turned to see which window Jill was behind. "Can you?"

"Say I'm overreacting," Dan said. "But I was just talking on the phone to someone I care a lot about, and heard some lunatic burst into her room shooting. It shook me up a little bit. Sue me." He raked his hands through his hair and took a step toward the motel. "Which room is it?"

"That one," Sid said. "One-fifteen. He came from 117 next door."

"There must be a crawl space in the attic, a window in the bathroom, *something!*"

"Where's Stan goin'?" Sid asked as Stan ran around the perimeter of squad cars. They watched as he went to the telephone van set up on the edge of the parking lot, tapping into the phone company's equipment on the corner of the property. Dan took off toward him, and Sid followed.

"The guy's making a phone call," one of the officers in the van was saying.

"Who's he talking to?" one of the FBI agents asked.

The agent monitoring the call shook his head and held up a hand to silence him. Dan wanted to jerk the earpiece away from him. He saw the tape recorder turning on the wall of the van. The cop monitoring the call turned up the volume, and Dan leaned in to hear.

"Honey . . ." The man's voice was overcome with emotion and wobbling.

"Jerry? Jerry, what are you doing? Where are you?" It was a woman's voice, and she was obviously upset. "Jerry, the police have been here. They're saying you blew up the post office. Just now, I heard on the radio that you were holding a hostage."

"I didn't do it, Debbie," Jerry said. "I'm telling you, you've got to believe me."

"Jerry, three people were killed!"

"Debbie, you believe me, don't you? I gotta know you believe me."

She began to sob. Jerry spoke again. "Debbie, honey, listen to me. Debbie, are you listening?"

"Yes," she choked out.

"Debbie, I want you to know that whatever happens, I love you. Please, no matter what people say I did, make sure the kids know that I'm not what they're saying."

"Jerry, you talk like you're gonna die!"

"It's a dangerous situation, Debbie. I'm surrounded by cops."

"Is it true you have a hostage?"

"Yes," he said. "I had no choice."

"Oh, Jerry, let her go!" she wailed. "*Please* let her go! This is getting worse and worse. How did it happen? What are you *doing?*"

"It's a long story," he said. "But I can't let her go. She's my only chance. I'm gonna ask them to get me a plane, and I'm gonna get out of here. Maybe by some chance . . ."

"Jerry, are you out of your mind? You can't play games with these people! They have guns!"

"I have a gun, too," he shot back. "My deer rifle that was in the truck."

"What are you saying? That you'll *use* it?"

He was quiet for a moment. "Debbie, please, promise me, that whatever happens you'll tell the kids that I'm not—"

"That you're not what, Jerry?" she yelled. "That you're not a killer? What if you *do* kill somebody? What if you kill that hostage? What if there's a shoot-out when you try to go to the plane?" Her voice broke again, and in a high-pitched voice, she said, "Jerry, don't you know what you're doing to yourself?"

He was silent for a long time, and Dan could hear the despair in his voice when he spoke again. "Debbie, I'm as much of an innocent bystander as that little boy whose mama got killed. You know I don't have this in me."

"Then let the hostage go, Jerry. Let her go and walk out of that room, and we'll get you a good lawyer . . . we'll do whatever we have to do. Just . . . please don't make it any worse. Please . . . I'm begging you."

He began to weep. After several moments, he said, "I love you. Just don't forget that."

The phone clicked.

"Call him back!" Stan said. "Maybe he'll be willing to come out now."

Someone dialed the number, and in the van, Dan heard the phone in room 115 begin to ring.

Chapter Twelve

● ● ●

The phone began to ring again, but Jerry made no attempt to answer it. Jill had been moved by the conversation she'd just heard. Though she hadn't been able to hear his wife's voice, she had seen her captor weeping. She knew by the pain on his face and the emotion in his voice that Jerry himself was in turmoil.

The phone's urgent ringing heightened the tension in the room, and she worried that it might send him over the edge. On the other hand, maybe he would decide to let her go and surrender. If she played her cards right, maybe she could push him toward that decision.

"Jerry, you could let me answer that phone," she said, just above a whisper. "I could tell them that you're coming out, that you haven't hurt me. I could tell them to put their guns down, that you didn't do it."

The phone kept ringing ... ringing ... ringing ...

His face was wet with tears, but he began to laugh. "Oh, yeah. They'll believe that."

"Why wouldn't they?" she asked. "Some of those cops out there are probably from Newpointe. They know me really well. They know I'm a good judge of character and that I wouldn't say this if it wasn't true."

"They know you're under duress and you'd say anything to get out of here," he told her.

The ringing continued, shrill, relentless ...

Her voice rose. "But if you're really innocent, they can substantiate your claims that you're not the one who planted that bomb."

"Oh, can they?" he asked. "How can they? Anyone who saw anything is probably dead."

"But if there were witnesses who saw your truck, then maybe they could confirm that you weren't there."

"But I *was* there. I just didn't know what he was doing!"

"What who was doing?"

He turned his back to her. The phone rang three times more as he stared at the wall, then quickly turned back around. "By now they've done a rap sheet on me and they know I served time for armed robbery. But it's been ten years since I got out, and I haven't had so much as a parking ticket since. And they'll find out I had post-traumatic stress disorder after Vietnam, and that I went for treatment. They'll call me crazy and say I've snapped. I know how this works."

"Well, excuse me for saying so," Jill ventured, "but you're not exactly acting sane right now."

Instead of getting angry, as she might have expected, he nodded his head in agreement. "You're absolutely right about that. But you see, I've never been in this position before. I don't quite know how to act." He wiped the sweat off of his temples and looked at the ringing phone. She hoped they wouldn't give up.

"What did your wife tell you to do?" she asked.

He looked up at the ceiling. "You can guess. She told me to let you go. That I was digging myself into a hole I couldn't get out of."

"Does she think you did it?"

His face twisted, and he swallowed hard. "She couldn't possibly. Not after being with me all these years. All she knows is she's hurting and scared right now." His face reddened, and as the anger seemed to rise up inside him like lava, he bared his teeth and kicked the bed table, knocking the phone off. Quickly, he hung it back up, as if the open line would give all his secrets away. Almost immediately, it began to ring again.

"Let me answer the phone, Jerry. Let me talk to them."

"No," he said. "I'm the only one who can talk to them. I've got to make some demands. I've got to have a plan." His hair was growing wet with perspiration, dripping down into his eyes, but still the air conditioner hummed and the telephone shrieked.

Finally, he bolted across the room and snatched up the phone. "I want an airplane," he said without prelude. "Get me a plane and a car that'll take me to the airport. If you don't meet my demands in two hours, I'll kill her, you got it? I have nothing else to lose."

He slammed the phone down, startling Jill. She stared up at him, letting the words sink in. Two hours, and he would kill her. She wasn't certain she believed him, but then, he was under extreme stress. There was no telling what he might do.

She decided she'd be quiet for a while, so that he could think his way out of this. Silently, she prayed for the men outside, that they would somehow know what to do.

Chapter Thirteen

• • •

Outside, it began to drizzle. The blue grill lights of Stan's unmarked car, and the unmarked cars of the FBI men, flashed along with those of the local police cars filling the parking lot. Dan's heart was flailing after hearing the man say he would kill Jill in an hour.

The Chalmette police and federal agents were arguing about whether to meet his demands to buy time, whether to try to go into the building, or whether to call him back and reason with him. Dan tried to stay back, out of the way, but the inaction was beginning to drive him mad.

"Why don't you jerks get busy and do something?" he shouted. "Time's ticking away. He may not even wait the full two hours!"

The head of the FBI contingency shot Stan an unappreciative look. "Somebody get him out of here."

Sid rolled his eyes and took Dan's arm. "Come on, buddy."

"They're just *sitting there*, like they have all the time in the world."

"No, they ain't just sittin' there. They're tryin' to make some rational decisions. Brother, you need to get back in the car, just to keep you from shootin' your mouth off where it ain't welcome. You need to stay out of the way, like we do when you fight fires."

He refused to get into the car, but leaned back on the hood. His head was beginning to ache, so he clutched it with both hands. "Are they gonna get the plane or what?"

"Maybe. Maybe not. It's their call, not yours."

"What about the wife?" Dan asked. "What if someone brought her here?"

Sid stared at him for a moment, processing the idea. "Now, that might be a good idea. The first one you've had all night. And if you stay here and don't start yappin' and yellin' again, I'll go throw that idea out to them. Can I trust you to do that?"

"Don't talk to me like some kind of idiot, Sid." Dan's face began to redden. "I've risked my life right alongside you, more times than I can count. Condescension isn't called for here."

"Neither is panic."

He banged his palm on the hood of the car. "I'm not panicked."

"Ain't you?"

"No! I just seem to be the only one concerned about Jill."

"You're the *most* concerned about Jill—I'll give you that. But you ain't the only one." Sid headed back to the others.

Dan stood on the fringes of the forces, feeling more helpless than he'd ever felt before. He saw some of the cops going into the motel's office, then heard that they were cutting off the circuit breaker that powered the air conditioner. It was eighty-five degrees out. Soon it would get so hot in there that Jerry Ingalls would be begging to come out. But so would Jill. He saw several of the cops clustering around the surveillance van again, and Stan seemed to be at the center. Slowly, he headed toward it, hoping he wouldn't be noticed. He saw that an FBI agent was calling Jerry again, letting it ring, ring, ring . . .

He started to suggest, loudly, that they not do anything else to increase the killer's tension, but just before he could get the first word out, the man inside picked up the phone and yelled, *"What?"*

Dan wiped the sweat from his face on the sleeve of his shirt and stepped closer, listening.

"Jerry, I think you know you're surrounded, and that the FBI is in on this, because blowing up a post office is a federal rap."

"I'm quite aware of that," Jerry snapped back.

"Then why don't you give yourself up, come on out, and spare your family any more pain?"

"I want you to listen to me," Jerry said, his voice quivering with rage. "I want you to get me that plane. I don't need a pilot. I can fly it, if you just have it waiting for me at the airport. I'm not bluffing, man. You've got two hours or she's dead."

"We're working on getting the plane, Jerry. But remember, she's an innocent bystander. You're not a cold-blooded killer."

Dan searched the agent's face, saw that he was feeling his way, trying to appeal to the human side of the man they'd heard in the phone call to his wife.

"You've got a lot more to lose than you think. Your family. . ."

"I've already lost my family," Jerry shouted. "You've taken them away from me. I'm gonna have to get on a plane and fly to who-knows-where, looking over my shoulder constantly, when I know I didn't do anything. So don't throw my family at me. Just do what I say." He slammed the phone down.

Dan shook his head.

"Okay," one of the agents told Sid. "Go ahead and get someone out to the wife's house and bring her here, fast. We'll bluff our way to the airport if we have to, but maybe the wife can buy us some time."

Stan and Sid got out of the van and headed for Stan's car. It began to drizzle, but that did nothing to help the sweltering temperatures. It only made it feel like a steam bath.

Dan stood close to Stan's car as he radioed the order back to Newpointe. When he'd finished, Stan looked up at Dan. "You okay?"

Dan could only shrug and look toward that motel room again.

"She's okay, you know," Stan said. "He hasn't hurt her yet."

"How do you know he hasn't? She's been in there over an hour and a half. We don't know what he's done to her."

"I just don't think he has."

Dan couldn't respond as he stared at the lighted window.

"You know, you and Jill haven't been an item for months. But you're acting like a husband negotiating for his wife. What gives?"

Dan breathed a sigh that spoke volumes. "I always knew she was okay. That I could pick up the phone and reach her if I wanted to."

"But you didn't want to."

Dan swallowed. It was too complicated to explain. He couldn't even sort out his feelings for his own sake.

"Now that she's being held hostage at gunpoint, you suddenly have feelings for her?"

"It's not sudden," Dan said. "Quit playing shrink and just get her out of there."

Chapter Fourteen

● ● ●

Inside the motel room, Jerry Ingalls went to the air conditioner and tried to make it come on, but it wouldn't. While he'd been on the phone it had gone off, and the room's temperature seemed to be rising dramatically as a result.

Jill heard rain drumming against the window, making the air even more humid than it had been. Jerry was drenched with sweat, and Jill was perspiring, too. So far, she'd stayed on the bed, her arms around her knees, protecting herself. Now she worried that the heat and his discomfort would add to his instability.

Slowly, she unfolded from her crouch and eyed the door to determine how long it might take her to rush to the door, turn the bolt, and push out into the night before he shot her. *Too long*, she thought. She'd never make it.

She peered into the darkened bathroom. No windows. And the ceiling in the small, stifling room was made of sheetrock. There was no way to push through to escape. Her eyes drifted back to the door. Maybe if she could just get closer to it, she would have an opportunity to run.

Cautiously, she got off of the bed and went to the air conditioner unit. "It must be broken."

He shook his head and slammed the cover down. "They did it. They want me to be as uncomfortable as I can be."

"How could they do that?" she asked. "They'd have to cut off all the electricity to do that, wouldn't they? The lights are still on."

"They could have tripped a breaker." He stood at a slit in the curtain, peered out, then turned back to her. He was still holding the rifle on her, but his finger wasn't poised over the trigger.

She crossed her arms nonchalantly and tried to get between him and the door. "Can I look out?"

"No," he said. "Get back over there."

His voice was tentative, almost timid, but he still waved that gun. She backed away, but didn't go all the way over to the bed.

"Did you mean that? What you said on the phone, about killing me in two hours?"

"Of course I meant it."

"But I thought you swore you weren't a killer."

"I'm not. But when you're surrounded by cops and falsely accused, you tend to do things you might not ordinarily do."

"And killing me will help you how?"

He gave her a disgusted look. "Just get back on the bed and shut up."

She sat on the edge of the bed but kept her eyes trained on him. He sat down, holding the rifle pointed at her, but his eyes seemed to move back and forth across the room, as his mind worked the problem over.

After several moments had passed, he turned back to the window. She thought of trying to rush him while his back was turned, but that finger was too close to the trigger. "It's sweaty," he said.

"What is?"

"The air." He turned back to her and looked at the floor. "It's what my little boy says. 'It's sweaty in here.' Like the air has the sweat floating around in it."

She forced a smile. "He sounds sweet."

His throat bobbed. "He is." His mouth twitched as emotion covered his face, and she knew he was wondering if he'd get to see his boy again. "You have kids?"

She shook her head, thinking that was probably a negative in his book. If she could say she was a mother, maybe he'd go easier on her. But somehow she felt he would know if she lied. She didn't think she looked much like a mother, or even a wife, for that matter. "I'm not married," she said.

"Engaged? Going steady?" It was the first hint of humor she'd encountered in him, but she didn't find it amusing. Neither did he. It was simply conversation designed to make the minutes tick by with fewer jolts.

"No." She began to realize it was a mistake to admit that to him. If she had no one who would mourn her murder, it would be easier for him to end her life. "But ... there's this firefighter I've kind of been involved with ..." It was a lie. She and Dan hadn't been involved in the last eight months, but she was still attached to him in some way. She thought about him more times during a day than she would ever admit to anyone. She wondered what he was thinking tonight after her bizarre phone call.

"That who you were talking to when I came in?"

She nodded. "Yes."

"Guess he's a basket case, if he heard all that."

Again, silence. He sat back in the chair at the window, and looked down at the floor, then at his watch, then at the phone.

She seized the opportunity to lean forward, ready to pounce toward the door as soon as she had the nerve. "Jerry, I could represent you, if you let me go. I could prove to them that you're innocent."

"But you don't believe that I am."

"Of course I do," she lied. "I could tell them that you haven't touched me ..." Her words faded out as quickly as she'd uttered them. She didn't want to give him any ideas. "I ... I could find the real killer."

"No, you couldn't. You'll never find him."

Jill frowned. "But with your help—"

Something she'd said was wrong, because his face hardened and he got up and turned back to the window again.

"Because all you have to do is tell them, and—"

"Shut up," he told her. "That's enough."

She checked her watch. Time was running too fast. "Jerry, please."

"I said shut up!" he yelled, swinging around. He looked at his watch, then peered out the curtain again. "What are they *doing?* They're just *sitting* there."

"They can't very well fly that plane into the parking lot," she said. "They're probably taking care of it by phone and radio."

He turned around and leaned his head back against the wall. "What if they think I won't really kill you? That it's a bluff? Maybe I need to shoot just to show them that I mean it." He began to pace across the floor, from the window to the bathroom, and back again. She sensed that he was getting more and more uneasy, more and more panicked, like a caged animal.

She eyed the door again, and watched him walk past her. He turned back around, like a sentry keeping guard, and passed her again. She sat up straighter, preparing to bolt. She had to get out of here, she thought. She had to at least try. She had to take the chance.

"One hour and twenty minutes," he said, grabbing a towel out of the bathroom and mopping his face. "They have one hour and twenty minutes."

"Jerry . . ." It came as a whisper, almost inaudible. In less than two hours he would pull the trigger. What did she have to lose by running now?

When he passed her to go back toward the bathroom, she took a deep breath and prayed a silent, pleading prayer. Then she pushed off from the bed and launched out for the door. He swung around with the rifle and yelled, "Don't!"

She turned the dead bolt and pulled the door open, but it caught on the chain.

Jerry crossed the room and slammed his gun against the door. It went off in his hand, shooting straight up into the ceiling.

She screamed and fell back, and he turned the gun on her. "Get back on that bed or I'll do it now!"

The phone began to ring, and still holding the gun to her, he sat down beside her and picked it up. He thrust it against her ear. "Tell them you're okay," he said.

She trembled as he pressed the phone to one side of her head, and the gun to her throat. "Hello?" she whispered.

"Jill, are you all right? We heard a gunshot . . ."

She glanced at Jerry and tried to find her voice. "I'm fine."

"Ask them about the plane," Jerry prompted.

"The plane . . ." she said, breathless. "Do you have the plane?"

"We're working on it. Jill, has he hurt you in any way? Are you—"

Jerry removed the phone and put it to his ear. "You've got an hour," he said, and hung it up.

Chapter Fifteen

● ● ●

On the east side of Newpointe, Debbie Ingalls saw the flashing lights of the police car through her window. She sat paralyzed in the dark of her living room as the walls went from blue-to-black, from blue-to-black. Had Jerry killed the hostage? Had they come to tell her he was dead?

"Mommy."

She jumped at the sound of her child's voice. Five-year-old Seth stood at the door with his hair all cowlicked and tousled, and those big freckles illuminated and darkened by the lights coming in the window. "Mommy, what's that light?"

"Come here, honey," she said, getting up and pulling her son to the back room with her. Her three-year-old daughter slept soundly there, and she crawled onto the bed next to her and held Seth with all her might.

"Why are you crying?" Seth asked in a whisper.

"Because . . . Daddy's in trouble."

"Why?"

"I don't know," she said, shaking her head. She pressed her forehead against her son's freckled face. She loved those freckles. She often told him they were angel kisses.

The doorbell rang, and she caught her breath and tried to calm herself.

"Who's that?" Seth asked.

"Um . . . Honey, I want you to stay here with Christy. Mommy has to go talk to . . . somebody."

She put the child down next to his sleeping sister and got off of the bed.

The doorbell sounded again.

Wiping her face with shaking hands, Debbie headed for the door. She touched the knob, pressed her forehead against the door, and gave in to another round of sobs. When the bell rang again, she forced herself to open it.

"Mrs. Ingalls?" the police officer asked, his hat dripping with rainwater. It wasn't the same officer who had been here earlier, to tell her that her husband was a terrorist.

She closed her eyes and nodded, pressing her hand against her mouth.

"Mrs. Ingalls, I'm Sergeant R.J. Albright, ma'am. I know you're aware that your husband is in some trouble. I also know he's been in touch with you . . ."

"Yes," she whispered.

"I was wonderin' if you would come with me to Chalmette and talk to him. We were thinkin' that if you could be there in person, maybe you could convince him to let his hostage go."

She opened her eyes wide and looked at him fully. "He's . . . he's not dead?"

"No. I'm sorry, did you think . . . ?"

"Yes." She collapsed against the door's casing, weeping.

The squad car's door slammed, and she saw a black woman storming up the sidewalk to her house, her silhouette stark against the flashing blue light. "You poor woman!" She reached the door and pulled Debbie into her arms. Debbie collapsed against her like a child running into the arms of its mother.

"Uh . . . ma'am, this is Susan Ford," the officer said awkwardly, as if the embrace embarrassed him. "She's the fire chief's wife. Her brother-in-law, Sid, is a police officer on the scene in Chalmette."

Susan kept holding her. "He asked me to come see about watchin' your kids while you go deal with your hubby, darlin'."

"We're kind of in a hurry," the officer said.

"Give her a minute, R.J.!" Susan snapped, handing Debbie a handkerchief. "Can't you see she's upset?"

"He's given us a deadline," R.J. insisted. "We need to get you there as soon as possible."

Debbie straightened, and tried to steady her breathing. She took the proffered handkerchief from the woman, then quickly flicked on the light behind her. She looked the woman over. She was pretty and small, and her face was full of compassion. Debbie felt like she'd known her for years. "I'll go," she said. "The children are in the back bedroom. Seth is awake. He'll be scared when I leave. Tell them . . . tell them I'll be back soon."

"Don't you worry about a thing. Me and the babies, we'll have us a big time."

Debbie tried not to look back as she headed out to the squad car.

• • •

The rain was falling harder as they reached the Flagstaff Motel after a hair-raising, siren-blaring, light-flashing drive from Newpointe. Debbie looked around and saw the New Orleans television station vans broadcasting live with bright lights that lit up their field reporters. Over to the side stood a group of people that were, no doubt, motel guests who'd been evacuated after the gunfire.

Everywhere, she saw uniformed police officers and FBI agents. She began to cry again.

The sky flashed with lightning, and a thunderbolt crashed right behind it. R.J. ushered her out of the police car, and the crowd seemed to part for her. She kept her eyes on the one motel room that everyone's attention seemed to be focused on. "How much time left?" R.J. asked as they approached someone at a van. She recognized him to be Stan Shepherd. She had seen his picture in the papers.

"Thirty minutes," he said, turning around. "You Debbie Ingalls?"

"Yes," she said.

"Will you talk to him if we can get him on the phone?"

"Of course. I don't know if he'll listen . . ."

"He's demanded a plane, and he wants us to give him a car so he can drive to the airport. He says he'll fly it himself."

"Where does he intend to go?"

"We don't know that. But he's digging himself deep, Mrs. Ingalls. If you talk him out of all this, he'll be a lot better off."

She'd already figured that out for herself. "Where's the phone?"

Two agents filed out of the van to make room for her, and they gave her a seat next to the phone, where she could talk and still see out the windshield. She heard it start to ring, and realized that everyone was listening to the conversation. "Do you have to listen in?" she asked. "I . . . I feel a little nervous . . ."

"Just do the best you can," he said. "And yes, we do have to listen in."

She accepted that with resignation and put the phone to her ear. On the third ring, Jerry picked it up. "The clock is ticking," he said.

She winced at the words. "Jerry?"

He hesitated. *"Debbie?"*

"Jerry . . . I'm outside." She looked through the windshield to the motel room window. "They brought me here so I could talk to you."

"You're here?" he asked, and she saw the curtain in the room pull back slightly. She saw some of the rifles being lifted, and she grabbed the arm of the cop next to her. He signaled for them to hold their fire. "Where?"

"In the van," she said. "Over to the right of the parking lot. Jerry, this is crazy! You can't do this. You can't just get on a plane and fly out of here and never look back. We love you."

"I can't believe they're using you like this." His voice was deadly calm, quietly angry.

"I wanted to come," she said.

"Where are the kids? They're not out there watching all this, too, are they?"

"No, they're at home. The police sent a baby-sitter. But I'm here, Jerry. Don't make *me* watch it."

"Debbie, I'm doing what I have to do. I can't go back there. They'll stick me with terrorism and murder, and I haven't done anything wrong. They'll put me in Angola for the rest of my life."

The sky flashed again, cracking the line. "Jerry, we can prove your innocence if you come out now."

"Have they got the plane?"

She looked at the agent who seemed to be in charge, and he mouthed that they needed a little more time. "Jerry, they need a little more time. Besides, it's not flying weather. It's dangerous—"

She heard something crash. The police officers in the parking lot bent behind their cars and aimed their guns. She guessed there must be two dozen weapons aimed at that window in front of her husband.

"They think I'm bluffing," he said.

"Jerry, calm down. The plane is almost there. But you can't take a hostage and threaten to kill her, then hop on a plane and fly off in a thunderstorm and think you'll get away with it. Jerry, somehow we can prove you didn't do the post office bombing. So far, you haven't killed anyone. But if you hurt your hostage . . . if you add another victim . . . so help me, Jerry, I'll never know what to believe. I'll never know what to tell the children."

She heard him weeping into the phone, heard him sucking in a wet breath. "Debbie, I can't surrender. They won't listen."

"Yes, they will. Jerry, you have to try. I didn't marry a quitter. I didn't marry somebody who runs when things get hot. I married a fighter. An honest man. A *sane* man."

"Debbie, I want you to go home. They can't hold you here."

"I'm not going!" she shouted. "Jerry, don't make me watch you come out of that room with a hostage! Please!"

"Debbie, I said to go home."

"No!" she screamed. "Jerry, so help me, if you do this, I'll never forgive you. Don't you *dare* leave me. Don't you *dare* ruin your children's lives!"

He was silent for a moment, then finally, the phone clicked off and she was left with nothing but a dial tone.

"Aw . . . He's mad," the man behind her said, raking his hands nervously through his hair. "He's agitated. You gotta let me go in. Stan, tell them . . ."

Stan stared at the motel room, his eyes intent on it, as if he could see into it. "Maybe we do need to send somebody in at this point," he said. "But not you, Dan."

"Send somebody in?" Debbie asked. "And do what? Shoot him?"

"We have to protect Jill," Dan said. "He's unpredictable . . ."

"Shut up!" one of the agents ordered. "You're not a cop. You don't belong here!"

Dan backed away, shaking his head. He looked as nervous as she. "Is he . . . the hostage's husband?" Debbie asked Stan.

"No," Stan said. "Just . . . a good friend."

She looked back at the distraught man, then at the motel room, and knew that the man they called Dan was in love with the woman inside. It was written all over his face, even if no one else could see it. Suddenly, she had overwhelming sympathy for him, and for the woman inside. "Maybe I need to be the one to go in there," she said.

They all turned. "What do you mean?"

"I could knock on the door. Tell him it's me. Maybe he'd let me in. Maybe I could talk him into coming out."

"You're willing to do that?"

Dan approached the van again, his face growing hopeful. "Yes."

"But he's dangerous right now. He's armed."

"He's my husband," she said, lifting her chin. "He won't hurt me, no matter how desperate he is."

"Are you sure?"

She looked toward the motel room as if weighing the possibility, then finally, said, "Yes, I'm sure. Let me go in."

"I'm gonna warn him you're coming."

"All right." She got out of the van and waited in the rain with her arms crossed. Dan was watching her, and she knew he could see how hard she was trembling. Someone called the room, listened as it rang, but Jerry wasn't going to answer it. Finally, an agent brought the bullhorn to his mouth. "Jerry, your wife is coming to the door. Look out the window and you'll see her coming. Let her in."

Debbie started walking toward the door as the rain pounded on her and lightning bolted, and she saw the curtains being jerked back. Jerry motioned for her to go away, but she didn't stop until she was at the door. As long as she stood in front of his room, she knew they wouldn't shoot him through the window and risk killing her and the hostage.

She knocked and waited, but the door didn't open. "Jerry, let me in," she cried. "Open the door, Jerry." As she called through, her voice became more urgent, more emotional. "Jerry, please. Don't do this to me. Please, open the door. Look at me! I'm alone. Don't leave me out in this storm with all those guns pointed at me."

Several minutes passed, and finally, the door opened just a crack. Debbie pushed inside, and it closed again behind her.

Chapter Sixteen

• • •

Jill couldn't believe Jerry's wife had pushed her way in, and as their eyes met, the tiny woman seemed to be assessing her for injuries. She stood no more than five-feet-three, and had eyes that were too big for her face and wet hair that dripped into her eyes. She burst into tears again at the sight of Jerry's rifle. Jerry paid no regard to the fact that she was rain-soaked. He crushed her against him as she wept into his shirt, both hands clenched in fists against his chest. "Jerry . . . Jerry . . ."

Jill waited, breath held, praying that his wife would have the clout to get him to let her go.

Jerry turned Debbie's face up to his and gazed sadly down at her. "I need for you to go back out there."

"No, I won't go," she said. "Not until you let her go and turn yourself in."

"I can't do that."

"Jerry, how could you do this? You're going to make a widow out of me. I'll never see you again."

"No, I'm not. It'll all work out. When I get where I'm going, I'll find work and send you money, and you and the kids can join me."

"Jerry, they'll come after you, if they don't shoot you down before you ever get on that plane. You can't be naive enough to think you'll get away with this."

"I have no choice."

"Yes, you do!" She pushed him away from her. "You can be a man and fight this. You can walk out there and turn yourself in, and we can prove that you didn't blow up the post office! You won't be labeled a murderer." She grabbed his shoulders and stared up at him. "How did this happen, Jerry? Why do they think you were there?"

"Because I *was*," he said. "I was there right before the explosion. But I didn't know. I wasn't involved."

She wiped her face with both hands. "Jerry, the friend you were meeting. Was it him?"

Jerry turned away.

"Who was it?" she screamed. "Jerry, tell me!"

Jill waited, breath held.

"I can't," he said.

Debbie banged her fists on his chest. "Jerry, are you gonna die for this? If you do, you'll be the one considered a killer. They'll never even look past you."

It felt like an oven in the room, and Jill wiped her face on her sleeve. Jerry sank down into a chair, glistening with sweat, and shook his head wearily. "It's out of my hands."

"No! It *can't* be!" Debbie turned to Jill. "She'll tell them, won't you? You'll tell them that he hasn't touched you! It should carry some weight."

"How do you know he hasn't?" Jill asked.

Jerry's eyes whiplashed to Jill's.

Debbie's chin came up and her lips compressed. "I know my husband. He's a gentle, sweet man ... a good husband and father ... He'd never blow up a post office or kill innocent people or hurt anyone ..."

The words seemed to chisel away at his constitution, and he wilted further with each one.

Jill sat straighter. "You're right. He hasn't hurt me. Yes ... I'll tell them."

Debbie turned back to him and leaned down to him. "See? Jerry, this can still be all right."

"They'll put me in jail," he said. "Maybe Angola again. Are you sure you can stand to go through that?"

"Yes! At least I'll know where you are. At least there's hope."

"Hope," he repeated. "I don't know if there *is* any hope."

"Of course there is. There's always a chance, if you're here to fight. Jerry, I'll fight with you."

"I fought last time."

"I wasn't *there* last time. You were fighting alone."

Jerry seemed moved by that, and he stood back up and reached for her. She reached up to touch his face as their eyes met, and Jill held her breath, certain that he was about to acquiesce and let her go.

When he seemed to struggle with an answer, Jill decided to speak. "I told him I'm a lawyer, that I would represent him."

Debbie's eyes widened as they turned to her. "Really? See, Jerry? Look how much influence she would have, if she was the hostage you were charged with taking, and she wound up representing you! Jerry, don't you see how much help she could be?"

He looked at Jill, as if assessing her for honesty. She looked away.

"Jerry, I've never asked you for much," Debbie cried. "But I'm asking you now. If you love me . . . if you've ever loved me . . . if you love the children . . . I need you . . . we need you . . . to let her go and walk out there without that gun."

Jill began to pray silently as Jerry gazed down at his wife.

Chapter Seventeen

● ● ●

Outside, the lightning bolting angrily in the sky mirrored the energy coursing through Dan's soul. He could hardly breathe as he waited in the rain for something to happen. Moments passed, and he began pacing, never taking his eyes from the door. Overcome with emotion, he prayed silently for Jerry Ingalls, that he'd have a change of heart and mind and let Jill go, that Debbie would have enough influence over him, that Jill would remain unharmed ...

Suddenly, the door opened, just a crack, then a little more, and Dan froze as a crack of thunder heralded the change. Officers all around the parking lot ducked behind the barricades of their cars and aimed their weapons. Headlights lit up the door, and they all waited. Then the storm grew silent for a moment.

Then Jill appeared, holding the rifle over her head.

"It's Jill!" Stan shouted. "Hold your fire!"

She broke into a run and headed toward them. Dan paid no regard to the guns aimed at her and took off between the cars to meet her. It wasn't until she was well past the headlights that she was able to see him, but she bolted into his arms and clung to him with all her might. Someone grabbed the rifle from her hands, and police officers surrounded her and pulled them out of harm's way.

"Where're the Ingalls?" Stan asked, keeping his eyes on the door.

"They're coming," Jill yelled. "They're unarmed. Don't shoot them."

They held their fire as the door opened again, and Jerry Ingalls came out with one arm around his wife and the other high in the air. Both of Debbie's arms were around him.

Slowly, they walked toward the police, one step at a time, as if they each expected to be gunned down at any second. When they were sure they weren't armed, the cops ran forward, pulled Debbie away, and threw Jerry down on the ground. Debbie began to scream that they were hurting him.

Suddenly, half of the reporters were shining their cameras on the scuffle, and the other half surrounded Jill.

"Miss Clark, are you all right?"

"Did he hurt you in any way?"

"What made him release you?"

She pulled away from Dan and stepped back as the rain drenched her. "No, he didn't hurt me. He let me go because his wife convinced him to."

"Why did he take you hostage?"

"Because he claims he's innocent of the post office bombing. He panicked when the police came."

She heard Debbie Ingalls sobbing hysterically, and looked back at her over her shoulder. "Wait! Stop!" Debbie screamed. "He has a lawyer! She's going to represent him! Jill Clark is my husband's lawyer!"

One of the agents pulled Jerry to his feet and began to drag him toward his car. Stan approached Jill. "That true, Jill?"

Dan let her go and stared down at her, and she was overcome with the sense that everyone here was looking at her, waiting for an answer. Even Jerry and his wife. A million conflicting emotions raged through her. "I ... I don't know what she's talking about," she said.

Debbie heard that and began to wail even more loudly, and Jerry looked at her with an anguished, betrayed expression. She put her back to them and looked up at Dan. "Will you drive me home?"

"I came with Stan," Dan said. "Besides, they'll want to take you back to the station. You'll have to give them a statement."

"I . . . I will," she said. "Just . . . drive my car. I just need some quiet. Just a few minutes."

"But they want to examine you, make sure you aren't hurt."

"I'm fine," she said. "Please, Dan. Get them to let me leave. I want to get out of here."

Dan secured permission to drive Jill alone in her car as two Newpointe squad cars escorted them back. She sat shivering in the air conditioning as her wet clothes clung to her skin.

Dan was quiet, and Jill got lost in her own thoughts. Why did she feel like a traitor? She had made a promise to Jerry and his wife, after all, but did a promise made under duress have to be kept?

She leaned her head back on the seat, breathing in the stream of cold air coming in from the air conditioner vents. "Jill, do you want the air conditioner off? You're shivering."

She shook her head. "No. It's been like a steam bath."

"But you're wet. You'll get sick."

She turned the vent away from her. "I'll be fine." She saw the concerned way he looked at her, and knew what must be going through his mind. "Really, Dan, he didn't touch me."

"Then why are you so quiet?"

She shook her head. "I was just thinking. He swears he's not guilty, wanted me to represent him."

"That would be a little crazy, if you ask me."

"Yeah, I think so, too. But I kind of had to make a promise to get out of there."

"Is that why he let you out?"

"One of the reasons." She thought back over the conversation with Debbie, her promise to help him, his final agreement to do as his wife had asked. "Maybe I should represent him, since I said I would. But what if he's guilty?"

"I guarantee you he wouldn't be holed up in a motel with a gun and a hostage if he wasn't. Any idea what his motive was?"

"I couldn't say. But he seemed concerned about the people who were killed, and Pete Hampton ..."

"So he's a killer with a heart?"

Jill stared at the rain-splattered windshield. Steam rose up like a fog from the road in front of them. "Something like that."

"At least he didn't pull that trigger. When I heard that gun go off, I thought my heart was gonna explode through my chest."

She regarded his wet clothes and the pained expression on his face. It suddenly occurred to her that he wasn't supposed to have been there. This wasn't Newpointe, where firefighters were called to every emergency. "Dan, why were you there?"

He didn't answer for a moment, just drove into the night, across the long, lonely bridge over Lake Pontchartrain. "When I heard what happened on the telephone, there was no way I could just stay put. I had to find out what was going on."

"Yeah, I guess that was pretty scary," she said.

"Shook me up real bad."

"I guess anybody I had on the phone would have felt the same way."

"Maybe," he said.

Again, there was deafening silence between them, as Dan seemed to struggle with his words. "I was praying while I was out there," he said. "I was about to jump out of my skin. I just knew you were gonna get killed by that maniac. I just knew I was never gonna see you again."

She thought of asking him why that would have impacted him at all, since she rarely saw him now. But fatigue was coloring her perceptions and her thoughts, and it wasn't a good time to get into them.

"I made some bargains with God when I was waiting in the parking lot."

"Bargains?" she asked. "What kind of bargains?"

"Well, the most obvious kind, I guess." He seemed to be battling with the feelings he was trying to express.

"And what might those be?" she asked.

"I just started to realize that I'd missed you," he said, and glanced over at her. "And I told God that if you walked out of there alive, unharmed, I would quit second-guessing my feelings for you."

She gaped at him. "You have feelings for me?" It was asked almost sarcastically, and she hated herself for it.

He looked at her across the darkness. "Jill, you know I do."

"I thought you did," she said. "But they sort of fizzled out, didn't they?"

"Not for me." He looked at the road in front of him again. The windshield wipers stroked back and forth, back and forth across the window. "I told God that I'd quit trying to find ways out of our relationship. That I'd try to resume things with you."

The dread implied in that made her angry. "And what did God say to that?"

"He brought you out alive and unharmed."

She laughed bitterly. "So now you're obligated? Is that it?"

She could see that her levity bothered him. He shot her a puzzled look.

"Don't worry about it, Dan," she said, looking out her window again. "Don't you remember? A promise made under duress isn't binding."

"I mean for it to be binding," Dan said.

She shook her head and her smile faded. "Well, excuse me, but it takes two to tango, and I don't think I'm interested."

She knew his thoughts gravitated back to the way she had run into his arms and clung to him.

"It's been months," Jill said. "I had feelings for you before, but . . . well, I've had to move on with my life."

"You're not seeing anyone else," Dan said. "I'd know if you were."

She shook her head, unable to believe they were having this conversation. "It doesn't make any difference, Dan. I'm letting you off the hook. You don't have to resume things with me. I'm sure God won't hold you to it if I don't cooperate."

Again, Dan grew silent as they drove along, and Jill felt tears rushing to her eyes. She hadn't cried at all since she'd been held hostage. In the room fearing for her life, she'd been able to control her emotions. Now, suddenly, when her body was safe but her heart was threatened, the tears crept up on her, making it impossible for her to push them away. She began to cry, quiet tears at first, then deep, hard sobs that came straight from her heart and soul and seemed to have no place to go. After a moment, she felt Dan's hand on her shoulder.

She was too weak to resist as he pulled her head against him. His shirt was soaked—but it didn't bother her as she wept against his neck.

"Jill, you don't have to be a tough guy," he whispered as he drove. "I know it's upsetting being roughed up by some crazy guy who takes you hostage. No one expects your frame of mind to be level and unemotional right now."

She wanted to yell that she wasn't crying just because of Jerry Ingalls and being held hostage, that she was crying for Dan and for eight months of wasted days and nights.

But she couldn't say any of that. Slowly, she sat back up and wiped the tears from her face. "It's been a long day."

"It's about to get longer. When we get to the police station, they're gonna want to question you for hours."

"I can handle that," she said. "As long as it's dry and they have the air conditioner on. Maybe some dry clothes."

"If you'll give me your keys, I'll go to your house and get you some."

She shook her head. "Frankly, I'd rather stay in these than have you see the condition of my house right now. It's kind of a mess."

"Okay, then. I could call Allie and ask her to go. Or I could just run to my house and change, and get you something of mine to wear."

"Okay," she said.

"Which thing?"

She was too drained to make a decision. "I don't know. I'll decide before we get there."

"You know, you don't have to be embarrassed if your house is a little messy. You're a busy lady. I wouldn't think less of you."

She didn't answer. He reached across the seat to take her hand, laced his fingers through hers. She wondered why that mere touch meant so much . . . why that hug moments earlier had melted her heart . . . why his arms around her when she ran from the motel room had felt like heaven itself.

"So when were you the most afraid?" he asked.

She thought that over for a moment. "When I heard him set a deadline for killing me."

He swallowed and squeezed her hand. His eyes grew misty as he said, "Yeah, me too. Did you think he would?"

"He didn't seem to be the type," she said. "But I couldn't be sure. I don't know his mental condition, his ups and downs. I couldn't predict his behavior."

"Did he seem crazy?"

"Not really," she said. "He seemed like a very scared man who'd been accused of something he hadn't done. He just happened to be waving a gun in my face."

As they reached the outskirts of Newpointe, Dan glanced in the rearview mirror. "Some of the TV vans are following us," he said. "They'll want to interview you."

"I'm exhausted," she said quietly. "Telling the police all that happened is about all I can handle, and I still have to go back to Chalmette tomorrow and take more depositions for the case I'm working on."

"Jill, can't you take the day off in light of what's happened?"

"No, I can't. I have too much work."

He grew quiet. She knew her commitment to her work was one of the reasons things had cooled between them. Her heart sank further as any hope flew away like a carelessly blown dandelion puff. As they reached Jacquard Street, the main drag through town, Jill realized they were near the post office.

"Would you take a detour?" she asked. "Before we go to the police station, I want to see the post office."

"Sure, we can do that." He passed Purchase Street, where the fire and police stations were, cut through Second Street and LaSalle Boulevard, and reached Bonaparte. As they approached, they saw other cars parked along the curb, along with media vans. Lights from the reporters' spotlights illuminated the devastation, and Jill found herself unable to breathe.

"Pretty bad, huh?"

She felt the blood draining from her face. "They never had a chance. What was he trying to do? Blow up the whole block?"

"The windows were blown out across the street, but thankfully, there aren't many other properties around here. We had a tough time putting out the fire. It took hours. You think it was hot in that motel. I thought my coat was gonna melt right off of me. I've never seen anything like it."

She looked back at the devastated structure. People had placed flowers around the crime scene tape that kept them away from the building. Already, a pile had formed.

"Where ... where was Pete found?"

He pointed to the corner of the parking lot. "Over there, where they've piled all those teddy bears."

The sight of the stuffed animals assaulted her heart, and she covered her face with both hands. "The man who was holding me ... really did this?"

"That's what they think."

"But ... it seems so impossible."

He stopped the car and let it idle for a moment. "Do you want to get out?" he asked.

"No. Let's just go to the station. If he did it, they need to book him. We don't need any delays."

"You want me to fight the media off of you?"

She looked out the back window and saw that they were still being followed. "That's okay. I'll just make a quick statement. Don't you have to get back to work?"

"I've probably been fired by now," he said, chuckling lightly. "I think Ray'll understand, though."

"I appreciate your coming, Dan."

"I appreciate you not getting yourself killed." He squeezed her hand again. This time, she squeezed back.

They reached Purchase Street and the Newpointe Police Department, and he pulled her car to the curb. "I'll walk you in."

Already the police cars were parking in front of and behind them, and she knew she would have no shortage of escorts. "It's okay, Dan. I can take it from here."

He leaned over and pulled her into a hug. She breathed in the scent of him—rain and soap and the slightest scent of smoke. The stubble on his jaw brushed her face, reminding her of other times ... She hated to think how much she'd missed him over the past eight months ... and how much she would miss him tonight, when she felt so shaken and alone.

"So what about the clothes?" he asked as their foreheads touched.

"I'll call Allie when I get inside," she said. "She probably needs to hear from me, anyway, if she's heard about this."

"All right." He touched her face and looked at her with adoring eyes that made her want to cry again. "You take care now. Call me if you need me, anytime night or day."

"I will, thanks." It seemed like such a cold, awkward response, but she couldn't manage more. He helped her out of the car, and Sid came to her side.

"You okay, hun?"

"I'm fine, Sid."

"We need you to come in and make a statement."

"I plan to."

As the reporters got out, microphones in hands and cameras on their heels, she was blocked from hurrying up the steps. She paused and watched Dan cut across the lawn before she began to answer their questions.

Chapter Eighteen

● ● ●

Frank Harper sat in the run-down motel in the seediest part of the French Quarter, watching his static-ridden television blare the news across the screen. Reruns of the tape of the post office just after the explosion replayed over and over on every station. He was so proud he could hardly contain it.

He watched as the reporter standing outside of the Flagstaff Motel in Chalmette described the surrender scene. Jerry had turned himself in. What a fool. It occurred to him that he might tell them what had happened, but then that old sense of peace fell over him. He knew Jerry wouldn't say a word. He knew he could count on him.

He had known it an hour earlier, when he'd stolen a car from a rest area as someone went in to use the facilities. As he'd listened to the play-by-play on the radio, he had known that Jerry would never talk.

Frank turned back to the papers on the table, picked up the ballpoint pen he'd found lying on the street, and returned to the most important work of his life. His manifesto. The reason for his blowing up the post office. There was no use committing an act that great without specifying his reason. To do less would mean cowardice, and he was not a coward.

He began writing as the news droned on about Jerry Ingalls's surrender, about his wife's part in the drama, about the woman he'd been holding hostage. Jill Clark was her name.

He looked up as they began to interview her. She looked shaken and sick, as if the day had taken its toll on her in more ways than one. Her brown hair was wet and beaded down into her face, and her nose was red as if she'd been crying.

"How many hours were you in there with him?" she was asked.

"Three or four. I'm not sure."

"Did he talk?"

"Yes."

"Did he say why he blew up the post office?"

"He claims he's innocent," she said, looking into the camera. "He says that someone else did it."

"Do you believe him?"

She didn't know quite how to answer that, and obvious seconds ticked by as she thought that one over.

"Did he say who did it?" someone else asked.

And suddenly Frank Harper's smugness fled, and he was certain beyond the shadow of a doubt that Jill Clark knew his name and had sent the authorities after him. Jerry Ingalls had given him away to save his own hide. The shock, the despair in that rose up inside him, and he knocked his manifesto off the desk.

He got up and raked both hands through his hair, suddenly paranoid, convinced they were surrounding his room even now. He went to the window and pulled back the curtain. Nobody was there.

He turned back to the television, and saw that woman, the hostage, still standing in front of the camera.

"Is it true that you're thinking of representing him?"

"It's true that he asked me to," she said. "Excuse me. I have to—"

"Miss Clark, are you going to represent him?"

"No comment," she said. She headed back into the police department.

She knew, Frank Harper told himself. If she was even considering representing the man who had taken her hostage, then he must have told her. That left him only one choice. He was going to have to kill her next, and he didn't have much time to waste.

Chapter Nineteen

• • •

Issie Mattreaux lay in her bed, staring at the ceiling, unable to sleep. Each time she dozed, she heard the explosion again, felt the world shaking, saw the flames and the smoke. Every time she closed her eyes, she saw five-year-old Pete Hampton, covered with cuts and blood, asking for his mother while he struggled to get a breath.

Somehow, she felt this was her fault. In some indirect, roundabout way, she had played a part in all that had happened.

She got up and went into her bathroom, turned on the light, and stared into the mirror. She looked younger with her dark hair down and tousled around her face. The little girl who used to watch as her mother slathered on her make-up was not so far removed from the twenty-five-year-old she saw reflected here. But who was she? The flirtatious, sophisticated woman who played by her own rules, or the sad little girl who didn't have any rules at all?

She left her reflection and went into her living room, opened the drawer where she kept pictures in several Kodak envelopes, and began to flip through them. She saw picture after picture of herself with men. Most of them were men her mother would have warned her from. Some of them were married.

Like Larry Hampton.

She came to the picture she had kept of herself and him together. It had to be four years ago, when Pete was a baby. She had gotten to know him at Joe's Place, the bar that felt like home to her. She hadn't been that attracted to him at first, but then one day she had seen him with his wife. Mary was pretty and gentle, and a good mother, and she made him look good. Issie remembered the spirit of competition that had risen inside her at the thought that she might be able to turn Larry's head from his wife and baby.

Winning him would have been no big deal, if it had been just the two of them at Joe's Place. She had always been relatively successful with men. But the addition of his wife and child in the battle had raised the stakes. If she could win him from a pretty woman and a happy marriage, then she would be victorious, indeed.

So she had set about to win him.

She closed her eyes as she recalled that she was his first infidelity. He'd found it to be easy and harmless with her. They'd had their fling, and then she had moved on to someone else. But he liked the feeling of cheating, and he hadn't stopped with her. She hadn't been surprised when, a couple of years later, he had disappeared from town with his latest mistress.

What if she hadn't flirted with him at Joe's Place, lured him into unfaithfulness, started a pattern of cheating and lying? What if he had still been with his wife right here in Newpointe? Maybe she wouldn't have been at the post office that day. Maybe Pete Hampton wouldn't have experienced two losses in his young little life. Maybe Issie wouldn't have such guilt.

She knew her feelings weren't rational, that changing her behavior probably would not have stopped the bombing, but at the very least, Pete's father might have been here when he needed him most.

She wondered what Nick Foster would say about all this. All that forgiveness he preached . . . would he still believe in it with such guilt coursing through her? Or would he finally hit that wall of intolerance, and decide that she was one of those who had gone too far?

She couldn't stand her thoughts, so she headed back into her room and got dressed, pulled on her shoes, and grabbed her purse. She would go to Joe's Place and drown her troubles away. There were always people there to help her get her mind off her troubles. The men were especially happy to oblige.

Then she'd come home with her brain fuzzy and her body tired, and she'd fall into sleep without any problems at all. The alcohol could hold the nightmares at bay. And maybe it would cover the guilt, as well.

Chapter Twenty

● ● ●

Dan Nichols was met with a lukewarm reception when he returned to the station. Ray, the chief, was angry that Dan had run off without a word, but he had called Cale Larkins to replace him when he realized he wasn't coming back. Cale and some of the others were annoyed that Dan would create such hardship. But Mark Branning and Nick Foster were more concerned about Jill.

He filled them all in about what had happened, and before he knew it, the angry ones had forgotten their anger and were astounded at Jill's adventure.

When he'd finished describing the scene to them, he went out to the truck bay, which hadn't yet been closed for the night, and sat in a chair next to the pumper. From here, he could see Jill's car where he had parked it on the street. Media vans had pulled in around it, and some reporters still milled around in front of the station waiting for her to come out. He whispered a silent prayer for Jill, that she'd have the energy to get through the questioning from the federal agents tonight. She deserved to go home and relax, but he knew that wasn't going to happen for a while.

Mark came out of the TV room into the bay, and pulled a chair next to him. "Inquiring minds want to know," he said. "Are you and Jill about to be an item again?"

Dan had known the question was coming. He leaned his chair back on two legs and looked at his friend. "Inquiring minds. That wouldn't be Allie, would it?"

"Hey, my wife is her best friend. She's been rooting for the two of you to get back together."

"Yeah, when she hasn't cursed the day I was born."

"So she was a little ticked when you dumped Jill. She's defensive about her. But she's gotten over it. You know Allie loves you."

He drew in a deep breath to buy time, then dropped the chair down and leaned on his knees. "I don't know if we're starting up again or not, Mark. All I know is, when I heard that gun go off over the phone, and things crashing and Jill screaming ... Well, nothing else mattered, you know? Every protective instinct in my body went into high gear."

"Now, that's how I've felt when Allie was in trouble. But I didn't really feel that way about Jill tonight, as good a friend as she is. I prayed for her, worried for her, rooted for her. But I wasn't rushing to the scene and thinking how I could take a bullet for her. But you did. See, that sounds like true love to me."

Dan grinned at his best friend's probing. "So are you trying to define it for Allie or yourself?"

"Both of us, I guess. It's kind of a hazard that comes with marriage. That feminine curiosity kind of eats into your brain cells, and male or not, next thing you know you're interested in people's love lives. Go figure."

"And this is a condition you recommend?"

"Sure, I recommend it. There's nothing like it. God knew what he was doing when he invented wives."

Dan looked at her car again, and slowly straightened. "I don't know where it's headed, Mark. It was a weird night. There's no telling what will come of it."

"But what do you want to come of it?" Mark asked. Dan shot him a look, and Mark laughed and held up innocent hands. "Hey, Allie's gonna ask."

"Tell Allie that I've been missing Jill. That tonight scared the hesitation out of me. That if it's at all in my power, I'm ready to have that fourth date."

"Fourth date? Man, you had way more dates with her than that when you were seeing her before."

"Yeah, but Allie'll know what I mean."

Mark thought about that for a minute, then began to laugh. "Oh, I get it. The guy with the three-date limit ... fourth date ... Allie'll love that."

"Tell Allie that it all depends on Jill."

"Uh-oh. The catch. I knew there had to be one."

"The catch is, does she want to be caught?"

"If I know Jill, she does. But she may not be willing to chase hard enough to catch you."

"Chase me? What do you mean by that?"

Mark chuckled. "Did you see your messages? You had three calls from women while you were gone tonight."

Dan waved that off as if it had no relevance. "They were just interested in the post office."

"Right, and they never call on other shifts." Mark's sarcasm caught Dan's attention.

"Okay, so they call. But that doesn't mean anything to me. I've never taken any of them on a fourth date. I wouldn't have rushed to Chalmette for them. I wouldn't have been begging the cops to let me go in and take on the gunman for any of them."

"So why did you?"

"Because it was Jill," he said, looking his friend fully in the eye. "She's different. She means ..." His voice broke, and he swallowed and looked off to the side. Finally, he met Mark's eyes again. "She means a lot to me."

Mark's amusement faded, and he nodded, as if he understood. "Like I said, buddy, sounds like true love to me."

Chapter Twenty-One

● ● ●

Hours passed as FBI agents questioned Jill about Jerry's behavior in the motel room, the things he had said to her, the threats he had made. When she'd told the story at least a dozen times, in as many different ways, they were finally finished with her.

When she and Stan were the only two left in the room, Jill leaned back in her chair and rubbed her eyes. Thankfully, Allie had brought her a change of clothes, and her hair had dried, but she felt bone-weary and wanted desperately to go home.

"So are you considering representing him?" Stan asked quietly.

"No," she said. "How can you ask that?"

"I know you," Stan said. "That, and the fact that he's still telling everybody that you're his lawyer. He's refusing to answer any questions until you're present."

She looked up at the ceiling and rolled her eyes. "I can't believe this. I told him that I'd represent him, just so he'd let me go. Surely he doesn't really think . . ." Her voice trailed off and she shook her head. "Stan, there's got to be another lawyer in town who would represent him."

"There are only two, Jill. You know that. Frank Manning just passed the bar, and he's doing mostly contract work. Then there's Clive Martin. I guess he could represent him, but Ingalls wants you."

Jill was beginning to get angry, and she narrowed her eyes at Stan. "Don't you think it's a conflict of interest? I mean, how hard am I gonna fight for a guy who held a gun to my head and kept me hostage for hours?"

"That's what I tried to tell him," Stan said. "And no, I don't think you should. I was just asking."

She threw up her hands, got up, and went to the window. It was too dark to see anything on the outside, but raindrops still ran in rivulets down the glass. "I'd be afraid that if he didn't like the way things were going, he'd grab me around the neck and start making demands."

"I don't blame you," Stan said. "It would be hard."

"Hard?" she asked. "That's an understatement." Her eyes filled with tears and she motioned in the direction of the post office. "I got Dan to drive me by the post office on the way home. I can't believe the devastation. People are dead, Stan. This guy probably did it. I don't care what he says. I can't represent a person who might have done a thing like that."

"You don't have to."

She breathed in a deep breath and let it out in a huff, then slapped both hands on the table. "Then why are you badgering me about it?"

"Badgering you?" He breathed a laugh. "Why do you think I'm badgering you? I just asked you a question."

"You think I should keep my word, don't you? You think, since I told him I'd represent him, that I should do it." Her face was reddening.

"No, I don't, Jill." He leaned forward on the table. "Look, I think you need some rest."

"Don't condescend to me," she bit out. "Don't treat me like some distraught woman who's changed her mind! I have reasons. *Valid* reasons."

He was getting angry himself. "For what?"

"For not keeping my word!"

Stan looked as if he didn't know what to say to her. "Jill, you're putting words in my mouth. I'm not condescending, but I'm also not gonna sit here and let you chew me out for things I didn't say or think."

She wilted. "I'm sorry." She looked up at him across the table. "Okay? I'm really sorry. I'm just very tired."

"That's what I said."

"Yeah, that is what you said." She took a deep breath. "So can I go home now? I'm exhausted, and I have to get up early tomorrow. I have to go back to Chalmette to take some more depositions."

"I wish you'd stay in town in case we have more questions."

"What could you possibly have questions about? I've given you a play-by-play of every minute he had me in there. I have work to do, and I'm not gonna let some terrorist get in my way."

"All right, all right," Stan said. "I'll call your secretary if I need you. She'll be able to get in touch with you?"

"Of course. If Sheila can't find me, she hunts me down like an animal just for the sport of it."

He wasn't amused. He just stared at her with serious eyes. "Jill, at the risk of sounding 'condescending,' let me take off my cop hat for a minute and put on my friend hat. You know, you could stand to rest tomorrow. This is one of those days when no one would fault you—"

"Stan, I appreciate your concern, but I have to be there tomorrow." She was growing more and more exhausted, and her head was beginning to ache. "I'm going home now, okay?"

He nodded and got up. "We'll call if we have any more questions."

"Yeah," she said without much enthusiasm. "You do that."

"You sure you're all right?"

"Yep. Nothing a couple of Tylenol and a soak in a hot bath won't cure."

Chapter Twenty-Two

● ● ●

But neither the Tylenol nor the hot bath helped Jill to sleep that night. She kept having nightmares of a man bursting through her closet door with a rifle aimed at her face. A man leaving a box in her home, a box that exploded as soon as she discovered it. A man pulling her up from a deep sleep and attacking her.

She woke up for the fourth time, covered in sweat and trembling, and finally realized that she wasn't going to rest tonight. She sat up in her bed and looked wearily around at the shadows cast by clothes hanging over her chair and draped over her exercise bike. She'd been keeping so busy that she hadn't hung anything in her closet in days. Now each draped outfit looked like a crazed terrorist waiting to attack. She got up and turned on the lights as she went through the house, looking behind doors and in closets, making sure no one was lurking there, waiting to jump out and ambush her. Even as she did so, she realized the silliness of all this fear. She was not the type to be paranoid, yet something she had never expected to happen to her had happened today. It wasn't something she could get over easily.

Her den was somewhat neater than her bedroom, though old, unread newspapers lay rolled on the floor beside the couch, and unopened mail was stacked on the coffee table. She sat down on the couch, staring at the wall, trying to analyze her feelings. She was a mature adult, she told herself. A lawyer. She dealt with frightening people all the time. What was different about this?

It was that she had been out of control when Jerry Ingalls had shot his way into her room, she thought. She still felt out of control. Part of that, she realized, had to do with Dan, who seemed to be moving back into her life. She didn't understand his renewed interest, except that it had to do with his rescuing a damsel in distress—a role she hated playing. Why hadn't he called her in the last several months? There had been nights that no one knew about, nights she'd spent at home, watching movies alone and feeling as if she was drowning. He hadn't come to rescue her then.

She looked around at her messy home and realized she had lost control of it, as well. Nothing in her life was working very well. Now she wished the phone would ring, but she knew it would not. In the wee hours of morning, no one suspected that the big, bold attorney might need someone to hold her hand tonight. She coped. It was what she did.

The house creaked, and she grew more tense. Her eyes darted from corner to shadow. Her ears listened for a sound that broke the silence, a body that might burst through a door. But this was ridiculous. Jerry Ingalls was in jail, and no one was after her.

Oh, yeah. She was a big, bold attorney. Coping. But she couldn't stand to be here alone.

Finally realizing that she *wasn't* coping, that she was falling apart, she picked up the phone and dialed Allie Branning. She was her best friend, and she would understand more than most, even though Jill hadn't even revealed her deepest vulnerabilities to her. Anyone would understand her paranoias tonight. Allie would let her sleep on her couch.

It rang four times before Allie picked up. "Hello?"

"Allie, it's Jill."

"Jill, are you okay?"

Jill hesitated a moment as emotion blocked her throat. Finally, she forced herself to answer. "No, actually. I'm having a hard time. Do you think I could come over there and sleep on the couch?"

"Of course," Allie said. "Come on. I'm up feeding Justin anyway. I'll turn the porch light on for you."

Relieved, Jill hung up the phone, packed a quick overnight bag, and headed out to her garage. She got in the car and started the engine before opening the garage door. If someone was waiting there for her, she'd run over them, she thought.

Kicking herself for being so paranoid, she backed out, her eyes sweeping from side to side as the headlights lit up the front of the house. She closed the garage with her remote, backed out into the street, and headed for Allie's.

The porch light was on when she got there, and Allie opened the door before she even had a chance to knock. "Come on in." She was holding her eight-month-old baby in one arm, his little head on her shoulder, sound asleep, and she reached out to hug Jill with her other. "I'm so glad you're all right. I was so scared, I didn't know what to do." She took Jill's bag from her and led her into the den. "I was just about to put him down."

Jill waited as Allie put the baby back to bed. She loved being in Allie's little house. It smelled of flowers, probably because Allie and Mark owned a floral shop, and she brought fresh cut flowers home every day. She'd never been here when there weren't flowers and knickknacks and bric-a-brac and trinkets everywhere. But she had to admit that there were fewer now than there had been before they'd had a baby. In fact, the Blooms 'N Blossoms Florist was for sale, but they hadn't found a buyer yet.

When Allie came back in, she pulled her into another hug. "You look like you've been tied to the back of a truck and dragged for about a hundred miles."

"Not that bad," Jill said.

Allie laughed. "Well, maybe not. But you look awfully tired."

"As tired as you looked the first few months after you had Justin?"

"Worse," Allie said. "Come on. I've got your bed ready in the guest room."

"The guest room?" Jill grinned. "Allie, this is a two-bedroom house. I told you, I'm happy to sleep on the couch."

"No, there's an extra bed in Justin's room. I rolled his crib into our room so you could have the room to yourself."

"Oh, Allie, you didn't have to go to all that trouble."

"I'm happy to do it," she said. "Mark's on duty tonight. I didn't want you staying by yourself tonight, anyway. Jill, I'd be a wreck if what happened to you happened to me. No way I'd stay in my house alone."

"But I'm supposed to be this tough attorney, who doesn't crumble and copes with the best of them."

"You are the best of them. And forget all that coping stuff. You should have come straight here and not gone home at all. Did you get to eat?"

Jill realized she hadn't. "I ate before I checked into the motel."

"And you didn't lose it when . . . never mind. That was hours ago. Let me fix you something." She went into the kitchen, and Jill followed wearily behind her. As Allie moved around in the kitchen, fixing her a sandwich, Jill sank into a chair at the table.

"So Mark calls to tell me to turn on the television, that you've been taken hostage. And he says that Dan ran out of the fire station, just disappeared and left them shorthanded, and next thing they know, he's there at the Flagstaff. So are you two back together?"

"Hardly." Jill propped her chin on her hand and closed her eyes. "Actually, I don't know what to think."

"Jill, I've been telling you for months that Dan is still in love with you."

"He has a funny way of showing it."

"Exactly," Allie said. "He does have a funny way of showing it. When you were seeing each other, he was scared to death he was going to lose you."

"So he went ahead and threw me away?"

"Something like that." She handed her the plate and went back to the refrigerator. "It has a certain logic if you look at it from his point of view. I never said he was rational."

"Well, it's not like he's just been sitting around alone all this time. He has been seeing other people."

Allie poured her a glass of milk, then took it to the table. "Yeah, but he's back to his no-more-than-three-date rule. In fact, I don't think I've seen him with anybody twice."

"Well, that's just peachy," Jill said, taking the glass Allie handed her. "So many women, so little time." She bit into the sandwich.

"You're missing the point," Allie said, pulling out the chair across from her. "You're the only person I've ever known who could make him break his three-date rule. He never dated anyone over three times because he thought people would think of them as a couple. But he dated you dozens of times. *He* was the one thinking of you as a couple."

"He wasn't thinking of that when he decided to cool things down."

"I know," Allie said. "Right there in the hospital after I had Justin, he was mad at you for being so busy and leaving him out. I never thought that breakup would last."

"It's lasted eight months," she said. "Whoever said Dan couldn't keep his commitments?"

"Look, he could have stayed here today and monitored things from television. He didn't. He was right there."

Jill took another bite of her sandwich and stared into her glass of milk. "He cares about people. He would have been there if it had been you or Mark or any of his other friends."

"That may be true, but so would a lot of other people, and you didn't see them rushing to Chalmette. It was dangerous and we'd have been in the way. But that didn't stop Dan."

Jill realized she didn't have much appetite. She pushed her plate away.

"Mark said Dan drove you home," Allie said. "So did he talk about resuming things?"

"Not really. Well, sort of. In the context of a bargain he made with God."

"A bargain?"

"Yeah. Something like, 'God, if you get Jill out of there, I'll date her again.' Like the Lord has a dating service and Dan's sacrifice helped things along."

Allie wilted. "Jill, he didn't really say it like that, did he?"

Jill smiled. "Well, not exactly."

"I'm sorry. I didn't mean to sound so shallow. I just meant, wasn't anything mentioned about how he felt, why he was there, *anything?*"

"Well, he did mention that he was scared to death."

Allie's eyebrows shot up. "Scared to death. That's good."

"But he seemed ticked off that I was going to work tomorrow, that I have to go back to Chalmette. He tried to talk me out of it."

"And did he?"

"No, I *have* to be there. And once again, I'm too busy to do what he wants me to do, which is the reason we broke up in the first place. He was jealous of my time. Had a hard time believing I could be thinking about him when I was working hard."

"I don't really think that was all of it," Allie said. "I think he was mainly scared of losing you."

"Well, he did. He saw to it." Jill slid her chair back and took her plate to the sink. "And as soon as the emotional surge wears off and the danger has passed, he'll be back surfing his little black book and holding to his three-date rule."

"What if he calls me and asks about you?" Allie asked.

"Tell him I'm tall and have brown hair."

"I'm serious."

Jill sighed. "I don't know what to tell him, Allie. I don't have the energy to worry about Dan right now. And I don't feel like being in a relationship where I have to do double the work. Either someone wants me, or they don't." She rinsed out her glass and put it into the dishwasher. "Thanks for the food. I'm sorry I'm so cranky. I'm just tired and depressed . . . we drove by the post office on the way home. I saw all those teddy bears."

That deep compassion filled Allie's eyes again. "Yeah, I went to the hospital today to see Pete."

"How is he?"

"Not good. He's comatose, has a fractured skull, a broken arm, cuts all over him . . . Our biggest concern is that when he wakes up, somebody has to tell him his mother is dead."

"Who's with him now?"

"Celia."

"Good. That'll give him some comfort. And she has all those maternal hormones pumping through her. I'm glad she realized he needed her."

She nodded and assessed Jill's face. "You go on to bed. There's an alarm clock next to the bed, but you'll have to set it."

"I will," she said. "I'll probably be out of here before you get up in the morning."

"Wanna bet? Justin wakes up at the crack of dawn. Plus, I have a busy day at the florist tomorrow because of the deaths. I've got people working, but I feel like I need to be there. I'm taking Justin with me."

"I'm going to get up at five." Jill checked her watch. "That's only three hours. I'd better get to sleep." She squeezed her friend's hand. "Thanks for letting me come over. I was really having a hard time."

"Anytime. I'm always glad for company, especially when Mark's at the station."

Jill went into the baby's bedroom. It smelled of baby powder, a scent that brought back those feelings of being out of control again . . . defeated feelings that her life wasn't going the way she wanted it to. There were things lacking, things that would never be hers, things she could never count on.

But she did have good friends who loved her. Feeling more secure than she had in her own home, she got into the bed and pulled the covers up, wishing it was already morning.

Chapter Twenty-Three

• • •

As soon as Stan finished with Jerry Ingalls, he headed for the hospital in New Orleans, where Celia still kept vigil beside the bed of little Pete Hampton. Though he was in intensive care, they had allowed Celia to sit with him. A lot of exceptions had been made for the orphaned survivor of the post office bombing. She was exhausted, and her eyes were shaded with dark circles. When Stan walked in, she was lying on her side on the little vinyl sofa beside the boy's bed, and she seemed to be sleeping.

He stooped down in front of her and pressed a kiss on her cheek. She woke up slowly. "Stan . . ."

"Honey, are you okay?" he asked, stroking her cheek with his knuckles. "You need to go home and get in bed. You and the baby need rest."

"But I don't know what to do about Pete," she said, sitting up. "His family should be here soon. He needs somebody."

"Has he woken up yet?"

"Not at all." She burst into tears and reached out to pull Stan into a crushing hug. "I'm afraid he's gonna die, Stan. I've been praying for him all day, but I don't know whether to pray for him to live or die, because he's going to be in so much grief when he wakes up. He's just so young."

"Do you believe he's in God's hands?"

"Yes, I do," she wept. "It's just so hard to see him like this and know about Mary."

He could see that she had been battling these questions all night, and was exhausted with emotion, grief, and worry. Knowing that he couldn't offer her answers right now, he got up and sat down next to her, pulled her against him so that her head was leaning on his shoulder. All he could give her was comfort, and he felt she needed that the most. "Tell you what," he said, kissing her temple. "You go back to sleep, and I'll just sit here and hold you."

"Not yet," she said. "Tell me about the bomber. The guy at the Flagstaff."

Stan sighed. "His name is Jerry Ingalls. He and his family live in Newpointe, believe it or not. Nobody I've run into knows them, though. They moved here six months ago when Inez Pepper died. She was a relative of theirs and left them her house."

"Where does he work?"

"At home. Has some kind of business designing websites. I guess that's why we don't know them. New in town, working at home, kids not yet in school. I'll talk to their neighbors tomorrow."

"Why did he do it?" Celia asked.

He let out a heavy sigh. "I don't know. We can't get anything out of him."

She touched his stubbled jaw. "I'm glad you're okay. Jill, too."

"She's fine." He stroked her stomach gently. The baby wasn't moving. "Go to sleep now."

"Will you wake me up when his grandmother gets here?"

"Of course I will."

"And if he wakes up . . ."

"Nope. Not going to wake you up if he wakes up. I'm going to play a game of Go-fish with him and keep you in the dark."

She elbowed him hard. "You'd better—"

"Of course I'll wake you up. Go to sleep, now."

In seconds, he could feel her body relaxing into sleep, and he closed his eyes, as well.

• • •

It wasn't more than a couple of hours later that Pete Hampton's grandmother and uncle bustled into the room. Celia woke up instantly and sprang to her feet. They were tired, bedraggled, and their eyes were red as if they'd both been weeping much of the way.

Mrs. Lewis burst into tears as she saw her grandbaby lying there comatose with a tube running into his mouth. "What's that in his mouth?" she demanded.

"It's the ventilator. It's keeping him breathing."

"He's on life support?" the woman cried. "No, that can't be!" She leaned over the bed to gently touch his face, then kissed it, as tears fell onto it. "Pete, Pete! You wake up, you hear? You don't need this ole contraption. You can breathe on your own, can't you?"

The child didn't respond.

"Is he gonna wake up?" she asked. "We're not gonna lose him, too, are we?"

The uncle covered his mouth with his hands and bent over the bed. He began to sob, and Stan and Celia both felt as if they were intruders on a private moment. Finally, Stan touched the man's shoulder.

"I'm gonna take my wife home now. She's been here ever since Pete got here . . ."

The grandmother left the bed and hugged Celia. "Celia, thank you so much for taking care of him. I don't know what we would have done if we hadn't known you'd be here."

"I'll be back tomorrow," she said.

"You take care of your baby," the woman said. "He needs his mama." With that, she burst into tears again.

Chapter Twenty-Four

● ● ●

Frank Harper finished his manifesto and, while he still could, abandoned the sleazy New Orleans motel. He was certain that the police would surround the room at any moment, just like they had done with Jerry at the Flagstaff. They would pretend that he was the bad guy, make everyone think that they were trying to protect society. Then they would take him prisoner of war, and lock him up like they'd done for the past twenty-five years.

He headed for the bar across the street, its neon sign flashing in the night, and found a truck that wasn't locked. Like a gift, it had a rifle in the gun rack on the back window, and a box of cartridges lay on the passenger seat. He quickly hot-wired it, a skill he'd learned in his teenaged years, and headed back to Newpointe. He had to find Jill Clark. She knew too much. He couldn't let her ruin his plans, not when he'd finally gotten free and had the chance to save his country.

It was really very simple.

He would find her and kill her tonight.

In rapid-fire language, like some kind of holy tongue, he quoted the Bill of Rights as he drove, and tears came to his eyes as he thought of the sacrifices he'd made for his land. He wished the war would end. It had gone on for too long already, but the people were deceived, and didn't know. They thought they lived in peace. They didn't know of the battles being fought without their knowledge, the prisoners being held and tortured, the communist plans to get the people fat and lazy, then change their way of life into something that was intolerable.

He wouldn't let it happen.

He reached the outskirts of Newpointe and went into a convenience store to buy a map. As he paid, he asked the clerk where a local bar might be. The clerk told him about Joe's Place, a few blocks away.

The bars were part of their plan, he told himself. They were put there to lull the people into a false sense of happiness. He wouldn't be fooled. But he needed the bar tonight so that he could find Jill Clark. All it would take was a few loose tongues, a couple of drunk braggarts, and he'd have her address in no time.

He went in to the smoke-filled room and cringed at the sound of zydeco music pouring from the speakers. It was another communist weapon, he told himself. That, and heavy metal. And country music. And rap. He was certain they had all been carefully created by the regimes that wanted to pull the country down.

He looked across the bar and saw a heavy man, nodding in his beer. He took the stool next to him. The man looked up.

"How's it going?" he asked.

The man nodded. "Long day."

"Yeah?" He reached out a hand. "My name's Dirk Henderson."

"Sergeant R.J. Albright," the man slurred.

"Sergeant?" Frank asked. "You in the military?"

"Nope. Cop."

"Oh." Frank swiveled on his stool to face him. "So you people have had some kind of day, haven't you? What with the bombing and all."

"Yep."

"And didn't I hear something about a hostage situation?"

"Yep. The guy who blew up the post office took Jill Clark hostage."

The bartender brought his ginger ale, and Frank gulped it like it was scotch. "Isn't she a lawyer or something?"

"Yep."

"You know her?"

"She's a good friend of mine."

"Oh, yeah? Was she hurt?"

The bartender leaned across the bar. "Jill don't get hurt. She knows how to take care of herself."

"Somebody has to," R.J. said.

Frank lit up a cigarette and inhaled deeply. "Why? She married?"

"Nope. Lives all by her lonesome."

"Yeah," Frank said, tapping his cigarette on an ashtray. "Doesn't she live up on the north side of town?"

"Naw, man. She lives over on Clearview."

"Oh, that's right," he said, as if he knew. "Big blue house?"

The bartender chuckled. "Hardly. Littlest house on the block. You'd think she could afford more, with all the work she does." He wiped the counter as Frank finished his drink.

Frank smoked another cigarette, listening to more of the banter about the bombing and Jill Clark and Jerry Ingalls, holed up in the Newpointe Jail. He paid his tab and slipped out.

He checked his map and headed for Clearview Street. In just a few minutes, he thought, Jill Clark would be one less of his worries.

He found the street and drove slowly up it, trying to decide which was the smallest house. When he came to a little one-story house, he saw the name *Clark* on the mailbox. He couldn't believe his luck.

He parked a few houses down and loaded the rifle. It was 4 A.M. He could pick her lock and slip inside. She'd be dead by 4:15, and then he could get on with his work.

He left the truck and ran from tree to tree, the grunt on the alert, ready to do what was necessary for the sake of the war. He reached her backyard. Quickly, deftly, he picked the lock and slipped inside.

The only light on in the house was one glowing on the stove, but in the faint light it cast, he could see her bedroom off the hall. He made his way to the door and looked inside.

The bed was rumpled, empty. No one was home.

The clock on her bed table flashed 4:10. Where was she? Had she anticipated that he would come?

He tried to decide whether to wait for her here or go back out to the truck.

What if it was a trap? Any minute now police could surround him and cage him inside . . .

He decided to chance going back to the truck. He went back out, bracing himself for gunfire. None came, so he sprinted back to the truck. He decided to wait in case she came home. He couldn't forge ahead with his plans until he took care of her.

Chapter Twenty-Five

● ● ●

Jill didn't sleep until her alarm clock went off. She woke up with the first cries of the baby at 4:30, and decided to go ahead and get up. She had to prepare for Chalmette, anyway.

Allie was nursing Justin when Jill came out of the bedroom. "Jill, he woke you up! I'm so sorry. He's not usually up quite this early, but he's teething."

"Don't be sorry," Jill said. She leaned over the baby and grabbed his hand. "It's your house, isn't it, Justin? Besides, I wasn't sleeping that well."

"Well, have some coffee and sit down with me. I'll make you breakfast . . ."

"No way," Jill said. "You've done enough for me, Allie. I really need to get going, anyway. I brought clothes to wear in Chalmette, but I forgot to get the shoes I need. If you don't mind, I'm just gonna jump in the shower, then run home real quick and change shoes before I head for Chalmette."

"That's fine," Allie said. "The towels are in the hall closet."

Half an hour later, Jill headed for her house. The sun hadn't come up yet, and as her headlights lit up she shivered with the fear that had driven her to Allie's. She opened the door with her remote opener, and punched it closed again even before she was all the way in. Leaving the car running, she dashed into the dark house, cut through to her bedroom, and swapped shoes. Then, as if she expected someone to jump out of a closet, she went back to her car. She hoped the Chalmette courthouse would be open early. She had a lot to review before she got started today. And she wouldn't feel safe until she was around people again.

•   •   •

Frank Harper couldn't believe his luck when he saw Jill coming home. Still parked up the street, he waited until she closed the garage behind her. Then he got out of the truck, and carrying the deer rifle, ran the few yards up the street until he was at her back door.

It was still dark outside, so he stood there, unseen, as she turned on her light and ran through the house. He waited for the light to go back out, or for her to settle in her bedroom before he picked the lock again, but in seconds, she was dashing back through the house and into the garage again.

Confused, he ran back around to the front of the house and saw her garage door opening. She backed out and headed south before he could even get her in the gun's sights.

Frustrated, he ran back to the stolen truck and followed her as closely as he could without being seen. He was surprised when she headed out of town, then got onto the bridge across Lake Pontchartrain. Where was she going?

The sun began to come up, and other early-morning commuters appeared on the road. He hadn't expected to follow her the hour's drive to Chalmette, but he supposed it was worth it if he accomplished what he'd set out to do. When she got to the courthouse, he found a parking place and watched as she went in. Was she going to court? Would she be there all day?

He decided that, no matter how long it took, he'd wait her out. But first, he'd make sure she didn't go anywhere. He got out of his car and went to hers. It was still early, and the parking lot was not full. The sun had now fully risen, but he didn't care. As long as he looked like he knew what he was doing, no one would notice him.

He went to her car and got down on the ground, slid underneath it. He made a few modifications, made more difficult because of his missing fingers. But he was used to accommodating. When he'd finished, he went back to his stolen truck. When she came out, at whatever time she did, her car would not start. He would then offer to help her, and he could quiet her before it was too late.

Time passed slowly, and finally, around midmorning, he began to doze. Parked safely in the courthouse parking lot, he slept for several hours. When he woke, he was startled to see that it was already late afternoon. But Jill's car was still there.

He hadn't lost her yet. There was still plenty of time to get her where he wanted her.

• • •

It was after 8 P.M. and almost dark before Jill came back out to her car. She was exhausted, but she and the attorneys for the defendant had finished taking depositions. She made her way back out to her car, tossed her briefcase onto the backseat, then shrugged out of her blazer and slid into the car. She tried to start it, but it wouldn't roll over. She tried again. Still nothing.

Frustrated, she dug through her purse for her cell phone, and called information for the local number of the auto club she belonged to. They weren't represented here, so she called the 800 number and asked how long it would take for them to come. They suggested that it was too late, that she should call a tow truck and try again tomorrow.

She was physically, mentally, and emotionally exhausted, unable to deal with this latest minicrisis. She sat there a moment, trying to decide what to do. Dan came to mind, as he had so many times that day, but she shoved the thought away. She didn't want him to think she was depending on him for anything, or that his actions last night had made her presume anything. But she couldn't call Allie, because she was so busy at the florist today. And Celia was probably still tied up with Pete Hampton. Sheila, her secretary, had probably already gone home for the day, and would make her life miserable if she asked her to come and get her.

Her mind drifted back to Dan again. He was the least encumbered of all her friends. Besides, she would feel safe with him. Reluctantly, she dialed his number.

"Hello?" He sounded out of breath.

"Dan, it's me. Jill. Is this a bad time?"

"No, not at all." He sounded glad to hear from her. "I've been running. I just came in. I tried calling you earlier. Are you home?"

"No. My car is broken down in Chalmette, and the auto club I belong to is turning out to be pretty worthless. I really hate to ask you this, Dan . . . but do you think you could possibly come and get me? I can have the car towed back to Newpointe, but I'm a little nervous about strangers right now, and I don't think I'd feel very comfortable riding with the tow-truck guy."

"Of course. I'm on my way."

"No hurry. If you need to shower and cool off—"

"No way. I'm coming now. Should be there within half an hour."

"Dan, it'll take longer."

"Not for me, it won't. I don't want you alone there."

When she hung up, she felt that warm feeling that she didn't want to feel. She was too tired to put up an emotional fight against her own feelings. Regardless of her better judgment, her heart looked forward to seeing Dan tonight. He was one of her biggest weaknesses. She wondered if she would ever overcome it.

She wished she didn't have to.

She laid her head back on the seat, locked her doors, and drifted off to sleep as she waited for Dan.

• • •

Frank Harper saw Jill sitting in her car, but only a few feet away from her, two deputies conversed as if they had absolutely nothing better to do.

He watched her carefully, knowing that he couldn't approach her to help her until she got out of the car and opened her hood—not unless the cops went away. But one of them leaned back against his squad car, settling in as he gave a play-by-play of last night's activities at the Flagstaff. She hadn't given any indication that her car wouldn't start. Why was she just sitting there?

What if she had called someone? What if she was waiting for someone to come?

It didn't matter, he thought, growing irritated. Whoever came to rescue her, their life would be at risk, too. He had to get rid of her, and anyone she may have told about him. He couldn't take the chance that anyone knew he was the one who'd left the bomb in the post office. Everyone who knew had to go. He didn't care if he had to take them each one at a time.

It would be well worth it to protect his privacy and enable him to get on with the serious work of defending his country.

Chapter Twenty-Six

● ● ●

When Dan reached the Chalmette courthouse parking lot, he saw two sheriff's deputies standing together, talking intently. He started to ask them where she was, but then he spotted her car. He pulled his Bronco close to it. She was there, her eyes closed and her head leaned against the window and the back of her seat, and her eyes were closed, as if . . .

His heart jolted. Then he realized how tired he had been today, and how tired she was last night . . . She had probably gotten up at the crack of dawn and worked here all day. She was only sleeping.

She had been through too much in the last twenty-four hours, and today Mark had told him that she'd spent the night at his house with Allie, because she was afraid. His heart kicked, giving him a personal indictment that he couldn't explain. Somehow, he felt responsible to protect her, even if she didn't want him to.

He pulled into the space next to her, then got out and knocked lightly on her window. She woke up with a start, then quickly opened the door. "Dan, hey."

He leaned in. "You okay?"

"Must have fallen asleep." She got out and tried to look alert and professional, but her business suit was crumpled and her hair was sticking out on one side. He fought the urge to smooth it back down.

"I've called a tow truck, but they haven't come yet," she said. "Then again, they may have, and I just didn't see them because I was sound asleep."

He slipped into the driver's seat and tried to start the car. The engine wouldn't turn over. "Have you been having problems before this?"

"No, not at all. The car's only a year old."

They heard the sound of the tow truck, and looked out toward the street. "There it is now." Dan waved it down, and the truck pulled into the almost empty parking lot.

When the tow truck had the car in tow and on its way back to Newpointe, Jill got into Dan's Bronco. "Dan, I really shouldn't have called you. I could have ridden in the tow truck."

Dan set his wrist on the wheel and looked over at her. "Jill, I would have been hurt if you'd called anybody but me."

"Thanks," she said. "I feel like I'm turning into a basket case. I couldn't even sleep at home last night. Truth is, I didn't sleep much, even at Mark and Allie's."

"I didn't sleep much myself," he said, "and I wasn't even the one held hostage last night. Why don't you just kick back and get comfortable?"

She relaxed back into the seat. As her eyes drifted closed again, Dan pulled the car out of the parking lot, and headed back to Newpointe.

She was asleep again by the time they reached the edge of the I–10 bridge over Lake Pontchartrain. Looking in his rearview mirror, Dan began to realize that the beat-up pickup with one headlight had been following them since they'd left Chalmette. He had noticed him first pulling out of the parking lot at the courthouse. Now he wondered if that person had been watching Jill.

Jill seemed to sense a difference in the way he was driving, and she woke up. "Something wrong?" she asked.

"No, nothing." He glanced in the rearview mirror again. "Everything's fine."

"Why do you look so worried?"

He looked over at her, then back to the rearview mirror. "Do you know who that is in the pickup behind us?"

She looked out the rear window. "Never seen that truck before. Why?"

"I think he's following us."

"Are you sure?"

"No. It just seems—"

"Why would anyone be following us? Jerry Ingalls is in jail."

"I don't know. Maybe it's a reporter, trying to get an exclusive."

"Oh, for heaven's sake. It's not like I'm tabloid fodder."

"If I speed up, maybe I'll lose him. That junk heap won't be able to keep up." But as he sped up, so did the truck behind them.

Suddenly, he realized that they weren't just being followed, they were being chased.

He touched his brakes to slow down, and the man almost hit him. "Uh-oh, I think I've made him mad now," Dan said, watching in the rearview mirror as the man pulled into the opposite lane and passed him. Dan sped up to be even with him, and tried to see the driver. It was too dark to see into the truck, but as they drove side by side, the driver turned his wheel and grazed Dan's Bronco.

Dan erupted. "What is he, crazy? He did that deliberately!"

"Slow down, Dan."

The car swerved and hit them again. "What's he doing?" Dan yelled.

"Trying to run us off the road," she said. "Stop! Stop the car!"

"I can't. What if he has a gun or something? He's insane!" He grabbed his cell phone and dialed 911. He didn't know to which dispatcher the call would go, but he hoped they would send the closest highway patrolman quickly. Before the emergency dispatcher had them on the phone, the truck rammed them again, this time crumpling Dan's door. The impact forced the front of the Bronco to slide to the right and scrape into the wall of the bridge. Jill screamed as metal sparked against concrete. Dan fought with the steering wheel and tried to move the Bronco away from the wall.

The truck picked up speed and made a hard right turn, crashing into Dan's fender and stopping them. They sat there for a moment ... waiting. "I'm getting out," Jill said, panicked.

"No!" Dan stopped her as the truck backed up again. The maniac shifted into drive, and headed for his left fender again.

Frantic, Jill opened the passenger door as the Bronco was shoved against the wall again, and her arm twisted. She yelled.

Somehow, Dan managed to grab the cell phone again. The dispatcher answered, "911, may I help you? Hello? Is anyone there?" But he dropped the phone and Jill scrambled to pick it up.

"Help! Somebody's trying to kill us on the northbound side of the I–10 bridge over the lake! He's ramming our car, trying to make us go over. Do you have anybody in this area?"

"We'll send someone right away," the dispatcher said.

The truck bashed them again. "We're almost to the end of the bridge!" Dan shouted to the phone. There was nothing but wooden rail between them and the lake. Their front right tire hung precariously off the bridge, its weight threatening to pull them over.

"We have to get out," Dan whispered. Jill started to come up from the floor board, but suddenly, there was one more ram, and the car fell further over the side, its other front wheel suspended in air.

They heard a siren coming from behind them, and the truck took off as fast as it could go, leaving a trail of black smoke behind it.

Dan didn't have time to worry about him. He had to get Jill out of the Bronco. "Climb over the seat and get out the back," he shouted.

She was almost hysterical, so he grabbed her hands and made her look at him. "Jill, climb over the seat! We have to get out."

She nodded, then got on her feet and crawled over the seat. The left side of the car was bashed in, but there was just enough room to get through. Dan pushed the button to disengage the back door, but it was stuck.

"Dan, I can't open it!" she cried. "Hurry!"

He crawled back, his way made more difficult by his size and the injuries he was just beginning to feel. He felt the car rocking, felt its weight shifting, heard Jill screaming for him to hurry. The police cars screeched to a halt as the Bronco began to bob ...

Finally, with one last thrust, he got the door open.

Jill fell into his arms as they stumbled out of the Bronco, and clinging together, they watched as it rocked ...

Once ...

Twice ...

Then fell over the bridge into Lake Pontchartrain.

Chapter Twenty-Seven

● ● ●

Jill couldn't stop shaking. She sat in the rescue unit as they splinted her swelling wrist—which was, miraculously, the only injury she'd suffered—and watched the highway patrolmen who had converged on the scene, directing traffic across the bridge. An all-points bulletin had gone out on the man who had run them off the road. They had found the beat-up truck abandoned not far from the bridge, but the man had apparently fled into the woods on foot. When they traced the truck, they learned it had been reported stolen early that morning. Police were combing the woods on the other side of the bridge, but they weren't having any luck. Somehow, the man had gotten away.

Jill fought back the tears, knowing that if she gave into even one, she wouldn't be able to stop crying for days. She watched as Dan stood on the edge of the bridge, his arm in a sling. He was in pain, she could tell, and probably had a broken collarbone, but he had refused to let the rescue unit transport him to the hospital just yet. He had too much to tell the police about what had happened, and he was determined to see the man caught. The blue flashing lights of the police cars lit one side of his face as he gave as much information as he could to the police.

Jill tore her eyes from him. Had she brought this trouble on him? If so, he was going to rue the day he'd ever met her. Hostage situations, car accidents . . . What would happen next? She wasn't safe to be around.

Finally, when Dan was satisfied that he'd told the police everything he could, he allowed the rescue unit to transport them to Newpointe Hospital, where there was a noncritical care emergency room. They couldn't treat head traumas or gunshot wounds, but they could do X-rays and set broken bones.

As they rode, Dan pulled Jill close. "You okay?" he asked for the hundredth time tonight. "How's your wrist feel?"

"Okay," she said. "I feel sure I don't have any broken bones."

"Sprains hurt plenty."

"I'll take a sprain any day. I'm supposed to be dead. That guy was after me."

"How do you know it wasn't me he wanted dead? He wasn't real discriminating in the way he came after us."

"It had something to do with yesterday," she said without doubt. "Something to do with Jerry Ingalls."

"You don't think Ingalls is behind this, do you?"

She thought it over for a moment. "Why? Because I refused to represent him?"

"Maybe that's enough. Maybe it's revenge."

"Or intimidation to make me give in."

Dan wasn't convinced. "Don't look now, but that was no threat. I think you and I were both supposed to be dead on the bottom of Lake Pontchartrain by now. If he wanted to make you represent him, he's not helping his cause."

The thought sent chills down her spine. "It's so confusing. I was with Jerry Ingalls for several hours yesterday. I mean, I know he had a gun to my head, but I just don't think he's the kind of person who would have someone hunt me down to kill me."

"What about his wife? Do you think she would send someone after you?"

"No! She was as meek as a mouse. Besides, wouldn't they know that they would be the number-one suspects? What good would it do them to kill two more people?"

"What good would it do them to blow up a post office? We're not dealing with rational people here."

"I don't know. I just don't know."

They rode in silence for several moments, and finally Jill looked up at Dan. "I want to talk to him."

"To who? Jerry Ingalls?"

"Yes," she said. "I want to find out what's going on. And I want to talk to his wife."

"Why? They'll just lie. They aren't going to tell you."

"But I'll know," she said. "I'll be able to look into their eyes and tell if they're lying. I'm a pretty good judge of character. People lie to me all the time. I'll know, Dan. I'll be able to tell."

"But what point would it serve?"

"It might give me a clue as to who tried to kill us, and who it is that's still out there. He failed, Dan, so he may come back and try again. I want to find him before he finds us." She turned her anguished eyes up to his. "I'm so sorry to drag you into this, Dan. If I were you, I wouldn't get within ten feet of me."

He tightened his embrace and kissed her. "Do I look like I'm afraid to be near you?"

She steeled her heart against his kiss. "If you're smart, you are."

"Well, I've never been accused of being all that smart."

She knew that wasn't true, but he made his point. Still, she didn't expect him to hang around much longer.

Chapter Twenty-Eight

● ● ●

Frank Harper had swum several miles down Lake Pontchar-train by the time he took the chance to look back at the lights flashing on the bridge. Police were everywhere, and he could hear dogs barking and voices yelling.

Clutching the rifle, he went back underwater and swam far-ther, then came up at the edge of a campsite. He saw campers with their lights shining through windows, and the sounds of singing coming from a rec building at the back of the grounds.

Slowly, cautiously, he came up out of the water, thankful it was July. Dripping, he skirted the edge of the lake and zigzagged through pine trees and over downed logs, until he came to the parking lot.

He went from vehicle to vehicle, looking for one that wasn't locked. When he finally came upon an unlocked van, he slipped in through the side door.

The van was plush, comfortable, a good place to get some sleep. First, he had to get it out of here, though. If those cops and their dogs made it this far, the dogs would sniff him out for sure. No, he had to be far away.

He saw a duffel bag lying on the backseat, and hurried to open it. A man's T-shirt and some gym shorts and flip-flops were stuffed in there, along with a water bottle and a racquetball racket. Unable to believe this stroke of luck, he laughed out loud and began pulling off his wet clothes to don the dry ones.

Then he slipped between the front seats and bent down to hot-wire the car. It cranked to life, and he shifted into reverse. Without turning the lights on, he pulled out of the parking lot and headed for the road.

He knew they would probably have a roadblock west of the campground, so he turned east.

As he drove farther and farther from the scene, he wondered if he had succeeded in killing Jill Clark and her friend. He had seen the Bronco go over the bridge and had felt a moment of joy. He turned on the radio to see if there were any reports.

He flicked from a country song to a Cajun tune, to Christian music, to a rock sound, then finally came upon the news. He listened carefully through news of the Asian economy, the illness of the Russian president, Congress's latest bill to pass . . .

Finally, they got to the local news out of New Orleans, and he turned it up. *"Police are investigating a murder attempt that took place earlier this evening when an unidentified suspect ran two people off of the I–10 bridge over Lake Pontchartrain. The driver's Bronco went over the bridge, but, amazingly, the two escaped before going with it. The suspect, who was driving a stolen pickup, escaped on foot. Police are still looking for the unidentified man, and warn residents in that area to stay inside and keep their doors locked. The assailant is said to be armed. And in other news . . ."*

Frank Harper slammed his fist on the steering wheel and cursed. So they had gotten away. He would have to try it again, and this time he had no room for mistakes.

He turned the van around and headed north to Newpointe, hoping he could find them before the police found him.

Chapter Twenty-Nine

• • •

The Newpointe Hospital sent Jill and Dan home after confirming that no bones had been broken. Dan had one arm in a sling and a bottle of painkillers clutched in his hand. He had a dislocated shoulder and some torn ligaments, and the pain of resetting it had been worse than if a bone had been broken. They warned him against working for at least a week.

Mark and Allie picked them up and took them to rent a car. Jill's had been towed to her mechanic in Newpointe, and she hoped it would be repaired tomorrow. She was certain that the man who had run them off the road had tampered with her car. She wondered what he would have done if she hadn't called Dan to help her.

Dan insisted on driving Jill home in the rental car, since they had both been asked to stop by the Newpointe Police Department to make a statement about what had happened, in case it was related to the post office bombing. As they went back into the station, Jill couldn't believe she was back for the second time in twenty-four hours.

"This is becoming a nightly event for you," Dan said.

"Tonight'll be different, though," Jill said. "I'm gonna talk to Jerry Ingalls before I leave."

Dan stopped in his tracks. "Jill, it's been a long night. Don't do that."

"I am," she said. "I have to look him in the eye. I have to see if he had anything to do with this."

"It's after midnight. They probably won't even let you in."

"Watch," she said.

They found Sid and Stan sitting head to head at Stan's desk with a couple of the FBI agents from yesterday. They all stood up when Jill and Dan approached.

"Are y'all all right?" Stan asked.

"We'll live," Dan said. "You wanted a statement?"

"Yeah, if you don't mind. We'll just move into the interrogation room . . ."

Jill hung back. "I'll give you a statement, Stan," she said. "But first I need to see my client."

"Your what?"

"My client. Jerry Ingalls. He doesn't have a lawyer yet, does he?"

Stan and Sid looked at each other. "Well, no, but . . . You're not really gonna represent him, are you, Jill?"

She took a deep breath. "Let's just say I need to talk to him before I can commit. But I need to talk to him now."

"But it's after midnight. He's asleep."

"I'll wake him up," she said. She waited, chin up, for one of them to make the decision to let her in. "Come on, Sid, Stan. I've had a rough couple of days. Give me this, will you?"

"Are you sure you ain't gon' walk in there and pull out a pistol?" Sid asked.

"Let LaTonya search me. I just want to talk to him."

"And then you'll represent him?" Sid asked.

"I told you, I won't commit until I talk to him."

Sid shot Stan and the agents a look. "Well, maybe if she does agree to represent him, he'll finally talk to us. I say we go ahead and let her wake him up."

"All right," Stan said, "but we're not letting you in his cell. You stand outside the bars and say what you have to say. Dan can start with his statement while you're doing that."

Jill nodded and shot Dan a victorious look, but he only shook his head. "Be careful, Jill. Real careful. Stay way back. Sid, don't let her get too close."

"I won't," Sid said. "All right, Counselor. Let's go."

Since Ingalls was the only one incarcerated right now, Sid opened the jail, turned on the light, and allowed her to go in. Sid came in with her and stayed seated in a folding chair at the end of the hallway. She walked across the concrete, her heels clicking irreverently in the night. She saw Jerry Ingalls sound asleep on his cot.

Anger exploded inside her. For all he knew, she could be dead now. She went to the bars. "Wake up, Jerry Ingalls," she shouted.

He stirred and squinted in the light. He saw her and slowly sat up. "What's going on?"

"I want to talk to you," she said. "Get up."

He rubbed his eyes. "What time is it?"

"After midnight. I would have come earlier, but I was too busy giving a statement to the police and getting patched up at the hospital. This may not come as a surprise to you, but somebody tried to kill me tonight. I want to know who it was."

He got up and walked toward her. "How am I supposed to know?"

"Because I have a feeling you had something to do with it."

His brain seemed to clear, and a slow frown darkened his face. "I have no idea what you're talking about."

"Tell me who's working with you," she demanded.

Jerry only stared at her for a moment, then looked down at his feet. "What did he do?" he asked finally.

The question surprised her. Was he admitting that he knew who had done it? "He ran us off the bridge over Lake Pontchartrain. We barely got out of the car before it went over the side. We're supposed to be dead right now. I want to know why."

Jerry slowly brought his eyes back to hers. "I have no idea."

That answer enraged her even more. "Did you have any-thing to do with this or not?"

He looked pale, suddenly, as he stepped closer to the bars. He grabbed them in his fists, and she took a step back. "Look, I know you must be shaken up," he said, "but you've got to believe me. I didn't have a thing to do with it."

Her eyes were beginning to fill with angry tears. "Are you threatening me into representing you?" she asked. "Is that what this is about?"

"No!" he said. "I gotta admit I was disappointed that you wouldn't, since you said you would. In my life, a person's word means something."

"So it *was* revenge?"

"No! How could I do that from in here? I'm not gonna kill you because you broke your word. How would that do me any good?"

"I don't know that it *has* to do you any good. Just like blow-ing up a post office didn't do you any good . . . killing three people and maiming a child."

"*I didn't do that!*" he yelled at her. "I told you, I was set up!"

"By whom?" she demanded just as loudly.

He shook his head and turned away. "Look, I didn't send anyone to kill you, I didn't blow up the post office . . . I need a lawyer, and if you're not going to represent me, then I need to find somebody else."

"I'm *not* going to represent you," she said through her teeth. "I don't represent killers. Especially when they've come after me twice."

"You're wrong," he said, more quietly. "Did I once hurt you yesterday? Did I so much as leave a scratch on you? I could have. We were in there for hours."

"So I'm supposed to give you a round of applause and pledge my life and my vocation to you because you didn't hurt me? Maybe you're a coward," she said. "Maybe you don't like to hurt people when they can look you in the eye. Maybe you prefer to do it differently, like running them off a bridge."

"*I am in jail!*" he yelled, throwing up his hands. "Does it look to you like I could run anybody off the road tonight?"

"Some people have connections," she said. "I don't know how you would have gotten in touch with them or why, or whether there's some allegiance in this that's making them help you out, but *somebody* is trying to kill me. I take that real personally."

He went back to his cot and sank down, looking between his knees down at the floor. "Look, I know you don't believe this," he said, not looking up at her, "but yesterday I was minding my own business, working at my job, not planning to hurt a single soul, and the next thing I knew I was being charged with terrorism and murder, and now you think I tried to kill you. I don't know how to convince you that I'm innocent, that I've been set up. Maybe I *can't* convince you."

Her face grew hot as her voice rose. "If someone set you up and you know who it is, why haven't you given them a name? That's the only thing that will get you out of here."

"There are reasons why I can't," he said.

"What kind of reasons?"

He looked up at her again. "Reasons that someone like you couldn't understand anything about. It has to do with keeping promises."

She wanted to scream. "I find it amazing that you can malign *my* character this way, when *you* are the one accused of heinous crimes. I haven't blown up any post offices. I haven't killed anybody."

"And neither have I." He got back up and faced her across the cell. "Look, it occurs to me that you seem to be caught up in this whether you like it or not. All I can tell you is to be careful."

"Then you *are* threatening me?"

He looked frustrated. "I told you to be careful, and you interpret that as a threat?"

She didn't know if she did or not. Suddenly, her head hurt, and she raised her hands to her temples. He saw the splint on her wrist.

"Did you break any bones?"

"No," she said. "It's a sprain."

"Any other injuries?"

She tried to filter out the kindness she heard in his voice. "The man who was with me dislocated his shoulder." She swallowed back the anger in her throat. "Look, I just came here to warn you to call off the dogs. So help me, if there's another attempt on my life, I'll make sure you pay for the rest of your life."

"And what if I'm the wrong guy to pay?"

"I don't think you are." With that, she clicked away from the cell.

"Don't go home," he said, stopping her.

She turned back to the cell. "What?"

"I said, don't go home. Whoever this is . . . he'll come back. He'll find you. I don't think he'll give up easily."

A foreboding chill went over her, and she stared at him for a long time.

"No, it's not a threat," he said, as if winded. "It's just good advice. You don't need to go home tonight. If I were you, I wouldn't go anywhere I usually go. Be careful."

Her anger seemed to dissipate like escaping air from a balloon. She walked out past Sid and back into the stairwell. Then, as Sid locked up, she stood at the bottom of the steps and took in a few deep breaths before she went back up to the police station.

She was exhausted and terribly afraid. She wondered if Mark and Allie really didn't mind if she slept in Justin's room again. They had insisted, but weren't *they* afraid to have her near them? She supposed they wouldn't have suggested it if they didn't want her there.

She only hoped the killer didn't somehow get wind of where she was. The last thing she wanted was to draw Mark and Allie into danger, too.

Chapter Thirty

● ● ●

Mark and Allie were both still up when Dan brought Jill to their house. When they saw saw the exhaustion on Jill's face, Allie quickly ushered her to the baby's room where she was going to sleep. Mark, worried about the pain and tension on Dan's face, stepped out on the front porch with him.

"You okay, buddy?" Mark asked.

"No, I'm not okay," Dan said. "I don't want to leave her alone."

"Man, she's not alone. I'm here with her."

"Yeah, but there's no telling what could happen. Somebody's out there, Mark. He got away. I'm scared for her." He turned around quickly as a thought came to his mind. "How would it be if I just slept on your couch?"

"Dan, you don't need to sleep on the couch. Not unless you're worried about him coming after you. I mean, you're welcome to stay here, but I don't think it's necessary."

"I don't know what I'm thinking," Dan said. "You'd be crazy to want both of us here, making you a sitting duck."

Mark frowned. "That's not it at all. That guy is probably still hiding out in the woods around Lake Pontchartrain somewhere. He doesn't know to look for her here, anyway. What about you? You think he knows who you are?"

"I don't know." His hand went up to his shoulder, and a pained look came across his face.

"Maybe you need to take a pain pill. Want to come in and get some water?"

He shook his head. "No. I don't want to be out of it if something else happens. Mark, are you sure you can protect her if—"

"Yes. Relax. I have it under control."

Dan began pacing in front of the porch steps. He looked as though he had more to say, but he seemed to catch himself. Taking a deep, weary breath, he said, "I guess I'll go and let y'all get some sleep. I could use some myself." He started out to the rental car.

"Hey, Dan?"

Dan stopped midstride and turned around. "Don't worry, man."

Dan didn't answer as he got into the car.

Chapter Thirty-One

● ● ●

Dan had trouble sleeping because the pain was too great, and he didn't want to take a pain pill with a killer on the loose. The phone woke him at about 9 A.M. Startled, he jerked it up. It was someone from the highway department, telling him they had retrieved his Bronco from the bottom of Lake Pontchartrain. They wanted to know where to have it towed.

He got up and called his insurance company, and they promised to take a look at the car as soon as it got to Newpointe. He didn't have to hear from them to know it was totaled. As many times as the maniac had rammed it, it was totaled even before it had gone into the lake.

He showered, then decided to go to the fire station to tell Ray, the fire chief, about his dislocated shoulder. He supposed it was for the best that he couldn't work for a while. It would keep him available to look out for Jill until the killer was caught.

As he headed to the station, he racked his brain for answers about the killer. If Jerry Ingalls was locked up, who could have run them off the road? Curious, he pulled over to a pay phone and, in the phone book hanging at the booth, he located Jerry Ingalls's address. He didn't know why he needed to see the Ingallses' house, but he supposed it came from the same place as whatever had sent Jill down to Jerry's jail cell last night.

He changed his route and headed for Spencer Street on the north side of town. He counted out the addresses, then slowed down when he got to the Ingallses'. It was a little house, no bigger than where Mark and Allie lived. For a moment, he just sat there and stared up at the frame structure with wisteria vines growing up the porch post and full ferns hanging from hooks. It boggled his mind that a man who lived in a neat little house like this, with a tricycle on the side and a ball lying beside the front door, could actually be a killer. And it puzzled him even more that he might have others working with him. Maybe his wife was the one who had run them off the road last night. The wife who hung the ferns and swept the porch and planted the flowers. He had assumed the culprit was a man, but in the darkness he hadn't been sure.

Frustrated, he went to the station, tempted to take off his sling so he wouldn't call attention to his injury. He was known as the one in great shape, the one who never had a problem with his weight, the one who jogged five miles a day and bench-pressed more than anybody in the department. He didn't suppose he would be bench-pressing anything for a while.

He found Ray Ford in the office they had recently built on to the back of the Midtown Station. Dan broke the news that he wouldn't be able to come in for a while, and was barraged with questions from Ray about what had happened last night. Dan gave him a few sketchy answers, then headed into the kitchen.

Nick—his coworker and preacher—was sitting at the table with books and papers spread out in front of him. "Whatcha doing? Writing your sermon for Sunday?"

Nick looked up at him. "No, I'm getting ready to do two of the funerals tomorrow." He nodded toward the sling on Dan's arm. "I'm sure glad it won't be yours, man."

"You and me both." Dan pulled out a chair and sank down. "Pretty stupid, but I guess I forgot about the funerals. So much has been going on."

"Wanna talk about it?" Nick asked.

Dan shook his head. "Don't know what to say. Don't even know what to think."

"Well, we could start with why you've made yourself Jill's rescuer."

"I haven't rescued her," Dan argued. "Night before last, that man could have blown her away and I couldn't have stopped him. Last night she called because her car broke down, which wasn't a coincidence. The scumbag did something so it wouldn't run. If I hadn't shown up, he might have killed her right there."

"But you did show up. And then you got her out of the car before it went over the bridge. I'd call that a rescue."

Dan couldn't help feeling defensive. "So what should I have done? Let her go over?"

"No, of course not. But that kind of danger does kind of bond you, doesn't it?"

"Yeah, it does." Dan stared down at the wood grain on the table. "Nick, have you ever considered marrying a woman just so you could protect her?"

Nick started laughing, and Dan grinned. After a moment, both of their smiles faded. "I'm laughing, but it's not so funny. Truth is, I *can* understand the feeling."

"Really?" Dan asked. He stood up and went to the refrigerator, got out some orange juice. "'Cause see, I know that Jill's not safe. And I have this overwhelming, irrational feeling that I'm the only one who can protect her. But I can't move in with her and hover over her. I know it. So it's actually been crossing my mind that maybe I should marry her so I could be there." He got out a glass and began to pour. "Like she would even consider that in the first place. She's not even sure she wants to date me yet, much less marry me."

Nick's grin returned. "I don't think I have to tell you that's the wrong reason to get married, and I would not do the ceremony."

"But you said you understood it."

"I do," Nick said. "There's this woman that I think about . . ." His voice faded out, and Dan came back to the table.

"Yeah? You've got a thing for a woman?"

Nick shot him a look. "Being a preacher doesn't exempt you from normal feelings, Dan. I wouldn't call it 'a thing.' I just think about her sometimes."

Dan was riveted. "Go on."

Nick couldn't meet Dan's eyes as he spoke. "She's not a Christian, and she's a little reckless, and I keep feeling this heavy burden for her, like I'm the only one who can save her. Only she doesn't listen to me. But so often, I'm tempted to ask her out to dinner or something . . . but then I know that if I did I might get more involved with her, I wouldn't think clearly . . ." He looked up at Dan again. "The idea of rescuing someone is not a good basis for a relationship. Especially not a marriage."

Dan looked into his glass, as if the answers swirled there in the pulp. A wry grin stole across his face. "So you wouldn't marry us," Dan said, thinking out loud. "We could go to the justice of the peace. Who's got that job now? Jesse Pruitt?"

"Yeah, I think he's still holding it. Come on, Dan. You don't want to do that. You don't want to marry her on a technicality. You want to get married under God."

Dan chuckled, considering that as he took a drink. "Well, all right. So what if I thought it over and realized that I really wanted to marry her for the right reasons? Because I want to take care of her for the rest of her life."

"You're not ready," Nick said.

Dan's grin fled. "How do you know?"

"Because I've watched you and Jill for the last year. I've watched all the women you've taken out over the last few months, and all the ways you've avoided her. Just because she's in danger now is no reason to start shopping for rings. Marriage isn't going to protect her. Even if you're married, you can't be with her every minute."

"I know that," Dan said. "It's more than protection. For the past few months, I've been thinking about her a lot. Wishing I could call her. But there was part of me that just couldn't. I didn't want to start it up again, because I knew . . ."

Nick's eyes bored into his. "You knew what?"

"I knew that if I called her one time, if I went out with her, if I gave an inch, that I'd be in for the long haul."

"The long haul?" Nick asked. "Now, that's a healthy way to look at marriage. And if it took a crazy man with a gun to get you to make that move—"

"So it takes a lot to break through this tough skull of mine."

"What does it take to break through hers? You said she doesn't even know if she wants to date you."

Dan realized he had a point. "But she did call me when she was in trouble last night. There were a million people she could have called, right? But she called me."

"That's a good sign," Nick said. "But how many successful marriages claim close calls with death as the foundation? On the other hand, she's vulnerable right now. So are you. Maybe you should just see how it goes. Spend some more time with her. Some time that isn't filled with stress."

"If people would stop taking her hostage and running her off bridges, maybe we could do that." Dan shook his head. "I don't know why he wants her dead. I don't understand it. She never does anything but help people. She spends her whole life trying to keep people out of jail. Keeping them from being sued, keeping them from getting taken. Why did they come after her so brutally?"

"They came after you, too, pal."

"Only because I was with her," he said.

"That would make most guys avoid her like the plague," Nick said. "But not you."

Dan shook his head. "I stayed away too long already."

Chapter Thirty-Two

● ● ●

Jill had been so tired the night before that she had not set the alarm, and she slept right through the baby's crying and didn't wake up until nine. The moment she noted the time, she leaped out of bed, threw on her robe, and ran out of the room.

"Morning, Jill," Allie said, standing in the kitchen with the baby on her hip.

"I overslept!" Jill said, rushing for the telephone.

"That's okay," she said. "You're the boss."

"But I had appointments." She punched out her office number, then winced at the pain in her wrist.

"Jill Clark's office," her secretary said.

"Sheila, this is Jill."

"You're still alive?" Sheila asked.

Jill swallowed back the aggravation she often felt when talking to the woman. If she wasn't so competent, Jill would have replaced her years ago. The one time she'd fired her, she'd learned that there wasn't anyone else in town as capable, so she'd hired her back. "No, I'm not dead," she said. "Did you hear that I was?"

"No, if I'd heard that I probably would have taken the day off."

"Sorry I spoiled your fun." She raked her fingers through her hair. "Look, I overslept. I'll be in shortly."

"If you don't mind my saying so, I don't want to be within a mile of you today, and I don't think any of your clients do, either. They've got enough problems."

Jill frowned and opened her mouth to argue, then realized that Sheila was right. "All right, Sheila," she said. "Cancel my appointments. I guess I could use a day off."

"What a relief. I'll go home, too."

Jill closed her eyes. "You're right. Why don't you forward the calls to your house? I hadn't thought about it, but my office probably isn't the safest place to be right now."

"Sure thing."

"And don't tell anybody where I am."

"Where *are* you?"

Jill closed her eyes. "Never mind. Don't worry about it."

"What if somebody really wants to know?"

"Then I want you to *really* not tell them."

"And what if they come after me and torture the information out of me?"

"Then you'll be safe, because you won't know."

She heard Sheila pause long enough to light up a cigarette. The woman constantly denied that she ever smoked in the office, but every time she came in she was certain she smelled smoke.

"My doctor thinks I'm under too much stress as it is," Sheila said. "I don't need bombs going off around me and bullets flying . . ."

"Sheila, I said you could go home."

"Well, if you'd let me off the phone, I could go."

Jill slammed the phone down and bounced down on the couch. Allie was standing in the doorway watching her. "When are you going to fire her?" she asked. "She treats you with so little respect."

"Even smart alecks have to work somewhere," Jill said wearily. "Besides, she's a whiz in the office. I don't have to like her very much."

Allie put Justin on the floor near a play center, and Jill got down on the floor next to him. He grinned up at her as he chewed on a set of plastic keys. He handed them to her, and she arched her eyebrows. "Thank you, Justin!" She looked up at Jill as she stroked his soft hair. "He gets sweeter every day."

"You need to get you one," Allie said with a smile.

"Nope," Jill said. "I think I'm called to be single."

"Yeah, right."

"You don't think people can be called to the single life?"

"Oh, sure I do. Paul the apostle apparently was. Lots of people are. Just not you. And if you're not, then Dan just might be the guy."

"And if I can prove he's not, will you leave me alone about this?"

"Hey, you don't have a mother nagging you for grand-children," Allie said. "So I have to do it."

Jill's expression faded. She missed her mother, who had died while she was in college, and wished she could be here to talk to. Allie saw her expression and instantly regretted her words.

"Oh, Jill. I'm so sorry. I didn't mean to sound so flip about your mom."

"It's okay," she said, holding a mirror up for Justin. He saw his reflection and grabbed at it. "So my children will be your grand-children? Do I need to remind you that I'm older than you are?"

Allie laughed. "I'd always hoped we were going to have chil-dren grow up together. It's not too late, you know."

Jill shook her head. "You're hopeless."

"Actually, I'm full of hope. You're the one who's afraid to dream. Besides, there's nothing I love more than a good wedding."

Chapter Thirty-Three

● ● ●

Lately there was nothing Aunt Aggie loved more than a good funeral. She cut through the funeral home to the visitation room to get a look at Sue Ellen Hanover before they closed the coffin. But to her chagrin, it hadn't been opened. So she wandered into the room next door, where a ninety-eight-year-old woman lay. Aunt Aggie recognized her right away, and pretended she had come to pay her respects as the family greeted her. The funeral director came into the room, as he always did when Aunt Aggie was on the premises. It was as if he was a security guard hired to keep her in line.

"Who did her makeup, *sha?*" she asked him.

"Paula Bouchillon," he said.

"When I go, I want her," she told him. "Now don't you let them put no silly wig on me, nor poof my hair up like Dolly Parton. I want to look natural, me. And I want to wear my tiara from the beauty contest." Aunt Aggie had been Miss Louisiana in 1938, and she never let anyone forget it.

"Yes ma'am. I'll put it in your file." He had been taking notes like this on Aunt Aggie's funeral for the last several months, since she'd become obsessed with her own death.

"Now T-Celia gon' want to put me in my purple dress," she went on, "but I don't like that dress. I don't know yet what I want to wear, but I'll let you know before the time."

"Yes, ma'am."

Celia, who had been looking for her, spotted her and hurried into the room. "Aunt Aggie, we need to sit down."

Aunt Aggie followed dutifully as Celia led her into the chapel where the funerals were held. "Aunt Aggie, you've got to stop planning your funeral. You need to be concentrating on the grieving family, and Sue Ellen, instead of all this morbid talk."

People started filling in around them, but Aunt Aggie didn't speak to any of them. They were carrying the closed coffin into the room, and her eyes followed it. "This is the quietest I ever saw her," Aunt Aggie said. "Didn't know she had it in her, me."

Celia was mortified and looked around to see if anyone had heard. "Aunt Aggie, she's *dead*."

"Might be, might not be. Sue Ellen would do 'most anything to get attention." The man in front of them shot them a disgusted look over his shoulder, and Celia looked as if she might crawl under the pew. "*Aunt Aggie!*"

"I didn't know he could hear me," she said. "But you know it's true." She patted Celia's leg. "I don't want that kind o' coffin, me," she said. "It ain't worth it. I want the cheap kind, 'cause there's no use spendin' all that cash on the dead . . ."

"Aunt Aggie, please quit talking about your death!" Celia sat back and set her hand on her belly. "You know, I think I'll go to Mary's funeral alone. I just don't want to sit through it with you if you're going to do this."

"Why you so upset when I talk about dyin'?" Aunt Aggie demanded. "Ain't like I'm gonna be floatin' down the river Hades. If I die, I'm gon' shoot right straight up to heaven, so why you actin' like it's some awful thing, *sha?*"

Celia managed to smile. "You're right, Aunt Aggie." She had been trying to disciple her aunt since she'd come to know the Lord a few months earlier. But the old woman was still a babe in Christ. Her faith in the basics—that Jesus Christ had died for her and rose again so that she could go to heaven when she died—had not wavered. "I just don't want you to go yet."

"Well, I ain't got no intentions," she said, "so don't you worry yourself." Allie and Mark slipped into the pew next to

Celia, and Aunt Aggie wrenched her neck to see around Celia. "Allie . . ."

"Hey, Aunt Aggie," Allie said, as if the old woman had greeted her. "How are you?"

"Don't mind that," Aunt Aggie said, waving her off. "Who sent that spray over there?"

Allie looked at the spray of flowers Aunt Aggie was pointing to. "Uh . . . Grant Hargis."

"*Sha*, if they want to order mums for my funeral, you tell 'em I hate 'em. You hear?"

Celia groaned.

"Aunt Aggie, you're gonna live to be a hundred and thirty years old," Allie said. "Quit planning your funeral, for heaven's sake."

"It's only because I'm allergic, me. Make me sneeze."

"You won't sneeze if you're lying in a coffin," Celia whispered.

"I might." Aunt Aggie leaned further around Celia, then got up and moved between her and Allie. "And I want you to put the flowers around the coffin so folks don't stand too close. Keep folks from breathin' down on me with they rancid breath—"

"Aunt Aggie, people are going to hear you!" Allie said.

Offended, Aunt Aggie got up again. "Well, then, I'll go sit with somebody who appreciates what I got to say." With that she slid out of the pew and headed for the cluster of firefighters she saw at the back of the room. Regally, she walked back to them, and they all got to their feet and hugged her. She felt like the most popular girl at the school dance.

She was just about to sit down when she saw Hank from the newspaper coming in with a camera around his neck and a pad and pencil in his hand. "Hank, you ain't botherin' folks for a story, is you?" she asked.

Hank looked cornered. "Uh . . . yes ma'am, Aunt Aggie. I thought the funerals would be a good human interest story after the bombing."

"Well, you take care that you don't upset these folks now, you hear? This is a serious occasion."

Several of the mourners shot her disgusted looks as she sat between two of her firemen.

Chapter Thirty-Four

● ● ●

Jill knew she should have gone to the funerals, but she just couldn't manage to pull herself together enough to do it. She was exhausted and still nervous about getting out in public, where she could be an open target for reporters and curiosity seekers, not to mention whoever had tried to kill them last night.

Allie and Mark had taken the baby and gone to the Blooms 'N Blossoms shop early to make all the sprays that would be sent to the funerals. They were also attending the funerals, but she had opted to stay at their house alone.

When her cell phone rang, she answered it quickly. "You got an urgent message," Sheila said, as if she was the boss and Jill had been negligent about her job.

"Who's it from?" Jill asked, doubting the real urgency of anything today.

"It was from a Debbie Ingalls." Jill caught her breath. "She sounded very nervous and insistent that she talk to you today."

"Debbie Ingalls?" Jill repeated.

"Ingalls . . . isn't that the name of the guy who's in jail for roughing you up?"

"He didn't rough me up. He just held me hostage for a few hours."

"So how did he run you off the bridge if he's still in jail?"

"Apparently, he didn't," Jill said. "We don't know if he's working alone or with someone else, which is why you're at home today, remember?"

"Oh, yeah. Anyway, this Debbie woman . . . is she his wife?"

"Yes."

"So what does she want with you?"

Jill figured it had something to do with Jerry's desire for her to represent him. "I won't know until I call her back. What's the number?"

Sheila barked out the number, then added, "I work in the middle of the hot seat and nobody wants to tell me anything. I'll just be an uninformed sitting duck. Don't worry about it."

"Sheila, if there's anything I need to tell you after I talk to her, I will. I won't make you a sitting duck."

Sheila muttered something that Jill was glad she couldn't hear and hung up. Jill took a deep breath, then dialed the number on her cell phone.

"Hello?" The voice sounded anxious, upset.

"Debbie, this is Jill Clark. I understand you tried to call me."

"Yes! Oh, thank you for calling back, Jill." It sounded as if Debbie burst into tears. "Jill, I need to talk to you. Please, it's very important."

"Why?"

"It's about Jerry, and all this mess. Please, Jill, can you come and see me? Can we talk somewhere? I could come to your office."

Every red flag in Jill's mind sprang up. "No. I'm not in the office today."

"Just tell me where. I'll come anywhere, as long as I can bring the children. I don't have anyone to keep them."

Jill frowned. Could a woman with two preschoolers really be dangerous? "Look, I'm a little nervous about meeting with any of you. Somebody tried to run me off the bridge into Lake Pontchartrain last night, and I'm not feeling exactly congenial right now."

"Someone tried to run you off the road? Jill, don't you see? That's proof that Jerry isn't involved."

Jill didn't answer.

"Jill, please . . . there are some things I could explain to you. Things that might help you understand. You seemed like a decent person when I saw you the other night, and you know that my husband didn't do anything to hurt you. You gave your word about something and you didn't keep it. That's okay, because I understand, but there are some things that you need to understand. Please. I'm begging you."

Jill closed her eyes as the guilt rose within her again, and those red flags fell to half-mast. If she refused to represent Jerry Ingalls, the least she could do was meet with this woman. She seemed like a harmless person. She was the one, after all, who had talked Jerry into letting her go. She supposed she owed her that much. "All right," she said finally. "I'll come to your house."

"You would do that?" Debbie exclaimed. "Oh, Jill, I would appreciate that so much. That way I could get the children down for a nap before you come, and we could talk."

"What time?"

"How about three? They should be sound asleep by then."

"All right. I'll be there." She hung up the phone and leaned her head back on the couch, her eyes closed. She couldn't believe she had agreed to do this. What in the world would Debbie have to tell her? There was nothing more that she wanted to know about Jerry Ingalls, and Debbie didn't have a prayer of convincing her to represent him. Besides that, she was worried what it might mean to go into his home. What if it was a trap of some kind?

She got up and paced across the floor, raking her fingers through her hair. She tried to think it through, then began to pray that God would give her direction. Would he stop her from going if it was a trap? Would he intervene somehow? She honestly didn't know, but by the time she finished praying, she felt an urgent need to keep this appointment with Debbie. Maybe that was God speaking to her. Maybe if it was the wrong thing to do, God would have let her know it. She just wasn't sure about her feelings anymore. Sometimes they made no sense, and sometimes they led her wrong.

The phone rang and she jumped. She tried to catch her breath as she picked it up. "Hello?"

"Jill, it's Dan."

She breathed out a sigh of relief. What had she expected? For the killer to call her to let her know he'd found her? Somehow, she'd have to get over this paranoia. "Hi, Dan."

"You sound a little out of breath," he said. "Anything wrong?"

"No," she said quickly. "The phone just startled me."

He was quiet for a moment. "I just wanted to let you know that they've set a time for Mary Hampton's funeral. Tomorrow at ten o'clock. I wondered if you wanted to go with me."

She closed her eyes and sank back onto the couch. "I don't know, Dan. I'll have to think about it. It's not that I don't want to go pay my respects . . ."

"I know," he said. "All the questions about the hostage thing and the bridge . . . I kind of dreaded that, too."

"And I don't know if I'm up to going out in public with this person still out there. I missed Sue Ellen's . . ."

"Me, too. What happened last night kind of has its lingering effects, doesn't it?"

She nodded, though she knew he couldn't hear.

"Have you eaten?"

"No. I was just about to go to the kitchen and see what Allie and Mark have in the fridge."

"Why don't I just bring you something over?" he asked. "It's lunchtime, and we both have to eat."

The thought of his company made her feel instantly better. "Okay," she said, "but I have an appointment at three, so I'll have to cut it short."

"An appointment?" he asked. "You're working today? I went by the office earlier and nobody was there."

"Yeah, well. I decided not to go in, and I sent Sheila home. Just in case." She was quiet for a moment, then finally said, "Debbie Ingalls wants to meet with me."

Disapproval screamed out of his silence.

"Dan . . . are you there?"

"Yeah, I'm here," he said. "You're not actually considering meeting with her, are you?"

"Actually, yes."

Silence again. "Look, I'll be over there in thirty minutes, and we can talk about it then." He had hung up before she had the chance to respond, and for a moment she sat there with the phone in her hand, staring at it angrily, almost rebelliously thinking that he had no right to talk to her about anything, that this had nothing to do with him.

She remembered the arguments they'd had when they'd been seeing each other before, when she had spent long hours working on a client's behalf. Dan had complained that she took too many risks and worked too many hours. Then he had just lost interest altogether.

"I'm not the kind of guy who really hooks up with one woman very long, Jill. You know that about me," he had told her. And then it had been over. Tragically, humiliatingly over.

Now he was back . . . temporarily, she assumed. Again, making her feel vulnerable and guilty for doing her job.

She was still turning the thoughts over in her mind when the doorbell rang. She looked outside and saw his rental car in Allie and Mark's driveway. As she opened the door, her anger melted away. He was too handsome for his own good, and the sling on his arm just gave him an endearing air of vulnerability. He was still the catch of the town, and she thought of all the women who would be sick to know he was bringing her lunch again.

Their eyes connected and her heart jolted. She hated the fact that he still had this effect on her.

"How ya doing?" he asked.

"Fine," she said. She stepped back from the door and allowed him in, and he set the bags on the table. "I got you sweet and sour chicken. I remembered you liked that."

"Yeah, it's my favorite."

Their eyes locked for a moment longer, and finally, he swallowed hard and looked at the floor. "Look . . . I had a long lonely night, and all these thoughts have gone through my mind about last night and how close we came . . ." His voice broke off and he looked up at her again. "A hug would be really nice right now."

A smile crept across her mouth as she stepped into his arms. He held her tightly, in a way she didn't think she'd ever been held before, almost as if she was cherished or . . . loved. Emotions both confusing and painful welled inside her, and she suddenly wanted to cry.

This, she told herself, was even more dangerous than walking into Debbie Ingalls's home.

Their eyes met again, and she tried not to let herself read the eloquence in his. She couldn't trust anything her heart translated for her. Quickly, she turned and went to Allie's cabinet and got out two glasses and some silverware. He stood there with his hands in his pockets, watching her with his head slightly tilted as she moved around the kitchen.

They sat down and he said grace, and then they began to eat in silence.

"So are we gonna talk about this?" Dan asked finally.

She looked up at him. "Talk about what?"

"About your going to Debbie Ingalls's house."

She looked back down at her food. "I don't really know why we would have to talk about it," she said. "It's just something I'm gonna do, that's all."

He seemed stung by the words, and she noticed a pink hue flushing over his face. "I'm not trying to get in your way," he said, "or to tell you what to do or anything like that. I'm just concerned. Last night somebody tried to kill you."

"You, too."

"Yeah, but it's you they were after. Your car was sabotaged. You're the one who was held hostage two nights ago."

She couldn't take her eyes off her food. He touched her hand to make her look at him again. When they met, his were probing, intense. "Jill, someone is still trying to kill you, and I don't want them to succeed. I really, really don't want that to happen."

She moved her hand away. "I don't want it to happen, either, Dan."

"Then why are you meeting with her?"

"Because I think she's a decent person," she said. "I met her the other night, and she's the one who talked Jerry into letting me go. She's a young, pretty mother who loves her husband."

"And what does she want with you?"

"Probably to try to talk me into representing him," she said, "which I'm not going to do under any circumstances, but I felt I at least owed it to her to give her a chance to have her say, since she is the one who got me out of that situation."

"Do you understand that you could be walking into a trap? If Jerry Ingalls does have people working for him . . . if he is the one behind that guy running us off the road last night, then Debbie Ingalls could be in on it, too. She's on her husband's side, Jill. Whatever their agenda is, she could be right there with him."

"They have two little kids," Jill said. "Why would she do that?"

"Why would anybody do anything?" he asked. "There are three people dead because he blew up the post office. There would be two more dead if he'd succeeded last night."

"I just have a gut feeling about this," she said. "I don't think Debbie is involved. She's just fighting for her husband and her life, and the lives of her children."

"But you can't always follow your gut feelings," Dan said. "Jill, look at me."

Grudgingly, she looked up at him. "Jill, you're an emotional person. I've known you long enough to know that your emotions do get tangled up with people. That's a good thing. It gives you compassion. But it also makes you exhaust yourself and spend yourself completely, and sometimes your emotions are wrong."

She felt the heat rising to her face, and her anger returned. "Tell me about it," she said.

"What's that supposed to mean?"

"It means that you're right. Sometimes my emotions are wrong. Like eight months ago when I started to fall for you."

He looked surprised that she would throw that at him. "What makes that wrong?"

"Well, it kind of became obvious when you told me that you're not the kind of guy who hooks up with one woman very long. It was pretty obvious then that my emotions were leading me wrong." She could see that her words had stung him, and she hated herself. What was wrong with her? Why would she lay her cards on the table like that?

"Jill, I know what you must have been thinking for the last several months. But there's a reason why I don't hook up with people very long."

"No kidding," she said. "Dan, I figured these things out about you a long time ago. You don't like to get attached. You don't want to love anyone."

Now it was his turn to look down. He had yet to touch his food, but he stirred it around on his plate as if he intended to.

"Jill," he said in a soft voice, "I didn't sleep much last night or the night before. This has been really hard for me. But it's been hard for the last eight months. I've thought about you every day, and I've wanted to pick up the phone ..."

"But you never did," she said.

"It was a fight," he told her.

She hated the tears that sprang to her eyes. She looked down to hide them. "And you're so strong. You were able to win that battle."

He leaned forward and coaxed her cheek up with his finger. Slowly, their eyes met. She gave herself a desperate reminder that she didn't want to be in love with Dan Nichols. That was the last thing in the world she needed right now.

"Jill, my not calling you had nothing to do with strength. It's a weakness, I'll admit."

"A weakness for other women?"

"No, not for other women."

"Because I distinctly remember seeing you with ... what ... two, three dozen? Your never-a-fourth-date rule seems to be working very well for you. I didn't know there were that many single women in Newpointe." She couldn't believe the jealousy seeping out of her own tone.

Dan sat back in his chair, and Jill gazed across the table at him.

"Jill, the reason I wanted to stop seeing you was exactly this kind of thing right here."

"What? That I speak my own mind?" she asked. "That I say what I feel?"

"No," he said, leaning forward, his eyes intent on hers. "Not that at all. That's what I like about you. But what I don't like about you is your walking into danger, putting your life at risk. Maybe you're not used to knowing that other people care about you. Maybe it doesn't matter to you. But I didn't want to lose you."

"Dan, excuse me for not understanding the rationale of your breaking up because you didn't want to lose me."

"Okay, so it wasn't rational!" he admitted. "Nobody ever said it had to be. But I was scared and I didn't want to lose you. But the minute I knew you were in real danger, I couldn't control myself anymore. I had to get involved."

"Don't do me any favors," Jill said.

Dan's face was redder than she'd ever seen it, and he got up and headed for the door. For a moment she thought he was going to leave, and dread fell over her. It was just as she could have predicted.

But Dan didn't leave. Instead, he stopped and turned back to her. "Look, I'm trying to be honest, here. This isn't easy for me."

She sighed, knowing he was right. He was not usually that direct or open with his feelings. This must be hard for him. "Look, I know what's going to happen, here," she said in a softer voice. "I don't even blame you for it, Dan. It's just like Celia hanging around little Pete Hampton's bed. She feels a sense of responsibility to him because she's his Sunday school teacher. You feel a sense of responsibility to me because we once meant something to each other. And when you heard I was in danger, you came to my aid. It's a guy thing," she said. "You can't help yourself. Last night, I shouldn't have called you when my car broke down. I should have called someone else. I just thought of you—"

He looked down at her, and she could almost see the hope in his eyes that she would say she needed him. But she wouldn't let herself say that.

"And then when we were run off the road, you felt protective again. You saved my life, Dan. You're off the hook."

He shook his head slowly, then came back and bent over her. He put his hands on the armrests of her chair. His face was only inches from hers. "I don't want to be off the hook, Jill," he said. "That's what I'm trying to tell you."

She didn't know why his nearness made her heart ache so much. "Then what's all this about your not wanting to be involved with somebody who takes risks?"

"Not wanting to and not doing it are two different things," he said. "Besides, the irony hasn't escaped me. I'm the one who works as a firefighter, and you're not making ultimatums to me."

"It hasn't escaped me, either."

"So how come you keep getting into more trouble than I do?"

She grinned slowly. "Just lucky, I guess."

He didn't seem to find that funny. He gazed down at her with misty eyes. "I tried to forget about you. I tried to go out with other women. I tried to tell myself all the ways that you and I are incompatible."

"So did I," she whispered.

"But then when I heard you were in trouble, I almost couldn't stand it, and all these regrets came rushing through me. Regrets that I had been so stupid to give up the time I could have spent with you, and here you were about to be snatched away and I'd never have that chance again. It was a selfish thing, Jill. That's why I showed up there that night. Not as much to save you as to save myself."

Somehow, that admission changed everything.

"I know I'm not making a lot of sense," he said. "But bottom line is, I want to resume things with you. I care about you, Jill. I haven't been able to get you off my mind, and now I'm beginning to realize that it's stupid of me to deprive myself of you because I'm afraid I might lose you. It makes no sense. It's totally irrational, and I don't want to live like that anymore."

A tear stole through her lashes and crept down her cheek. She wiped it away. She couldn't believe he was admitting this. It was something she had dreamed of him saying at night when she had no control over her thoughts, but she hadn't believed he ever would.

"I want us to be a couple," he said. "I want to take you out more than three times. I want to break my record again." He grinned slightly, and she couldn't help meeting that grin through her tears. "But this kind of stuff just drives me crazy," he went on. "Knowing that you're walking into danger, possibly a trap, that you could be killed. That after I've finally said this to you, and you're right in my grasp . . ." He dropped down into the chair next to her. "What am I saying?" he asked. "You may not even *want* to resume things. This all may be totally moot."

Again, she wiped at her tears. "Don't jump to conclusions," she said.

"What's that mean?"

She smiled. "It means that I want to resume things, too. But I want to understand you. I want to understand what happened before."

He leaned back hard in his chair and looked at the ceiling, as if he could find the answers there, written out concisely, in a way they could both understand. "I don't want to be left behind," he said.

She frowned. "Left behind? What do you mean?"

He shook his head, got up, and turned his back to her. "When I was a kid, we had all that money."

She nodded. It was common knowledge that the Nicholses were one of the wealthiest families in town.

"My parents hired nannies," he said. "And they went off and traveled to Europe and to the Middle East and to Aspen. They were never home on Christmas," he said. "I was left behind. I told myself when I grew up, I would never be left behind again."

It all made sense as the words processed through her mind, and she softened. She got up and touched his back. He turned around and looked down at her. "Don't look at me like that. There's no reason for pity. My background made me who I am today, but it just made me want certain things and not want others."

"I can understand that."

"But I think I can get over it, if you'll just be patient with me."

She smiled.

"It's not gonna be easy," he admitted. "I'll be a basket case if you go to her house today. It's gonna be painful." He plopped back into the chair.

She sat across from him and scooted her chair close to his until their knees were touching. Their foreheads met, and she looked down and took his hand lying in the sling. There was so much she would love to say to him, about how she wished for him at night, and occasionally allowed herself to pray that he would have a change of heart. She had never expected that prayer to be answered.

Big tears dropped off on their hands, and finally, he looked up at her and wiped the wet spot under her eyes. Then he looked down at her lips and kissed her. It was as if the months of longing had built up in her soul, and she suddenly missed him with all her heart, and thought that if this was the last kiss between them, she would never be able to stand it.

When the kiss broke, he touched her face, and she met his eyes. "Dan, how would it be if you came with me to Debbie Ingalls's house?" she asked.

He dropped his hands and pulled back to look at her more clearly. "You wouldn't mind that?"

"No," she said. "I think it would make me feel safer."

His eyes lit up into a grin. "That would make me feel a lot better."

"Just this time," she said. "And I won't ask you to take me on your firefighting calls."

He chuckled, then pressed a kiss on her lips again. "Thank you," he whispered.

"Thank *you*," she countered softly.

And then he kissed her again.

Chapter Thirty-Five

● ● ●

It was midmorning when Frank Harper finally woke at the wildlife refuge just east of Newpointe. The captain's chair in the middle of the stolen van had made his back ache. He stretched and tried to think. He was hungry, but he had no money. He dug around through the glove compartment of the van, and into the overhead compartments, until he came up with a folded ten-dollar bill. He yelled jubilantly, thrilled that he could now buy enough food to get him through the day.

He would drive through a fast-food place and get some breakfast, and then he could think better to find Jill Clark. Brain food was what he needed. Brain food and a little more time.

He headed back toward Slidell, wondering if anyone from the campground had noticed the van was missing yet. If they had reported it, would they have already made the connection that he could have been the one who took it?

The thought filled him with urgency, and he realized that he needed to lose the van if he didn't want to be found. He needed another car, one that was nondescript, just like a million other cars on the road today.

He drove for another twenty minutes before he reached Slidell and navigated his way to the Piggly Wiggly. The parking lot was scattered with people: a young woman trying to keep three toddlers together as she unloaded her basket; an elderly woman tipping a bag boy; three teenagers loading an ice chest. No one seemed unduly interested in him.

He sat in the van for a moment, scanning the different choices of cars, and saw at least six Honda Civics. One of them had to be unlocked, he told himself, so he grabbed his almost dry clothes and shoes from the floor of the van, stuffed them into the duffel bag, pulled his rifle to his side, and left the van behind. It took only three tries for him to find a green Civic that wasn't locked, and in seconds, he had the engine running and was on his way.

He headed back to Newpointe. He would pay his respects to Jerry Ingalls's wife. Maybe she could tell him where Jill Clark would be, and who the man was in the Bronco with her. Maybe he could send Jerry Ingalls a strong warning through her—a warning to keep his mouth shut, or his wife would suffer.

He reached the edge of Newpointe and headed for the Ingallses' house.

Chapter Thirty-Six

● ● ●

The little house where Jerry Ingalls lived was immaculate, except for a tricycle on the porch and a ball lying in the yard. Jill could hardly believe that they were standing at the front door of the man who, quite possibly, had blown up the post office.

The house looked freshly painted, and a garden of impatiens lined the sidewalk. Dan stood next to her, his face looking tense and concerned as his eyes scanned the property as if he might find a hidden bomb there or a grenade launcher hiding behind a bush. "I don't know what I expected," she said. "But not this."

"I know," he said. "I drove by here earlier and felt the same way. I think I expected a dirt floor shack like the Unabomber had. Not flowers and toys."

Jill rapped hard on the door, trying to look more like an attorney than a victim.

Behind her, Dan touched her shoulder, and she felt the reassurance of his presence and the warmth of his need to be with her. The door opened and she came face to face with Debbie Ingalls again. The woman was smaller than she, with delicate features that suggested fragility. She probably weighed a hundred pounds and stood about five-foot-three. Her hair was black and pulled into a loose chignon at the back of her head, but the dark circles beneath her eyes and the lines around her mouth made it apparent that this ordeal had been taking its toll on her.

She gave Jill a shaky smile. "Thank you for coming," she said. "I worried that you might change your mind."

Her smile was endearing, but Jill tried to ignore it. She didn't want to like her. "This is Dan Nichols," she said. "He's a good friend. I hope you don't mind that he came with me."

"Not at all," Debbie said, reaching out to shake Dan's hand. "Come on in. The kids are asleep."

They walked cautiously into the house, and Jill was surprised at the amount of sunlight coming through the back windows. The house was decorated with live plants and craftsy items that she suspected Debbie had made herself. It reminded her of Allie's house, and again she was amazed that Jerry Ingalls lived here.

"Sit down," Debbie said, and Jill noted that her hands were shaking as she gestured toward the couch.

Nervous herself, Jill went to sit on the couch, but Dan remained standing for a moment. Jill knew he still wasn't sure this was aboveboard. All of this—Debbie's nervousness, the lovely little house—could have been a clever scheme to give them a false sense of security.

Debbie looked up at Dan's sling. "Broken arm?"

"Dislocated shoulder," he said.

"Ouch. I'm sorry."

"You should be."

Debbie stiffened. "What do you mean?"

"I told you, we were run off of the bridge last night," Jill said. "Somebody was trying to kill us."

Debbie's mouth came open in a look of defensive disgust. "You can't possibly think that Jerry had anything to do with this."

"Well," Jill said, "he obviously wasn't in the car. But you've got to admit, it's a coincidence."

"If he'd had his way," Dan added, "they would have been dragging the lake for us this morning."

"Jerry doesn't want that," Debbie said. "You've got to believe that. He wants you alive so you can keep your word to him!"

"My word?" Jill repeated.

"Yes. You told him if he would let you go the other night you would defend him. I was there. I talked him into it based on your promise."

"Give me a break! You would have said anything, too, to get him out of there. He had threatened to kill me."

"In our family, when you give your word, you keep it. Jerry feels real strong about that. We've come to expect it from people."

Jill was stung, but Dan breathed a sarcastic laugh. "Real honorable," he said. "But that's not really worth a hill of beans when you go around blowing up post offices."

Debbie's eyes flashed. "My husband did not blow up the post office."

"You weren't so sure of that the other night."

"Yes, I was. I've always been sure of that. Jerry doesn't have that in him." She got up, paced across the floor, turned back to them. "Look, I don't blame you for breaking your word. To you, Jerry's a criminal. But he's *my* husband. Jill, I know you don't have any reason to represent him, especially if you think he's guilty. But I wanted you to come here today so I could explain some things about his past, so you could understand who this man is and why I love him."

Jill looked at the floor. She didn't want to see the tears in Debbie's eyes. Dan sat down next to her. "I'm not sure there's anything you could tell me, Debbie. A killer is a killer, no matter what made him that way. I'm not of the school of thought that says it's society's fault and everybody's a victim."

"Neither am I," she said. "And Jerry isn't, either. That's not what I meant. He's not a killer, so I don't have to make excuses or explain that away." She started pacing frantically back and forth across the room. "I didn't know Jerry before he went to Vietnam, but everyone who did says he was the sweetest guy you'd ever want to meet. Everyone loved him. But when he came back from Vietnam, he was a different person. He'd been through some terrible things. And he had a hard time coping."

"Most Vietnam vets are productive citizens," Dan said. "Lots of them had harrowing experiences. You don't see them killing people."

"Please, just listen! That's not what I meant. What I'm trying to tell you is that he went through a series of jobs and had a really hard time staying focused. He finally got involved with the wrong people and started doing drugs and other things he shouldn't have done. He wound up being a part of a group that robbed a liquor store one night, and he was the one that got caught."

The admission caught Jill off guard. She had expected her to wax poetic about his virtues, not share his criminal record.

"He did mention he'd been in prison," Jill said, bringing her eyes back up to Debbie.

"That's right," Debbie said. "He's an ex-con. He served five years for armed robbery. But he considers it the biggest blessing of his life."

"Prison?" Dan asked. "You've got to be kidding!"

"No," she said. She came back to her chair and sank down, intent on making them understand. "There was a prison ministry that came in three times a week and they told him about Jesus." Her voice broke. "I don't know if you're believers, but Jerry is now. He became a Christian while he was in prison. And when he got out, that sweet spirit that he once had was back. He had been changed forever. I met him after that."

Jill's brows furrowed together. She had seen lots of prison conversions, but she had trouble trusting them.

Dan wasn't sold either. "And that was before he took up terrorism?"

Debbie didn't appreciate the comment. She ignored it and addressed Jill instead. "The first five years after he got out of prison he went to therapy. He'd had some terrible experiences in

Vietnam, was badly wounded, and he still had nightmares. But he started to get better. Eventually, he was helping the other people in his group. Leading them to Christ and discipling them."

Dan shot Jill a skeptical look, but she kept quiet. It didn't sound like a bill of goods. It sounded real.

"Jill, my husband is innocent. Someone else blew up that post office, and he doesn't even know why."

"So what happened?" Jill asked. "Why was his pickup on the scene? Why was he in the motel? Why did he shoot his way into my room?"

"I've asked myself those questions a dozen times," she said. "I wish I could explain all of that to you, but there are things that I don't know. Things he won't tell me."

"You better believe there's something he won't tell you," Dan said. "By the way, honey, I have this little hobby . . ."

"No, you don't understand," she said, cutting him off. "That morning, the day the post office bombing happened, Jerry got a phone call. He seemed a little shaken up by it. When he got off the phone, he told me he had to go to meet a friend from his unit in Vietnam. I didn't really like the idea, because now and then he still has nightmares, and I didn't want all those memories dragged up again. Stuff that he couldn't even talk about with me. But he insisted. He said this was a really close friend. Somebody that he cared a lot about, and hadn't seen in years. He wanted to make sure that he was all right, because the man sounded like he was in a little trouble."

"Who was the friend?"

"He wouldn't say. He just told me to trust him."

"He didn't say what kind of trouble the guy was in?" Dan asked.

"No, he sure didn't. I don't think he *knew* what kind of trouble."

"Didn't you wonder why he couldn't invite the man here? Let you meet him, if they were such great friends?"

"I asked that," Debbie said. "He told me the man was kind of rough around the edges, and might scare the kids. He said it was best if he met him alone. I didn't see him for the rest of the day. The next thing I know, the FBI are at my house asking about Jerry . . . I honestly didn't have a clue. Then I realized . . . they thought he did it. Then I saw the reports about the hostage situation, and Jill . . ."

"You're *sure* you don't know who this friend was?" Dan demanded again.

"I don't know," she said, " he wouldn't tell me his name. He still won't tell me. I don't know why he would cover for him after he committed such an awful crime and got Jerry thrown in jail. But I think he is covering for him. You've got to believe me!"

"It's hard to believe," Jill said, "you have to admit."

"Of course it is. I'm aware of that. *But my husband is not a killer!* He's a wonderful father and a wonderful husband. He's active in our church. He's active in prison ministry. He goes to Angola twice a month and does Bible studies there. I think something must have happened that day, something he couldn't control. He got backed into a corner and he didn't know what to do but to come out shooting. But he didn't shoot *anybody*, Jill. Nobody got hurt."

"Except three people are dead at the post office."

"I would bet my life on his innocence!" she yelled.

Silence fell like a curtain around them. Finally, Jill spoke again. "What do you want from me?"

Debbie covered her face and tried to calm herself. "I want you to talk to him again."

"I did talk to him. Late last night. Didn't he tell you?"

Debbie looked at her over her fingertips. "No. I haven't been able to talk to him today. Did he tell you anything?"

"Not really, but I told *him* a few things. I was sure he was involved in what had just happened to us."

"Think about it," Debbie said. "This guy, whoever he is. He's still out there. He's the one who wants you dead. I don't know why. I can't imagine, but you've got to consider that Jerry doesn't have anything at all to do with it."

"If he was innocent, why wouldn't he be the first to tell who really did it?" Dan asked. "He has you and the kids. Why would he sit in jail like that, and not say a word?"

"I don't know," Debbie said, "but that's how Jerry is! He takes his friendships very seriously. And all that happened in Vietnam was so serious that he hasn't even been able to share it with me! But it's like a big scar right through the middle of his heart. I think maybe he thought he could turn this person around or something. Somehow he got sucked into this, and he doesn't know how to get out of it."

"Mommy? Are you crying?"

Jill was startled as the little boy came out of the bedroom, rubbing his eyes. His brown hair was tousled, and he had wrinkle prints on his face.

Instantly, Debbie's expression changed from pleading to pleasant. "No honey, I'm fine. Come here." The five-year-old padded barefoot across the carpet. Debbie pulled him into her lap.

"Seth, I want you to meet Ms. Clark and Mr ..."

"Nichols," Dan said.

"Nichols," Debbie repeated. "They're our friends."

"Hey," the child said.

Dan got up and shook the little boy's hand with a flourish of respect. "How you doing, buddy?"

"Fine, thank you."

Jill's heart melted. She wouldn't have expected a killer to have polite children.

"Did you have a good nap?" Debbie asked.

"Yes, ma'am." They heard a child crying from the other room, and she put the little boy down. "Just a minute. Let me go check on your sister." She looked up at Jill and Dan as she got to her feet. "My three-year-old. Excuse me."

She left the room and the little boy sat in her chair, staring across at Jill and Dan, like a grown-up at a meeting.

And Jill felt a sudden sense of dread that this child would soon face the stigma of having a father who was known as a terrorist.

Chapter Thirty-Seven

• • •

Frank Harper saw the rental car parked out in front of Jerry Ingalls's house, and decided now was not the time to go in. Instead, he parked in the driveway of an apparently vacant house a few doors down and watched for the visitors to come out.

He angled his rearview mirror so he could watch without wrenching his neck, but time rolled on and on. Whoever was there was staying an awfully long time. He wondered who it was, what she was telling them. Did she know about him? Was she telling them everything Jerry knew?

Someone knocked on the glass, and he jumped. An old woman stood at the window, smiling congenially and waving in at him.

Dread overcame him, but slowly, he rolled the window down.

"Hello," the woman said. "I'm Dora Higgins, next door. I couldn't help noticing you waiting over here. Are you waiting for your realtor to show you this house?"

He nodded. "Yes, ma'am."

"Well, I certainly will be glad to have a neighbor. It's a little creepy having it vacant, if you know what I mean. Would you like a piece of pie while you wait? I just took a fresh apple pie out of the oven. My grandchildren are coming this afternoon, and I like to have something sweet for them."

He shook his head. "Uh ... no, ma'am. Thank you."

She looked disappointed. "Well, I reckon you can't go takin' apple pie from ever'body who offers you some. Not with the kind of things goes on around here. Guess you heard about our neighbor over there, Jerry Ingalls. Blew up the post office a couple days ago. Such a nice man, too, and those children ... oh my, they don't deserve what they've gotten. But I can assure you that the rest of us on this street are decent people. Are you interested in this house for rental property, or will you be living here?"

He glanced back in the rearview mirror. No one had come out of the Ingallses' house just yet. "Uh ... I haven't decided yet."

"Well, all it needs is a little yard work and a few repairs on the inside. The lady who lived here was one of my dearest friends. She lived here for years before she died. It fell into a little bit of disrepair at the end because she was ill and couldn't do much, but oh, in her day, she was able to keep this garden blooming all the time."

"Yes, ma'am."

"Are you sure you don't want some pie? It looks like your realtor is late. You could call them from my house."

He shook his head hard. "No, ma'am. I'll just wait a little longer."

"All right, then. So nice to meet you."

He watched her as she headed back to her home, and thought how her whole house probably smelled of baked apples. A memory assaulted him, a memory of his paternal grandmother when he was only four or five, pulling an apple pie out of the oven and letting him cut his own piece, as big as he wanted. She had died when he was six, and there hadn't been anyone in his life like her.

He missed her. For a moment, he eyed the vacant house, wondering what it would be like to have her as a neighbor. He fantasized about flowers in the garden, a pie cooling on the windowsill, a perfect lawn. Those were dreams that weren't available to him, he thought with contempt. They hadn't been since the communist threat peeled the blinders from his eyes. Instead, he'd had to give the best of himself for his country, and he was still giving. But it was for people like Dora Higgins that he fought. So she would have the freedom to bake apple pies for her grandchildren.

He glanced in the rearview mirror and hoped that he didn't have much longer to wait. He had too much to do, and he needed to get on with it.

Chapter Thirty-Eight

• • •

"Do you know my daddy?" Seth Ingalls asked them as his mother went to get his sister.

Jill gave Dan a sad look. "We've met."

"Do you know when he's coming home?"

"No, I don't, honey. I'm sorry."

"Mommy cries at night," he said. "She misses Daddy."

"What about you?" Dan asked. "Don't you miss your daddy?"

Jill supposed the question was designed to expose Jerry's evil. Maybe Dan expected the child to scream out that he'd been abused by his father for years, and hoped he would never come back. Instead, the corners of his mouth began to droop and his eyes filled with tears. He began to rub them as he nodded his head. "He read to me at night."

Jill's own eyes filled, and she met Dan's eyes. He looked stricken, as if he knew he'd made the wrong call. She turned back to the child. "What would he read?" she asked.

"*Charlotte's Web*," he said. "Last time, *Winnie the Pooh*. My sister loves Tigger. He's her favorite. She cries, too."

"Have you been able to talk to your daddy?" Jill asked softly.

"I can't," he said. "He's on vacation." He rubbed his eyes again. "He shoulda took us."

Jill couldn't fight the tears welling up in her eyes. Dan squeezed her hand, as if to tell her that the child was no reflection of the father . . . that you could have a killer for a dad and still be a sweet kid.

Debbie came back into the room carrying the little girl. She was a tiny replica of her and looked too shy to speak to them. She buried her face in her mother's chest as the boy gave the chair back to his mother. "Sorry I took so long. Christy's a little shy, and she didn't want to come in here." She glanced at the boy, saw that he'd been crying, and shot Jill and Dan an accusing look. "Honey, what's wrong?"

"He was just telling us he misses his daddy," Jill said softly.

Debbie kept one arm around the sleepy little girl, and slid the other around him. She hugged him tightly, and when she looked at them again, her eyes were full of tears. So were Jill's.

"This is a hard time for our family," she whispered.

Jill got up. "We should go now." Dan stood up beside her.

"Jill, I'm begging you," Debbie said. "Won't you please reconsider? Somehow we'll pay you. We'll come up with the money. He just needs a good lawyer."

"It's not the money," Jill said. "Why me? Why not someone who's unbiased, objective?"

"Because you know he didn't hurt you. You were with him for several hours and you know what he's like."

"I don't know anything of the kind," Jill said. "I met him for a few hours in some strange circumstances—"

"That's right!" Debbie cut in. "You've got to realize what kind of stress he was under or he would've never—" She caught herself and looked self-consciously down at her children. "Otherwise, he would never have done anything like that." She brought her eyes back to Jill's. "Jill, I truly believe you're a woman we could trust. That you saw my husband's character. In your heart, you know . . ."

"You'd be a whole lot better off with someone else."

"Well, we don't *have* someone else," she said. "He wants you and I want you. There was something about you," she said.

"Something that made me think you were a woman of honor and integrity, even though you didn't keep your word."

Jill rubbed her temples. She was beginning to get a headache. "I can't promise to represent him, Debbie."

Debbie covered her mouth and sobbed. The little boy reached up and touched her face. "Mommy, don't cry," he whispered.

When he couldn't stop his mother's tears, he turned his angry little face to Jill and Dan. "My daddy is good," he said. "He wouldn't do anything bad."

"Honey, that's all right," Debbie said. "They know."

Jill bent down to the child. "It's sweet of you to defend your daddy that way." She breathed in a deep breath and let it out quickly. Dan squeezed the back of her neck. "I'm sorry, Debbie," she said finally, straightening again. "I believe that you believe in your husband. And I believe that you don't know what's going on. But I can't do it."

Debbie squeezed her eyes shut, then finally nodded her head. "All right," she said. "I guess there's nothing more I can say."

"No." Jill and Dan headed for the door before that little boy won her heart, before that little girl, so shy and sleepy, sitting in her mother's lap, began to affect her ... before Debbie Ingalls convinced her to change her mind.

"Thank you," Dan said as they drove home, "for deciding not to let her emotionally blackmail you."

"I hope I did the right thing."

"You did," he said. "Just because a guy has a cute kid and a sweet wife, doesn't mean he's not a killer."

"I know," she said. "But I've got to tell you, I wish he wasn't."

"Yeah, it would be nice to find out that he was innocent. But things don't always happen that way."

"I know they don't."

"Besides that," he said, "his wife could have been putting on an Oscar caliber act."

Her gaze drifted out the window. "I guess."

"You just never know."

But Jill felt that deep in her heart she did know. Debbie Ingalls hadn't been putting on an act.

• • •

Frank Harper watched as Jill Clark and her boyfriend came out of Jerry Ingalls's house, and suddenly overwhelming rage filled him. The sense of stark betrayal by Jerry's wife, a woman he didn't even know, was so fierce that he wanted to hurt her.

But he had no time right now. He would have to wait until later. Meanwhile, he had to follow the man and woman until he could finish what he'd started last night.

He wasn't going to sit still for betrayal. Vengeance had to be paid, or the war would never be won.

Chapter Thirty-Nine

• • •

Celia stayed with Pete Hampton while his grandmother and uncle made arrangements for his mother's funeral. Celia had been praying since the explosion that he would wake up with no lasting brain damage, but now she caught herself praying that he would not come around while his family was away from the hospital. Her greatest fear right now was that she would be forced into telling him that his mother was dead.

She couldn't think of a more horrible task.

But as the hours ticked by, he began to give indications that he was coming out of his coma. First, just an arm moved, then his head rolled, and he brought a hand up to scratch his face.

She stood frozen in front of him, trying to decide whether to try to reach his grandmother at the funeral home. Before she could make the decision, his eyes fluttered open.

Her heart jolted. "Pete? Can you hear me? Pete?"

His eyes closed again, and he was out. Celia went around the bed to call the nurse, but his eyes opened again. She stopped at the side of the bed and leaned over, waiting. "Pete? Can you hear me, honey?"

This time, his eyes focused on her. "Pete?" she said more loudly.

He opened his mouth to speak, but the tube in his throat prevented him.

"Don't talk, honey," Celia said. "There's something in your throat helping you breathe. Just nod if you know who I am."

He nodded. She breathed a laugh and stroked the side of his face. Her eyes filled with tears, and she realized that, if he knew—if he really knew—there might not be any brain damage.

"Then let's take a little test," she said softly. "I'll give you a name, and you nod if that's who I am. I'm Aunt Aggie Gaston."

He shook his head.

"I'm Miss Allie."

He shook his head again.

"I'm Miss Celia, from Sunday school."

He nodded.

"That's right!" she said. "You know me, don't you?" Maybe he would be all right, she thought. She reached for the buzzer, pressed it once, then a second time just to punctuate the urgency.

Pete tried to talk again, but the tube kept him from it.

"Shhh, honey, don't talk."

But he kept trying, and she could see from his lips moving what he wanted to say. "Mama."

She swallowed and stepped back. Her mind raced as she sought the right answer. She couldn't tell him, she thought. She needed help. *He* needed help. She pressed the buzzer again.

"Yes?" one of the nurses asked on the intercom.

"Pete's awake!" she said. "Please hurry."

Within seconds the two nurses were in the room standing over him checking his vital signs, asking him questions that he answered appropriately. Celia stood back as tears ran down her face in anticipation of the question she was going to have to answer. She prayed that his grandmother would return soon.

Her heart ached as she waited for the nurses to finish with him, and she tried to think of the best ways to tell him. Would it be better just blurted right out? Or should she pretend his mother just wasn't here, that she would be back later? No, she didn't believe in lying to children. But the truth was just too painful.

As the nurses worked on him, he became agitated and tried to pull the tube from his throat. His face looked panicked and scared as Celia came back to the bed, and he kept trying to speak. "Ma-ma ..."

Celia bent over him. "Honey, she's. ... not here." She wiped at the tears under her eyes. "Pete, does your head hurt? Are you in any pain?"

He fought to pull the tube out of his throat. The nurses got his hands away and strapped them down. Tears began to pour from his eyes, and his face reddened with his frustration.

A doctor rushed into the room and leaned over the bed and spoke to Pete, and began examining his eyes and asking him questions. Still crying, Pete answered with nods and shakes of his head, but that word kept forming on his mute lips. "Mama."

The doctor looked back over his shoulder and prompted Celia to answer him. She shook her head, indicating that she couldn't. A sob rose up in her throat, and she muffled her mouth to keep from frightening the child.

This is silly, she told herself. She was being a coward. The boy was confused, and she could clear that confusion up.

She tried to level her emotion and took a step toward the bed.

Just then, his grandmother came through the door, and Celia felt as if she'd been delivered. "He's awake, and he recognizes me. But I haven't told him yet ..."

Pete's grandmother burst into tears and rushed to his bed. He struggled to free his arms.

"Oh darlin', we're so glad you're awake," she said. "We thought we'd lost you. How do you feel?"

Again, he mouthed the word and tried to free his hands to pull out the tube.

"Why is he strapped down?" she demanded.

"He was trying to take the tube out," Celia said. "They couldn't get him to stop."

"Oh, no, honey," his grandmother said. "You have to leave that in so you can breathe." She bent over the child and stroked his hair back from his eyes. He looked up at her, his big eyes focusing on her with every ounce of energy he had. "Honey, do you remember what happened at the post office?"

He shook his head.

"There was an explosion," she said. "That's why you're here. You were in it."

He looked as if he couldn't quite grasp that.

"And so was your mama."

Celia stepped up behind the grandmother and put her hand on her shoulder, encouraging her to go on.

"Honey, your mama's gone to heaven."

He looked at her for a moment, not quite grasping what she'd told him. And then his eyes changed to an expression of horror. His face began to redden, and he shook his head viciously.

"She got hurt real bad," his grandmother said. Her voice cracked as she tried to go on. "Honey, Mama died."

He sat up, shaking his head and fighting the straps that held his hands. One broke free from the Velcro that held them, and he pulled the tube out and began to yell in a hoarse voice, "You're lyin', Grandma! Why are you lyin' to me?"

He collapsed back on the bed, struggling to breathe, and the nurses and doctor rushed back to him and began trying to calm him down. He couldn't breathe, so he stopped fighting. They put the tube back down his throat, and when he was calm and breathing again, his grandmother took his limp little hand.

"Oh, honey. I'm so sorry I upset you. But I wouldn't lie about a thing like that."

He was too weak to fight, so he just closed his eyes as the tears squeezed out through his lashes.

They all stood there helplessly until he cried himself to sleep.

It was hours later, after Pete had fallen asleep and awakened again, that they had been able to convince him that it wasn't a cruel joke. His mother had been killed, and he had been left behind. Celia didn't have the heart to leave him, partly because his grandmother looked so torn and alone. Mary's brother Zack was busy taking care of the funeral arrangements and calling relatives, so he wasn't able to be there with her. So Celia hung around, trying to be whatever help she could be.

She was glad to see Stan arrive, but the tense look on his face told her he hadn't come to keep vigil with her. "I need to interview Pete," he said.

"No," she said. "Stan, this is not the time. He's not ready for this. He can't even talk while he's on the ventilator."

Mrs. Lewis got to her feet and moved closer to the bed, as if to protect Pete from him. He tried to smile at the distraught-looking grandmother. "Excuse me. I need to speak to my wife in the hall."

Celia followed him, ready to put up a fight to protect the little boy. "Stan, he just found out his mother is dead. He doesn't want to talk about the post office. He doesn't even remember any of it. I don't want him getting upset again."

"Honey, I know you're feeling real protective of him right now," Stan said. "It's a tragic situation, but I have to talk to him, because he's our only eyewitness to a terrorist act. Now, if I can get enough information from him, maybe we can head off the FBI agents who also want to interview him."

"But you've got the guy in jail."

"We have reason to think there's someone else who acted with him. Last night, Dan and Jill were almost killed on the I–10 bridge. I don't think it's a coincidence that that would happen the day after the bombing. Someone is still out there, and Pete might be able to identify him. Jill's life could be at stake, and Dan's, and who knows who else's?"

She sighed heavily. "All right, Stan, but so help me, you'd better be gentle with him. He's just a little boy."

Stan promised, so she led him back into the room. "Mrs. Lewis, I'm so sorry, but my husband needs to talk to Pete for a minute."

"Well, okay, but don't expect him to talk back." She took the boy's hand protectively.

Pete looked despondent when he looked up at Stan, nothing at all like the bright-eyed youngster he had delighted in. "How you doing there, Pete?"

The boy shrugged.

"Pete, I've got to ask you something about the explosion at the post office. You're the only one who can help us. Just nod or shake your head, okay? Do you remember being at the post office?"

Pete thought for a moment, then nodded his head. His mouth pulled down at the corners, and he covered his eyes with fists to hide his tears. His grandmother squeezed his hand.

"Did you see anyone you didn't know in there?" Stan asked. "Someone bringing a package or anything that wasn't where it was supposed to be?"

Pete nodded.

Stan stiffened. "Was it a man?"

Pete nodded.

"Did he mail anything?"

Pete shook his head.

"Did you see anything with him?"

Pete nodded and looked around. He pointed to the box of tissues on his table.

"Tissue?"

He shook his head and pointed to the box.

"He means box," Celia said.

Pete nodded that she was right.

"So the man came in and brought a box." Stan pulled Jerry Ingalls's mug shot from his coat pocket. "Pete, was it this man?"

Pete looked at the picture, then frowned and shook his head.

"No? Are you sure?"

Pete nodded and held up his hands. Two fingers on each hand were bent down. Stan frowned up at Celia. She didn't know how to interpret that.

Pete took the picture and pointed to Jerry Ingalls's fingers holding the sign with his number on it. Then he held one hand up with two fingers bent down again, and pointed at those with his other hand.

"Something about fingers?" Celia asked.

Pete nodded.

"He didn't have none?" the grandmother asked.

Pete shook his head.

"The man didn't have some of his fingers?" Stan asked.

Pete pointed at him, indicating that he'd gotten it right.

"So Jerry Ingalls didn't bring the bomb." He studied the picture. "Pete, is there anything else about the man? Were his eyes brown? Blue? Gray?"

Pete shrugged, but then he pointed to his face and made a full gesture.

"He had a beard?"

Pete nodded.

"What color beard? Blonde? Gray? Brown?"

Pete nodded at the color brown.

"Was his hair brown, too?"

Pete nodded and indicated that it was a little long.

Stan let that sink in for a moment. "Pete, I need to know if anyone was with him. Did you see anyone inside the post office with him?"

Pete shook his head, then pointed to the door.

"Outside?" Celia asked. "Someone was outside?"

He shook his head and held his hands like he was holding a steering wheel.

"In his truck?" Stan asked. "Someone was in the truck?"

Pete nodded.

The truck that Jerry Ingalls drove was blue, so he decided to give Pete another test. "Pete, was it a gray truck?"

Pete shook his head.

"Was it white?"

Again, he said no.

"Was it blue?"

Pete nodded.

"Which side of the truck did he get in on?" Stan asked. "Right? Or left?"

His grandmother looked up at Stan. "He doesn't know his left from his right," she said quietly. "Why don't you draw a picture?"

Stan grabbed the pad out of his pocket and sketched a truck. "Was the truck going this way, Pete?"

He shook his head.

"The other way?"

He said yes.

"And which side did the man get in on?"

The boy pointed to the passenger side.

"So, he wasn't driving. It was Jerry Ingalls's truck, but this mystery guy is the one who brought the package in."

"So, who was he?" Celia asked.

"I don't know," Stan said. "And Jerry Ingalls doesn't seem real inclined to tell us." He looked at the child again. "Pete, you've been a big help. We might be able to catch the guy who did this because of the information you just gave us."

The little boy closed his eyes again, and fresh tears squeezed out.

Stan leaned over the rail on his bed, and his face softened. "You must be pretty special, because God saved your life when you could have been killed. He must have something real important for you to do some day."

Big tears rolled down the boy's face, and he wiped them away.

Celia stepped up to the opposite side of the bed, and defensively touched his hand. The boys lips twisted. His grandmother leaned over and pulled him into a hug.

Stan shot his wife an apologetic look. He could see that the day had taken its toll on her. "Celia, I want you to go home and get some rest," he said quietly.

"I was about to. I'll just follow you home."

They said their good-byes, and walked together to the elevator. Celia was wiping her eyes as she got on.

"Honey, I'm worried about you. You don't need to be going through this with them."

"Just until tomorrow," she said. "I'm going to sit with him, while his grandmother and his uncle go to the funeral."

"This is way beyond the call of duty for a Sunday school teacher," he said.

"That's okay. He's worth it." She sighed and looked up at him. "So . . . Did the missing fingers ring any bells for you?"

"Nope. But at least that's something to start with," he said. "At least we know that Jerry Ingalls isn't the one who delivered the package into the post office. Maybe he's telling the truth. That he gave somebody a ride to the post office and didn't know what he was delivering."

"Not on your life," Celia said, growing angry again. "Don't you let that man go, Stan. He killed people we know, friends of ours. Little Pete is an orphan because of him."

"Celia, you of all people should understand my concern about locking up an innocent man."

"He isn't innocent if he drove the car. He was involved, Stan."

"There's no question he was involved. The question is, whether he knew about the bomb. And why he won't tell us who he was driving that day."

"You think he didn't know him?" Celia asked. "Just picked him up somewhere and gave him a ride to deliver the bomb? How likely is that? And why wouldn't he give you a description?"

"Got me."

They got off the elevator and walked out into the parking lot. "So what's the next step?" Celia asked.

"With this new information about his fingers, maybe someone can identify him. Meanwhile, we keep questioning Jerry Ingalls. But he swears he won't talk until he has a lawyer. And he wants Jill Clark."

"She's not considering it, is she, Stan? She'd have to be out of her mind to represent the man who took her hostage."

"I don't know," he said. "Jill doesn't always think like the rest of us. There's really no telling what she might do."

They walked across the parking lot until they reached Celia's car. He opened the door for her, helped her in, then reached in and gave her a long, sweet kiss.

She smiled and leaned her head back on the seat. "Stan, can I ask you a big, big favor? One of the biggest I've ever asked?"

"Anything."

"Find Pete's dad. You can do it. Somebody needs to. Pete needs his dad back."

"I've already set the wheels in motion," he said. "I've got a few leads."

She reached up and kissed him again. "I knew I could count on you."

Chapter Forty

● ● ●

Frank Harper followed the car Jill Clark was in for several miles before he panicked. He saw her talking on her cell phone, and could have sworn that the man driving was watching him in his rearview mirror. Had they spotted him? Was she calling the police?

He was a lot of things, Frank thought, but he wasn't stupid. No, he wasn't going to be drawn into a trap. Quickly, he changed lanes, almost grazing the car next to him. Then without signaling, he took a right turn and got out of town as fast as he could.

● ● ●

In the rental car, Jill spoke to Pete Hampton's grandmother and learned that the boy was awake and had been moved out of ICU. He had been told about his mother and was despondent. Jill wanted to go see him.

"It's not wise right now," Dan said. "You'd be crazy to cross that bridge again tonight. Let me just take you back to Mark and Allie's."

She let out a deep sigh. "I guess you're right. Celia's been at the hospital most of the day. Anyway, he probably just needs quiet tonight." She stared out the window. "It's a terrible thing to lose your mother."

Dan glanced over at her. "It is, isn't it? I guess you would know."

She nodded. "Mom's been dead for almost ten years. But I still miss her so much sometimes. There are so many things I need to tell her. So many things I need help with."

"Ironic," Dan said. "You want yours and can't have her, and mine's alive somewhere and I haven't talked to her in ten years."

She studied his expression for a moment. "Do you miss her?"

He shrugged. "You can't miss something you never had. My mother wasn't like yours, Jill."

"How do you know? You never met my mother."

"She wasn't like most mothers."

"Are your parents still married?"

"Dad died eight years ago," he said. "A heart attack at Pebble Beach. Right on the golf course."

"I'm sorry."

"My mother cried her eyes out. And it occurred to me that she would have never cried that hard for me."

"I bet she would."

He shook his head. "Nope." He stopped at a red light but kept his eyes on the road in front of him. "I think I kind of hoped she would hang around Newpointe a little more after he died. You know, since it was just the two of us." He breathed a laugh. "She hasn't been back since."

"Do you hear from her?"

"No," he said. "But that's okay."

"Is it?"

"Yeah," he said. "I don't have any expectations anymore. That makes it okay."

She turned that over in her mind for a long moment, realizing how sad it was not to have any expectations of people you were supposed to love. People who were supposed to love you. She wanted him to have expectations of her, and she wanted to fulfill them.

But she wasn't sure he could fulfill any of hers.

• • •

Frank Harper stole another car. It was like laundering money, he thought. You just kept it moving so no one could ever trace it back to you. With the cars, he just kept swapping them back, and the thefts were blended into the car theft count without any-one ever tracing them to him. When they found them unharmed, they probably assumed some kid had stolen them for a joy ride and never even tried to find the thief.

When he had found an Accord, he tried, but failed, to locate Jill. As he drove around town trying to find her, he realized that he had probably been paranoid when he stopped following her earlier. Just because she'd been on the phone didn't mean she had spotted him. In fact, now that he thought back, they hadn't acted as if they'd seen him, except for the instant in which her friend had looked in the rearview mirror. Now that he ran it back through his mind, he was pretty sure that the man had been straightening his hair. He wouldn't have done that if he'd been panicked about someone following him.

No, he had just overreacted. And now he couldn't figure out where she was or what she was doing. He didn't know how he was going to get to her in time to kill her tonight, and he didn't have much time to waste.

He decided he wasn't going to waste any of it looking for her. Instead, he would get a message to Debbie Ingalls about how dangerous it was to talk to his enemies. It would be a loud, clear message.

Doing something—anything—made him feel better than doing nothing, so he drove out of town to Slidell and bought the supplies he would need for the message. Then he drove back to the Ingallses' house and sat out front, watching for the lights to go out.

When all had gone out, except for the one in the front bedroom, he began to get ready. Just a few more minutes, and Debbie Ingalls would know what it meant to betray him.

Chapter Forty-One

● ● ●

Inside the house, Debbie Ingalls sat in the front bedroom rocking her little girl to sleep. She was lonely, so desperately lonely that she didn't know how she was going to survive it. She wished that Jerry could call her from jail and reassure her that everything was going to be all right, but she had a strong feeling that it wouldn't.

She held Christy close and rocked. The baby was already asleep, but Debbie didn't have the heart to put her down. She needed the contact, the sweet comfort provided by her children. Seth was sound asleep already, and she didn't want to experience the silence of the house, nor the fears that kept barreling through her mind. If only she had been able to convince Jill to represent Jerry, there might be hope.

Leaning her head back on the rocker, she tried to pray, but the words just wouldn't come. Her heart was too heavy, and her hopes were too thin.

Then outside, she heard tires screeching as they rounded the corner. The glass at the window shattered as something flew into the room. She screamed and jumped up, knocking the rocker over and waking the child. Christy began to shriek.

Then Debbie saw it. Some kind of flaming device beginning to lap in flames across the carpet. She screamed louder and ran from the room, closing the door behind her.

"Seth!" she cried. "Get up, honey!"

She bolted into his room and jerked him out of bed.

"Hold Mommy's robe and follow me!"

Christy kept screaming, and Seth began to wail. She grabbed the cordless phone as they ran out into the night. Blocks away she could hear the car screeching around corners, fleeing from the neighborhood.

She took the children to the far side of the yard, then frantically dialed 911. "Someone just threw a bomb through my window," she cried. "My house is on fire. 203 Spencer. Hurry!"

The dispatcher told her they'd have someone there quickly, and she pulled her children to the side of the house, in the shadows, so that they wouldn't be open targets if the person came back. Sitting down on the edge of the yard, she began to weep as her children huddled closely against her.

Chapter Forty-Two

● ● ●

Dan heard the call on Mark's scanner as he and Jill were eating dinner with the Brannings, and he and Mark sprang out of their seats. "I'm going," Mark said.

"Me, too," Dan echoed.

"But your shoulder!" Jill cried. "Dan, you're on leave until it heals. They aren't going to let you fight a fire!"

"I just want to be there," he said. "I'll be back when it's over."

Jill and Allie stood at the door with their mouths open as Mark and Dan pulled out of the driveway. "You'd think it was a volunteer fire department and they couldn't do without them."

"Yep," Allie said. "Welcome to the world of firefighters."

"Next time, I'm going to insist they keep that scanner turned off."

"Get used to it. Mark has a scanner in both of our cars and in the house. He never wants to miss a call."

"But if he's not on duty ..."

"If he's not on duty, he'll overlook the cats in trees. But if there's ever a fire, he's outa here."

"Even with an injury?"

"They can keep him from being officially on duty," Allie said. "But these guys are never really off duty."

"And he's worried about *me* taking chances." She came back into the house and locked the dead bolt. "Now what? Do we save their dinner for later, or just throw it out?"

"Save it," Allie said. "Always save it. They'll come home starving to death, and Aunt Aggie doesn't make house calls."

Chapter Forty-Three

• • •

D an didn't realize the call was to Debbie Ingalls's house until they rounded the corner and saw where the emergency vehicles were. The woman who had fought so hard today on her husband's behalf was sitting out on the grass in her robe, holding both of her children on her lap. The little girl was screaming, but the boy seemed enamored of the flashing lights and the sirens as the trucks and squad cars pulled onto the scene.

Dan crossed the yard to Debbie. "Are you okay?" he asked.

She looked at him like he was an accessory to the crimes that had been committed against her. "Yes, I'm fine."

"What happened?"

Her voice trembled. "I was rocking Christy, and some lunatic threw a bomb or something through the window."

"A bomb?" he asked. "Did it explode?"

"No. It just scared me to death . . . it was on fire and caught the carpet on fire, and before I knew it, it had climbed up the curtains . . ."

"Did you see what the car looked like?"

"No," she said. "I was busy getting the kids out." Her clipped tone suggested that she wasn't interested in his sympathy, not after their visit today. It occurred to him that her stress level had been even greater than his and Jill's, and tonight's events had only made things worse. Still, in the back of his mind, suspicions lurked.

Sid Ford and R.J. Albright, from the police department, cut across the yard to question Debbie, and Dan stepped aside. He looked at the house, where the current shift of firefighters worked. He wanted to help, as Mark was, but without the full use of his arm, his presence could actually hinder things.

Mark came out of the house, no longer hurrying.

Dan met him at the sidewalk. Lowering his voice, he asked, "How's it look?"

"Looks like the fire was confined to that one front room, and we've put it out. The rest of the house can be saved. The smoke damage is minimal."

"Did you notice the glass fragments where the window broke? Did they fall inside or outside the house?"

"I saw them inside," Mark said. "Why?"

"Just wondering if this was a trick."

"Why would it be a trick?"

"To get Jill's sympathy. Make us think she couldn't possibly be involved if someone's trying to kill her, too."

Mark looked over at the woman still sitting on the grass, clinging to her children. "I don't see her jeopardizing her kids that way."

Dan followed his gaze, then shook his head. "No, me either. But I had to consider it." He looked at Mark again. "So the glass fell inside, huh? Just like she said, something came into the room through the window."

"Looks that way. Could have been a lot worse."

"Guess so," Dan said. "Meanwhile, what do we do with her? She'd be nuts to stay here. If it's the same guy I had a run-in with last night, I don't think he's gonna give up that easy."

Ray Ford, the fire chief, was just coming out of the building. He wasn't required to fight fires, either, except when they were understaffed. But like Mark and Dan, he rarely missed an opportunity. "So this is that Ingalls guy's house?" he asked in a low voice.

"Yes," Dan said. "I was just here this afternoon with Jill. Ray, we probably need to help her make some arrangements tonight."

"No kiddin'," Ray said. "I'm a step ahead of you. I already called Susan."

Dan wondered what Ray's wife had to do with this. "What's she gonna do?"

"She gon' get Ben's room ready for 'em. I'm gon' take her to my house tonight."

"You sure you want her sleeping in your house?" he asked. "I mean, she is the wife of the guy who blew up the post office."

"Somebody's got to do it," Ray said. "Might as well be me. Besides, she don't look much like a killer."

"They never do."

Ray chuckled. "Spoken like a man who got run off a bridge last night."

"You better believe it. I don't trust anybody right now."

"Well," Ray said, "the way I figure it, if she's what she seems . . . an innocent victim . . . then Susan will nurse her back to normal. And if she's an accessory or even a killer herself, Susan'll have her baptized by the end of the week."

Dan couldn't help chuckling. He just hoped Susan understood what she was getting into.

Chapter Forty-Four

• • •

Dan's and Mark's food was still waiting when they returned back home, and Allie warmed it up for them while they filled them in about Debbie Ingalls's latest problems.

"It just shook them up a little. Ray Ford took them home to Susan, and they'll be staying there tonight."

Jill gaped at him. "Dan, who did this?"

"Obviously not her husband," he said. "I don't know why he'd do that to his own family . . . his own house."

"You think it was the guy who ran us off the bridge?"

"Probably," he said. "But she didn't see the car."

Jill was silent for a long moment as she stared down at the table. Dan took her hand. "You okay?"

She looked up at him. "Dan, what if he's telling the truth?"

"Who?"

"Jerry Ingalls. What if he's telling the truth about not being involved? About somebody else being the one to blow up the post office?"

"Even if he did, you don't have to get involved, Jill. It's not your job."

"But somebody has to. I want to know who did this, Dan. I want to get to the bottom of it before someone else winds up dead."

"You can do that without being his lawyer."

"Maybe not," she said. "I don't know. I'm so confused." She rubbed her face hard, then dropped both hands on the table. "I'm gonna go to the Fordses' house and talk to Debbie."

"Now?" Dan asked. "Jill, it's pretty late. They might be in bed."

"If there aren't any lights on, I won't knock. But I need to talk to her one more time."

"I don't like the idea of you out on the street at night."

"Me, either," Allie agreed.

Jill threw up her hands. "I'm a lawyer," she said with frustration. "I have to do what I have to do."

"All right," he said, holding up his palms in surrender. "Would you consider . . . Jill, could I come with you?"

Frustrated, she looked from Dan to Allie to Mark, then back to Dan. "All right," she said. "You can drop me off so I won't have to drive myself. But I'm not making this a habit."

He grinned and mouthed the word *yes*, then took his plate to the sink and rinsed it off. Quickly, he followed Jill out the door.

● ● ●

Susan Ford opened the door when Jill and Dan got there. "*Girl!*" She reached out to hug her and brought her right in. "Jill, what are you doin' out at a time like this? You shouldn't be out by yourself this late."

"I'm not," Jill said. "Dan is waiting in the car. Susan, I heard about the fire and I needed to see Debbie."

"She's right in the kitchen," she said. "I been trying to calm her down. We been praying together."

Jill's eyes locked into Susan's. She fought the urge to ask if Susan thought this could be an elaborate, expensive act. Was it all a play for sympathy? But she knew Susan never thought the worst of people. She would defend Debbie just because she felt sorry for her.

Jill walked into the kitchen, and Debbie looked up. "Jill! You and Susan know each other?"

"Honey, everybody in Newpointe knows each other."

"Except you," Jill said. "Nobody knows much at all about you."

"Oh, I don't know," Debbie said bitterly. "We seem to be the talk of the town right now."

Jill saw the tears come to Debbie's eyes, and she ducked her head, suddenly ashamed of her careless remark. Debbie looked shaken, and it didn't seem to be an act. The woman looked like she hung onto control by one fraying filament.

"Tell Jill what happened, Debbie," Susan said as she gestured for Jill to take a chair.

Debbie touched her forehead and swallowed hard. "I had put Seth to bed and I was rocking Christy, when all of a sudden something crashed through the window. The next thing I knew my house was on fire, and I had to get the kids out . . ." Her voice broke off. "If I'd been in bed, or if I'd put Christy down before Seth . . . He must have aimed for the only room with the light in it, but I always leave a lamp on in there, because she's afraid of the dark. If I hadn't been in there, the fire could have engulfed her before I even realized it. It *must* be the same guy who blew up the post office, but why is he after me now? My husband is taking the heat! I haven't done anything."

Jill pulled out a chair and sat down, her suspicions beginning to melt away. Would Jerry have had someone throw a bomb through his child's window? Not the man who'd shown her their pictures when he was holding her hostage, and worried what they would be told. Then again, whoever he was involved with could have acted without his approval. "Debbie, do you think Jerry knows who did this?"

"I don't even know if he's being told about it," she said. "Every now and then they let him call me, but I haven't heard from him today."

"That doesn't answer my question," Jill said. "Do you think he knows who did this?" She didn't know why she bothered to ask. She fully expected Debbie to cover for her husband at all cost.

Debbie dropped her face into her hands for a long moment, then looked up at Jill again. "Yes, I think he does."

Jill hadn't expected that answer. "Do you think he'll tell the police?"

"I don't know," Debbie said. "I don't know why he wouldn't tell after the post office was bombed. He has this loyalty thing sometimes. He means to do the right thing. I don't know."

Jill stared at her for a moment. "I'm gonna go talk to him tomorrow, okay, Debbie? I'll consider representing him."

"You will?" Debbie's mouth fell open, and she gaped at her. "Oh, I'm so happy to hear that."

Susan patted Jill's hand. "Good for you, honey."

"I didn't say I would. I said I'd consider it. I want to hear what he has to say about the guy who did all these things. I want to hear what he thinks about who started the fire in your house. I want to see his face when he says it."

Debbie's eyes were bright with tears. "You'll see, Jill. You'll see that he's not a killer. You'll see that he didn't have anything to do with this. And when he finds out about me and the kids—"

"When he finds out, if he still won't tell, Debbie, it isn't going to look very good."

"He has to," she said. "He just has to."

Chapter Forty-Five

● ● ●

As Dan drove Jill back to Allie and Mark's house, she kept looking behind them to see if anyone was following them. She realized that the killer could follow just as easily in daytime, but for some reason night seemed more threatening. Especially this night, when he had already been active in another part of town. She doubted he had called it a night and gone home to watch a movie.

But it didn't appear that anyone was following them. When they got to the Brannings', Dan walked her to the door and kissed her good night.

Allie was nursing the baby in her bedroom when Jill came in, so she told Mark good night and went on to Justin's room to get ready for bed.

When Allie put the baby down, she knocked and peeked into the room. Jill was sitting on the bed, staring at the air. "Everything okay?" she asked.

Jill shrugged. "As good as it can be with an insane killer on the loose. I thought they had him locked up, but now it looks like there's one still out there."

Allie sat down in the rocking chair. "I wish they'd catch him before Mary Hampton's funeral tomorrow. It would go a long way toward healing that family."

Jill felt sick. "Are they taking Pete?"

"No. He's still on the ventilator; he can't leave the hospital. Celia's staying with him while the grandmother and uncle go."

"Are you going?"

"Yeah, I plan to."

"I'm not going," Jill said, looking at her feet. "I just don't feel safe yet, out in public."

Allie's compassionate eyes rested on her. "Do you feel vulnerable to another attack?"

"A little," she said. "But I've got to get over it. I have a lot to do tomorrow, and I don't have time to slink around in hiding."

"I thought you were taking the rest of the week off."

"I'm going to the jail to talk to Jerry Ingalls. I may decide to represent him."

Allie just stared at her for a moment. "Did you tell Dan?"

"No. He won't like it. But I have to do it anyway."

"Why?"

"Because it might be the right thing. The man who held me hostage the other night ... he doesn't seem like the type to do these things ..."

"He sure had a gun to your head, Jill. They were real bullets."

"But he didn't pull the trigger. Not on me. He showed me pictures of his children. When his wife came in, he let her talk him out of it. I could tell he loved her."

"And because he loves his wife, you don't think he was even an accessory to the bombing?"

Jill considered that and realized it didn't make sense. "I'm just considering that he may not have been."

Allie came to the bed to hug her. "You've always had good instincts," she said. "All I know to do is pray for you."

"That's the best thing. And as for Dan ... well, I'll just have to deal with that as it comes. Our relationship is kind of fragile right now. I don't know. He may decide it's not worth it."

"Can you live with that?" Allie asked.

"I don't want to," Jill said. "But either we're compatible or we're not. We might as well find out now."

Chapter Forty-Six

● ● ●

The police station was abuzz with activity after the last strike by the killer, and Jill walked in and looked around. She didn't see Stan or Sid anywhere, so she headed for the front desk and asked to see Jerry Ingalls in an interrogation room where she could question him privately.

"Are you questionin' him as his attorney, Jill?" R.J. Albright asked her.

"I think so," she said.

"Didn't you do that the other night? Sid says you chewed Ingalls up one side and down the other, and still didn't commit to representing him."

"Well, maybe I'll commit today."

"Why?"

"Because he needs an attorney, and they're about to appoint one."

"Don't have to be you."

"Maybe it does," she said. "Which room can I have, R.J.?"

He pointed to the first room at the back of the station, and she headed back to wait for him. She went in and dropped her briefcase on the mahogany table, and went to the barred window to peer out. There wasn't much to see, even though they kept the back lawn lit up. There was an eight-foot wall that went around the jail's recreation area, obstructing the view from the police station to the bayou behind them. But she supposed the prisoners needed sunshine now and then, so she didn't blame them for the wall.

The door to the room opened, and Jill turned around. She crossed her arms as Jerry came in. He was unshaven and looked as if he hadn't slept in days. Wearily, he sat down and slumped at the table. "Did you come to ream me again?" he asked.

"No, not really." She waited for the door to close, then fought the chill running down her back. This was the man who had threatened to kill her just a few days ago.

"For somebody who refuses to represent me, you sure are showing up here a lot," he said.

She sat down and leaned forward on the table, meeting his eyes. "I'm still not sure I'll represent you, but I wanted to talk to you."

"About what?"

"About what happened to your wife and children last night."

He looked confused, and she studied his face earnestly for some sign of guile. There was none. "What do you mean, what happened to my wife and children?"

"No one's told you?" she asked.

He stiffened, and his eyes grew wide as his face reddened. "Is my family all right?"

"Yes, they're fine," she said. "But last night, while Debbie was rocking Christy in the front bedroom, someone threw something through the window and started the house on fire—"

He sprang up out of his chair, knocking it over, and backed against the wall with both hands to his head. "He didn't! Tell me he didn't!"

"*Who* didn't?" Jill demanded through stiff lips.

His hands fell limp to his sides, and he came back to the table and bent over it, breathing hard. "Just ... did they catch him?"

"No," she said. "He got away. We don't know how he keeps escaping, but somehow he does. Jerry, if Debbie hadn't been in there with Christy at the time, if she'd been sitting a little closer to the window . . . they could be dead now. You've got to tell us who this is."

He began to pace across the room. A fine layer of perspiration glistened on his skin. "Where are they now?"

"They're staying with some friends of mine. Ray's the fire chief in town, and his wife Susan . . . she's the one who took care of the kids when Debbie came to the motel . . ."

His eyes shifted from side to side across the room, as if considering all his options. "I don't know what to do! My family—"

"Tell the truth," she said. "If you're not involved, Jerry, your only hope is to tell us who did this."

He slammed his hands on the table. "But he can't help it. It's not his fault."

"Why isn't it his fault, Jerry?"

He turned his face to the wall, banged a fist on it. Someone opened the door to see if Jill was in danger. She waved them away.

"I can't believe he would do that. We had a covenant. We're supposed to protect each other's families."

"A covenant? What do you mean by that?"

"I mean that we—" He stopped cold and turned back around, as if he'd said too much already. "Nothing. I didn't mean anything."

She couldn't believe he was going to clam up now. She got to her feet and came around the table. "Jerry, your children could be in danger. Your wife could be a target for him. He's still out there. He isn't giving up. He's tried to kill me, your wife, your kids, and he *did* kill three people and orphan and injure a little boy!"

"How is that boy?" he asked.

She hesitated a moment, surprised by his concern. "He woke up yesterday. He's grieving because they're burying his mother today."

Jerry looked away and rubbed his eyes roughly. "I don't believe this. This wasn't supposed to happen."

"Jerry, are you protecting this man out of some sense of honor?"

He shook his head, unable to answer.

"Because there's no honor in protecting a crazed killer. No honor at all."

"A covenant is a covenant," he bit out.

She frowned. "Jerry, look at me."

For a moment, he kept his back to her, then finally, he turned around and met her eyes.

"If you want me to represent you, you're going to have to be straight with me. You're going to have to tell me a whole lot more than this."

He rubbed his temples, then stepped toward the table and sank back into his chair. He looked as if the last drop of energy had just drained right out of him. "What do you know about covenants?" he asked.

She thought this was another challenge about her not keeping her word. "I know it's an agreement. I know about honor and all that—"

"No," he cut in. "I mean, what do you really know about the Jewish custom of cutting covenant?"

She twisted her face at the question. "Well, nothing, I guess."

"I didn't think so." He got up again and began pacing across the room, thinking hard as he spoke. "They used to take animals and cut them in half, longwise, and lay them opposite each other, and walk between the two pieces. It was how they sealed a covenant."

Jill remembered she had heard that before. "Yeah. Just like in Genesis when God told Abraham to cut the animals in half."

"Yes!" Jerry said, pointing to her, as if she—a simpleton—had just understood a complicated concept. "And God was the one who walked between the pieces of flesh, in the form of a smoking oven and a flaming torch. And that was the Abrahamic covenant."

Jill wondered how in the world this could possibly have anything to do with Jerry's case. She hoped he was going to tell her.

"At Jewish wedding ceremonies, the fathers would do the same things."

"What things?"

"They would cut the animals in half and lay them opposite each other, and the father of the bride and the father of the groom would walk between the pieces. In doing that, they were saying, 'I will give my life for this covenant. If my child fails to keep it, may the Lord do the same to me that I did to these animals.'"

"I still don't understand what this has to do with the post office—"

"Just listen," he said, sitting back down opposite her at the table, his eyes boring into hers. "When people made a covenant, they kept it, because it's witnessed by God. It's very serious."

"I understand that," she said. "Now, you tell me. Are you in a covenant with this person?"

He got up and turned his back to her again. Frustrated, Jill leaned on the table. "Jerry, if you are obstructing justice and enabling him to commit more crimes, maybe against your own family, God will not honor that."

"Just listen," he said. "Jonathan, Saul's son, entered into covenant with David. They swore to protect each other with their lives. Everything that was Jonathan's became David's, and everything that was David's became Jonathan's. They were identified with each other."

She shook her head. Maybe he was unstable, she thought. Maybe he needed to be hospitalized. She rubbed her forehead. "Jerry, you don't have to keep telling me these things."

"When Saul, Jonathan's father, set out to kill David, you didn't see Jonathan siding with Saul. He had a covenant with David, and that superceded his relationship with his father. He was sworn to protect David. That's what it means when you enter covenant with someone. You keep it. You take it seriously. You defend and protect them. You give them what's yours . . ."

"And is this what you did with this person?"

He closed his eyes and sat down again, and she could see the struggle on his face, as if he was fighting a memory. A terrible, painful memory.

"Jerry, if this is what binds you to this person, he didn't keep his end of the bargain. He betrayed you when he went after your family."

"The covenant stands, even if it's one-sided," he said. "God kept his covenant, even though the Israelites broke it over and over."

"You're not God!" She slid her hands down her face and looked at him over the fingertips. "Jerry, do you or do you not know who blew up the post office?"

He banged his fists on the table again. "I'm telling you, when you walk between the pieces, you're in covenant."

Now it was her turn to slam her hands on the table. "So you take the fall for some maniac and go to prison for the rest of your life for something you didn't do? What about your covenant with your wife?"

He closed his eyes as he struggled with that thought. "Yes. I do have to put that first. My wife and children . . . But what if this was a message to me? A warning not to talk? What if I give you his name and he goes after Debbie and the kids for revenge?"

"Jerry, he's a crazy, unpredictable, reckless killer. Your family will be much better off if we know who he is so we can find him and stop him."

"But he'll feel justified in his revenge if he thinks I broke covenant. He has a rationale for everything." His voice broke and emotion twisted his face. "We went between the pieces. I didn't walk. I was carried." He stopped and swallowed, trying to rein those emotions in.

Her eyes narrowed. "What do you mean 'carried'?"

"I was bleeding to death," he bit out. "I wasn't the only one. But he came back for me. I do owe him."

It was the first thing he'd said that made any sense to her. Had it happened in war? Had the killer saved Jerry's life? "Jerry, are you talking about Vietnam?"

He didn't answer, which was answer enough. He leaned on the table and stared into her face. "Some people can't be held accountable," he said. "Some people don't have the mental faculties, and sometimes . . . that's our fault. We have to protect them because we swore we would."

"Jerry, you're the one who sounds like you have mental problems. This sounds crazy. They're just gonna think you're insane, that you blew up the post office because you don't know right from wrong. I'll only represent you if you're innocent, Jerry. I'm not going to do the 'guilty by reason of insanity' defense. If you would just give me the name, tell me what really happened, the last time you saw him, why it was your pickup at the post office, why you were at the motel . . ."

He covered his face and shook his head harder with each question she posed to him.

"Jerry, your arraignment is the end of the week. They're going to appoint an attorney for you if I won't represent you."

"You could do it," he cried. "You said you would. That's why I let you go."

"And what would you have done if I hadn't? Killed me? What did you expect me to do?"

"Some people, when they give their word, they stand by it."

"When it's done under duress, I don't think it counts."

"Read about the Gibeonites," he said. "Read about the deceitful way they got Israel to enter into covenant with them.

Joshua kept it, anyway, even when they knew they'd been deceived, because Joshua knew how serious covenant was."

Jill didn't remember any of these stories. She vowed to herself that tonight she would start reading the Old Testament again. "I don't know anything about Gibeonites, Jerry. I don't know anything about Joshua's covenant with them. All I know is that I am not obligated to represent you, and if I don't feel that you're being straight with me, I'm not going to. So you have a choice. You can either tell me who did this, or you can get yourself another attorney."

When he didn't answer, she took her legal pad and pen and her laptop, which were spread out on the desk, and began to pack them back into her briefcase. She got up and started to the door, then turned back around midstride. "I only came here because your wife convinced me to. She's very persuasive. When I saw that there had been an attempt against your family, I hoped you weren't involved. I started to believe you, Jerry."

"You can believe me now, too."

"Still, I don't know the whole story. I can't represent you with only half of it. Meanwhile, whether I represent you or not, I can't go home. I have to look over my shoulder every minute, scared to death he's going to come out of nowhere. Even where your family is, Jerry, he could find them. This guy seems to be everywhere . . . and then nowhere . . . While you're in your cell waxing poetic about this glorious covenant of yours, he could be out there blowing up another post office. Or a football stadium with kids in it, or an airport!"

"It's not that hard to figure out!" Jerry shouted. "You can do it without my betraying him!"

She dropped her hand from the doorknob and stared at him, dumbfounded. "So you're telling me that if I figure out who he is, that's one thing, but you're not going to help me?"

"You can figure it out," he said.

"All right. Fine. I'll go tell your wife you said that. While she's sitting up, unable to sleep tonight for fear of some flaming, flying thing crashing through her window, killing her baby . . ." She brought her trembling hand to her forehead and tried to calm her voice. "Jerry, you should care more about your own family and the innocent bystanders who have been drawn in and may be killed because of this. Talk about honor . . . Jerry, *you* pulled *me* into this. I didn't ask for it. You *owe* it to *me* to tell me who wants me dead before they finish the job."

He stared down at the floor, struggling with the tears in his eyes. "He was in my unit. He saved my life. He won a Purple Heart and a Congressional Medal of Honor."

"I don't care if he won a Nobel Prize!" she yelled.

"He had brain damage because he came back for me! It doesn't take a genius to figure this out!"

Suddenly, she realized he was feeding her information. It wasn't a name, but it was close.

He got up and went to the door, opened it. "I'm ready to go back," he told the guard.

Jill stood frozen, watching him leave.

"Tell Debbie I love her," he choked out. And then he was gone.

It took a few moments for Jill to get her thoughts back in line. She grabbed her briefcase, stepped out into the noise of the police department, and scanned the room for Stan.

Chapter Forty-Seven

● ● ●

Jill spotted Stan at the doorway of Chief Shoemaker's office, with several men she didn't recognize.

She cut through the desks, stepping around people, and made her way back to where Stan stood. He caught her eye, and she mouthed, "I need to talk to you." He nodded, then excused himself and headed to his desk. She met him there and plopped down in the chair across from him.

"I'm sorry if I interrupted something," she said.

"Don't worry about it. It's just the feds trying to make our lives miserable. If they'd get out of our way we might solve these crimes."

She looked back over her shoulder at the group of men still talking to the chief of police and Sid Ford. "Is this about Jerry Ingalls?"

"You got it. If he had to blow up something, I sure wish it hadn't been a federal building. It got the FBI involved, and there's a certain amount of head-bashing involved in working on a case with them."

Jill leaned forward, propping her elbows on his desk. Lowering her voice, she said, "That's why I'm here, Stan. I just talked to Jerry, and I think he gave me some vital information."

"Oh, yeah?"

"Yeah, but I'll give it to you as a trade. I'll give you what I know, but you have to repay the favor."

Stan didn't commit. "What did he tell you, Jill?"

Jill knew Stan well enough to know that he would help her whether he committed to or not. "He has some kind of covenant agreement with this person, and out of some sense of honor, he won't give a name. But I gathered that the guy is someone who served with him in Vietnam. He has a Purple Heart *and* a Congressional Medal of Honor, so it couldn't be too hard to narrow him down. He apparently was wounded saving Jerry's life. Brain damage. Jerry feels real conflicted about betraying him because of that."

Stan leaned back hard in his chair. "Anything else?"

"No, nothing. I still don't know how Jerry is involved, but at least you can get a name and maybe a picture, and catch this guy. The FBI could probably get that information in minutes. I want to know when they do."

"I can't promise you that, Jill. A lot is out of my control here."

"Stan, my life is in danger. I want to know this guy if I run into him. And Pete Hampton's life could be in danger, too."

A deep frown furrowed Stan's brow. "Jill, do you have good reason for thinking that?"

"It's just common sense, Stan. If he thinks that little boy is a witness, then he'll come after him, just like he came after me, and just like he came after Debbie Ingalls."

"I hope not."

"Find him, Stan. Lock him up."

Stan got up. "Wait here. I'll go get the agents on this. Maybe they'll prove competent, after all."

Jill waited, fidgeting all the while and watching the front door as Stan, Sid, and the FBI agents made phone calls and pounded on their computers. Every time someone walked into the station, she eyed them with suspicion, wondering if they were the right age to be a Vietnam vet. Anyone could walk in and hang around without being noticed. There were people everywhere: cops and perpetrators and people filing complaints.

After ten minutes, Stan came back to his desk. "We're still working on it, Jill, but we did just get a list of the men in Jerry's unit. A lot of them were killed in action." He handed her the printout. "That's all I have so far."

"I'll take it," she said.

As Stan crossed the room and returned to the FBI agents working near the chief's office, she took a pen from his desk and crossed off the names with the word *deceased* beside them, and saw that there were only five left. Jerry Ingalls, Jack Canady, Frank Harper, Michael Mills, Cliff Bertrand . . .

Her breath caught in her throat. Cliff Bertrand, the postmaster, had been in Jerry's unit? She got up and looked for Stan. He was standing beside an agent as he was talking on the phone and punching a computer keyboard. She almost tripped over a chair as she made her way to him.

"Stan, did you see this list?" she asked. "Cliff Bertrand—"

"Yeah, Jill, we saw it. There's gotta be a connection here. We're working on it right now."

"Do you think he targeted the post office because of this connection?"

"Could be."

Jill realized she wasn't going to get very far with Stan in front of the agents, so she went back to his desk. She crossed through Cliff's name, and Jerry Ingalls's name, and studied the three remaining names. Jack Canady, Frank Harper, Michael Mills . . .

She knew better than to use the police computer, so she got out her laptop and plugged in her modem, got on the Internet, and began searching the databases she had at her disposal, for information about which one of these men had won a Congressional Medal of Honor. When she wasn't able to find it, she tried keying in all three names and searching for a phone number. Jack Canady's name came up, and she saw that he lived in Vermont. She picked up the phone and dialed it. An operator's voice came on and said that the phone had been disconnected.

Not one to give up easily, she did a search on the next person on her list, but found nothing. She was typing in the third name when two hands fell on her shoulders.

She jumped and knocked over a glass of water. Grabbing a tissue to mop it up, she glanced back and saw that it was Dan.

"Jill, why are you here?" he demanded.

The question seemed unreasonable. "What?"

"Did you come here to talk to Jerry Ingalls again?"

"Yes," she said. "And he gave me some leads, Dan."

"Jill, he's dangerous. And it's dangerous for you to be here. Do you realize anybody can walk into this place?"

Though she'd already considered that, she acted as if she hadn't. "It's the police station, Dan. Where could I be safer?"

"Probably anywhere but here. These cops aren't worth the tin their little toy badges are made from if somebody starts shooting or leaves a bomb. You've got to get out of here, Jill. Have you forgotten how crazy this guy is?"

"What did you do, anyway? Just drive by to check on me?"

"No. We were coming back from a call and I happened to see your car out front."

"Dan, the FBI agents are this close to finding the guy's name, and probably a picture of him. I'm staying until I see it." She glanced at his arm. "What were you doing out on a call, anyway? You're not supposed to be working."

"I just heard it on the scanner, so I went. I didn't do anything much." Dan looked at his watch. "I have a doctor's appointment later today. I'm hoping to get my medical release so I can go back to work."

"Dan, you're not ready."

"Sure, I am. The shoulder's feeling fine. Now, if you insist on staying here," he said, setting his foot in a chair and leaning on his knee, "then I'll just have to stay here with you."

She struggled not to grin. "Fine. If you think you're a better guard than a couple dozen cops, you can guard me."

Dan pointed to the sergeant whose desk was beside the front door. Technically, no one should get in without going through him. But the paunch-laden officer was reading a magazine. "Look at that guy," he said. "Sitting down on the job, reading a magazine. You tell me how he's gonna protect you if that killer bolts in? What's he gonna do? Beat him with a copy of *TV Guide?*"

"He's got a gun."

"He's not gonna have time to use it, Jill. This guy is too good."

"Dan, I'm not leaving here until I know something, and that's that." She went back to her computer, torn between anger and the mildly pleasant feeling of having someone care about her.

"All right," he said. "Then I'll just sit right here with you." She didn't argue, but got back on the Internet. She found the number of the third guy on the list, and dialed it. A machine picked up.

She moaned as a man's voice told her he wasn't home but that he'd get back to her as soon as he could. She thought of leaving a message, but something told her not to. If this was the man who had blown up the post office, and run her off the road, and tried to blow up Debbie Ingalls's house, she sure didn't want him to know she was checking up on him.

She hung up the phone and moaned.

"Who are you calling?" Dan asked.

She looked up at him. "I'm trying to get in touch with someone from Jerry Ingalls's unit in Vietnam. The killer won a Congressional Medal of Honor. I have three names, I just don't know how to find out which one it is. I thought if I talked to one of them . . ."

"No way," Dan said. "You can't just call them up. What if word gets back to him that you're close?"

"It could," she said. "You're right." She studied the list again. "Dan, I found out that Cliff Bertrand was in their unit."

He frowned. "Cliff was in the army?"

"Yep. I don't think it was a coincidence that it was his post office that was targeted, do you?"

"No." He thought for a moment, then began to look at the screen over her shoulder. "There's gotta be an easy way to find out about a Congressional Medal of Honor."

She looked behind her at the group of agents and cops around the computers near the chief's office. "I'll bet Stan knows by now, and he's not telling me."

"Stan? I'll get it out of him."

Jill realized that he might have more clout with Stan, as a comember of Protective Services. He got up and headed toward the activity, but Jill couldn't stay back. She hurried to catch up with him.

"Stan, have you got the name of the killer yet?" he asked point-blank as he reached the police detective.

Stan shot them a look that said he couldn't talk in front of the agents. But thankfully, one of them turned around and addressed Jill. "So Ingalls told you the guy had brain damage? Did he say anything about any physical abnormalities?"

Jill shook her head. "No. What kind of abnormality?"

"Missing fingers," the agent said, turning back to his screen as a list scrolled across it.

"No, he didn't say anything about that."

"The kid did," the agent said. He sat straighter. "Here we go. Guys, we have a match."

"Which name?" Stan asked.

"Frank Harper." He typed in a few more things, then looked up at the other agents. "We've got to track down a picture of this guy and get it to the television stations immediately, along with an 800 number so people who've seen him can call."

Jill's heart threatened to pound right through her chest. She had known the killer was out there before, but somehow, knowing his name and his history made it all the more urgent.

"One problem," the agent said, typing frantically on the keyboard. "He's been in the psychiatric ward of a Veterans Administration Hospital in Jackson, Mississippi, for twenty-five years. If he's there, how could he have done the bombing?"

Stan jerked up a telephone and got the number of the VA hospital in Jackson.

"No wonder Jerry is so loyal to him," Jill said softly. "I guess you'd feel pretty loyal to a guy who saved your life and wound up in a mental hospital for the rest of his life."

Stan routed his call to the administrator and identified himself as a police officer in Newpointe, Louisiana. "I'm looking for information on a patient of yours. Frank Harper. Could you tell me if he's still a patient there?"

Stan listened, frowning. "What do you mean, technically? You're kidding. Disappeared how?"

Jill looked at Dan. They had their man.

"Then you do consider him violent. Do the police you reported this to have any information on where he's been? Can you tell me who I can get in touch with about that?" He bent over and began to write the name of a Jackson police officer. He stood back up. "Could you tell me the nature of his illness?"

He took a few more notes. "How did this happen?"

More notes.

"Could you tell me ... does he have all of his fingers?" He glanced at the agent who was looking up at him, listening, and shook his head that he didn't.

"I appreciate your help. Yes, please do. And I'll get in touch with the Jackson PD. Thank you." He hung up and looked down at the federal agents who were staring up at him, then at Dan and Jill. "He escaped a couple of weeks ago. Overcame an aid and got away. Apparently stole about a hundred dollars from a petty cash drawer in one of the offices. He's there because of a brain injury sustained in Vietnam after he saved some of his buddies. A mine went off. Somehow it blew some of his fingers, and he hasn't been right in the head since. He's normally heavily medicated with antipsychotics and antidepressants, but of course, he hasn't taken them since he broke out."

One of the agents grabbed up a phone and Stan's notes. "This the number of the PD in Jackson?"

"Yeah," Stan said. "They've managed to trace him to a few places, but haven't caught up with him yet."

"I got a picture!" one of the other agents said, turning his monitor so that they could see. "This one was of their unit in Vietnam, but it's really old. Here's one from the hospital a couple of years ago."

Jill went to the screen and stared down at it. She had never seen that face before. His hair was scraggly and long and peppered with gray, and his eyes looked drugged and vacant. He wore a beard which needed a trim. If he'd shaven or cut his hair, he could look totally different. But the fingers were unmistakable. He couldn't disguise those easily.

"You know this man?" the agent asked her.

"No," she said. "So this is the one who tried to kill me?"

The agent didn't answer. He was printing the photographs out and calling a television station.

Jill felt sick and rushed to the ladies' room. She threw up in the toilet bowl, then washed her mouth out at the sink. She looked in the mirror. She was white, and dark circles underscored her eyes. What had come over her? Just the sight of the killer had turned her stomach upside down.

Dan was waiting beside the door when she came out. "You okay?"

She nodded. "Yeah. It just ... kind of caught me off guard." She looked up at him. "Dan, I'm going to represent Jerry Ingalls."

He looked pained. "Jill, you can't."

"Why not? Now that I know who did it ..."

"Jerry Ingalls could still be involved. There could be a whole group of them."

"But I don't think he is. I think he's an innocent bystander who feels a debt to this man because of some covenant he made with him once. He needs a lawyer, Dan."

"But not you, Jill. It's not your job."

"Then whose is it?"

"I don't know," he said, his face reddening. "But you've gotta know that if you do this, you'll make this Harper guy even madder than he was before. This may be exactly what he was afraid of. The reason he wanted you dead. He'll come after you with everything he's got. He's mentally ill, Jill. I don't want you in his path."

Jill didn't especially want to be in his path, either. "Dan, I appreciate your feelings. Really, I do. But I can't help thinking that God put me in that motel room for a reason, and that he yoked me with the Ingalls family for a reason. Like it or not, he did."

"I can't believe God is telling you to do this."

"But you're not listening objectively."

His face softened, and he took her hands and pressed his forehead against hers. "You're right, kiddo. I'm not."

It was as close to an admission of love as he had given her, and warmth flowed through her. It was almost enough to make her back down. But not quite. "Will you trust me on this? Will you not go berzerko if I follow my gut on this?"

He closed his eyes. "All right, Jill. Go tell Stan that you're going to represent him. But I can't promise that I'll let you out of my sight until Frank Harper is caught."

"Come on, Dan. Your job is much more dangerous than mine, and I can't make you stay away, even with a torn shoulder. You walk into fires, into caving buildings, deal with explosions ..."

A slow grin crept over his face, conceding defeat. "Okay, you win. I'll try to quit hovering."

She shook her head and pressed a kiss on his lips. "Don't do that. I kind of like it."

Holding hands, they went to tell Stan.

Chapter Forty-Eight

● ● ●

Issie Mattreaux knocked on the door to Ray Ford's office, which was attached by a breezeway to the Midtown Fire Station. Ray yelled, "Come in," so she pushed through the door.

"What's up, Issie?" he asked, only glancing up for a moment before going back to his paperwork.

She sat down on the old couch facing his desk. Her uniform had a stain on the leg from an IV bag that had sprung a leak earlier, and brown streaks of iodine stained the front of her shirt. "I was ... just wondering if you'd had the chance to find Pete Hampton's dad."

Ray set his pen down and leaned back hard in his chair. "I've made a few calls. Talked to his sister, who I remembered lived over in Baton Rouge. She was pretty shook up when she heard about Mary. I think if she knows where he is, she'll find him."

Issie looked down at her hands. "So you think he would return your call?"

"He might," Ray said. "I knew him okay when he lived here. He went to my church. I guess you could say we were friends. 'Course, he kind of kissed all his friends good-bye when he hauled off and left his wife. I don't know what in the world gets into some people."

Issie contemplated that for a moment. There had been a time when she had been among the "some people" he spoke of. The things that had thrilled her before seemed suddenly too heavy to carry.

"Maybe I'll try her again today," Ray said. "She's probably been thinkin' things over. She's a decent person, I think. Maybe she's come up with some ideas where he might be."

"Too bad you can't go over to the police station and get some of the feds to find him."

"Not a bad idea," he said. "Maybe I could get Stan to do it. Thing is, he's been so busy with the bombin' and findin' the dude who almost killed Dan and Jill, that he ain't had time to think."

"But he has a vested interest," Issie said. "Celia's at that hospital night and day. If he found the dad, maybe she could come back home and take care of herself."

"Good point," Ray said. "I'll call him."

She slapped her knees and got up. "Well, I just wanted to check. Poor kid's been on my mind a lot." Her lips trembled as she got those words out, and Ray regarded her with thoughtful eyes.

"Issie, do you need to talk to a counselor? That bombin' was pretty heavy, and you ain't the only one havin' some problems. I've had some others come in here real shook up, and they're bigger and tougher than you."

She shook her head. "No, I'm fine. Really."

"I hear you been spendin' a lot of time at Joe's Place."

She grinned. "I always spend a lot of time at Joe's Place."

"Yeah, but you ain't been puttin' 'em away like you been doin'."

Her grin faded. "Do people really have nothing better to do than to talk about what I do when I'm off duty?"

"There are people who care about you."

She laughed aloud, but there was no joy in it. "I don't need that kind of caring." She opened the door and started out, then turned back. "Let me know if you find Larry Hampton, will you?"

Ray had a puzzled, concerned expression on his face as he watched her leave.

Chapter Forty-Nine

● ● ●

Jerry Ingalls's eyes were more alive than she'd seen them since she had met him. He'd been told that Jill had agreed to represent him, and now he had hope as he sat with her in the interrogation room.

"Jerry, I want you to know that I've decided to represent you for one reason. I figured out who it is you're covering for."

He looked down at the wood grain on the table, obviously not surprised.

"It's Frank Harper," she said. She didn't know why it was necessary to say the name out loud. Maybe she just wanted to see the reaction on his face.

He got up, putting his back to her, but didn't say a word.

"I admire your loyalty to the man who saved your life, Jerry," she said. "He was a hero. But he's not a hero anymore. The Frank Harper who blew up the post office and ran me off the bridge and caught your house on fire is not the same man who saved your life in Vietnam."

"Tell me about it," he said, swinging around to face her. "He gave his life for me, and that *means* something to me."

"I know," she said. "It means something to me, too. I'm a Christian. I know about someone giving his life for me."

"No, you don't." He pulled the chair back out and plopped into it, looking smugly across the table at her. "You don't know about that. If you did, it would change every area of your life. Not a day would go by, not an hour, that you weren't thankful for what he did for you. You'd wear it like a robe. It would be all over your face. His light would shine out of you. But you don't."

She felt as if she'd been slapped. "How dare you? You don't know me. You don't know what I'm like."

"I know that you don't have much faith. You have enough honor to take me for a client, but it didn't bother you at all to break your promise to me at first."

She was getting angry. "Then why do you even want me for your lawyer?"

"Because I believe God threw us together for a reason."

If she hadn't uttered those same words to Dan less than an hour ago, his comment wouldn't have had much impact. Now it sounded like a sign. Was God speaking to her through Jerry? She honestly didn't know.

She threw her hands up. "Jerry, you make me feel really helpless. I don't even know where to start with you."

"Start by understanding what I understand."

"I can't make myself understand something that has no basis in logic!"

"How much time do you spend each day studying God's Word?" The question came like a spear through the air, impaling her right through the heart.

"I'm a busy woman, Jerry. I have people running me off of bridges and putting guns to my head ..."

"When life is normal," he said. "How much time? Fifteen minutes? Thirty?"

"Sometimes," she said.

"Sometimes what? Fifteen or thirty? And how much time do you spend in prayer?"

"I pray!" she said. It was getting hot in the room, and she got up and turned on the fan in the corner. "You know, Jerry, meeting with you just wears me out."

"Just think about it," he said. "A man gave his life for you, and you mostly ignore him."

"I do *not* ignore him! I'm in church three times a week . . ."

"So you think he died for you so you could walk in and out of his house three times a week?"

She knew her face was red. She snatched up her briefcase. "Look, just forget it. I thought I could represent you, but now I see that I can't—"

"Why? Because I say what I see? Because I pointed out that you can't possibly understand my loyalty to the man who saved my skin, since you obviously don't have much for the one who saved yours?"

"No! Because we need to be talking about the case, not about my spiritual life . . . which happens to be just fine, thank you very much!"

"Okay," he said, holding up his hands innocently. "I'm sorry. I'll leave you alone. Just . . . don't leave."

She sat down and looked at the table until she could calm her thoughts. Finally, she said, "We have to talk about your arraignment tomorrow."

"All right," he said. "Let's talk."

Jill only hoped she could get through their conversation without losing her temper.

• • •

When she'd finished with Jerry, Jill stopped by Stan's desk. He was just getting off the phone and looked up at her as he hung it up. "Everything go okay in there?" he asked. "You look a little ragged."

She felt more ragged than she'd ever felt, and she wasn't sure why. "Everything went fine. Did you find out anything about Frank Harper?"

"Yes. He checked in at a little hole-in-the-wall motel in the French Quarter the night of the bombing, but didn't stay all night. We also found out that he was here, at Joe's Place, early that morning. R.J. Albright talked to him, but couldn't remember anything specific they'd talked about."

She shivered. "I don't know why that bothers me. I mean, I figured he had been here. But to know he was that close."

Stan studied her for a moment. "Jill, are you sure you're all right?"

"Yeah. I'm fine. Just ... trying to process my meeting with Jerry. He's not an easy man to get along with."

Stan's phone rang, so he picked it up. "Stan Shepherd."

"I'll see you later," Jill whispered. "Call on my cell phone if you need me."

He nodded and waved.

She stepped out into the light and took in a breath of hot, humid air. She glanced next door at the fire station. Dan's rental car was there, and she knew he was back on duty, waiting for the opportunity to destroy his shoulder again, since it wasn't ready to be tested. She wondered how he had gotten the doctor to give him a medical release.

Irritated, she cut across the lawn.

Aunt Aggie was in the kitchen ordering everyone to the table. Jill stood in the doorway and looked at her watch. She hadn't even realized it was dinnertime yet.

The old woman was the first to spot her. "Jill, *sha*, bring yourself on in and have some eats with us. We got plenty!"

Dan heard Jill's name and appeared from another room. "Jill, how'd it go?"

"Fine," she said. "Uh ... I'm not hungry. I can't stay ..."

"Yes, she can, Aunt Aggie. She needs to eat. Jill, humor me on this one thing, okay?"

Jill grinned, then became aware of the eyes of all her firefighter friends on her. They were assessing her relationship with Dan, trying to decide if they were fully on again. She hoped they didn't ask her, because she wasn't sure herself.

"All right. Maybe I am a little hungry."

"You don't want to hurt an old woman's feelin's," Aunt Aggie said. "Now sit yourself down here and let me get you a plate. Preacher, you want to say the prayer?"

Jill still had trouble picturing Aunt Aggie as a Christian. The last few times she'd eaten here, Aunt Aggie had seemed resentful of Nick Foster's insistence on prayer before eating. It was strange to see her asking for it.

Jill bowed her head as Nick thanked God for Aunt Aggie and for her cooking, and for the food they were about to share. As he went on talking to God about protection on their calls, Jerry Ingalls's words came back to her. Had he been right about her spiritual life? Were there things she needed to examine? And if so, when would she find the time?

She decided at that moment that she needed to be alone with God tonight, and it couldn't happen at the Brannings' house.

She ate quietly, conversing neither with Dan nor with his coworkers. She sensed Dan's tension next to her, as if he knew something was wrong. Once when she looked up, she saw Nick Foster, her preacher, looking at her. She wondered if he was assessing her heart, as well.

After they had eaten, Dan walked Jill into the truck bay. "Are you sure you're all right?"

"Yeah, fine."

"You're sure quiet. Are you mad that I came back on duty? Because I got my medical release, you know. They said I could come back."

"I admit, I was a little aggravated when I saw that. You know your arm isn't ready, Dan."

He propped his good arm over her head and leaned against the wall. "It's fine. I'm still stronger than most of the guys here."

"At least you're modest."

He grinned and gazed down at her. "So tell me the truth. How did the meeting with Jerry Ingalls go?"

She crossed her arms, then realized how defensive that looked and let them drop to her sides. "I'm just smarting a little. Jerry challenged my biblical knowledge and my prayer life. It kind of stung."

"A known terrorist is questioning *your* beliefs?"

"Yeah. You believe that?"

"I told you he was crazy."

She pushed off from the wall and put some distance between them, as her arms crossed again. She looked down at the concrete floor. "The thing is, he isn't, really. The things he said, they made an awful lot of sense."

"Things like *what?*"

"Things like the attention I give to Christ. Things like how important he is in my life. Things like this concept of covenant that I don't know anything about, even though I've been a Christian for years."

"Jill, I don't think Jerry Ingalls's level of spirituality is something you should aspire to."

"I know," she said. "But as he was talking, I started feeling really defensive. See, I think God can speak to us through all kinds of people. Even people like Jerry. Before, when he was talking about all those Old Testament covenant stories, it rang true, Dan. This isn't about Jerry. It's about me, and my relationship with God."

He slid his hands into his pockets. "All right. I can't argue with that."

"I'm going to read all about covenant tonight," she said. "Everything I can find. I just want to know . . . to understand. If it's there, in the Bible—and I guess it is—then it must be important, don't you think?"

"Maybe. Or maybe Ingalls is one of those kooks who makes mountains out of molehills."

"I don't think this is a molehill, Dan."

"Okay," he said. "Whatever you say. We can look it over tomorrow after I get off. I'll bring my concordance."

She looked up at him, shaking her head. "I can't wait until tomorrow. I need to know tonight."

"Well, okay. I'll dig some tonight, too."

"Okay. I just . . . feel really fragmented lately . . . scattered . . . I could use a little grounding, and some serious quiet time with God."

"I guess we could all use some of that. You could probably stand some time without me, too. I've been hovering over you pretty good lately."

She didn't object as adamantly as she should have. "No, Dan. It's not that."

"Are you sure?" his tone was flat, as if he didn't believe her.

"Yes, of course."

The fire phone rang, and seconds later, the alarm went off, alerting all the firefighters that there was work to be done. She stepped back against the wall, out of the way, as Dan and the others ran to get geared up. When they had pulled out of the bay, she hurried back to her car, hoping she could continue this with Dan later.

Chapter Fifty

● ● ●

Jill called T.J. Porter, a cop who took jobs as a security guard whenever he could, and hired him to stand guard outside a hotel room so that she could be alone. Allie didn't like the idea.

"Jill, are you sure you're ready to stay in a hotel with that man out there looking for you?"

"Yes," Allie said. "I'll rent a room at the Biltmore in Slidell. I have some things to think about, and I need to be alone."

She hadn't considered how Allie might take that, until she saw her reaction. "I'm sorry if we're too noisy for you."

"No, no!" Jill said. "Nothing like that. It's just ..." She dropped her bag on the floor and looked down at it. "Oh, I might as well tell you. Jerry Ingalls threw some stones at me today. Some spiritual stones."

"I don't understand."

"He challenged my Christianity."

"He what? The guy who held you hostage for hours is challenging *you?*" Allie moved the baby from one hip to the other. "Well, that just goes to show you that he doesn't have a clue. He doesn't know you at all."

Jill wasn't so sure. "Maybe he does. He had some good points. I want to be alone so I can do some studying. I don't read my Bible very much, Allie, and I don't take much time to pray ... I just ... need to reevaluate some things."

Allie began to look worried. "You're not questioning your salvation, are you?"

"No," Jill said. "Not that at all. But I am questioning my relationship with the man who died for me. I think I *need* to question it."

"Well, okay. Then you do need to be alone. But couldn't you just lock yourself in Justin's room? We'd be quiet."

"No, Allie. It's not you. I just need to be totally alone."

Allie sighed and shook her head. "All right. Call me in the morning, okay? Let me know you're all right."

"Okay." She leaned over and pressed a kiss on Justin's fat cheek. "I'll see you two later. If Dan calls, tell him to call me on my cell phone, okay? I'll just let him think I'm still here."

"Why won't you tell him where you really are?"

"Because then there would be this big argument over it, and I really want to concentrate on the Bible tonight."

"All right, I guess I can do that."

Jill smiled. "Thanks so much for being here for me. What would I have done without you?"

"It's not over yet, Jill. The invitation always stands. After you get this spiritual thing worked out, you're welcome to come back."

Chapter Fifty-One

• • •

Jill felt safe with the armed guard outside her hotel room door, but she wasn't sure if it was his presence that calmed her, or the distraction of Jerry Ingalls's accusations about her spiritual life. She hadn't had to go home for her Bible. It had been lying on the backseat of her car, exactly where she'd left it after church last Sunday. Dismally, she realized that was where she kept it most of the time.

She threw herself onto the bed and wondered where in the world to start reading. Should she start with the four Gospels, or the Epistles, or go back to the Old Testament? Then she remembered Jerry's mention of the Abrahamic covenant.

She looked in her concordance for the word *covenant* and found the first reference in Genesis. She turned to the story of Noah and began reading.

She was completely absorbed when the cell phone rang. It was Dan.

"Don't tell me," Jill said. "You've dislocated your shoulder again and you're on your way to the hospital."

"Nope. It's been a real slow night, and my arm is great. I've been doing a little reading . . ."

"Me, too," she said.

"I've also been talking to Nick. I think I've gotten a little insight on what Jerry might be thinking about this covenant stuff. Wanna hear it?"

"Yes, of course."

"All right. Well, see, there were these two guys who were best friends. I mean, really, really close friends. Closer than brothers. They wind up going to war together, and they sort of bond, you know?"

She frowned, assuming he was talking about Jerry and Frank Harper. "Yeah. I can understand that."

"So one day Friend One tells Friend Two that he wants them to have a covenant with each other, right? He wants to know that whatever happens, Friend Two will protect him. And he promises to do the same. He also wants to be sure that, if anything happens to him, his friend will protect his family, and take care of them. Again, he promises the same. Are you with me?"

"Yes," she said, sitting up on the edge of the bed. "I'm with you."

"So as a symbol of this covenant, they swap clothes."

"Clothes?" she asked. "Isn't that a little crazy?"

"Just stay with me. See, Friend One is a higher rank than Friend Two, so when he gives Friend Two his clothes, it's like he's giving him all the privileges and rights of that rank. When his subordinates see him, they think he's the other guy. But his enemies consider him a greater target than he was when he wore his own clothes. So with the privilege comes awesome responsibility."

"Wait," Jill said. "That's not allowed in the military. You can't just swap each other's uniforms."

"But they did," he said. "And what it symbolized to each of them was this: 'I'm in you, and you're in me.' They were so closely identified that they were literally willing to give their lives for each other. Over and over, the higher ranking friend protects his subordinate friend."

"Yeah, go on."

"Then one day, a great tragedy befalls Friend One's family, and he's killed along with his wife and children ..."

She got to her feet. "I thought you were talking about Jerry and Frank Harper. Dan, who *are* you talking about?"

She could tell he was grinning, and his tone was escalating, as if he couldn't wait to get the whole story out. "Just listen. Friend Two grieves deeply, and just about never gets over it. He gets promoted, big-time, and is very successful, but he still never gets over the death of his friend. Then one day, years later, he finds out that Friend One has a son that is still living. He's excited, right? Because he thought all the children had been killed.

"He finds out that this son was injured in the tragedy that came on his family, and it crippled him. But his nanny got him out of harm's way, and she's raised him ever since. Now he's an adult, living in poverty, still crippled."

Jill had stopped trying to figure out who these people were. Instead, she was captivated. She felt like a kid waiting for the next chapter of the storybook. "Uh huh."

"So Friend Two asks the son to come talk to him. The son is frightened. He's not sure if this man is a friend or an enemy, and let's face it, he's got a little touch of paranoia because of what happened to his family when he was a kid. But he agrees to come. And when he sees him, Friend Two tells him that he was in covenant with his father, and that he is sworn to protect him, too. So he invites him to move into his expensive home, and eat at his table, and live like one of his own sons. In one day, the son is transformed from being a poverty-stricken, crippled recluse to having all the riches that Friend Two can offer."

Jill smiled. "That's a beautiful story, Dan. Who are the people?"

He paused, just long enough to raise her anticipation. "They were Jonathan and David, from the Bible. And the son was Mephibosheth. Second Samuel chapter nine."

She closed her eyes, ashamed that she hadn't recognized it. "No wonder it sounds familiar. Jerry told me parts of the same story."

"Really? Well, I was telling Nick about all this covenant stuff, and he showed it to me. Whoever said the Bible isn't a great read?"

She turned to 1 Samuel in her Bible, and flipped through until she found the first passage about Jonathan and David. "It sure is. I can't believe I haven't been reading it."

"But there's more," Dan said. "The coolest part. Nick showed me in Galatians 3 where it says we're clothed with Christ, so when we accept Christ, we take his robe, so to speak. And we're identified with him. His family is our family. His enemies, Satan and all who fight with him, are our enemies. Jill, we just gloss right over Jesus saying this is the new covenant in his blood. But *we* are in covenant with Christ. Isn't that great?"

Tears filled her eyes. "Yes. That is great." She swallowed. "I was just reading about the Abrahamic covenant, where God passed between the pieces of flesh ..."

"Yes!" Dan was getting more excited. "Nick said that we do that when we enter into covenant with Christ. We symbolically pass between the pieces of Christ's flesh. He showed me in Hebrews 10:20, where it says we can enter the holy place through—and I quote—the veil, that is, Jesus' flesh. So you see? We do walk between the pieces. We are in covenant with Christ, in just that way. This is the coolest thing!"

She nodded, unable to speak. "I sure don't live like much of a covenant partner."

"Neither do I." He was silent for a moment. "Listen, I just wanted to share this with you, because it seemed important to you today."

"It is." She wiped her tears. "But all this doesn't explain why Jerry would still defend Frank Harper after he started killing people." She frowned and tried to remember what Jerry had said. "He told me something about the Gideonites or somebody, who deceived the Israelites. Oh, I should have taken notes."

"I'll ask Nick."

"Okay. Call me back on the cell phone if you find out."

"Will do. Say hi to Allie for me."

She felt a slight pang of guilt that he didn't know where she was, but she wasn't prepared to tell the truth and get into a long, distracting discussion. She wanted to bask in this new information she had about her savior. "I'll talk to you later, Dan. And thanks for the story. I needed that tonight."

She hung up and stared down at the pages of her Bible. There was so much she needed to know, so much she had never understood. How would she ever be able to absorb it all?

She had a good, repentant cry, then prayed a while before going back to the Bible. And as she read, a gentle peace fell over her, even as more questions about Jerry and Frank were raised.

Chapter Fifty-Two

● ● ●

Ray Ford's kitchen was alive with the sounds of laughing children playing on the floor in the corner. His sixteen-year-old daughter Vanessa sat cross-legged on the linoleum. He came into the room and smiled down at her. He hadn't seen her playing in years. She wouldn't have done so now, if her mother hadn't put her in charge of the Ingalls children while Susan and Debbie cleaned up the supper dishes, then relaxed with a cup of coffee. Vanessa still sat there with them, though she probably could have turned them back over to their mother at any time along the way. He enjoyed watching her delight in the children.

"Debbie got a contractor to come look at the repairs on the house today," Susan told him. "It's gonna take a lot longer to get it fixed than we thought."

"You stay as long as you need to," Ray said. "Don't you worry about us. We got plenty of room here."

Debbie smiled that humble smile that made him feel even more sympathy for her plight. "I don't know why you're being so kind to me, but I appreciate it."

The phone rang before Ray could answer, and he turned around and picked it up. "Yello?"

There was a long pause, then . . .

"Ray Ford? Is that you?"

Ray didn't recognize the voice. "Yeah, it's me. Who's this?"

"Larry. Larry Hampton."

Ray slowly straightened from his end-of-day slump and shot Susan a look. "I been tryin' to find you," he said into the phone.

Again, a long pause. "My sister told me."

"She said she didn't know where you were," Ray said.

"She didn't, exactly. But she knew how she could get in touch with me."

"Well, did she tell you why I called?"

Again, silence. When Larry spoke again, his voice was broken. "She said . . . that Mary . . ." He couldn't finish the words. He swallowed back the emotion in his voice, and cleared his throat. "How's Pete?"

"Well, he ain't doin' so good. He's in the hospital and still on a ventilator. He got some cracks on his skull, cuts and bruises all over his body, but that ain't the worst part. The hole in his heart is the part we're most worried about."

"How's he taking it? His mom's death . . ."

"How do you *think* he's takin' it?"

Larry was silent for a long moment. "I know what you must think of me, Ray. But trust me, there's nothing you can think about me that I haven't thought about myself."

Ray leaned back on the counter. "I ain't here to make judgments, man. I just want to reunite a family."

"Maybe it's too late for that."

"Well, sure it is with you and Mary. It's past too late. But you got a kid, you know. A kid who right now thinks he's a orphan."

Larry's voice was full of tears and regret. "I want to come back . . . get him . . . but his grandmother . . ."

"You think his grammaw gon' turn you away, when you the only parent he got left?"

"She should," Larry said. "The way I left town. I never planned on showing my face there again."

"Well, you need to change your plans," Ray said. "Comes a time in life when you need to worry about your own kid more than your reputation."

"That's easy for you to say," Larry told him. "I'm just not sure that Pete isn't better off with his grandma."

"Grammaws are nice," Ray said. "She'll do fine, if she's all he's got. After a couple years, he'll get over the pain, move on, grow up. That crack in his skull'll heal, his bones will get strong again, them cuts and bruises'll go back to normal, but that hole in his life, it ain't ever gon' go away. He needs his daddy."

"But what will I tell him?" Larry asked.

"Tell him you love him. Tell him you won't leave him again."

Larry's raspy voice came with much effort. "I don't trust myself to keep that promise."

Clutching the phone, Ray glanced at Susan and Debbie, then stepped into the laundry room, pulling the cord as tight as he could for privacy. "You know, all this regret is real movin' and all, but it don't mean nothin' if you don't come back and take care of your boy."

"I called, didn't I?"

"Yeah, you called. But that don't make you a man."

"What do you mean, it doesn't make me a man? I'm thirty-five years old."

"Only a coward would stay away when his boy needed him like this. I never took you for a coward, Larry, till you up and left your family. But it ain't too late to change things."

"Well, if I had been trying to be your champion, I guess I wouldn't have left."

"You ought to be your boy's champion. That's what fathers are s'posed to be." He knew he was making Larry mad, that it was quite possible that he'd get ticked off and hang up the phone, and Ray would never be able to get in touch with him again. But it needed saying. And he didn't have a lot of patience for tact these days. "Are you coming back, or ain't you?"

"I don't know," Larry said. "Just tell me where he is. What room?"

"He's in the Pendleton Memorial Hospital in New Orleans." Again, that choked emotion in his voice. "Has he been asking for me?"

"Are you kiddin' me?" Ray asked. "He don't know to ask for you. He don't know where you are. All he knows is you took off and left him one day. And it was just him and his mama, and now his mama took off and left him. Now it's just him and his grammaw."

"I can't take care of him. I can't raise him. Not by myself. My life is a mess right now, Ray. It's upside down."

"You don't think *his* life is upside down?" Ray asked. "All I'm askin' you to do is come back here and show that boy that he ain't a orphan. Let him know you didn't leave him without lookin' back. Let him know he's still got one parent alive on this earth who loves him."

Silence on the phone line was almost audible. Ray thought back over his history with Larry. They'd never been close friends, but they'd played Little League baseball on the worst team in the league. They'd both played in the band in high school. They'd been in the same vacation Bible school class year after year. They knew much of the same Scripture. "Man, I know the guilt is eatin' you up. I know you think it's too late to ever make things right with your boy. But you remember all the Scripture they taught us way back in Bible school? You remember that verse they taught us in fourth grade? Romans 5:8? They hammered it into us so we'd never forget it. It was practically tattooed on our foreheads."

"But God demonstrates his own love for us in this," Larry whispered. "While we were still sinners, Christ died for us." His voice broke off, and Ray heard him weeping.

"You remember the way home," Ray said. "Come on home, Larry. People need you here."

Finally, Ray heard a barely discernible click, followed by a dial tone. Larry had hung up.

Ray breathed a deep sigh and closed his eyes, wishing he hadn't been so hard on him. Maybe a little gentleness, instead of anger, could have lured him back. He went back into the kitchen to hang up the phone.

Susan was waiting. "Was that Larry Hampton?"

Ray stared down at the cord still swinging against the wall. "Yeah, that was him, all right."

"What did he say? Is he coming back to see Pete?"

He stared down at the floor between his feet. "Got me. I did my best."

"Pete Hampton," Debbie said. "Is that the little boy who was in the explosion?"

"That's right," Ray said, looking down at her. He started to add that it was the explosion her husband was probably a part of. The one they had spent hours fighting. The one that had killed three of their friends. But he knew it wasn't Debbie's fault. When they had taken her in, he and Susan had made a decision to minister to her and the kids without any condemnation. He wasn't going to start condemning now.

"His daddy left him a couple of years ago," Susan explained. "We've been tryin' to find him."

"How sad."

"Yeah, it's awful," Susan agreed.

"Susan, I don't know if he might call back," Ray said. "But if he does, and I ain't here, you get a number, if you can. I need to be able to call him back."

"He didn't give you one this time?"

Ray shook his head. "There's no tellin' how I might get in touch with him again. At least he's been told."

"So you don't think he'll come back?"

"It depends," Ray said, "on how much a coward he's come to be."

Chapter Fifty-Three

● ● ●

Dan couldn't sleep that night as thoughts of his conversations with Nick and Jill about covenant kept reeling through his mind. Finally, he quit trying to sleep, got up and dressed again, then went into the workout room and began to lift weights with his good arm. It was how he always worked out his frustrations and his anxieties; he tried some form of self-improvement. But he didn't understand why the subject of covenants, while it brought such joy, also brought such anxiety. Was there something in him that needed repentance?

Then his mind drifted back to Jill. Covenant. Wasn't that what people entered when they married? Was that why this subject inspired such anxiety? Was it the fear that someday he might enter into a covenant with Jill, or the fear that he wouldn't? Was it the fear that he wouldn't have the guts, or the fear that he couldn't keep the promise?

He saw a light come on in the kitchen. He put the weights back in their places, then stepped into the doorway to see who was there. He saw Nick sitting at the table with his Bible and papers spread out in front of him. He was, no doubt, working on his sermon for next Sunday.

Nick looked up and saw Dan standing in the doorway. "Couldn't sleep?" he asked.

"Nope," Dan said. "I've got a lot of things on my mind."

"The stuff we talked about?" Nick asked.

Dan nodded and took the seat across from Nick at the table.

"Did something I said bother you?" Nick asked. "Anything you didn't understand?"

"No, I understand it all," Dan said. "I passed it on to Jill. It's really pretty exciting stuff."

"Sure is," Nick said. "But most of us preachers don't talk about it much from the pulpit. I guess we feel like it's too much stuff to fit into a thirty-minute sermon."

"Maybe you need to go overtime."

"Right," Nick said. "They'd be nodding off all over the room. No, in this sound-bite culture, I can't hold them that long."

"Maybe you could do a series on it."

"That's what I was thinking," Nick said. "That's why I decided to get up and work. It was fresh on my mind. I'm working on a covenant series right now."

"Good," Dan said. "I think I need to hear that." He regarded Nick for a moment, wondering if he should tell him what was on his mind about covenants and Jill . . . and the fear he had of failing. But suddenly the door opened, and Issie Mattreaux, one of the paramedics who got off at eleven, came in and headed for the refrigerator.

She started when she saw them. "Oh, hey. I didn't think anybody was in here."

Nick seemed to sit straighter, and smiled up at her. "You just get off?"

Dan noticed something between them—a tension in the way they avoided each other's eyes and spoke in short phrases.

"Yeah. I just needed to get something out of the fridge."

Dan looked up at her. She was a beautiful woman with silky black hair, tanned skin, and the build of a teenager. She probably wore a little too much makeup, more than Dan's taste, but she certainly stood out in a crowd.

He watched Nick's eyes following her across the room.

"So what are you guys doing?" Issie asked as she pulled her drink out of the fridge.

"I'm working on a sermon," Nick said. "You should come hear it."

She grinned. "You know I don't do church." She took a drink, then headed back to the door. "Well, I guess I'll go home."

"You gotta be somewhere?" he asked.

She turned around. "No, I just thought I'd go get some sleep."

"Why don't you pull up a chair and talk for a while?"

Dan knew right away that something was up. It wasn't like Nick to waylay a beautiful woman unless he had an agenda. He suspected the agenda had more to do with his heart than his head. Issie Mattreaux was bad news.

Instead of sitting beside Nick, she sat next to Dan. "So, Dan, what's up with you? Anybody tried to run you off a bridge lately?"

Dan didn't find that amusing. "Been a couple of days."

"So what did you do about your car?"

"They totaled it. The insurance is giving me a check tomorrow. Guess I'll be shopping for a new one."

Nick kept looking from Dan to Issie, as if there was something he wanted to say, and suddenly Dan felt as if he was in the way. He slapped his hands down on the table and stood up slowly. "Well, guess I'll hit the sack."

Issie sprang to her feet, as if she didn't want to be left alone with Nick. "Me, too. I gotta go. See you both later."

She headed out as quickly as she'd come in, and Nick's eyes followed her to the door. "She's not going home," he said when the door had closed. "She's going to Joe's Place."

Dan sat back down. "Why do you say that?"

"Because that's what she does. That's where she goes every night when she gets off at eleven."

"How do you know?"

"I've seen her go there."

Dan stared at him, trying to evaluate why that would matter to him so. "She's a big girl. Makes her own choices."

"Yeah, I know," Nick said. "But I wish she wouldn't, because they hurt her."

Now, Dan's eyes narrowed, and he half-grinned at his preacher. "Nick, you're not interested in her, are you?"

Nick looked down at his Bible again, and stared at the words as if he was reading, but Dan knew better. The question was probably circling around in his mind, and he was framing it, trying to figure out how to answer . . . probably searching his soul for the truth, because he didn't know, himself. Finally, Nick looked up at him. "I can't be interested in her, Dan. But I do have a real burden for her. She's lost and unhappy, and she constantly gets herself into situations that get her into trouble. I worry about her."

"You know, it's not your job to be the caretaker of the whole world. That's God's job."

"I really do know that," Nick said. "But she's a special case."

"Why? Because she's good-looking?"

"No," Nick said. "Because she seems like such a sad person."

Dan made a face. "She doesn't seem that sad to me."

"That's because you don't know her that well."

He breathed a laugh. "And you do? You two could hardly look each other in the eye."

Nick looked at him as if he couldn't believe he'd said that. "That isn't true."

"It *is* true. If I didn't know better, I'd think you two had a crush on each other."

Nick laughed out loud, but it seemed a little overdone. "The last person in the world Issie would ever get involved with is a preacher. It's not just us Christians who don't want to be unequally yoked, you know. The unbelievers aren't real crazy about it, either. You're lucky, you know," Nick said. "You and Jill, you start off with a lot going for you. You care about the same things. You both want to be fruitful for God. You care about how he sees you. You'll both make Christ the center of your relationship. If you two got married, you'd start off way ahead of the game already."

"You act like we're engaged."

Nick stared into him. "Well, haven't you thought about it?"

Dan didn't want to answer that. It made him real uncomfortable. He shifted in his seat. "We're a long way from that."

"Oh. My mistake. I thought you two were getting along real well."

"Well, you don't marry someone just because you get along real well. At least you shouldn't. I mean, there has to be more to it, doesn't there? There has to be a lot of trust."

"You don't trust Jill?" Nick asked.

Dan rolled his eyes. "Oh, come on. Of course I do. But maybe not in that way. Not enough to know that she'll stay with me for the rest of my life."

"What about yourself? Do you trust *yourself* to stay with her for the rest of your life?"

Dan shook his head. "I don't know. I honestly don't."

"Are you thinking about it?" Nick asked.

Dan rubbed the stubble on his face. "Maybe. But this covenant stuff kind of got me thinking. It's pretty serious stuff ... that two-becoming-one business. I don't think most Christians realize how serious it is."

"I'd say you're right."

"I mean, if they realized that marriage really is a covenant ... and it's binding and can't be broken without ripping—"

The telephone rang suddenly and Dan jumped. He realized he was tense, perspiring. Did the subject get under his skin that much? Thankfully, he got up and answered the phone on the wall. "Midtown Station."

"Dan, is that you?" He recognized the voice of Lisa Manning, one of the women he'd taken out a time or two before Jill.

"Hey, Lisa. What's up?" He noticed that Nick looked accusingly up at him, as if Dan had solicited the call.

"I hate to call so late," she said. "But I figured you'd still be up. I have to go to this big dinner tomorrow night. One of those coat and tie functions, and I thought it was a shame to get all dressed up and not have a date."

He felt his muscles tightening. It was getting hotter in the room. He wondered if something was wrong with the air conditioning. He turned his back to Nick.

"So what do you say?" she asked. "You want to go as my date, or not?"

He breathed out a hard sigh. "I don't think I'd better, Lisa."

"You busy?" she asked.

He glanced back at Nick. The preacher wasn't hiding the fact that he was listening. "Yeah."

"Oh, I get it," she said. "It's Jill Clark, isn't it? Are you two on again?"

"You might say that."

"I heard you were with her when you had your accident the other night."

"Bad news travels fast."

"It's a small town. She's bringing you bad luck, you know."

Dan laughed. "I don't believe in luck." He glanced at Nick again, hoping that would please him.

"So you two are an item?"

"I don't know," he said. "I mean ... I'm not sure. I just ... don't think I can go tomorrow night."

The back door opened and Mark came in. Apparently, he'd been in the backyard of the station, talking on his cell phone, probably to Allie. Dan felt suddenly self-conscious. "Uh ... thanks for the invitation, though."

"No problem," she said. "I'll just find somebody else."

"All right. Thanks for calling."

He hung up and turned back to Nick and Mark as they both stared at him. "Who is that?" Mark asked.

Dan started to tell them they needed a hobby, that his life didn't need to be their sole source of entertainment, but he knew that was a little defensive. "It was Lisa Manning."

"Lisa Manning?" Mark asked. "What did *she* want?"

"She asked Dan out," Nick said.

"Thanks a lot," Dan shot back.

"Are you going?"

"Of course not." He pulled his towel from around his neck. "You know, I appreciate your concern, but you're not Jill's caretaker just because she's staying at your house." He walked away.

Mark frowned. "Jill's not staying at our house. At least, not tonight."

Dan turned back around. "What do you mean? Where is she?"

"She's staying in a hotel. Didn't she tell you?"

"No!" he said, his face reddening. "I just talked to her a little while ago."

"What did you do? Call her cell phone?"

"Well, yeah, after Allie told me to. I assumed she was there and just didn't want to tie up your line or something."

"She wasn't there. She was in a hotel."

Dan slammed his hand into the wall. "What in the world would possess her to do that? She knows this guy's still after her."

"She hired a guard to sit outside her room. It's okay."

"No, it's not okay," he said. "She's in danger."

"She said she needed to do some research for the case. She needed to be alone so she could focus. Something about the Bible."

"Why didn't she tell me she wasn't at your house?"

"Calm down," Nick said, coming to his feet. "Maybe there's a logical explanation."

"There's no excuse for her lying to me."

"*Did* she lie to you?" Mark asked. "Did she ever say she was at our house?"

"No," Dan said. "But she knew I thought she was still there, and she didn't tell me. To me that was lying." His face was crimson, and he headed for the phone and jerked it up. He jabbed out Jill's number.

"Hello?"

"Why didn't you tell me you were in a hotel room?"

There was a long pause. "Dan, I just didn't want you to worry. I knew you'd overreact."

"Overreact?" he asked. "Because I care about you? Because I'm looking out for you? You said you like that, that you didn't want me to stop."

"Dan, I have a guard right outside the door. Nobody can get past him."

"Unless he blows him away! Jill, you're a sitting duck for this guy!"

"I'm a sitting duck no matter where I am. I needed to be alone tonight, Dan. I needed some time to read about covenant and figure out what's going on with Jerry and Frank Harper. I needed some time to pray. I knew you wouldn't understand."

"You knew I wouldn't understand?" Dan repeated, incredulous. "Just because I don't approve means I'm so dense that I can't understand?"

"That's not what I meant, and you know it."

"I can't believe you'd lie to me!"

"I didn't lie. I just didn't tell you where I was. It didn't come up."

"So, let me get this straight," Dan said. "Just because I didn't think to ask you if you'd moved in the last twenty-four hours . . . Excuse me if I misinterpreted our relationship to be close enough that you, at least, told me where you slept at night."

"Dan, you're blowing this way out of proportion. This really has nothing to do with you."

"Oh, well, thanks a lot. Guess that puts me in my place." He slammed the phone down and pressed his forehead against it.

"That didn't go well, did it?" Mark asked.

Dan shot him a piercing look.

"Man, I'm sorry I started all this. I wouldn't have said anything if I'd known—"

"That she lied to me?" he asked. "No problem. You know why? Because there are other fish in the sea." He picked up the phone and began to dial again. "Lisa Manning is one of them."

"Man, don't do it." But Dan kept dialing. "Dan, you're making a big mistake."

Dan swung around. "Don't tell me what I'm doing. She's putting her life in danger, and she doesn't care what I think about it. She lied to me to keep me from reacting, and I'm not even important enough for her to consult about this at all."

"She doesn't have to consult with you, Dan! You're not married."

"We're not going to be, either."

"Dan, you can't run every time she disappoints you."

"This is the last time she's gonna disappoint me," he said.

Lisa answered the phone, and he snapped, "Yeah, Lisa. Listen, about that invitation. I think I will take you up on it."

"Good. Pick me up at seven."

"You pick me up," he countered. "I may not have a car yet."

"All right," she said. "I'll see you then."

When he hung up the phone, he turned back to his two friends. "Don't say a word," he said. "Jill Clark doesn't care about me or my feelings, so I'm not going to care about hers."

He started to storm away, but Mark grabbed his arm. "What are you doing?"

"What do you mean, what am I doing? You heard me."

"Are you and Jill still an item, or not?"

"I don't know."

"Well, who would know?" Mark asked sarcastically.

"Apparently, you!" Dan said. "Why don't you tell me?"

"I think you are an item, but that self-destructive part of you that is scared to death of a committed relationship is looking for the slightest little excuse to call it off. You pump iron until you look like Arnold Schwarzenegger, jog five miles a day, comb your hair every time you pass a mirror . . . But you're your own worst enemy. You sabotage yourself the minute things start going right for you. It's like part of you doesn't *want* to be happy."

"I don't need you playing shrink on me, Mark."

"All right, then," Mark said, glancing at Nick. "Then let Nick tell you. Tell him, Nick. You're his pastor. He'll listen to you."

"Oh, brother . . ." Dan said.

Nick got up and set his foot on a chair. "Dan, you were just talking about not trusting yourself with that kind of commitment. From the looks of things, you were right."

"Great," Dan said. "So much for pastor confidentiality. You two are amazing." He started to leave the room, then turned back to them. "Get this straight. I'm not going out with Lisa Manning because I'm so weak that I can't help straying. I'm going to make a point."

"To Jill, or to yourself?" Mark asked.

"Maybe both of us," he said. "If our relationship is so superficial that she doesn't even tell me when she's walking into the line of fire, then it's too superficial for us to have an exclusive relationship."

Mark's voice dripped with sarcasm. "You'll show her."

Dan went back to the weight room and began to pump iron with a vengeance.

Chapter Fifty-Four

● ● ●

The van that Frank Harper had stolen after Dan's car went off the bridge was found in Slidell's Piggly Wiggly parking lot that night, after the Civic was reported missing. It belonged to one of the employees inside, and he was distraught, cursing and pacing, as the police took the report. There were no witnesses who had seen the thief.

When someone from the Slidell Police Department learned that the van had been stolen from a campsite near the I-10 bridge, he called Stan Shepherd to tell him that the thief was probably Frank Harper himself, and that it was highly likely that he was driving a green Civic.

Stan put an APB out, alerting all the cops on duty in several surrounding counties that the killer may be in a green Civic. And as he cruised the town in his unmarked car, trying to think like an insane terrorist, he racked his brain for where Frank Harper might be.

He went to every motel in town and showed Frank's picture, asked if anyone had seen him. No one had. He cruised the parking lots of Delchamps, the Newpointe Library, the Bonaparte Court Apartments, the Bijoux movie theatre, looking for the stolen green Civic, but found nothing.

Where was this guy? What was he up to? Who was he going to try to kill tonight?

Around ten o'clock, he called home to check on Celia. "Hey, babe. Were you in bed?"

"No," she said. "I'm cleaning out the closets."

"Cleaning the closets? Why?"

"It needed doing. I want the house to be clean when we bring the baby home."

"But we still have two weeks."

"Maybe, maybe not."

He frowned. He had heard that women had a burst of energy before they went into labor, that they often got into a cleaning spree that was almost obsessive compulsive. "You're not nesting, are you?"

"Probably," she said, "but don't worry about it. It doesn't mean anything."

"You know, they say that you're supposed to get as much rest as you can, even if you don't feel like it, because if you do go into labor, you'll wind up being too tired to deliver."

"And what?" she asked, amused. "I'll have to carry the baby the rest of my life? Stan, honey, this baby is coming whether I'm tired or not."

"You still need your rest. Our closets are clean enough."

"Okay. I'll go to bed. When are you coming home?"

Before he could answer, he got a call on the radio. "Hold on," he said, and turned it up. Slidell police had spotted the Civic at a parking lot when they'd been called about another car theft. "What kind of car was stolen this time?" he asked.

"A maroon Cavalier," the dispatcher told him. "Tag number's SEW 365."

Quickly, Stan put an APB out on the maroon Cavalier and alerted all available police that Frank Harper was driving it and that he could be armed and dangerous. He picked the phone back up. "Honey, it's gonna be a while before I can get home. You just call me if you need me. I'll keep the phone on. And go to bed, will you?"

"Okay," she said. "I promise."

He clicked off the phone and drove past Jill's house. Nothing there. Then he drove to Debbie Ingalls's place. She still wasn't home.

An uneasy sense of having no control plagued him as he drove. Something was going to happen tonight. He could feel it. He only hoped he could stop it before it was too late.

Chapter Fifty-Five

• • •

Jill hadn't slept at all that night. Despite her need for rest, Dan's words tumbled through her mind. By the time she'd checked out of the hotel the next morning, paid T.J. Porter, and headed for the jail, she looked as exhausted as she felt. She had dark circles under her eyes, but she had applied her makeup to hide it.

Still, Jerry noticed right away. "You look like you didn't get much sleep last night," he said. "Have you been crying?"

"No," she lied. "I was just up late reading about covenant."

His eyebrows shot up. "Really? You read about covenant? Everything about it?"

"Everything I could find," she said. She sat down wearily and looked up at him. "But there's something I don't understand. You said something about the Gideonites. I looked and looked and I didn't see anything about the Gideonites having to do with covenant."

"No," he said. "Not the Gideonites. The Gibeonites."

"Who are they?"

She could see that Jerry was a born teacher. He leaned forward, and his face came alive. "Just before Joshua led the Israelites into the Promised Land, God told them not to make a covenant with anybody, and to destroy all of the people in the cities of the Promised Land. So the Gibeonites, who lived in the Promised Land, decided to trick the Israelites into entering into covenant with them. They got old wineskins and old clothes and dried pieces of bread, and made it look like they had come from a long way away to make covenant with them. They knew if the Israelites knew they were from the Promised Land, they'd never make covenant with them. So they lied. Joshua didn't consult God, and he fell for it. The Israelites entered into covenant with them, and it was binding."

"But it was deceitful, " she said. "If they were tricked, they wouldn't have to keep the covenant, would they?"

"Oh, but they did," Jerry said. "If you read about it you'll see that's exactly what happened. When they found out the Gibeonites just lived around the corner, they realized they'd been had. But the covenant itself meant more than the deceit. They had to honor it. When the Gibeonites were attacked by the Amorites, they called on the Israelites, and they had to defend them. So that tells me that it doesn't matter if one person deceives you in covenant, or if they break it. Regardless, you're obligated for your side of the bargain. There's another example of that, with Jacob and Leah. He worked seven years so he could marry Rachel, but after the wedding he found out he'd been had. Was the covenant he'd made with Leah broken? Nope. He had to honor that covenant."

"Okay," Jill said, trying to understand. "So even though Frank Harper is a maniac and is going around targeting people at random, including your family, who is part of your covenant with him ... you still have to keep your part of the covenant. Is that what you're saying?"

Now Jerry looked confused, and he slumped back in his chair. "No. That's not what I'm saying. My covenant with my wife is more important than that. But I've talked to her and she sounds like she's in good hands. And you know who blew up the post office, so I'm not keeping anything from you."

Jill rubbed her temples. They were beginning to ache. She was bone-tired, and her soul felt bruised. "All right, Jerry. Just a few more questions. I'm curious. You told me that you didn't become a Christian until after Vietnam, when you were in jail. So how did you have such a strong feeling about covenant before you even knew God?"

Jerry sat straight again. "See, Frank is a messianic Jew."

Jill frowned. "What do you mean? A Christian? Are you trying to tell me Frank Harper is a *Christian?*"

"That's right."

"No way!" She got to her feet and shook her head viciously. "Oh, no way! You've got some real distorted view of Christianity if you expect me to believe that a terrorist could be a Christian. A cold-blooded killer? The violent person who was chasing me on the causeway?"

"He's mentally ill, Jill. He's not himself."

"So . . . before this . . . this mine or whatever it was . . . he was a real Christian? A Jewish Christian?"

"Well, he was half Jewish. His mother was a Jew. He knew all about covenant. I did believe in God and I believed God punished people for breaking his laws. Frank taught me about the gravity of covenant, and about his covenant with Christ. He was very devout then. A great influence. He impacted so many people. I didn't accept Christ then, but he laid the groundwork in me. Later, when things changed for him, I couldn't forget that."

She didn't want to think that the same Christ who loved her also loved Frank Harper. She didn't want to think he had the same access to God that she had. "I'm sorry, but this is a little much."

"I don't know how God holds the mentally ill accountable," Jerry said. "All I know is that before he got blown up trying to save me, he loved Jesus. He hasn't been right since, but I think God must make allowance for that."

She felt sick again. She rubbed her eyes, unable to comprehend all of this. Since she couldn't grasp it, she decided to switch gears. She opened her briefcase. "Jerry, I'm going to do my best to represent you at the arraignment this morning, but they're not going to release you."

"I realize that," he said.

"Unless you intend to tell them about Frank Harper. Then maybe there's a chance they would be lenient . . ."

"I'm sure you've already told them," he said.

"But it would mean so much more coming from you. If you could just tell them the truth about how things worked, how you wound up at the post office, how you wound up at the Flagstaff."

"I can't do that," he said.

She slammed her hand on the table. "Why not? They need to know how Frank got you involved, Jerry. They need to know why your pickup was there, why you took a hostage, why he went after Cliff Bertrand."

"No, they don't. They only need his name, and they didn't get it from me. When he hears about it on the news, he won't hear that I spilled my guts. Maybe he'll realize I didn't tell them."

"Jerry, what difference does it make if you did? He knows his picture and name are all over the news."

"It makes a difference because he'll go after my family again if he thinks I broke covenant! He isn't sane, Jill. He isn't rational. I'm trying to protect my family!"

As frustrated as that left her, she knew she couldn't argue with his logic. She wasn't sure that he wasn't absolutely right. Unable to go on, she closed her briefcase, told him she would meet him in court, and left the room.

While she waited for court to convene, she went into the bathroom, pulled her phone out, and tried to call Dan. But there was no answer. She called Allie to see if Mark was off duty yet and if he knew where Dan was.

"No, he may be trying to get something worked out about replacing his car," Allie said.

Jill sighed. "We kind of got into a fight last night about my staying in the hotel. I just wanted to try to talk it out."

Allie was quiet for a moment. "Jill, there's something I need to tell you. I'm your best friend and I'm not going to let you find out about this from someone else."

She fought the urge to hang up. She didn't know how much more she could take. "Find out about what?"

"Jill, last night, Mark said that Dan was so mad at you that he kind of went off the deep end. Lisa Manning asked him to dinner tonight, and he said he'd go."

"He what?" She swallowed hard, trying not to let her emotions get the best of her before she went into court.

"I'm sorry. I don't know what's gotten into him, but the man has so much pride. And apparently, you wounded it when you didn't tell him where you were. So he's going out with Lisa. He's a jerk, Jill. That's all I can say. Just a big jerk."

Jill didn't know how to react. She felt tears pushing to her eyes, but she told herself she couldn't allow it. Not now. Not when she had to go into court and defend Jerry Ingalls.

"Well, I guess that speaks volumes," she managed to say.

"No, I don't think it does," Allie said. "Don't give up on him. I'm sure it's just an overreaction."

"You just called him a jerk. Which is it?"

"Well, he's a jerk that overreacts. Come on, Jill. I really like the two of you together. If you got married, we'd be best friends married to best friends. Don't let this ruin my dreams."

She knew Allie was teasing her, trying to make her laugh, but there didn't seem to be any mirth left in her. "You know, he can go out with anybody he wants. We don't have an understanding or anything. We're not engaged, for heaven's sake. We're not even going steady . . . or whatever they're calling it now." Her voice wobbled as she spoke, and she tried to steady it.

"Jill, I know you're hurt."

She squeezed her eyes shut as tears pushed out. She wouldn't be taking this so hard, she told herself, if she had slept last night. And she would have slept last night if she hadn't taken her fight with Dan so hard.

For a moment, she didn't answer. "I thought we had something. How stupid." She pinched her tear ducts, trying to stop the tears. Taking a deep breath, she said, "Look, I've got to go to court."

"Are you okay, Jill?"

"I'm as okay as I've ever been. You know me. I always land on my feet. Knock me down, I bounce right back up."

"Like one of those Weebles? You wobble but you don't fall down?"

Allie was still trying to get a smile out of her, but she didn't think she had one in her. "Yeah, something like that." Her voice cracked with every word. "I'll talk to you later, Allie."

She hung up the phone and leaned over the sink to splash water on her face. She tore a paper towel out of its dispenser and blotted her face as she looked in the mirror. Why had she ever believed she could hold someone like Dan Nichols? He needed someone like Lisa Manning, someone beautiful, young ...

Forcing her thoughts back to Jerry Ingalls, she grabbed her briefcase up and left the bathroom, determined not to think about Dan Nichols again for the rest of the day.

Chapter Fifty-Six

• • •

Stan got up early the next morning and drove to Jackson, to the Veterans Administration Hospital where Frank Harper had been a patient for so many years. Some of the FBI agents who were working with him on the case were waiting for him there. They had already cleared it with the administrator to search Frank's room.

Stan didn't know what he had expected, but the men on the ward looked relatively normal. He and the other agents came in, and an orderly pointed them to the bed Frank Harper had used. Next to it was a locker, and they opened it and saw dozens of articles taped to the inside walls, articles about Waco and Oklahoma City, and the Unabomber, ads for survivalist gear and articles about conspiracies in the government. They found handwritten manuscripts, pages and pages of the same theme. Frank Harper thought he was a prisoner of war, and believed communism had infiltrated the government. The FBI agents took the contents of the locker for evidence. As they tagged and bagged it, they ran across an address book. Jerry Ingalls's name was written in red ink with several tally marks beside it.

"Wonder what the tally marks are?" one of the agents said.

The psychologist who had worked with Frank for years had led them to his bed, and he stood back, out of the way, as they worked. "Can I take a look?" he asked the agent.

The agent showed him the marks. "That's the number of times he visited him," he said. "He kept score of who came and talked a lot about how only one of the men he saved kept in touch anymore."

The agent counted the tally marks. "He came fifteen times. Over how long?"

"Years," the doctor said. "There's no telling how long. But he trusted this Ingalls guy because of that."

"Maybe that's why he went to Newpointe and got Ingalls involved," Stan said. "He was the only one he trusted."

"So now that Ingalls is locked up," Stan asked, "where else could he be?"

Chapter Fifty-Seven

● ● ●

Jerry had a tearful reunion with Debbie in court before he pled not guilty. The judge accepted the plea, but denied Jill's request to send him home pending trial. It was as Jill had expected, but she still felt like a failure as they led him out of the courtroom.

When Debbie had left, Jill went back across the street to the police station, and saw Stan driving up. He was beginning to look as tired as she.

"Stan, have you found Frank Harper yet?" she asked.

He shook his head and led her into the station. "We found his trail. We know he's been in New Orleans, and there's evidence that he's been in Newpointe and Slidell, but we haven't been able to find him yet. We think he's driving a maroon Cavalier, but he's changing cars every few hours, so there's no telling."

"You've got to find him," Jill said. "Stan, he's ruining my life. Please." Her voice broke off, and she covered her face, desperately trying to hide the emotion. "I can't go home, I can't go to my office . . ."

He looked at her with surprise, then took her arm and led her to his desk. Urging her to sit down, he asked, "Jill, are you all right?"

Jill realized she was losing her professionalism. She had never done this before. "Yes, I'm all right." She wiped at the tears falling, and shook her head. "I don't know what's wrong with me. I just—"

Stan handed her a box of Kleenex. "Jill, you've been under a lot of pressure. This would be stressful for anybody. You may even have a little touch of post-traumatic stress disorder."

"Give me a break," she said, jerking a Kleenex out of the box and wiping her nose. "I'm fine, I told you."

"You don't look fine."

"Are you speaking as a detective? Collecting clues?"

"No," he said. He got up from his desk and came around to take her arm. Gently, he pulled her to her feet. "I'm speaking as your friend. Come on, let's go to the interrogation room so we can have a little privacy, and you can tell me what's got you so upset."

She didn't object, just allowed him to usher her into the room. When he closed the door behind them, she sank miserably into a chair. Stan leaned on the edge of the table and looked down at her. "So what's going on, Jill? I've known you to have all sorts of run-ins with danger, but I don't think I've ever seen you like this. Is it Dan?"

She shook her head, but her face belied her denial. Finally, she realized that there was no use denying it. She was as transparent as glass, and she felt that everyone saw clearly what was in her heart—good and bad. "Last night I had this great prayer time, and I came to understand God on a deeper level than I ever have before. And today, everything's falling apart. This case is cutting into my relationship with Dan," she said. "It's ruining everything."

"What is?" he asked.

"The fact that somebody's trying to kill me. It kind of throws a wet blanket on my mood."

Stan smiled. "So you think Dan's going to quit seeing you because of your mood?"

"I'm not any fun!" she shouted. "I'm high maintenance. Too much trouble."

"Wait," Stan said, holding up a hand to make her back up. "Has Dan told you this? Because he doesn't seem like the party animal type to me, and he's not that shallow. In fact, the Dan I know has been more interested in you *since* Jerry Ingalls took you hostage. I haven't seen him backing off because it put you in a bad mood."

She got up and shook her head, as if he could never understand. "I'm constantly butting heads with him. It's like he thinks I'm suicidal, like I'm going to throw myself in front of a bus, just to get that adrenaline rush."

"Dan is not that unreasonable," Stan said. "Jill, have you and Dan had a fight? Have you broken up again?"

She laughed hard, though there was no humor in it. "It's worse than that. It's gone past fighting to indifference. He's got another date tonight."

Stan frowned. "I find that hard to believe."

"Well, believe it," Jill said. "He's going out with Lisa Manning."

Stan's face went slack. "Lisa Manning? She's not his type at all."

"*Au contraire*," she said. "He obviously likes her better than me." She covered her face, hating herself for exposing her feelings this way. "Oh, Stan, look at me. I've never acted with anything less than total professionalism with you, and here I am falling apart like some kind of lovesick teenager. It's so stupid! I hate myself for this."

"Jill, you're too hard on yourself. I'm not just a cop you butt heads with. I'm your friend. Your brother in Christ. And I do happen to be your deacon, so technically, it's very normal for you to come to me with your problems." He hesitated as she looked hopefully up at him, then he felt suddenly inadequate. "The thing is, I don't have a clue what to tell you."

She couldn't help laughing through her tears. Poor Stan. He'd never bargained for any of this. He'd just been in the wrong place at the wrong time.

"Have you tried talking to Dan?"

"He's not answering my calls," she said. "And last night he was really upset. I think he's finished with me."

"Then he's not worthy of you."

"Right."

Stan looked down at the floor, as if racking his brain for wisdom. "Well ... he's not. If he takes off at the slightest little thing ..."

The door flew open just then, startling them both, and Sid Ford stuck his head in. "Stan, Celia's on the phone. I think it's an emergency."

"Excuse me," Stan said and dashed back to his desk. Jill followed, wiping her face.

"Celia?" he asked. "Honey, are you all right? Really? Are you sure? No, no, I'll be right there. Can you wait? Do you need an ambulance?"

Jill forgot her own problems. Her heart began to pound. Celia was in labor.

Stan slammed down the phone and yelled out, "We're having a baby!" Then he grabbed his keys and ran out of the building without another word.

Jill began to laugh as she watched him. Then her laughter melted into more tears, as she realized that the whole world was rotating and moving and changing all the time. But it was all passing her by. Friends were marrying, having babies, buying homes, saving for college ... And the only relationship she'd ever had with that kind of potential had just slipped through her fingers.

She thought of going to the hospital with them to get her mind off of Dan, but she knew it was no use. Celia would probably be in labor for hours, and she would just be in the way. No, she didn't belong there. She didn't really belong anywhere.

Feeling safer in the police station than anywhere else, she asked to borrow the phone at one of the empty desks. She called Sheila for her messages, then spent the next couple of hours returning calls, realizing that she was just marking time, waiting for the minutes to pass.

She wished with all her heart that she could go home, but she couldn't. Mark and Allie's was the closest to home she could go tonight. And as soon as she could pull herself together, that was exactly where she would go.

Chapter Fifty-Eight

● ● ●

A storm was moving in as Jill headed out to her car, and black clouds darkened the sky. Any minute, it would begin to rain. It would pound down on Dan and Lisa on their date, she thought, and if there was any justice, they would have forgotten their umbrellas. Lisa would get drenched and look like a wet cocker spaniel.

With her remote key, she clicked "unlock," and saw the light inside the car come on. She opened the back door and dropped her briefcase on the seat.

"Jill!"

She turned around and saw Nick standing in the truck bay at the fire station next door. She closed her door and headed across the lawn. "Hey, Nick. Don't you ever leave this place?"

Nick shrugged. "For some reason, we single guys are the ones they call when they want to trade shifts." He bent down and looked into her red, bloodshot eyes. "You've been crying."

"No, I haven't," she lied. "Why do you say that?"

"The Dan thing," he said. "I've been praying for you."

She rolled her eyes and looked away. "I guess everybody knows. He didn't even bother to tell me himself."

"I know. I'm sorry, Jill. But if it's any consolation, he's a miserable man right now."

She looked up at her preacher. "Yeah, that is some consolation. He deserves to be miserable."

Nick gave her a wry grin, but she couldn't seem to return it. "Don't give up on him."

"He gave up on me," she said.

"He's a complicated guy. Just hang in there. I still think you two are meant for each other."

"Whatever," she said. "Thanks for the encouragement, anyway."

"But you're not encouraged."

Tears came to her eyes again. "It's been a long few days." She choked back the emotion in her throat. "I'll see you later."

She crossed the lawn to her car. A mud-splattered pickup truck passed her as she got in, and she closed the door and started the car. The truck pulled to the side of the road as soon as she got behind him. He honked at her, and she wondered if she had done something to make him angry. Were her bright lights on? She checked and saw that she had not even turned her lights on. She passed him feeling uneasy. He pulled out behind her, tailgating her and honking and flashing his lights. A chill went through her.

Frank Harper had found her.

She slammed her foot on the accelerator and flew around the corner and into the left lane, almost hitting another car. The truck pulled up beside her, still honking and weaving, and she saw the man behind the wheel motioning to her to pull over. He didn't look like the pictures she'd seen of Frank—no beard, shorter hair—but he looked crazed, and that was enough for her. His eyes were wild and his teeth were bared, and his mouth moved in vicious dialogue as he tried to make her stop.

She made a quick left turn, and the truck cut across a busy lane of traffic and followed.

Trembling, she groped for her cell phone. She found it and pressed 911 with her thumb, then pressed *send*. The phone only beeped. She glanced down and saw the words "Low Battery" displayed on the small screen.

The truck bumped her, just like on the bridge, and she almost ran into the opposite lane of traffic. She crossed in front of him and got in the right lane, and again, he bumped her, trying to run her off the road.

She wove in and out of traffic, trying to decide what to do, but the truck stayed with her, weaving and honking and bumping her, trying to run her onto the shoulder. He didn't care who saw him, she thought. Cars were stopping and pulling off the road, and drivers were cursing and yelling as they flew by them. She skidded around a corner, and the truck came after her.

She had to find people out of their cars, she thought, people who could protect her. She had to drive into a well-lit area where lots of people were, and run for help. But her fear of stopping was too great.

The truck made its way up beside her, and the driver waved his hand at her, telling her furiously to pull over, as if the words would force her to comply.

She skidded around another corner, and was back on Jacquard, the main strip through town. But the traffic and visibility didn't stop him. He kept bumping her, urging her off the road, and she realized with a chill that he wasn't going to give up, and she couldn't lose him. She saw him reach under his seat, and he came up with a gun, waved it at her. She swallowed back a scream. Any minute now he would start shooting.

Not knowing what else to do, she skidded into the parking lot of a convenience store where several people stood outside at the gas pumps. She swerved to a stop, then threw the door open and ran for the door. The truck slid to a halt behind her, and the driver stumbled out.

Patricia Castor, the mayor, was inside paying for gas. She looked up as Jill bolted through the door.

"Help me!" Jill screamed. "He's after me! Please!"

The mayor pulled her into her arms, but her surprised eyes were locked on something outside the door.

"Call the police!" Jill screamed. "Hurry! That man—" She pointed out the doors, and saw the man from the truck. He wasn't running, and he wasn't coming in after her. Instead, with his gun in one hand, he opened her back car door and reached in, and jerked a man out of her backseat. It was Frank Harper.

Jill started screaming. He had been in her car. Frank Harper had been close enough to cut her throat, but that man . . . that truck driver . . . had stopped him. She couldn't stop screaming, and Pat Castor tried to calm her down. Outside, the men were struggling. Frank Harper knocked the gun out of his hand. He swung his right fist across the trucker's jaw, knocking him back, and took off running.

Jill bolted through the doors. "Catch him!" she screamed. "That's Frank Harper! Don't let him get away!"

A squad car pulled up with its siren on and lights flashing. Someone witnessing the traffic violations had probably called him, she thought, and R.J. Albright jumped out. "What's goin' on here?"

"R.J., go after him! Please, go after him. Frank Harper . . . He was . . . in my car . . . my backseat . . ."

R.J. ran back to his car and radioed for help.

The truck driver's lip was bleeding, and he stumbled toward Jill. "Lady, I was trying to tell you. I drove by you when you were getting in your car on Purchase Street, and your light came on and I saw him hunched in your backseat."

She covered her mouth, unable to stand the horror of such a chilling brush with death. "But I put my briefcase in the backseat. I looked. He wasn't there!" She realized then that she had left the car unlocked as she had talked to Nick. He must have gotten in then. "I thought you were him! You had a gun!"

"I'm a deputy in Ouachita Parish, so I always have a weapon. Ma'am, when you didn't stop, I thought I might have to shoot him myself. I could see him risin' up in the back."

She began to sob, and Pat Castor bustled out. "R.J.," the mayor said, "you go after that man, hear? Don't you let him get away."

"I'm not, ma'am," the chubby officer said. "I've got folks chasin' him down as we speak."

But something about that didn't sound good to Jill. R.J. was too out of shape to chase down a perpetrator, and she feared that too much time had been wasted. Frank Harper was going to get away again.

Chapter Fifty-Nine

● ● ●

Celia's contractions were ten minutes apart, but when Stan got to the house, he had spent half an hour looking for a baby blanket Celia insisted on taking with her. When he'd finally found it, he had hurried her into the car.

Celia didn't seem to understand the urgency as keenly as he did, a fact that baffled him. Didn't she know that this baby was coming with or without that blanket? Didn't she understand that they'd never make it to New Orleans on time if they didn't get on the road *now?* "You know, it's crazy, us taking time to go all the way to New Orleans, when we can be in Slidell in ten or fifteen minutes. I'm calling the doctor and telling him we can't make it."

"Don't you dare!" Celia said. "We *can* make it. We agreed that the latest technology and that neonatal unit were at the New Orleans hospital, and we wanted to make sure we had everything we needed in case of a problem."

"There isn't going to *be* a problem! Everything's great with the baby, so why can't we just—?"

"Stan, my doctor is in New Orleans. And Pete's at the same hospital, so I can check on him. Now, calm down."

His hands trembled as he cranked the car and pulled out of the driveway. He ran over the garbage can, bashed it in, and dragged it several feet before it rolled out from under the car.

"Stan, are you all right? Do you want me to drive?"

He shot her a disgusted look. "You can't drive. You're in too much pain. No, I'm fine."

"Actually, I'm not having that much pain yet."

"Then why are you sweating?"

"Because you haven't turned the air conditioner on."

He caught his breath and cut it on, then aimed the vent at her. "Is that good?"

"Fine," she said. "Uh, Stan, you're running a red light!"

He slammed on the brakes, almost sending her through the windshield. "I'm sorry, honey!"

"Stan, you may be a little too nervous to drive. Why don't you just let me?"

"I'll calm down," he said, panting. "I'll do better."

He turned on the radio, a classical station from New Orleans, hoping the music would calm him down. "They say Mozart makes babies more intelligent. I heard that in some states they give every mother a Mozart tape to take home from the hospital with her."

"Is that Mozart?" she asked.

He shrugged. "I have no idea. But it sounds good, doesn't it?"

She smiled. "Yes. It does." She reached across and took his hand.

They heard a siren pulling out of Purchase Street, and Stan quickly turned off the radio and cut on his scanner. He focused immediately on what was going on. Frank Harper had been seen at a convenience store on the corner of Jacquard and Clearview, but he got away. They were combing the woods, trying to catch him.

"They're gonna get him!" he shouted, then shot her an apologetic look. "I'm sorry, sweetheart. I didn't mean to yell."

She was still sweating, and leaning her head back on the seat. "You need to go there, don't you?"

"Go where? Don't be silly. We're going to the hospital."

"But this guy . . . you need to catch him. You know, you could turn around and go back to Aunt Aggie's, and she could take me.

It's probably going to be hours before I actually have the baby. By then you could lock this guy up and get to the hospital in time."

He hesitated a moment, giving that some serious thought. What he wouldn't give to be there when they caught Frank Harper. What if they weren't thorough and he got away? What if they didn't catch him?

Then he realized that worse than that would be missing the birth of his baby. No, he thought. He wouldn't turn back now. "There's nothing in the world that would make me turn back now. Not even the chance to wrap up this case."

"Are you sure? I really would understand."

He turned off the scanner and touched her stomach. He felt it slowly tightening as she entered a contraction. His baby would be here before the day was out. Suddenly, his heart soared joyfully, and he couldn't wait to hold it in his arms.

"I've never been more sure of anything," he said.

Chapter Sixty

● ● ●

The moment Lisa came to pick him up, Dan realized what a mistake he was making. The dark clouds in the sky gave him a foreboding sense of doom, as if this date was a mistake he would soon regret. He wasn't in the mood, didn't even like the idea of riding in the car with her, much less going to a dinner as her date. He didn't want to act charming or funny; he didn't want to laugh at her jokes, or tell her she looked nice.

They got to the dinner and were seated at a table of ten people. Then he realized what an idiot he was. His very presence here was a nail in the coffin of his relationship with Jill. What had he been thinking? Conversations abounded around him, and every now and then Lisa would look back at him and ask, "Are you all right?"

"Yeah," he'd say, irritated. "I'm fine." He was getting tired of her asking, but he supposed he didn't blame her. She wasn't being forced to go out with him, after all. If he hadn't accepted, she would have found someone else, and she would have had a better time.

He tried to concentrate on his food, but wound up just stirring it around on his plate, wondering where Jill was staying tonight, hoping she wasn't alone somewhere, hoping that she wasn't in danger. And then he realized that she *was* in danger, that Frank Harper could walk right into that hotel, shoot down the guard, bust through her door, and take her life before she even had a chance to react. His stomach tightened and his eyes misted over at the thought of that. Then how would he feel?

Vindicated, because he'd been right? Validated, because she'd deserved it?

She didn't deserve it. Nobody deserved it. He didn't deserve it, either. Yet he was doing this to himself. Instead, he could have been spending this evening with her, keeping her out of harm's way. Instead, he was sitting here with another woman, realizing what a cowardly jerk he was. He made himself sick.

He looked over at Lisa. "Uh . . . I need to make a phone call. I'll be right back."

She nodded as if she couldn't care less. He didn't blame her. As a date, he was sadly lacking tonight. But he couldn't help himself. He got up, went to the foyer, and found a pay phone. He deposited the coins and quickly dialed Jill's cell phone.

A recording came on. "The cellular customer you are trying to reach is not available at this time."

He slammed the phone down. She was trying to avoid him. He was sure Allie or Mark had told her about the date by now. Did he blame her for avoiding him? No, he didn't, he thought. But if she was avoiding him, why had she tried all day to call him? Maybe *his* avoidance of *her* had made her so angry that she'd given up on him entirely. What had he expected?

He dug some more coins out of his pocket, deposited them into the phone, then quickly dialed Mark and Allie's number.

"Hello?" It was Allie.

"Allie, is Jill there?"

Allie hesitated. "I thought you were having dinner with Lisa Manning."

"Allie, please let me talk to Jill."

"I didn't say she was here."

He didn't like the taunting tone in her voice. "Is she, or isn't she?"

"What do you care?" Allie asked.

"I *care*," he said. "That's why I'm calling. Please. Is she there or not?"

"You know, if you ever wanted a relationship with her, this is not the way to do it, Dan."

He tried to calm himself, and hit his forehead into the phone. "Look, I realize that. But I need to talk to her, okay? She made me really mad last night, but I've been worried about her, and I'm tired of worrying about her when I don't have to. If she would just be more careful and quit doing such stupid things!"

"*She* does such stupid things?" Allie asked. "What about when you went on calls before the doctor cleared you? You're one to talk, Dan."

"Okay, so I do it, too. But it doesn't make it easier when it's the person you're having a relationship with."

"Yeah, tell Jill about it!" Allie said. "But you didn't see her going out with another man just because she couldn't manipulate you into doing everything she wanted."

"Look, I'm not used to the constant struggle. She made me mad and I reacted."

"Well, grow up!" Allie shouted. "It's time you learned how to have a real relationship, and you don't do it by going out with some other woman every time you get mad at the person you care about."

He was sorry he'd called. "Look, if you see Jill, will you please tell her I called, and I'll call back later."

Before she could answer, he slammed the phone down.

Dan went back to the table and took a seat beside his date. She shot him an annoyed look. "Everything okay?"

"Uh ... no," he said, keeping his voice low so he wouldn't embarrass her. "It's not okay, as a matter of fact. I never should have come out with you tonight."

She grunted. "You sure know how to make a girl feel great."

"I'm sorry, but this has nothing to do with you. None of it. But I do have to go."

"Go? You're gonna leave me here?"

"You have your own car," he said. "I'll take a cab. You know a thousand people here. You're not alone."

"Well, sure, but it's a little embarrassing."

"I know," he said. "I'm sorry, but this was really stupid. The whole thing was stupid. I shouldn't have come here with you. I don't know what I was thinking . . ."

"All right, then," she snapped. "Go then. I'm sorry I called. You can bet I'll never do it again."

"That's good," he said. "I think that's the best thing."

She looked at him like he was crazy.

"Look, I'm out of here, okay? Thanks for inviting me. And . . . I'm really sorry." With that, he was out the door.

Chapter Sixty-One

● ● ●

Frank Harper heard the sirens and knew they were after him. He ran through the woods as fast as he could, determined to do what he did best: survive. But then he heard dogs barking and voices from several different directions. He pulled his shirt off, then flung it into the trees, hoping to slow them down as the dogs came upon it. Then he took off in another direction. But he saw flashlights coming toward him.

Somehow, he had to throw the dogs off. He ran, crouched, then leaped to a high branch and scurried up a tree. He crawled out on one of the strongest branches, then dropped his feet and hung there, swinging. The branch protruded over the bayou, and Spanish moss draped it on either side of him. He swung harder, making sure he had enough momentum to launch directly into the water without touching the ground. The dogs would smell him on the tree, but they wouldn't be able to tell where he'd come out.

He swung and let go, and fell into the warm, muddy water of the bayou. He came up on the opposite bank and ran, crouched down, from bush to bush and tree to tree.

The barking got closer, and he leaped to another branch and pulled himself up. His legs and arms were as strong as a cat's, and he knew that even the dogs couldn't keep up with him.

But then he saw a dozen flashlight beams crossing through the woods, too close to him. They came from all sides, and there were dogs on this side of the bayou, too. He was surrounded, and they were growing closer. His head hit a catalpa nest, and he brushed it off.

He swung again, trying to hit the water again and make a run for it, but the splash sent the dogs into a frenzy, and all of the flashlight beams shone on him. He let out a blood-curdling, torture-chamber yell, then tried to run through the water as its mud bottom pulled and sucked at his feet.

"It's him!" someone cried. "We got him!"

Someone grabbed him and fought him to his knees, the nasty seaweed and skin-sucking mud pulling at him harder. He was handcuffed and jerked to his feet, and someone read him his rights as they dragged him out of the water. All the while, he kept his eyes closed and his face down to his chest, refusing to engage with the enemy. He had been through this before. He knew how to hold his secrets.

Chapter Sixty-Two

• • •

Dan called a taxi, and Jacob Baxter, a fireman who moon-lighted with his cab, picked him up. They were halfway down Jacquard when he saw the traffic bottlenecked up ahead. He leaned forward on the seat. "What's going on up there, Jake? You know?"

Jacob rolled down his window and leaned out to get a better look. There were police lights flashing up ahead, and one cop was directing traffic toward a detour. "Don't look like a wreck. Looks like they're all at that convenience store."

"You got a scanner in here?"

"Yeah, but I don't use it with customers in here."

Dan shot him a look. "Turn the thing on, will you?"

Jacob reached under the dash and turned the scanner on, and immediately they heard the police activity. *"Subject has escaped on foot in the wooded area east of Jacquard, south of Le Fleur Boulevard."*

"He got away again? What's the matter with you people?"

"R.J. was first on the scene and claims he didn't go after him because he had to see about Jill Clark."

Dan's hands hit the dashboard. *"Jill?"* He looked at Jacob. "Something's going on with Jill! Let me out here. I'll run the rest of the way."

"But you didn't pay me!"

He reached into his pocket, got his wallet, and threw it at Jacob. "Take what I owe you." Then he took off, running between cars, zigzagging in and out of bottlenecked traffic, trying to get closer to the convenience store that seemed to be at the center of the crisis.

"You forgot your wallet!" Jacob yelled out the window. "Dan!"

But Dan ignored him, reached the yellow line at the center of the road, and began to run as fast as he could.

He reached the block that was roped off and jumped the crime scene tape. An ambulance was on the scene, its lights flashing, and he saw Sid Ford standing at the back of it as they loaded someone in.

His heart threatened to leap out of his chest as he tore around the ambulance. "Jill! Where's Jill?"

He saw that the person on the gurney was a big, burly man with a bloody nose, and he turned to Sid and grabbed him. *"Where is she, man? Where's Jill?"*

"I'm here, Dan."

He swung around and saw Jill coming around the ambulance. She was in one piece, unharmed, and he grabbed her and crushed her against him. He felt her weeping as she wrapped her arms around his neck, and he held her so tight that he lifted her feet from the ground. "Are you all right? I thought you were hurt, or worse. I didn't know . . ."

"I'm fine," she said. "He came after me, Dan. He was in my car, and I was driving and didn't know it. . . . He was going to kill me . . . But that man, that truck driver, he saved my life . . ."

Dan couldn't let her go. He closed his eyes and kept holding her, his hands stroking her hair and his face pressed against her neck. "Jill, I love you. I thought I'd lost you. I'm so sorry . . . so sorry . . . can you ever forgive me. . . . ?"

"Yes," she whispered.

It was the most beautiful word he'd ever heard. He loosened his embrace and looked at her, wiped the tears on her face. He didn't even realize he had tears of his own until she reached up and wiped his. "Jill, that Lisa thing was just childish revenge . . . I was mad at you about the hotel . . ."

"You were right about the hotel . . . He could have gotten me there if he'd wanted to . . . It was foolish . . ."

"But the date was just a stupid whim, and the minute I was with her I knew how miserable I was going to be, and I left her sitting there in the restaurant . . . like a real jerk . . . but all I could think about was getting back to you and making things right. I didn't know you were almost killed . . ."

She touched his lips with her fingertips. "Shhh. It's okay. I'm just so glad you're here. I thought I was going to fall apart." She breathed in a sob. "You feel so good."

He tightened his embrace of her again, and made the decision that he was never going to let her go.

Chapter Sixty-Three

● ● ●

Jerry Ingalls was lying on his bunk when the main door opened, and he heard them bringing someone in. He sat up and looked between his bars. The moment he saw Frank Harper, he sprang to his feet. "Frank?"

As they passed his cell, Frank held his arms over his head, as if protecting himself.

"Frank! It's me, Jerry!"

Frank slowly dropped his arms and peered at his friend over them. "Jerry?"

"Yes, it's me!"

They both stared at each other, surprised, as the police officer unlocked another cell and let Frank in, then locked it behind him.

"Frank, are you all right?" Jerry asked through the bars.

"No!" Frank yelled, his voice echoing off of the cement block walls. "They hunted me down like an animal, then beat me and brought me here."

In the dim light, Jerry tried to see evidence that Frank had been beaten, but saw none. His scraggly hair was wet, evidence that he'd had the usual shower they insisted on before processing new inmates. He doubted there had been any beating, unless Frank had put up a fight.

"I almost had her," Frank yelled. "I almost got her. I was gonna follow her to wherever she was going, but then the Lord gave her into my hands. She left the car unlocked and went to

294

talk to somebody, and I just left the car I was in and slipped into her backseat, as bold as you please. She didn't see me when she got in. I could have just put my hands around her throat, but the car was running out of control. I was gonna wait till she stopped."

Jerry frowned. "Who are you talking about?"

"You know who," Frank said. "Your lawyer lady. The one you've told so much. The one who's part of the whole government scheme ..."

Jerry shook his head. "Frank, I didn't tell her anything. Anything she knows she's found out on her own. And she's not part of some conspiracy."

"We had a covenant. You were supposed to keep your end."

"I did keep my end," Jerry said, grabbing the bars between their cells. "But you didn't keep yours. Especially when you targeted my wife and children."

"Only because she's in on it with your lawyer!" Frank shook his head frantically. "I can't sit still for people betraying our freedoms. *Somebody's got to do something.* I thought I could count on you, but I learned. I've known all along, since Nam, that someday you would betray me."

"Frank, it's been twenty-five years. I haven't yet betrayed you. I kept the covenant all these years, just like you taught me."

"But you told them. You told them that night, when you held her hostage, you told her everything. I knew you had, because they were after me, and they wouldn't have known about me if you hadn't told them."

"I didn't tell them, Frank. You've got to believe me. That's why I'm sitting in jail. They think I did it." He tried to calm his voice. "Frank, why did you set me up that way? Why would you get me to drive you to the post office, and not tell me you were gonna blow the stinking thing up?"

"Because I didn't want you to stop me," he said. "I had to do it. And once you were involved, I knew you would help. You were committed because you owed me, and you owed your country."

"Why did it have to be done?" Jerry demanded. "Why that post office?"

"Because of the captain. He betrayed me, too. After I was decorated, he handed me over to the enemy. He knew."

"Frank, Cliff Bertrand put you in the hospital. You needed to be there. The man was retired from the service. He was just working, earning a living. He didn't do anything to you."

"He was in on it. I had to get him out of the way." Frank got up and came close to the bars, grabbed them and leaned close to Jerry. "I had to get him out of the way so that I could get on with the important work. We have to make our mark, Jerry. We have to get out of here and finish the job. We have to hit other federal buildings, like that guy did before in Oklahoma. We have to take them out, before it's too late. The Viet Cong are part of this. They're on our soil now, infiltrating the government. You think the war is over, but it's not. It came home with us."

"You blew up a post office and killed three people. Wounded a little boy. He's an orphan now, Frank. His mother died. He's five years old, grieving with a fractured skull and who even knows what other injuries."

Frank's face seemed to change. "I tried to save him. I told him to go outside. Where is he now?"

"He's in the Pendleton Hospital in New Orleans, scared to death and no doubt in serious pain. One minute everything is fine, the next minute he's in the hospital and his whole life has changed. How can you think you're the good guy in that, Frank?"

"Every war has casualties. You ought to know that."

Jerry moaned. "Frank, you ran two people off of a bridge, and almost blew my wife and children up . . . Those people didn't have anything to do with communism, Frank! Do you realize what you're doing? This is not you. You're not thinking clearly. You're not making sense."

"I'm making more sense than you with your cute little house and your freshly cut lawn, and that little wife . . ."

Jerry shook his head. "Frank, maybe you need to go back to the hospital."

"I ain't going back to the hospital," he said. "I'm a free man. They can't hold me there forever. Bunch of fascists. I got away, and I'm never going back."

"You got away? You told me you were released. Frank, did you escape from there? Is that what happened?"

"Yes," he said. "I don't have to be a patsy for this communist country. I'm not going to be theirs anymore."

"Frank, we live in a republic. We're not communist."

"Yeah, but if they win the war it'll be communist. First it was Cambodia, now . . ."

"We're not in Vietnam, Frank, we're in Louisiana, and there aren't any communists around. This is not war!"

"It *is* war!" Frank shouted, kicking the bar. "Everything is war."

Jerry backed away from the bars and sank helplessly down on his bunk. It was no use. Frank was too far gone. Jerry knew Frank had been mentally disabled since the mine had exploded, but he'd never realized the severity of it until now. "Frank, you need help. Medication. You need that hospital."

"There's nothing wrong with me that another bomb won't fix!"

Jerry felt nauseous, and his heart ached with a deep, abiding sadness that his friend had come to this. "Frank," he said quietly, "you must be tired. Why don't you get some rest?"

"I can't sleep here," Frank said. "What if we get ambushed? What if they're out there?"

"They're not," Jerry said, "but just in case they are, I'll stand guard while you sleep."

"You will?" Frank asked suspiciously. "You won't let me down now, will you?"

"Of course not."

"We have a covenant, you know. I *carried* you between the pieces. There were dead bodies everywhere, blown to bits, and I came back for you when you were bleeding to death. I carried you through, with bullets flying and mines exploding. You have to protect me. What's yours is mine."

"I haven't forgotten," Jerry said sadly.

Frank went to his bunk and lay down on the top of the covers, without taking off his shoes. "I know I made you mad, what I did to your house and all. But I never intended to hurt anybody. It was just a little fire bomb. I knew she'd have plenty of time to get the kids out. It was just a warning."

Jerry looked up at him over his fingertips. "A warning about what?"

"Not to talk to anybody else. I wanted her to realize she couldn't do that."

"But we swore to protect each other's families, Frank. We had a deal."

"And that's what I did. I protected her."

"*How?*"

"I stopped her before she went too far."

"That's not the agreement, Frank. That's not what you promised. I trusted you with them."

"I didn't hurt them, I swear. They're not hurt, are they?"

"No, but they're scared to death, and my house is damaged . . ."

"But they're not hurt, are they?"

Jerry sighed heavily. "No, they're not hurt."

"See there?" He got comfortable on the bed. "Now you keep watch. I'll just get a few winks, and then I'll guard."

"Okay," Jerry said.

It wasn't long before Frank Harper was sound asleep, and Jerry could hear him snoring rhythmically.

Jerry muffled his mouth and began to weep. This man had saved his life so sacrificially, so heroically, when he was minutes from death. Frank Harper had run into a firefight with no regard for his own life, had thrown Jerry over his shoulder and had rushed him to the medics as bullets shot past him. He had gotten him safely to the gurney that would take him to the helicopter.

Then, as Frank had backed up and let the copter take off, the wind had knocked him back. He had caught himself with his hands. . . . directly on a mine. Jerry had never been able to forget the sight of that explosion that had almost killed his friend. He had lost several fingers and shattered his skull, and his brain had never recovered. How could he stop repaying? His friend was sick, and he didn't need to be in a jail cell or out on the street. He needed to be safe . . . medicated . . .

He knelt down beside his bunk and began to pray that Frank would get help before the justice system sealed his fate.

Chapter Sixty-Four

● ● ●

Jill wanted to kiss Sid Ford when he told her Frank Harper had been caught. Now she felt comfortable going back to her home, taking a shower, eating from her own kitchen, and lying in her bed for the first time in days. It was heaven. She'd never realized how precious her own home was.

She checked on Celia once before going to sleep, and was told that the baby still had not come. She tried again in the morning, and learned that Celia was still in labor. She decided to head for the hospital, anyway, with the hopes of visiting Pete if Celia hadn't delivered yet.

She drove to New Orleans, thankful that she didn't have to look over her shoulder for Frank Harper anymore. She was back in Dan's good graces, and he'd already asked her to hold tonight open for him. Things were looking up. Funny how much things could change in twenty-four hours. Yesterday she had been a basket case melting into tears at the slightest thought of Dan. Today she was floating.

She stopped along the way and bought Pete a gift. When she got to the hospital, she was told that Celia had just been taken to delivery. The baby should be born in mere moments. Unable to contain her excitement, she went to the waiting room and saw that Mark and Allie were waiting there. Aunt Aggie, she was told, had been with Celia and Stan all night. "How long have you been here?" she asked.

"An hour or so. Poor thing. It's been a long night for her."

She sat down. "Does Stan know about Frank Harper?"

"Yep. But he's a little distracted."

Allie went with her to Pete Hampton's room, and they found his grandmother sitting beside his bed, and the child lying under the ventilator mask. She walked in and smiled at the little boy. "Hi, Pete. How're you doing?"

He lifted his hand in a weak wave.

"Miss Celia's up here having her baby. Did you know that?"

He nodded.

"She came by when they first checked into the hospital," his grandmother said.

Jill leaned on the rail of his bed and smiled at his grandmother. "How are you holding up, Mrs. Lewis?"

She could see the remnants of grief on the old woman's face. "I'm doing fine. A good night's sleep would do me a lot of good ..."

"It's been a long week," Jill agreed.

Allie went to the other side of the bed and stroked the boy's hair. "So how's he doing? Are they going to take him off the ventilator soon?"

"Not for a while," his grandmother said, and the lines of worry grew more pronounced on her face. "He's not breathing right on his own yet. There's no telling how long he'll need it." Tears burst into the old woman's eyes, and she turned her back to the boy so he couldn't see.

He didn't have to see. He carried his own pain. He looked off in the distance, his eyes vacant, troubled ...

"I just wondered if you knew that the man who did ... this ... is in jail?" Jill asked.

The child looked up at her, suddenly interested. He held up his hands and pointed to his fingers.

"Yes, he was missing some fingers, just like you told Stan."

He nodded.

She knew the vacant look in his eyes reflected the thoughts that crept through his mind, thoughts of his dead mother and the explosion that had put him here. She reached into her bag and pulled out a gift she had bought him on the way here. It was a Game Boy with a Mario Brothers game inside.

His eyes widened.

She wished she could see a smile break through all the tragedy on his face. "Do you have one?"

He shook his head.

She handed it to him, and he turned it on. His eyes brightened instantly. He showed it to his grandmother with great interest.

"Well, I'll be," the old woman said. "Jill, you shouldn't have."

Jill looked down at little Pete, and saw that, at last, he was smiling through that mask. It was such a little thing, she thought. She wished there was something more she could do.

• • •

Celia still hadn't had the baby when Jill returned to Newpointe. She went to the office, revelling in her new freedom from Frank Harper.

Sheila was already there. "Sheila! I didn't expect you to be here."

"I thought I'd come back and catch up on some things, since your friend is locked up," she said, picking up a stack of files and heading for the file cabinet.

"He's not my friend," Jill assured her.

"Well, at least we don't have to worry about him throwing bombs through the window or trying to set the place on fire." She began to file the folders. "You know, you really have the jinx syndrome."

"What, pray tell, does that mean?"

"You're bad news. A danger to be around. A person could lose their life."

"You're perfectly safe with me now," Jill said.

"Hey, I'm just saying . . . a lot of bad stuff happens to you."

"Not anymore."

"So what's the deal with you and Dan Nichols? I heard the two of you were practically shopping for rings, and then I saw him out with Lisa Manning last night."

Jill wondered if there was anything in Newpointe that escaped Sheila's attention. "It's a long story."

"So you two are off again?"

Jill smiled. "No, actually. We're on again."

"And you don't care about his other women?"

Jill was not about to get into this with her. "Sheila, I'll be in my office if you need me."

"Because you can't just let him walk all over you, you know. You gotta lay the law down with these guys, or they'll think they can treat you any way they want. I've been through this, you know."

"So have I," Jill said. "I can handle it. But thanks." She went into the office, closed the door, and began to try to catch up on all the work she'd fallen behind on since the explosion.

Chapter Sixty-Five

• • •

At one o'clock, Sid Ford took Frank and Jerry out to the walled-in recreation area behind the police station where they could get some fresh air and sunshine. It was department policy ever since Patricia Castor, the mayor, was threatened with a lawsuit claiming the jails were unfit. She had immediately funded thousands of dollars to clean up the jails and build the recreation area. She had also wanted to outfit the cells with television sets and VCRs, but the city council had voted her down. They had also voted down the Nautilus machines she had proposed. It wouldn't do to turn the prisoners into puffed up, buffed up muscle men, they said.

So instead of weights, they had this yard, where they could soak up sunshine and feel the wind on their faces. It wasn't freedom by any means, but it was better than the cell. Jerry sat on the bench in the shade and watched as Frank paced like a nervous, caged animal from one corner of the wall to the other. Sid Ford was sitting in a folding chair by the door, reading the newspaper.

As Frank passed Jerry, he whispered, "I'm getting out of here."

"You're what?" Jerry asked.

Frank glanced back at Sid. He was absorbed in a newspaper article. "Getting out of here. They can't hold me."

"How do you figure that?"

"I'm gonna go over the wall. That's how I escaped from the POW camp in Jackson."

Jerry got to his feet. "Frank, don't try it. He's got a gun and he'll shoot you before you can get one foot over."

"No, he won't. I'll be gone before he knows it."

Frank glanced at Sid and saw that he was still engrossed. They weren't even in his view. "Frank, you're not going to get away with this," he said. "What are you gonna do? Go after Jill Clark again?"

"Yes, and anybody else who stands in my way. And that kid … I'm gonna take care of him."

Jerry shot him a look. "What do you mean?"

"I mean, I'm gonna make things right for him."

Jerry didn't know how much more he could take. "Frank, you're not gonna get out of here. You're only gonna make things worse for yourself."

"Watch me," Frank said.

Jerry knew he was going to give it a try, and probably get gunned down trying to climb over that wall. He had to talk him out of trying. "So you want to get out so you can see the boy? How are you planning to make things right?"

"Maybe he just doesn't need to hang on anymore," Frank said. "Maybe if he could be with his mama …"

As Jerry realized what he was saying, he covered his face. "Frank, you're a hero. Don't you remember in Vietnam, when you saved my life? Why would you want to go from being a hero to a killer?"

"Sometimes being a killer *is* being a hero," Frank said. His eyes were getting wild as he mentally measured the height of the wall. "I don't have a choice, anyway. I have a war to fight. That little boy can just make a peaceful exit, slip right on into heaven with his mama. Then I can finish the battle."

"What battle?"

"I'm gonna take out that hospital. Think of the statement. Think of all the attention it would call to what's really goin' on in our government."

"That is not a government building, Frank."

"That's what they want you to think. But they're all government buildings. They hold dozens and dozens of POWs in there, and they have their headquarters there and manipulate the multitudes in the name of good. When they find the kid dead, everybody will be there investigatin'. The FBI will fill the place up lookin' for me, and that detective and some of these Newpointe cops. . .I could get them all with one explosion."

He had little doubt that Frank could pull it off, if he could just get out of jail. But that seemed remote, and he was thankful to the point of tears. It occurred to him for a moment that he needed to get Sid's attention somehow, just in case Frank did manage to get over the wall. But then he told himself it was ridiculous. Frank would never make it. The very suggestion could get Frank into more trouble than he was already in, and Jerry wasn't about to bring that on him.

The sun was about to go down, and Jerry kept expecting Sid to take them back in, but he was apparently enjoying the cool of the day too much, and was letting them stay longer than usual. If it became dusk, he thought, and the sky began to darken, there was a possibility Frank would try. He couldn't let that happen. Somehow, he was going to have to stop him.

Chapter Sixty-Six

● ● ●

Dan called Jill at the office that afternoon. "I got my new wheels."

She grinned. "Really? What kind?"

"Another Bronco. The insurance almost covered all of it."

"Good for you."

"So ... what are you doing tonight?"

She sat back in her chair. "I really wanted to go to the hospital. Celia should have that baby any time."

He was quiet for a moment, as if he wasn't sure if that was an invitation. "Mind if I come along?"

She grinned. "I was hoping you'd take your new Bronco."

A few seconds passed as a million thoughts seemed to file through both of their minds. "Jill, I know I've said this already, but ... about Lisa last night ... I'm still so sorry."

She looked down at her hands and wondered at the way her heart hammered and her nerves raged when she talked to him. "Dan, I was hurt. Really, really hurt. But you came back, like my hero riding in on a white horse, just when I needed you. I forgive you, and I don't want to think about it again."

He seemed too moved to speak. "You know, I could look the world over, and I'd never find anybody like you."

She smiled. "That could be a good thing."

Again, silence lay like a breathing thing between them. "I don't know how to explain how I feel," he whispered. "This ... attachment to you ... it almost hurts."

A tear rolled down her cheek, and she wiped it away. "You don't have to explain it," she said. "I know just the feeling."

"What I said last night, when I found you. That I love you . . . Jill, I've never told another woman that before."

Her heart melted in gratitude, and she closed her eyes as more tears made their way out. Then fear crept in to crowd out the warmth in her heart, and she wondered if he regretted it now.

As if he read her thoughts, he went on. "I meant it, Jill. I meant it last night, and I mean it now, and I even meant it eight months ago when we stood in front of that nursery at the hospital and parted company. I didn't say it then. I couldn't. But I knew it every day that passed without you, and every phone call I wouldn't let myself make, and every time I drove past your house just to see if you were home, but wouldn't let myself stop . . ."

"You did that, too?" she asked.

"Jill, I love you."

She sucked in a deep, ragged, wet breath at the words. "I love you, too."

She could almost hear the smile on his face. "Good," he whispered. "That's good." He drew in a deep breath. "I'll be over there in a few minutes, okay?"

"Okay."

When Jill hung up the phone, she sat there for a moment, basking in the afterglow of the truth of his love. She pulled her knees up to her chest and dropped her forehead against them, and began to pray. She thanked God for Dan, and for the conversation they'd just had, for bringing them together . . .

She had a lot to talk to God about. There was so much grace to acknowledge. So much generosity. So much love.

Chapter Sixty-Seven

● ● ●

Still outside in the police yard, Frank began to eye one corner of the wall where some jasmine grew over it. He seemed to think he could get a running start and hurl himself over. Jerry knew he couldn't. No one could jump that high, and if he tried to climb, Sid would be on him in a second. But just as he was rationalizing his silence, one of the younger cops came bolting out. "Sid, Stan wants to talk to you. He thinks Celia will deliver in the next hour or so!"

Sid jumped to his feet. "Finally. I thought Stan was gon' tear up Pendleton Hospital waitin' for that baby! Man, ole Stan's gon' be a daddy. Which phone?"

"My desk," the rookie said.

Sid rushed inside to take the call, and the rookie picked up the paper and started to read.

"Now's my chance," Frank whispered.

Jerry looked at the uniformed cop with the weapon on his hip. "Frank, don't do it. They'll kill you before you get off the ground."

Frank seemed to enjoy that challenge. "I told you, watch me."

Jerry could feel the heat in his face. He didn't want to see his friend die. "Frank, I'm begging you. Please ... just wait ..."

"I can't wait. I have to go now."

"Frank ..."

"But don't worry. I'll see you again, Jerry."

Jerry fought the tears burning in his eyes. He knew his friend was crazy … had been for years. But he also knew that this man, this once heroic man, had given him a second chance to get his life right and fall in love and marry and have a family. Without him, none of that would have ever belonged to Jerry. Yet Frank had never known those things.

He grabbed his friend's arm and glanced at the rookie cop, wishing he could get his attention, make him call them back in. But the guy wasn't looking.

"Frank, things are gonna be all right, man. In this life or the next … You and me, we're brothers. We take care of each other, man. And I'm trying to take care of you."

"I'm taking care of myself," he said. "It's for you. For the whole country. My contribution." He stood stiffly, gave Jerry a salute, then took off running from one corner to another. He scaled the wall in the corner, one foot on each wall, pulling by the vines until he was over the top.

Jerry stood, stunned, waiting for the cop to start shooting, waiting for Frank to fall back down, for his problems to end … But Frank was stronger than he thought. He had the stealth of a cat, and he was going over.

The rookie heard Frank's shoes on the bricks and looked up as he reached the top of the wall. "Freeze!" he yelled, trying to get his gun out of his holster. But it was too late. Frank Harper was long gone.

Sid ran back out, and Jerry was pulled back in as sirens blared and police dispersed. It was just a matter of time before they would catch him, he thought. Just a matter of time before they gunned him down. Just a matter of time before Frank was released from the real prison that had held him all these years.

Chapter Sixty-Eight

● ● ●

Frank managed to cross the bayou and hot-wire a car before the dogs found his trail. He got out of town before they set up any roadblocks, and headed east to Hammond. He found a little Cajun Mom and Pop store on the outskirts of town and went in pretending to look for a gas treatment for his car. As they went to get it out of the back, he stole a pair of scissors and a pack of razors. He took one look at the gas treatment and told them he didn't like that brand.

He got out of there before they could get suspicious, then drove to a filthy gas station a mile away, locked himself in the bathroom, and cut his hair and shaved.

It had been years since he'd shaved, and he cut himself in several places, both on his jaws and his head. But by the time he was finished, his hair was piled in the trash can beside the sink, and his head and face were as smooth as marble.

He felt ten pounds lighter as he went back out to the car he'd stolen. The car next to him, at the gas pump, had a purse sitting on the seat. He looked around, and saw the driver inside paying for her gas. Without missing a beat, he opened her passenger door, grabbed the purse, threw it into his car, and drove off.

As he drove, he laughed at the treasure he had found. She had at least six credit cards, all in her husband's name, and about thirty dollars in cash. He was a different person, he thought. He had a different look, and a different identity. He could do anything he wanted. Nothing could stop him now.

Chapter Sixty-Nine

● ● ●

The rookie who had allowed Frank to escape threw Jerry Ingalls back into the cell and slammed it shut. "You've got to listen to me!" Jerry shouted. "He's headed for New Orleans! For the hospital where that boy is."

"Why should I believe you?" the cop demanded, kicking the bars. "You helped him escape! You been coverin' for him all this time. I'll probably lose my job over this. I've been here one month, and then you come along and—"

"I didn't help him! I didn't think in a million years he could get over that wall! You've got to listen to me. That's where he's going!"

"No, that ain't where he's goin'!" the kid yelled. "You heard us say that's where Stan was. You're just tryin' to throw us off!"

"He has some distorted idea that he could help the kid by killing him! A put-him-out-of-his-misery kind of thing. Please, listen to me. He said that when they find the boy dead, the FBI will come, and when they do, he's going to blow the place up."

"I'm not stupid!" the rookie shouted. "You're working with him. Everybody knows it. You covered for him the whole time we were looking for him. Why would you fink on him now?"

"Because . . . I see that I can't help him as long as he's out there. He needs help. He's sick. Please, you've got to stop him! Let me talk to the chief."

"Right. I'm really gonna call more attention to the fact that a prisoner got away while I was watching! Like I'm not in enough trouble already!"

Jerry didn't know how to get through to him. "Then call my lawyer. Call Jill Clark. I have a right to talk to my lawyer!"

But even as he spoke, the rookie left him alone, and he knew that he was going to cover his own tracks to save his job. They wouldn't catch Frank and wouldn't figure out where he was until it was too late.

"Hey!" he yelled, his voice reverberating over the room. "Somebody listen to me!"

But they were all too busy chasing the escaped prisoner.

Chapter Seventy

● ● ●

It was midafternoon when Frank got to the Pendleton Memorial Hospital in New Orleans. He didn't park at the front of the hospital; that was too dangerous. Instead, he parked in a crowded parking lot at the back and walked around until he found an unlocked entrance.

He knew better than to go to the lobby and ask the volunteers there for the Hampton kid's room, so instead, he went to a pay phone and dialed the hospital's number. He asked for the room number, and without a hitch, they gave it to him. "Would you like me to connect you?" the lady asked.

"No, thanks," he said. "I'll connect myself."

He hung up, and chuckling to himself, went to the stairwell and ran up to the third floor. No one paid him a bit of attention as he counted down the room numbers, then came to the child's open door.

His grandmother was in there, sound asleep in a rocking chair in the corner of the room. Pete lay limp on his back, a ventilator mask over his face, and its tube running down his throat. Frank's stomach lurched. The child was in bad shape. His head was bruised and misshapen where it had hit the pavement in the explosion, and he had tubes and cords running like webbing around him.

Frank suddenly wished he had grabbed the kid up when he'd seen him in the post office, and taken him with him. He even would have gotten the mother out if he could have done it over.

But it wasn't too late.

No, he couldn't bring the kid's mother back, and he couldn't heal the child. But there was a way to set things right. He could end his suffering. Stop the ache in that broken heart. He traced the tube from the oxygen mask back to the ventilator, then found the power cord and unplugged it. He heard the oxygen output ceasing.

He glanced across the bed to the grandmother. She was snoring lightly. In the corner, a television was turned down low, and he saw his picture flash across the screen. It alarmed him, but then he realized that he didn't look like that anymore. He looked into the mirror and didn't recognize himself. He grinned.

The little boy's eyes opened, and he coughed. He looked up at Frank, squinting as if trying to determine who he was. And then the boy saw his fingers.

He tried to gasp for breath, but the air wouldn't come. His face was beginning to drain of whatever color it had left.

Frank hurried out of the room so he wouldn't have to watch. If the grandmother could just stay asleep, maybe Pete would slip away. It would be so merciful . . . so kind. It would set things right once and for all. In just a few minutes, the kid would be with his mother.

He went back out into the hall, feeling more useful than he'd felt since he blew up the post office. He saw three security guards at the nurse's station, so he went the other way and slipped out into the stairwell.

He waited there for a moment, trying to think. The building smelled of antiseptic and brought back memories of his twenty-five years in captivity. The scent of iodine and blood filled his senses, along with the smell of cigarette smoke and body odor. His head began to hurt, and he sat down on the top step and clutched it.

He shouldn't have come here. But he had to help the kid.

And he had to do something about the government. And that detective. His wife was here somewhere having a baby. Where were they?

He went up to the fourth floor, looked out into the hall. It looked like the third floor, so he went up one more. He pushed into the hall and saw the nursery window a few yards away. And then he saw her. Jill Clark, standing there with the man he had almost killed with her.

He couldn't believe his luck.

They were all right here, right under his nose. Shortly, they would discover that Pete wasn't breathing, and they'd call the FBI and more police, and they'd all be here, like corralled sheep waiting for the end.

He ducked back into the stairwell and hurried down. When he got to the first floor, he bolted out, but his paranoia kept him from going through the lobby.

Were they looking for him? Did they know he was here?

He slipped into the cafeteria and headed back to the kitchen, as if he knew where he was going. The people in the kitchen were too busy to notice him as he cut through. There was a delivery door at the back left corner of the room where two guys were unloading some boxes of bread from a truck. He slipped behind a steel refrigerator, and waited until they began rolling the boxes further into the kitchen. When it was safe, he jumped on the truck and got behind a stack of boxes.

After a moment, the guys came back out and closed the doors of the truck. In moments, he felt the truck moving.

He laughed lightly to himself. He had escaped again. They were never going to catch him. As the truck pulled out of the hospital parking lot, he got up and peered out the small back windows. He saw a police car and convinced himself they were really the FBI, looking for him.

Perfect, he thought. The more the merrier. With everyone here, he could fulfill the rest of his mission. He could do away with all of them. He didn't have to worry about Pete Hampton anymore. By the time Frank got back, Pete would be gone.

He could get the feds, the detective who was having a baby, the communist doctors who ran the place, Jill Clark and her boyfriend, all of the ones who were responsible for the communism bleeding the country of its freedoms. All he would need was this truck, a few barrels of fertilizer, some diesel fuel, and a few other critical items. When he was finished, they'd give him another Medal of Honor.

All he had to do was wait until the drivers parked it for the day. Then he could take the truck and gather the ingredients he needed. Before dark, he'd have the whole place going up in flames.

Chapter Seventy-One

● ● ●

"One, two, three, *breathe!* One, two, three, *breathe!*" Stan wiped his forehead on the sleeve of his shirt. Celia squeezed his hand with all her might as she tried to follow his instructions.

He could see from the contraction monitor that her contractions were getting intense, and he couldn't imagine that this would go on much longer. When he saw the line peak out on the monitor and then begin to descend, he grabbed the wet towel next to her and began to dab at her face. "You okay, baby?"

She was relaxing now, letting go of his hand. "Yeah," she said, breathless. "That was a bad one."

"Sure you don't want an epidural?"

She closed her eyes. "I don't know. Maybe."

"It's not a contest, you know. You don't have to do this natural stuff."

"How much longer do you think it will be?"

"Not much longer."

She took in a deep, cleansing breath. "I don't want to slow things down. I can do it."

"The contractions are two minutes apart," he said gently.

He heard something crash out in the hall, then a man's voice rising. Over it all, he heard, "You let me through them doors or you gon' be all over that floor, you!"

He knew Aunt Aggie's voice. Celia met his eyes. "You might as well go in and rescue her," she said. "She's gonna get in here one way or another."

"Are you sure you're up to it?" Stan asked.

Celia nodded. "I love Aunt Aggie. Just let her come in and see that I'm okay, and then we'll get her out of here when the next contraction starts."

Stan hurried to the door and leaned out into the hall. "Aunt Aggie, what are you doing?"

"Tellin' me I need to stay in the waitin' room!" she spouted. "Don't nobody belong in there if I don't!"

Stan took her hand and pulled her into the room. "You can't stay very long, Aunt Aggie. Celia's having a real hard time."

"They call the doctor?" she demanded. "They told him she's havin' trouble?"

"Not trouble-trouble," Celia said, wiping the sweat from her forehead. "It's normal. I'm just getting to the end."

"The baby ready?" Aunt Aggie cut in. "Where's the doctor at? Why ain't he in here with you?"

"He'll be here shortly," Celia said. "They're checking on me regularly."

"Checking on you?" Aunt Aggie shouted. "If you wanted me and Stan to deliver that baby, we coulda did it at home, you. Don't need to pay no doctor for dancin' in here when he feels like it, and *checkin'* on you!"

Stan saw the line on the monitor beginning to rise, indicating another contraction, and Celia reached for his hand. "Aunt Aggie, you need to go now," he said gently. "Celia's having another contraction."

"I'll call the doctor!" the old woman said, heading for the door.

"No, you don't need to call the doctor. It's not time yet."

"Look at her!" Aunt Aggie said. "She's in agony! *Sha*, you gon' be all right?"

Celia was clenching her teeth and breathing hard.

"Come on, baby, let's count," Stan said. "One, two, three, *breathe!* One, two, three . . ."

"She don't need you countin' at her, you!" Aunt Aggie shouted.

Stan stopped counting and decided to do whatever it took to get Aunt Aggie out: "Go get the doctor, Aunt Aggie. Tell him the contractions are a minute and a half apart."

Without another word, Aunt Aggie rushed from the room, on a mission to bring a doctor back with her.

Chapter Seventy-Two

● ● ●

Jill and Dan got to the maternity floor just as Aunt Aggie came running out of the room. "Doctor! Doctor!"

Dan grabbed her arm. "Aunt Aggie, is everything okay?"

"She in there having that baby and ain't no doctor for miles!"

Dan shot Jill a disbelieving look. "Aunt Aggie, this is a hospital. I'm sure there are doctors around."

"Ain't none where she needs 'em." She shook loose of Dan's grasp and started up the hall. "I ain't got time for you. I gotta go find me a doctor."

Dan let her go. Just as she headed up the hall, a nurse came from the other direction. "Uh, nurse," Dan said. "I think they may need you in that room there."

She nodded. "I was going to check on her."

Dan stepped back, tense, as Jill came up and stood next to him. They waited, hoping that nothing had gone wrong. Then the nurse came back out.

"Everything okay?" he asked.

"Just fine," she said. "She's progressing nicely. Won't be long now."

"Nicely?" Jill asked. "But Aunt Aggie sounded like the baby was ready to come."

"She's still got a little way to go," the nurse said. "She's not exactly having fun in there, but things are going well."

"You don't think you need to call a doctor?"

The nurse looked up the hall in the direction Aunt Aggie had gone. "The doctor's on his way. He'll be here any minute."

"Well, I hope you know that if he isn't, he's gonna have Aunt Aggie to contend with."

The nurse chuckled and headed back to her station.

Jill relaxed, realizing that Celia was okay. She walked over to the big glass window with all the babies behind it. Dan came up behind her, slipped his arms around her, and nuzzled her neck. "Does this bring back any memories to you?" she asked.

He lifted his face. "Yeah, this is where you dumped me."

She turned around, shocked. "*I* dumped *you?* You've got to be kidding. You're the one who gave me that song and dance about how you weren't the kind of guy who hooks up with one woman very long."

He grinned. "You sure didn't put up a fight."

She turned back to the nursery. "Hey, when you're ready to leave, take off. You won't see me begging."

As he pulled her back against him, she felt him laughing quietly. She turned around again and looked up at him. "Are you laughing at me?"

He caught her lips unexpectedly and kissed her, right there in front of the glass and all those babies and the nurses that were attending them. Her heart's rhythm went out of control, and she was glad she was in a hospital.

When he broke the kiss, she stepped back and looked up at him. She didn't know what to say. He smiled at the nurses behind the window, gave them a cursory wave, then pulled Jill to an exit door at the end of the hall. "Where are you taking me?" she asked.

He settled into the corner of the landing and pulled her against him again. "Somewhere where we won't be stared at while I kiss you." Again, he caught her lips, and this time, she settled into the kiss, sliding her hands up around his neck, into his hair. Her heart was beating so fast that she feared it would explode, and she could feel his raging pulse as she touched his neck. They'd been together many times, had even kissed, but something about the declarations of love and the life being born just a few feet away made everything seem a little more urgent.

They broke the kiss, and Dan's breath was ragged as he touched her face. His lips hovered over hers as he whispered, "You know we're going to have to get married, don't you?"

Jill looked up at him, startled, but he kissed her eyelids, one at a time. "Married?" she whispered. "Is that some kind of proposal?"

He brushed his face gently against hers, his own eyes closed as he found her mouth again. When he could speak, he said, "Paul said in the Bible it was better to marry than to burn with passion. The way I figure it, I'd rather be married *and* burn with passion."

Something about that statement made her stomach flutter, and she swallowed and looked up at him, wondering if he was joking, if this was a flippant statement about their getting too close too fast. But as he met her eyes and looked down at her, framing her face with both hands, she realized that he was serious. His eyes began to mist with tears, reflecting her own as she gazed up at him. "I'm serious, Jill," he whispered. "Marry me. I don't think I can stand it if you don't."

It took her a moment to find her voice. "But what if the passion fades?" she whispered, tears welling in her eyes. "What if we settle in and get comfortable with each other, and the passion doesn't seem to burn as bright?"

He only smiled. "I want to settle in with you, Jill. I want to get comfortable. I want to have babies with you and go to PTA meetings and eat popcorn while we watch movies at night, and sit next to you every time we go to church."

One tear rolled out of her eye and traveled down her face.

"I want to lose my hair and have you pretend it's still there."

Another tear escaped, and she laughed as she wiped it away.

"I want to look over at you in bed when I'm ninety years old, and still be amazed that you'd hang out with a toothless guy like me. I want to make a covenant with you, Jill. I want to love and protect you and cherish you until the day I die."

There was no use wiping the tears away. They were coming too quickly now. He smeared them with his thumb. "Will you, Jill?" he asked. "Will you be my companion and my partner and my helpmeet for the rest of our lives? Will you marry me?"

"Yes," she whispered, and rose up to slide her arms around him again. "Yes!"

As he crushed her against him, she wept with all her heart.

Chapter Seventy-Three

● ● ●

Jerry paced the cell back and forth, back and forth, like a wild lion suddenly held captive in the zoo. Occasionally, he went to the bars and banged and yelled, but still no one came. His hands were bruised from banging on the bars, and his voice hoarse from yelling.

He couldn't believe this was happening. Frank would be at Pendleton Hospital and have a bomb assembled and planted before Jerry could get anyone to listen to him.

He took off his shoe and began beating the heel of it against the bars, praying that someone up there would have the intelligence to come back and question him about what had happened. If they would just listen ...

But still no one came.

Maybe they had caught him, he thought. Maybe he hadn't gotten far, and he was upstairs right now, being processed before being brought back down. Maybe the doors would open any minute, and Frank would be locked up again.

Or maybe Pendleton Memorial Hospital was going to be Frank's next project.

He started banging again, unable to give up. Eventually, someone had to come for him.

Chapter Seventy-Four

● ● ●

Outside, Larry Hampton pulled his early midlife crisis Camaro into a parking space and sat looking up at the huge, intimidating hospital. He was likely to see people he knew inside, people who knew he had abandoned his family for his secretary. What they didn't know was that the relationship had ended months ago, and he was now seeing a waitress who worked in the French Quarter. He'd been through three jobs, and now, looking back, he realized how funny it was that he had left his family so he could feel young and free again, but today he'd never felt older in his life.

He turned his car off, got out, and headed up to the hospital. His little boy was lying upstairs somewhere on life support. The fact that he'd even had to think about coming made him hate himself even more. He didn't deserve to be the boy's father. Yet ironically, except for his grandmother and a couple of uncles, he was all Pete had left.

He went to the information desk, asked for Pete Hampton's room, and was directed to the third floor. He went to the elevator and waited, then thought better of it. He didn't want to run into anyone he knew, so he decided to take the stairwell. The door echoed as it closed behind him, and he took the steps two by two.

He reached the third floor and stepped into the corridor. He looked up and down the hall for the right door number, and saw that Pete was just across from the nurse's station.

He slowed his step as he reached the door, dreading the moment of confrontation with his former mother-in-law. He hoped his visit didn't bring Pete any more pain.

The door was partially opened, and he pushed it slightly and peeked inside. Thelma, his former mother-in-law, was sitting up in a rocking chair, sound asleep. *Good*, he thought. That would give him a chance to look at his son, maybe give him a hello hug before she started throwing accusations at him.

He stepped tentatively inside, and saw the small form of his son lying on the bed beneath a tangle of wires and tubes. He wore a mask, and a tube ran through it into his mouth and down his throat. *The ventilator*, he thought. It was what was keeping his son alive, yet it looked so invasive, so painful, so alien …

He stepped closer to the bed and saw how pale and white the child's face was. He leaned over and pressed a kiss on his cheek as a tear rolled out of his eye. And then he heard the whistling, desperate sound of breaths not quite grasped.

The ventilator wasn't doing its job. Startled, Larry grabbed his little boy up from the bed and yelled, "Pete!"

The child's eyes opened, frantically, desperately, as he gasped for breath.

Thelma woke then, and sprang out of the chair at the sight of his father holding him. "Larry!"

"He's not breathing!" he yelled. "Quick, do something! Call the doctor! *Something!*"

In seconds, she had the nurses running in. One of them began breathing through the tube to give him air, as the others tried to determine why the ventilator had stopped. When they found the unplugged cord, they all moved into a new degree of frenzy.

It took several moments for them to get him breathing again, moments during which Larry stayed back against the wall, watching in horror as he realized that someone had unplugged the life support from his child. Suddenly, a fierce protectiveness rose up inside him, and any trepidation he'd had before about being back in his son's life vanished. He wasn't going to let anyone hurt him again.

When he saw his son breathing again with the tube running down his throat, he crumpled over and began to cry. There was no one there to comfort him. Instead, Thelma and the nurses shot him an occasional accusatory look. But it wasn't until the police officer came in and announced that Larry was under arrest that he realized they thought he had unplugged the ventilator.

He shook his head as they clamped the cuffs on his wrists. "I didn't do it. I came in here and he was gasping for breath."

Pete opened his eyes and reached a hand out, beckoning his dad closer to the bed. Tears rolled down his face as he tried to sit up, but he was too weak.

"Pete, I'll be back, son," he said. "I'm your daddy, and don't you forget you have one. I'll be back."

But Pete couldn't talk as they escorted Larry from the room.

Chapter Seventy-Five

● ● ●

As soon as Dan and Jill heard about what had happened to Pete, they came up to the room to see if there was anything they could do for his grandmother. They found her huddled over the bed, trying to make Pete stop crying, but he was distraught, and kept pointing to the door his dad had gone through, motioning for him to come back.

Jill felt sorry for the tired, ragged-looking old woman who hadn't bargained for any of this. "Thelma, I heard about Larry. Is there anything I can do?"

The woman looked up at her with tears in her eyes. "We were just so shocked to see him here, and now Pete can't get over it, but Larry's under arrest and I can't get him back."

The boy tried to pull his tubes loose, and the grandmother fought to hold his hands. Dan went to the edge of the bed, grabbed the boy's wrists, and held them firmly to his sides. "Take it easy, buddy. It's gonna be all right. You need that tube so you can breathe."

The boy was crying too hard to listen.

Thelma covered her face with her hands, and Jill pulled her into a hug.

The boy shook his head and Dan let one hand go. Pete pointed to the door again.

"What's he telling us? Something about his dad?"

Pete nodded his head. He pointed to the wall where the plug was, then held up his hand and bent some fingers. His grandmother saw that and pulled back from Jill.

"The fingers," she said. "Whenever he does that, he's talking about the man who planted the bomb. He saw him, and he said he didn't have some of his fingers."

Jill looked down at him. "Honey, that man is in jail. They caught him yesterday. He's locked up."

Pete shook his head and pointed to his hair. He moved his fingers like scissors on his hair, but Jill didn't understand. Again, he held up his hand and bent some of his fingers down.

A chill ran down Jill's spine, and she looked back up at Dan. He, too, seemed to seriously consider what Pete might be saying. Pete was getting more and more agitated, pointing to the door with tears rolling down his face. He wanted his daddy.

Suddenly, Jill felt overcome with the need to go and get Larry, but the police would never listen to her. Maybe they would listen to Stan, but he was still with Celia, waiting for his baby to come.

"I don't know what to do for him!" Thelma cried. "He's so upset. I wish Larry had never come back! And I'm so confused … Part of me thinks he couldn't have unplugged the ventilator, but if he didn't, who did?"

Pete had stopped trying to pull out his tube, so Dan let his hands go and began stroking his forehead, trying to calm him down. The boy continued to cry.

"Do you really think Larry could have done that?" Dan asked.

"I never thought of that man as a killer," Thelma said. "But I don't know anything about what he's turned into in the last couple of years."

Jill shook her head. "No, I knew him when he was in town. Unless he's just gone off the deep end or something, I can't see him coming in here for that. Besides, if he wanted to …" She couldn't say the words "kill him" in front of Pete, so she rephrased it. "If he wanted to unplug it, why would he try to …" She glanced at Pete, and saw that he was looking up at her, hanging on every word. "To fix things, at the last minute?"

"Maybe when I woke up he got caught and had to cover his tracks," Thelma said. "But he was already holding Pete. I'm not sure, but I think I woke up *because* he yelled." She shook her head. "Or maybe he wanted to look like the hero, coming in on a white horse to rescue his child."

Jill thought that over for a moment. Maybe it was possible, but even as she considered it, Pete started shaking his head again, pointing to the door, kicking his feet with weak energy as tears rolled down his face. He wasn't going to rest until his father came back.

A doctor who had seen the activity of his heart monitor rushed into the room. "Pete, what's the matter, son? You've got to calm down."

"He wants his daddy," Thelma said.

Pete stopped kicking and nodded, as if at last he had been understood.

"All right," the doctor said. "I'll see if I can catch him before they take him out of the building."

His grandmother stiffened, as if she didn't know if that was a good idea or not. Pete suddenly grew still at the prospect.

"He doesn't think his father did it," Dan whispered.

Jill leaned over the bed. "Pete, do you know who unplugged your breathing machine?"

Pete nodded.

"Was it your daddy?"

He shook his head no.

"Who was it then?"

He held up his hand and bent some of the fingers again. Jill straightened, frustrated. "That's impossible. Frank Harper is in jail."

Dan frowned. "You don't think ..."

"Let's go make a phone call," she said. "Pete, we'll be right back, okay? The doctor's going to get your daddy. You just rest for a minute, okay?"

Pete was growing tired and weak, and he nodded as they left the room.

Chapter Seventy-Six

● ● ●

It didn't take long for Jill to find out that Frank Harper had escaped from jail, and that they were looking for him in New-pointe at this very moment. Panicked, she ran up to the floor where Stan and Celia were having their baby. She began to pace frantically in front of the door, waiting for Stan to come out.

"Are you okay?" Dan asked her.

"Yes," she said, "but if Frank Harper has escaped from jail, and little Pete thinks that he saw him unplugging the ventilator, then that means he's here in this hospital!"

Dan was beginning to sweat. "You know, Jill, I'd really like to get you out of here. Let's just leave, okay?"

"But what about Pete? What about Stan and Celia? I mean, what is he up to? Why would he want to kill Pete?"

"Because he's a witness to the post office bombing," Dan said.

"Maybe," she said, still pacing. "We have to warn Stan. He could come after him. We have to tell the police . . ."

A nurse came through the door, and Jill almost attacked her. "Has the baby come yet?"

"Just about," she said. "It's crowning. Shouldn't be too much longer."

Jill wiped the perspiration forming on her forehead, and Dan took her hand and headed for the stairwell.

Chapter Seventy-Seven

● ● ●

It's a girl!" The baby's cry went up and filled the room, and Celia laughed with relief as she looked down at her beautiful daughter.

They put the baby into Stan's arms, and he began to mist up as he bent down to show his wife.

"She's beautiful," she said. "Oh, Stan, isn't she beautiful?"

"Just like her mama," Stan managed to say. He couldn't believe how blessed he was.

● ● ●

Jill and Dan found the police huddled just outside the hospital. Larry sat in a squad car as one officer questioned him.

"Excuse me. Sir, excuse me . . ." Jill pushed her way through the officers and reached the cop who was talking to Larry. "I just found out that Frank Harper escaped from Newpointe Jail this afternoon. I was just with Pete Hampton upstairs, and he's indicating that Harper is the one who unplugged the ventilator. I think Frank Harper is here, somewhere, in the building."

"Frank Harper?" Larry asked. "Isn't he one of the guys who blew up the post office?"

"Yes!" The cop seemed to be ignoring her. "Are you listening to me?" she asked him.

"Ma'am, they're looking for Frank Harper in Newpointe. He escaped on foot, and he couldn't have made it here."

"He could have if he stole a car, and that's one of the things he does well. I'm telling you, he's here. Pete saw him."

"I thought the boy couldn't talk."

"He can't. He motioned. Frank Harper is missing some fingers. Pete keeps holding up his hand like this." She showed him, and the man rolled his eyes.

"He wants his daddy. Now, why would he want his daddy if he was the one who tried to kill him?"

"Maybe he doesn't *know* he tried to kill him!" the cop shouted.

Larry was shaking his head. "They won't listen. They're convinced I came here to kill my son."

"People have done a lot of crazy things to keep from paying child support," the cop said.

"I don't *pay* child support!" the man shouted. "Never have. I've been hiding from my family for the last two years. Why would I come out of hiding now and make myself known to my son, just so I could kill him?"

Jill couldn't take anymore. She turned back to Dan. "Let's go back and find Stan. He'll listen."

"But the baby . . ."

"Stan needs to know that Frank Harper is in there!"

Dan nodded, took her hand, and pulled her back through the cluster of police.

They reached the fourth floor again, and were told that the baby had come. They asked the nurse to go tell Stan they needed to speak to him, that it was urgent. As they waited, they paced in front of the door, waiting for Stan to come out so they could tell him what had happened with Frank Harper. It seemed to take forever, but finally, he came through the door, grinning from ear to ear.

"It's a girl!"

"Yeah, we know. They told us."

Stan's grin faded. "What's the matter? You wanted a boy?"

Jill shook her head, unamused. "Stan, Frank Harper's escaped."

"He's *what?*"

"He's escaped. And I have reason to believe he's somewhere in this hospital, Stan."

"No way."

"Somebody unplugged Pete's ventilator and almost killed him. His father found him gasping for breath, and they've arrested him thinking he's the one who did it."

"No way," Stan repeated. "Larry Hampton may be a jerk of a father, but he's not gonna kill his little boy."

"Then you need to talk to them," Jill said, "and get him back up because Pete wants his daddy now that he knows he's here. But not only that, Stan. I'm scared to death of what Frank Harper is up to. The police downstairs won't listen to me. They're convinced that he couldn't be in New Orleans, but I know and you know that he could have stolen a car before they even got the dogs out. He's here. Little Pete kept holding up his hand with his fingers bent down . . ."

"He did?" Stan asked. "That would indicate Frank Harper, but how could he have gotten in without being recognized? His picture's been all over the news."

Dan put his arm around Jill's shoulders. "Stan, I'm thinking Harper may have cut his hair. Pete did a scissor-like motion on his hair, and kept holding up the hand with lost fingers."

Stan looked back at the door where his wife and child lay. "I don't like this," he said. He pulled the cell phone out of his pocket and called his office.

"LaTonya, it's me, Stan. What's going on with Frank Harper?"

He listened for a moment, then shot a look to Jill. "Let me talk to him." As he waited, he put his hand over the phone. "Some rookie who's been on the force for four weeks was guarding him when he escaped. She's going to get him so I can talk to him." Stan straightened again and looked down at the floor. "Yeah, I just wanted to know what Jerry Ingalls said about Frank's escape . . . What do you mean, what do I mean? You interviewed him, didn't you? Did you ask him what Frank told him before he escaped? . . . I don't care *how* busy you've been. I don't care if every cop in town is out looking for Harper. I want you down there talking to Jerry Ingalls. Call me back immediately! I want to hear from you as soon as you have any information."

By the time the rookie got back to him, Stan was pacing outside the door to Celia's room with the cell phone to his ear. Jill and Dan were huddled against the wall, waiting. "What did he say?" Stan asked the young cop.

"Well, he claims that Frank Harper is headed there. Where you are."

"What for?" Stan shouted.

"Something about wanting to put the kid out of his misery. Ingalls said he was feeling guilty about the kid's mother. And he said something else, Stan, but I don't know . . ."

"I didn't ask you to know or not know!" Stan said. "What did he say?"

"Ingalls said Harper talked about planting a bomb there."

"Oh . . . no . . ." Stan started to run even as he kept the phone to his ear, and Jill and Dan began to follow him into the stairwell, down the stairs, onto the first floor . . . He ran through the doors and found the cluster of cops still talking to Larry Hampton. Jill and Dan had trouble keeping up with him, but they managed to as Stan bolted through the cops and yelled, "Frank Harper is in the building! We've got to evacuate."

One cop turned around. "The guy who blew up the post office?"

"He's here," Stan said, out of breath. "We've got to get everybody out. Now. He told his cell mate that he was going to kill Pete Hampton, and that he might blow up the whole hospital." He pointed to Larry. "You've got the wrong guy."

The cop filling out the arrest report looked up.

"I told you what happened," Larry said. "He tried to kill my boy. Now, will you let me get back to him and make sure he's okay?"

"He didn't do anything wrong," Stan said. "He saved the boy. He'd be dead if his dad hadn't walked in."

Larry's eyes filled with tears. "I'm glad I came. I almost didn't." He turned back to the cops. "Can I go? Please, I have to get my son out of here."

When the cop hesitated, Stan stepped in. "You don't have time to take him in. You have to help me evacuate this building. It's gonna take all of us. We need to notify the FBI and alert the bomb division. We've got to find out if there's a bomb in this building, and we've got to find Harper, and we've got to get my wife and daughter out of here immediately."

"How much time do we have?" the cop asked.

"I have no idea. We'll just have to go on faith."

• • •

Unaware of what was going on in the hospital around her, Celia waited for them to bring her the baby after cleaning her up. Aunt Aggie was in her room with her, finally relaxed after the tension of the day.

"Where'd that Stan go?" Aunt Aggie asked. "He oughta be here with his wife."

Celia didn't know where Stan was, but she knew that if he wasn't here, there was a good reason. So she tried to be patient. "He'll be here, Aunt Aggie. Maybe he got a call or something. Or maybe he decided to contact relatives."

"I called arrybody who needs to know already."

"Did you call the Fords, Aunt Aggie?"

The old woman thought a moment. "Arrybody but the Fords."

Celia chuckled and picked up the phone. She dialed Susan's number in Newpointe.

Susan answered, and Celia could hear the children talking in the background.

"Hello?"

"Susan, it's me, Celia."

"Celia, honey! Where you callin' from?"

"I'm in the hospital! I had the baby."

A cry went out over the phone line. "Celia had her baby! Celia had her baby! Girl or boy?" she asked, coming back to the phone.

"It was a girl," Celia said. "She's beautiful. We're gonna name her Agatha Nicole."

"You're namin' her after Aunt Aggie! Oh, honey, I'm on my way."

Celia laughed. "No, you don't have to come. It's a long way."

"Forty minutes aren't anything," Susan said. "I'll be there. You just try and keep me away."

• • •

Susan hung up the phone and turned around to Debbie Ingalls. She looked tense and preoccupied, as she had since Ray had called to let them know that Frank Harper had escaped. "You haven't been out of this house in a couple of days. Why don't you pack up the kids and come with me to the South Shore to see Celia's baby?"

Debbie shook her head. "That's okay. We can stay here."

"Honey, as jumpy as you been, and with Frank Harper on the loose again? I don't think I'm gon' leave you by yourself. Now, you just get your stuff together and come with me. If they won't let the kids up, you can wait in the lobby, but at least you'll feel safe."

Debbie considered that for a moment, then looked back at her children. "I guess it wouldn't hurt. It would be a nice diversion."

"We'll get ice cream on the way," Susan said.

"They'll ruin your car."

Susan waved her off as if she didn't care. "We'll bring towels," she said. "There's nothin' they can do that a good washin' won't fix."

Chapter Seventy-Eight

● ● ●

Frank Harper was filthy from mixing fertilizer and diesel fuel with the other ingredients he needed to build his bomb. He had stolen a rifle from out of a pickup truck and pawned it to get the cash to buy the bomb materials from various hardware stores. He loaded the barrels onto the bread truck he had "borrowed" after the business had closed for the day. It had been so easy he couldn't believe it. And he had the detonator put together, and the timer ready to be set.

He headed back to the hospital. As he reached it, he saw the activity of the police cars and people being evacuated from the building. He realized they must have already found Pete and figured out he was here. Did that mean the boy had survived being unplugged from the ventilator? He hoped not. He wanted the boy to die peacefully, not in an explosion like his mother. But he supposed that dead was dead no matter how it happened.

The fact that he might have been found out didn't faze him as he crossed the parking lot in the bread truck. They were looking for someone going out, not coming in. He had the perfect cover.

He pulled the truck to the side of the building where he knew the kitchen was and pulled into the delivery drive. He climbed into the back of the truck and set the timer for fifteen minutes. Then grinning, he got out and left it there.

If he ran, he'd have plenty of time to get far enough away that the explosion wouldn't reach him, but he'd still be able to watch it. He looked around with pride as he saw the task force with their FBI T-shirts. A bomb squad had pulled up to the front door with the bomb robot, and they were taking it in as patients filed out of every exit.

They wouldn't get them all out, he thought. It was impossible. But he supposed that even those in the parking lot would be blown up. The statement would be loud and clear. And the people who heard would understand, and perhaps their eyes would be opened.

He took off from the side of the building and headed through the cars, trying not to run so he wouldn't call attention to himself. But he had to get out of here quickly.

Then he saw the car pulling into the parking space in front of him, and the black woman getting out. Two little white children climbed out of the backseat, and then he saw a woman he recognized. It was Debbie Ingalls. He couldn't miss her with that skinny face and those big eyes. Jerry had shown her picture to him every time he had come to visit him over the last few years.

Suddenly, he began to remember Jerry's words back at the jail, about how the covenant reached out to his family, how Frank had already violated it once. He had promised Jerry that he hadn't meant to hurt Debbie and the kids, that the fire bomb had just been a warning. Jerry trusted him.

Now he didn't know what to do. The women passed him without recognition, and were heading to a side entrance. Apparently, they hadn't seen the activity of the police at the entrance doors. He watched as the two women and children headed toward the hospital, and he wanted to yell out that they couldn't go in there, that they were evacuating because there was a bomb, that they needed to get as far away from there as possible.

But if he did that, the communist pigs he was trying to defeat would descend on him. He looked down at his watch. There were only twelve minutes left. He looked back at Jerry's family, and saw the two little kids holding hands and skipping beside their mother.

Jerry's kids.

He couldn't do it. He couldn't break his covenant with Jerry. It meant too much. It was too binding. They had sealed it by walking through the flesh. He had carried Jerry out on his back, between the dead and bleeding bodies, had gotten Jerry to the helicopter ... And then there had been that explosion, that surprising blast that seemed to come from nowhere, and then darkness ...

Jerry had been there when he'd come to, weeks later. They had hugged and wept together, and Jerry had promised to fulfill the covenant just as David had done for Jonathan. Frank had promised, too.

"Frank, things are gonna be all right, man. In this life or the next ... You and me, we're brothers. We take care of each other, man. And I'm trying to take care of you."

Jerry had uttered those words just hours ago. They were covenant words. And they weren't one-way. That covenant that was so strong between Jonathan and David, between Abraham and God, between Christ and his church ... that covenant that he had taught Jerry to honor ... He remembered the import of it, and he knew that he couldn't keep the covenant if he let that bomb go off with Debbie Ingalls in the hospital.

Without another thought, he took off running back to the truck. He had to go the long way because new police cars were filling in nearby. He went around the hospital, dripping with sweat, and came up behind the cars with the flashing lights. He reached the truck and got back into it, and looked down at the timer. There were ten minutes left.

He tried to think how to stop it, how to break the connection, how to make the clock stop ticking ... but he didn't have time to figure it out. Instead, he bent down and hot-wired the car again, started the engine, and backed out.

Chapter Seventy-Nine

● ● ●

Larry Hampton ran back into his son's room. Pete saw him and reached out to him. He went to the bed, unabashedly, and threw his arms around his little boy and began to weep over him. "Pete, I'm so sorry, I'm so sorry, I'm so sorry . . ."

The child clung to him with his weak little arms, and tears rolled down his temples. Larry wiped them away and looked up at Pete's grandmother standing at the side of the bed. "Hello, Thelma."

"Hey, Larry," she said.

"I'm so sorry," he told her, choking back the tears. "About Mary. And about . . . everything."

She nodded and smiled at the joy on the little boy's face as he held his daddy. "I know," she whispered. "The main thing is that you're back, and Pete needs you so much right now."

He wept at the sweetness of that forgiveness, and realized that grace wasn't just a word they threw out in church. It really existed. And now it had meaning for him.

A frazzled nurse rushed in. "We're evacuating the hospital," she said. "I've got them bringing a gurney in here for Pete, and we've got to keep his ventilator attached." As she spoke, she began disconnecting the cords that weren't vital. Her hands were shaking.

"We don't have to wait for the gurney," Larry said, picking Pete up. "I'll carry him, and his grandmother can carry the ventilator and the IV, can't you, Thelma?"

Thelma looked worried. "Well, yes. But what's going on?"

"It's a bomb threat," the nurse managed to get out. "Probably nothing, but we have to be safe." She disconnected the last of the cords and unhooked the IV bag. "Hold it up above him. And take the stairs. Hurry, please! Head for one of the ambulances so you can plug him back in. If he goes into respiratory distress, give him mouth-to-mouth."

They obeyed quickly.

•   •   •

Stan was trying to help Celia down the stairs with one arm and holding his baby in the other, when he heard Aunt Aggie shouting over the people in the lobby. "You don't let me go back up there and get my great-great-niece, you gon' wish you never been born, you."

Celia was pale and breathing hard, and Stan scanned the room for a free wheelchair as he yelled to Aunt Aggie. "I got them down, Aunt Aggie. Celia needs a wheelchair."

Aunt Aggie looked tremendously relieved, but much older than she had just hours before. She grabbed a wheelchair out of a nurse's hands and helped Celia into it. Stan handed Celia the baby and pushed the wheelchair out the doors as Aunt Aggie ran along beside them. He saw the people clustered around the outside of the building, but they weren't far enough away to avoid a blast. "Out there, Aunt Aggie," he yelled. "All the way across the parking lot."

He was running with the wheelchair, weaving between parked cars, trying desperately to get to the other side of the parking lot as orderlies ran by with patients on gurneys and IV poles rolling beside them. He saw Dan and Jill already on the other side, each pushing a wheelchair of a patient who couldn't help himself.

Cops tried to direct the flow of people, but they were ineffective as panicked loved ones fought to get patients out of harm's way. Stan knew he needed to help, but he wasn't going to turn back until he knew for sure that his wife and baby were safe.

And then he heard a scream and turned around. He saw the bread truck driving through the people, forcing them to leap and dive out of his way. The driver had a shaved head, but as the truck passed, Stan saw those eyes that he had seen in the pictures of Frank Harper ...

"Aunt Aggie, stay here with Celia!" he cried, and he started to run after the truck. He heard feet running behind him, and Dan caught up to him.

"That's him!" Dan cried. "That's Frank Harper!"

The truck bobbed and wove through the cars and the people, not slowing at all but picking up speed as it got closer to the parking lot exit. But there were two police cars blocking the way. Stan ran as fast as his legs could carry him, knowing that his child's life and his wife's life and the lives of all the people in the parking lot and still making their way out of the hospital depended on it. He saw the truck slow down as it reached the blockade, but then it picked up speed in one last burst, and crashed the front fenders of the two squad cars, breaking through and skidding out of sight.

Stan pulled out his badge and flashed it at one of the stunned police officers. "I need your car!" he said, breathless.

The cop didn't say a word as Stan jumped into it. Dan got in on the other side, but Stan didn't have time to make him get out. He jerked the car in reverse, and his tires squealed as he turned it around and began chasing the truck. It was a mile up ahead of them, sliding around corners and grazing cars as it drove. It headed toward the highway, then opened up, burning rubber as Frank Harper stood on the accelerator to reach the truck's maximum speed.

"You can catch him!" Dan yelled. "That truck won't go that fast!"

They were gaining on him, narrowing the distance between themselves and the truck. "He's done something!" Dan yelled.

"There's a bomb back there, all right. He's trying to get away as fast as he can. He knows it's about to go off!"

Stan prayed silently that Celia and the baby and Aunt Aggie and Jill were far enough away from the building, but his heart told him they weren't. He had the sudden urge to grab the automatic rifle from behind his head and start shooting until Frank Harper was down.

Suddenly, three police cars came out of a side street and flew out in front of him. "Look out!" Dan cried.

Stan slammed on brakes and slid sideways, out of control, trying to avoid hitting them. He spun and hit a telephone pole head on. Air bags blew out, knocking them back against their seats.

Stan punched the side of his door, furious that the New Orleans police had almost killed them. He would report them, he thought. He would make sure he had all of their badges.

"You all right?" he asked Dan.

Dan opened his door and saw the truck pull onto the highway. "They've caught up to him!" he yelled.

Stan leaned out his open window and saw that the truck was surrounded by the cars, with one on either side and one behind. The highway cleared of cars as drivers pulled off to the side.

But the truck just kept on going. Frank Harper wasn't going to be stopped.

Chapter Eighty

● ● ●

Frank Harper ignored the cops chasing him down the high-way. He glanced back at the timer, and saw that there were only fifteen seconds left. If he hurried, he could get far enough away that the hospital wouldn't be harmed . . . far enough so that Debbie Ingalls wouldn't have a scratch, and Jerry wouldn't think of him as a covenant-breaker . . .

Ten . . . nine . . . eight . . .

He realized that it was too late for him to get out of the truck, too late for him to stop and run far enough that he could escape the explosion. He realized it was a sacrifice he would have to make. A sacrifice worthy of the covenant it represented.

Three . . . two . . . one . . .

Bright, hot darkness closed over him, knocking him out, out, out into some other dimension . . . and Frank was hit with a clarity he hadn't seen in years.

And then there was the light, beckoning for him.

Chapter Eighty-One

● ● ●

They heard the bomb from the parking lot and every station inside the hospital and the stairwell and the elevator shafts. Jill felt as if the earth had shaken as people threw themselves on the ground to escape the blast. Debbie Ingalls was running through the parking lot when she heard the explosion, and she threw herself over her children. Celia screamed and threw herself over their new baby. Larry threw himself over Pete on the ambulance's gurney. Aunt Aggie marched out into the parking lot, raising her fist at the fireball that had threatened to destroy her family, and yelling at it as if it was some part of Frank Harper rising into the sky.

Panicked, Jill made her way to Celia. "Where ... where is Dan? Where did he go?"

"He went with Stan," Celia cried. "They were following that truck."

Jill couldn't even voice her fears. "Celia, they were ... where the explosion ..."

Celia looked in the direction of the black smoke filling the sky. "No," she said. "No, they weren't. They couldn't be."

"They were!" Jill cried. "I saw them get in a squad car. They chased the truck out of here."

"No!" Celia cried. "No, they couldn't have. They didn't go that way, Jill!"

"Yes, they did!" she screamed. "They did!" She scrambled to her feet and started running in the direction she had seen them go, not knowing how far they were or how close she could get or what she would do when she got there. All she knew was that she had to get to Dan. She had to find him and know . . .

And then she saw a police car turn onto the road leading to the hospital, heading toward her, and she began to run faster, faster . . .

"Jill!" Dan jumped out of the backseat of the car and bolted toward her. Jill almost collapsed as he swept her into his arms and held her in a crushing embrace.

"Keep driving!" Stan told the officer who had picked them up. "My wife is over there!"

As the car drove past, Jill cried, "I thought you were in the explosion! I thought you were . . ."

"I'm not," he said. "I'm here. We're both here. We're still here." He was crying, too, and holding her with all his might. "I thought he was trying to get away from the explosion, but he was taking it with him. The police that were chasing him . . . they went up in the blast."

"Why?" Jill asked. "Why would he do that? Why would he drive away?"

"Only one reason I can think of," he said. "Because God is still in control."

Chapter Eighty-Two

● ● ●

The wedding took place at Calvary Bible Church, and two-thirds of Newpointe turned out for the occasion. Mark and Allie had seen to it that the church was filled with every kind of flower in bloom. It was a celebration, not just of a marriage between two beloved people in Newpointe, but of life itself, for so many of the attendees had come so close to death.

Jerry Ingalls was still in jail awaiting trial for holding Jill hostage, but Jill hoped that the judge would be lenient in sentencing him. Yes, he would serve time for his stunt at the Flagstaff, but she hoped her representation of him and her own testimony at the sentencing would cause the judge to make it a light sentence.

She had spent time with Jerry in his cell after the explosion and Frank's death and had seen the grief that had overcome him at the news. When he learned that his own wife and children had been at the hospital, and that she had passed Frank without recognizing him in the parking lot, he told Jill that he knew why Frank had driven the bomb away. It was that unending covenant between them, that promise to protect even their families.

But even in his grief, he seemed glad that his friend was no longer tormented by the illness that had plagued him for years. Jerry had latched on, instead, to the faith that Frank Harper had before his brain had been damaged, to the fruit he had borne, to the witness he had been. Jerry clung to the hope that Frank was at peace, living in the promise of the covenant that had held him like a dearly loved child ... even when he had been unable to hold it.

As Jill and Dan exchanged vows, they remembered the gravity of the covenant into which they were entering. When they exchanged rings, Nick told their friends and loved ones that it was like the ancient ritual of exchanging robes, symbolizing the merging of their identities and all their possessions. When they exchanged vows, he told how serious and holy and binding the covenant was under God, and how they were bound to love and protect each other, care for each other's families, and fight each other's enemies. When they kissed, he told how their union made the two become one. When he announced "Mr. and Mrs. Dan Nichols," he explained that Jill's taking of Dan's name was another way of identifying herself with him, just as we all take the name of Christ when we enter into covenant with him. When they cut the cake at the reception, Nick explained how the exchanging of the pieces of cake, each fed to the other, was the same as the old covenant custom of eating something that represented the covenant partner, just as communion represented our eating of Christ's body and drinking of his blood, to remind us of the new covenant. Then Nick led the guests, and the bride and groom, in partaking of that communion ... the ultimate covenant meal.

And he declared the Lord to be at the center of Jill's and Dan's marriage.

•   •   •

As the tears of understanding gave way to joy, and the reception grew more festive around the bride and groom, Nick saw Issie Mattreaux slipping from the room. Quickly, he cut through the crowd and caught her in the hall. "Issie?"

She turned around, and he saw that she was crying.

"Are you all right?"

She nodded. "Yeah. Sure. I was just ... moved. That was the most beautiful wedding I've ever seen. All that stuff about the covenant. I've never heard any of that before."

"I'm glad you like it. It was all Dan's and Jill's idea. I've never really thought of tying it all together in a wedding ceremony like that." He took a few steps closer to her and saw that the tears were still rolling down her face. "Are you sure that's all?"

"Yeah," she said. "I just ... get a little teary-eyed at weddings." She breathed a laugh. "You know how it is. It's always somebody else's wedding ..."

He chuckled. "I have that feeling myself sometimes, believe it or not."

She shot him a doubtful look. "You? I thought you were all philosophical about your bachelorhood."

"Not always," he said. "Sometimes I think I'd like to have a companion. A helpmeet."

"Where do you get these words?" she asked on a laugh. "I'm still trying to figure out all that covenant stuff. No new concepts just yet, huh?"

His smile faded into a pensive frown. "Are you really trying to figure it all out, Issie?" he asked. "Because if you are, maybe we could go have a cup of coffee and talk about it."

She looked at him as if she didn't trust him. "You aren't planning to get me cornered and beat me up with a sermon, are you?"

"No, not at all," he said. "I just want you to understand it. Besides, my work is done here. It wouldn't hurt me to commiserate with another member of the 'always the bridesmaid' club. Who knows? We might just cheer each other up."

Issie shot him a grin, and he counted it a personal victory that she wasn't crying anymore. "Okay," she said. "Let's go."

And as they walked out into the night, Nick prayed silently for a way to show her the Light that would chase all the shadows out of her life.

Afterword

● ● ●

I love to read, which is probably why I love to write. But lately, I've been increasingly concerned that some readers spend hours a day reading novels, and little or no time reading God's Word. Yes, I want to build my readership, and I want readers to like what they read. I have a message in my books and want that message to get into as many hands as possible. I am also sometimes forced to measure my success by the number of people who buy my books. If no one buys them, the bookstores will stop carrying them. This process makes it easy for me to get my focus off of my true purpose.

But if the only spiritual education you get is through one of my novels, then I have failed. My sole purpose for writing what I write is to point you to Jesus Christ. It isn't enough for me to point and have you give God a cursory nod. If you aren't drawn to his Word through reading mine, then I have no business writing these books. And you have no business reading them.

I don't mean to sound harsh, but the Lord has been working on me about what I'm doing and why. So often, we Christians soak up messages and ideas, and sometimes we even come under conviction, and wince a time or two. But then we forget and move on to the next stimulus.

Yes, I try to pass along the hard lessons God has taught me, and I try to convey truth as the Lord has revealed it. But if you read my work and accept anything I say as sound doctrine, without comparing it to the true Word of God, then you are an excellent candidate for false teaching. I am only a sister traveling the same road as you, learning lessons just like you learn them, grappling with the same growing pains, the same fires, the same trials. I have only one source for truth, and that does not lie in anyone's novel, or anyone's devotional book, or anyone's sermon, no matter how clever or eloquently written. It lies only in Scripture, which is "living and active and sharper than any two-edged sword."

I do believe that God sometimes speaks to my readers through my books, that he sometimes uses me to impart messages to you. But the Holy Spirit can only do that if I'm getting out of his way, emptying myself and offering myself as a vessel to be used by him. I can tell you, that's no easy task for me. As I agonize over the words and the plot and the characters, it's easy to lose sight of the truth God wants me to pass along.

So don't trust my words—trust God's. Study the book he has given us so that you can't be swayed by any false teaching. Know his Word inside and out, so that no one can deceive you. Then, and only then, read a novel, or a devotional, or a doctrinal text, and see if you agree with the human author who's walking the same road as you, that human author for whose sins Christ hung on a cross and died. And when you and I are sitting side by side at the wedding feast of the Lamb, you'll see that I got there the same way you did: through believing the Word of God and acting on it. "But what does it say? 'The word is near you; it is in your mouth and in your heart,' that is, the word of faith we are proclaiming: That if you confess with your mouth, 'Jesus is Lord,' and believe in your heart that God raised him from the dead, you will be saved" (Romans 10:8–9).

God bless all of you!

Terri Blackstock

About the Author

● ● ●

Terri Blackstock is an award-winning novelist who has written for several major publishers including HarperCollins, Dell, Harlequin, and Silhouette. Published under two pseudonyms, her books have sold over 3.5 million copies worldwide.

With her success in secular publishing at its peak, Blackstock had what she calls "a spiritual awakening." A Christian since the age of fourteen, she realized she had not been using her gift as God intended. It was at that point that she recommitted her life to Christ, gave up her secular career, and made the decision to write only books that would point her readers to him.

"I wanted to be able to tell the truth in my stories," she said, "and not just be politically correct. It doesn't matter how many readers I have if I can't tell them what I know about the roots of their problems and the solutions that have literally saved my own life."

Her books are about flawed Christians in crisis and God's provisions for their mistakes and wrong choices. She claims to be extremely qualified to write such books, since she's had years of personal experience.

A native of nowhere, since she was raised in the Air Force, Blackstock makes Mississippi her home. She and her husband are the parents of three children—a blended family which she considers one more of God's provisions.

Acknowledgments

● ● ●

I would like to express deep gratitude to Angela Hunt, Alton Gansky, Jack Cavanaugh, Athol Dickson, and Lisa Samson for brainstorming with me on this plot. I feel so privileged to have such wonderful authors offering me ideas. During a novelists' retreat in Grand Rapids, Michigan, we sat together over breakfast, talking about villains, car chases, and bombs. Before we knew it, I had a conclusion to this book. I couldn't wait to get home and write it.

I'd also like to thank Zondervan Publishing House for bringing their novelists together to encourage each other. It was one of the highlights of my year.

And once again, I'd like to thank Dave Lambert, Sue Brower, and Lori VandenBosch for their untiring efforts to keep my books coming. I am very pleased to be able to work with such quality people.

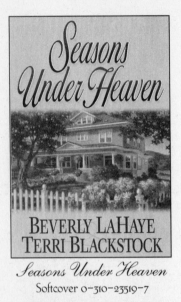

Terri Blackstock

Newpointe 911 Series

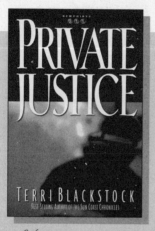

Softcover 0–310–21757–1

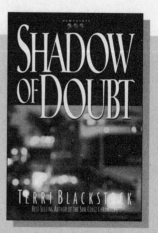

Softcover 0–310–21758–X

Softcover 0–310–21759–8   Softcover 0–310–21760–1   Softcover 0–310–25064–1

Check out these great books

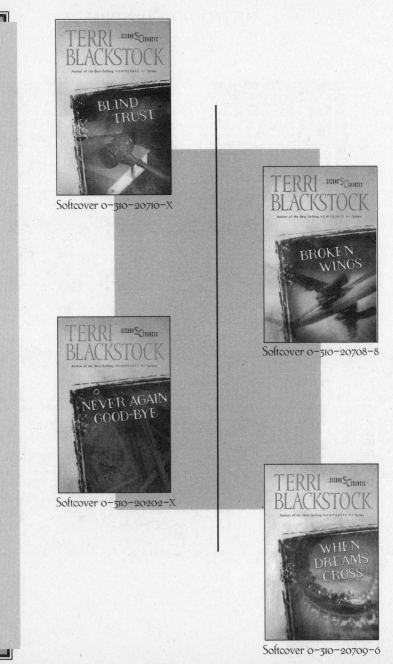

from Terri Blackstock, too!

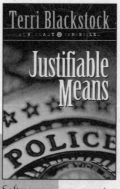

Softcover 0-310-20016-4

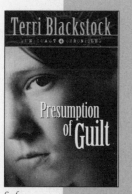

Softcover 0-310-20018-0

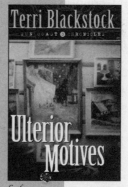

Softcover 0-310-20017-2

Softcover 0-310-20015-6

Seaside

Terri Blackstock

Seaside is a novella of the heart—poignant, gentle, true, offering an eloquent reminder that life is too precious a gift to be unwrapped in haste.

Sarah Rivers has it all: successful husband, healthy kids, beautiful home, meaningful church work.

Corinne, Sarah's sister, struggles to get by. From Web site development to jewelry sales, none of the pies she has her thumb stuck in contains a plum worth pulling.

No wonder Corinne envies Sarah. What she doesn't know is how jealous Sarah is of her. And what neither of them realizes is how their frantic drive for achievement is speeding them headlong past the things that matter most in life.

So when their mother, Maggie, purchases plane tickets for them to join her in a vacation on the Gulf of Mexico, they almost decline the offer. But circumstances force the issue, and the sisters soon find themselves first thrown together, then ultimately *drawn* together, in one memorable week in a cabin called "Seaside."

As Maggie, a professional photographer, sets out to capture on film the faces and moods of her daughters, more than film develops. A picture emerges of possibilities that come only by slowing down and savoring the simple treasures of the moment. It takes a mother's love and honesty to teach her two daughters a wiser, uncluttered way of life—one that can bring peace to their hearts and healing to their relationship. And though the lesson comes on wings of grief, the sadness is tempered with faith, restoration, and a joy that comes from the hand of God.

Hardcover: 0-310-23318-6

Mystery and suspense combine in this first book of an exciting new 4-book series by best-selling author Terri Blackstock

Cape Refuge

Terri Blackstock

Thelma and Wayne Owens run a bed and breakfast in Cape Refuge, Georgia. They minister to the seamen on the nearby docks and prisoners just out of nearby jails, holding services in an old warehouse and taking many of the "down-and-outers" into their home. They have two daughters: the dutiful Morgan who is married to Jonathan, a fisherman, and helps them out at the B & B, and Blair, the still-single town librarian, who would be beautiful if it weren't for the serious scar on the side of her face.

After a heated, public argument with his in-laws, Jonathan discovers Thelma and Wayne murdered in the warehouse where they held their church services. Considered the prime suspect, Jonathan is arrested. Grief-stricken, Morgan and Blair launch their own investigation to help Matthew Cade, the town's young police chief, find the real killer. Shady characters and a raft of suspects keep the plot twisting and the suspense building as we learn not only who murdered Thelma and Wayne, but also the secrets about their family's past and the true reason for Blair's disfigurement.

Softcover: 0-310-23592-8

Pickup up a copy at your favorite bookstore!

ZONDERVAN™

GRAND RAPIDS, MICHIGAN 49530 USA

WWW.ZONDERVAN.COM

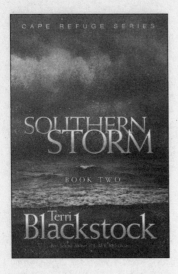

The Highly Anticipated Sequel
to *Cape Refuge*!

Southern Storm

Cape Refuge Series

Terri Blackstock

Police Chief Cade disappears after hitting and killing a man with his car. Without a trace, without a note, without taking clothes or his car or money, he is gone. When a witness says she saw Cade getting into a blue Buick with a woman before his disappearance, the newspapers report that Cade left town to be with her. Blair knows it doesn't make sense for Cade to leave without word for any reason. The dead man is identified, and it soon becomes clear that the woman Cade was seen with was the wife of the dead man. Newspapers begin to ask hard questions. Was the Cape Refuge Chief of Police having an affair with this woman? Did he deliberately kill her husband and then make it look like an accident? When the police department receives a handwritten note from Cade that he has run off to get married to a woman he's kept secret, everyone breathes a sigh of relief. But Blair notices his unusual signature: Matt Cade. Cade never goes by his first name, and he especially never calls himself "Matt." She thinks it's a signal from him that the contents of the note are false.

Meanwhile, around the south, there are news reports about babies being kidnapped from area hospitals. When a ransom call comes to Hanover House from the baby's kidnapper, they are all shocked to see that the phone it is traced to is Cade's cell phone. Is he involved in the baby's disappearance? Is that why he's disappeared?

Softcover: 0-310-23593-6

Pick up a copy today at your favorite bookstore!

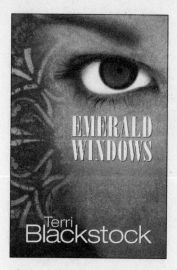

Emerald Windows

Terri Blackstock

Ten years ago, devastated by an ugly scandal, Brooke Martin fled the small town of Hayden to pursue a career as a stained glass artist. Now Brooke has returned on business to discover that some things never change. Her spotted reputation remains. Tongues still wag. And that makes what should be her dream assignment tough.

Brooke has been hired to design new stained glass windows at Hayden Bible Church. The job is a career windfall. But Nick Marcello is overseeing the project, and some in the church think Nick and Brooke's relationship is not entirely professional—and as before, there is no convincing those people otherwise.

In the face of mounting rumors, the two set out to produce the masterpiece Nick has conceived: a brilliant set of windows displaying God's covenants in the Bible. For Brooke, it is more than a project—it is a journey toward faith. But opposition is heating up. A vicious battle of words and will is about to tax Brooke's commitment to the limit. Only this time, she is determined not to run.

Softcover: 0-310-22807-7

Pick up a copy today at your favorite bookstore!

ZONDERVAN™

GRAND RAPIDS, MICHIGAN 49530 USA

WWW.ZONDERVAN.COM

We want to hear from you. Please send your comments about this book to us in care of zreview@zondervan.com. Thank you.

GRAND RAPIDS, MICHIGAN 49530 USA

WWW.ZONDERVAN.COM